All characters and events depicted in this book are entirely fictitious. Any similarity to actual events or persons, living or dead, is purely coincidental.

The following story contains mature themes, strong language, and explicit scenes, and is intended for mature readers.

Edited by Andie Edwards of Beyond the Proof
Proofread by Shannon Shacka
Ebook cover art by Cormar Covers
Model Dane de Bruin shot by Wandar Aguiar
Paperback chapter art by Ginotage Sandaru
Discreet paperback cover by Books & Mood
www.oliviahayle.com

ONE *wrong* MOVE

OLIVIA HAYLE

To everyone who wakes up one day and wonders when and where they lost themselves… and sets out to rediscover that person.

Prologue

Nate

I saw her first.

I'd just been given a not-so-subtle dressing down by my father. The head of the family and former CEO of Contron. Apparently, I'm not pulling my weight in the family company the way I should be.

Now, I'm sitting at the bar in the Village, drowning my sorrows in a gin and tonic. I haven't been here before. It's close to the university area, and the sound in the dimly lit locale is loud. Overflowing with laughter, drunken chatter, and music that has a pounding beat.

It makes me feel alive. Like I'm someone else for an hour or two—someone younger, someone idealistic and optimistic. Someone still in college.

I don't often miss that time of my life. But right now I do. Sleeping in, slacking off, and studying. Sometimes.

I miss the cold air that shrouds Boston this time of year and the weighted blanket of low expectations that came with having the perfect older brother.

These days, life is all suits and boardrooms. I'm good with it, but it drains energy. Too often, I feel like I'm a battery that's running on empty.

I take a sip of the drink and look around. Dean is still in

the bathroom, having downed his third beer. It gives me plenty of time to people-watch.

A group of friends sit in a nearby booth, beer bottles on the tabletop in front of them. One of the guys is drinking what seems to be whiskey or scotch, and he scratches at the nonexistent beard on his chin.

My gaze slides over, along the tables at the back. Past the abandoned jukebox and the stage that must, on occasion, host live performers.

I see a girl sitting alone at a table.

There's a halo of blonde curls around her face, falling just past her shoulders. A dark headband crowns the locks. She's in an oversized cable-knit sweater with sleeves that are too long. One of them is pulled down over her hand, like she's using it as a barrier to hold her cold beer. It looks untouched.

She glances around. Her eyes are alert and a bit pensive. A pointed chin, almost elfin, but there's nothing doll-like about her face. Her skin is flushed, as if she just came in from the cold.

College student, I think. She has to be. Which makes her a decade younger than me, maybe more.

She glances up at the ceiling and cocks her head, just slightly, like she's studying something intensely. I look up, but there's nothing there. Just spotlights that have been dimmed to a low setting. Somewhere in the background, an old eighties rock song begins to play. The woman taps along with the tune, her free hand drumming against the worn wooden table.

I take a long sip of my gin and tonic. It feels pretentious, suddenly, to have a cocktail in a dingy college bar.

I wonder if she's waiting for her date.

I wonder what her voice sounds like.

I wonder what her smile looks like.

And I wonder, looking at her across the crowded bar, if I'll ever be able to forget the sight of her. The question seems outrageous at the moment. How could I?

I feel as if I've been struck.

Putting down the glass, I undo the button of my suit jacket. It feels all wrong now, too. Something that belongs to the man I am during the day, the man I'm expected to be, but not me. Not really.

I shrug out of it. Leaving it on the chair beside me, the chair Dean vacated, and move to rise out of my own. There's no way I can leave here without at least saying hi to her. Without asking what she's thinking about.

A hand lands on my upper back. "Don't," Dean says, "stop by the table with all the jocks on the way to the restroom. They're so fucking riled up, I swear. They saw my suit and wanted to ask me about stocks. Couldn't tell if they were joking or not, so I gave them terrible advice, just in case."

I turn to him. "How noble."

He grins and nudges my shoulder with his. "We have to teach the pups some manners."

"And you're the old dog in this scenario, are you? We're not even thirty-five."

"Oh, but we've been in the game a long time." He leans against the bartop beside me. I've known him since college, a friend forged through too much alcohol, too little sleep, and endless anxiety about exams.

I glance over his shoulder at the girl.

She's still sitting alone. Unlike most people, she hasn't pulled out her phone to pass the time, to avoid even a second of boredom. She's looking around like she's analyzing the environment she's in. An observer rather than a participant.

Dean follows my gaze. "What... oh," he says. Then he smiles. "She's cute, isn't she?"

I pick my gin and tonic back up. "She's a college student."

"So? Even old dogs, and all that." He bumps my shoulder with his again and then he walks off. Meandering through the crowd. My buddy, Dean, who can be blunt but also charming. Who is good-looking, sporting a short buzz cut, and who has a passion for sailing and real estate. Heading straight toward the table where she's sitting—radiant and alone—gripping an untouched bottle of beer.

And she looks up at him… and smiles.

So, even though I saw her first, he was the one who spoke to her first.

And that made all the difference.

Chapter 1

Harper, four years later

The gallery is large, white, and entirely impersonal, excluding the bright-colored art pieces lining the walls. Standing next to my new coworker, Aadhya, I feel incredibly out of place. Not only is she tall, she's fabulous, too. And *British,* dressed in a sleek outfit that's nothing like my own red maxi dress. She's gorgeous and already knows the ropes around here. I find her *incredibly* intimidating.

She walks me through the client roster. The codes that open the different offices. The protocol for event organizing.

Her overview is at a breakneck pace, and I try my best to follow along.

"Now you try," she says, stepping to the side and gesturing at the computer. Aadhya watches me for a few seconds as I try to replicate her steps. "So, you really just got here a week ago?"

"Yes," I say.

"From New York?"

"Yeah. I love the City, but needed a change of pace," I say. It's an understatement. I needed an *escape,* and London and this gallery provided it. I applied to this paid junior traineeship a few months ago, without telling anyone. And when the acceptance letter arrived in my email inbox a few weeks ago…

I'd seen a way out. A chance at a new existence. I'd jumped at it and left everything behind.

"New York, though," Aadhya says. Her tone is contemplative. "I can't imagine ever leaving that city. I was born and raised in London, and this city is never getting rid of me."

"This gallery was just calling my name," I say. "So how does this system work? With the access codes?"

She comes to stand beside me and shows me what to do with brisk competence. For my first day, it's thankfully pretty slow, with only a few clients scheduled for appointments to browse the art. I know my tasks. Shadow Aadhya all day and make sure the clients are happy, satisfied, and have a glass of champagne in hand if they want it.

Around us hangs art worth millions of pounds. Excitement is a steady beat inside of me, all day long. To get to work with this. To get to *see* it every day.

A few men are standing on the other side of the gallery. I recognize one immediately. Eitan White. The owner and executive head of the Sterling Gallery. He's a short man with thick, curly black hair, and the most intimidating gaze I've ever encountered.

His voice is warm as he speaks to a tall man in a suit.

I look back to Aadhya. "A potential customer? Already?" I whisper.

She nods and flips a page of the art collection catalog. She's looking for one of the abstracts. "Yes, he was here bang on time as the gallery opened. He's an existing client. Always gets the royal treatment and personal tours from Eitan."

I glance over at the pair again. There's something familiar... A deep, unsettling feeling washes over me when the man turns, and I catch sight of his profile.

Oh no.

No, no, no.

I had known he was in London. Of course I knew, but I didn't think I would bump into him. Hadn't really thought about it at all. Not since I packed a bag and booked a flight.

But it's true that he's always been interested in contemporary art. Had frequently asked me about existing and up-and-coming artists every time he's gone to dinner with Dean and me. It had been one of the few things we had in common. I loved telling him about the artists I thought had a bright future, and he seemed like he enjoyed listening to me go on about it.

"Harper?" Aadhya asks. She's chewing gum, and her long, black ponytail gleams under the soft glow of recessed lighting. She's beautiful. Brown skin, expertly applied makeup, and a fantastic accent. "You are staring a bit, you know."

"Oh, I'm sorry."

"Don't be. He's fit. I know that first hand." She grins and inclines her head slightly in his direction. "One of the gallery's best customers, too, so you know he's got deep pockets."

"Right, that makes sense. You kinda have to if you're into art," I say. My voice comes out high, laced with nervousness.

Aadhya taps her manicured nails against the closed cover of the Sterling Gallery's collection catalog. "He makes Eitan very happy, at least, whenever he visits. I've tried to score a date for months."

My eyebrows rise. "You have?"

"Of course," she says with a smile. "Do you know how rare it is to have fit customers?"

I look back at Nate, where he's chatting with our eccentric boss, a legend in the art industry and someone I remember hearing about in college.

The two of them start strolling through the gallery toward where Aadhya and I are lingering.

Shit.

My heart rate speeds up with every step they take. Dean and Nate have been friends for nearly twenty years. They went to college together, and Nate had been over at our place plenty of times for dinner.

He was also supposed to be Dean's best man at our wedding.

The last time I saw him was at a dinner party, months ago. He'd been sitting across the table from me, surrounded by Dean's family and friends and so much candlelight that it sucked all the air out of the room until I felt like I was about to suffocate. But everyone else near me laughed on, oblivious to the danger.

Dean must have sent him.

Sure, he's interested in art, but what are the odds of Nate being here on my second day?

I grab one of the gallery's oversized coffee table books, resting it upright on top of the sleek desk that holds our single computer, and drop onto the lone chair facing the screen. In a panic, I open up the hardcover and concentrate intently on the pages.

"We have more from Vesper in the room across here," Eitan says. "If you're interested in some of their more fluid expressions, there's a piece in purple that I personally find very expressive."

Nate gives a thoughtful hum.

"Good afternoon," Aadhya says warmly. "As always, just let me know if you two want anything while you browse. A cup of coffee?"

"I'm good, thank you," Nate says. His voice is so close. Right in front of me, above the edges of a glossy Monet I'm barely looking at. My breaths feel too fast, my heart beat too rapid.

Footsteps start up again, and I breathe a sigh of relief.

"Harper?" he asks. "Is that you?"

Shit.

I lower the enormous book to find three pairs of eyes staring at me. Eitan, with barely concealed surprise. Aadhya, with her mouth gaping wide. And Nate, standing on the other side of the desk, his dark eyes intent on me.

I give him a small smile. "Hi, Nate."

"What a lovely surprise," he says. His voice is deep and assured, and not the least bit surprised. *He knew,* I think. The suspicion grows thicker in my throat, and fear lodges deep.

He wouldn't come here on Dean's orders. *Would he?*

"You know our new colleague," Eitan says. His voice is impossible to decipher, and I glance from my ex-fiancé's best friend to my new boss.

"I do, indeed," Nate says. "How have you been, Harper?"

"Great. Yeah, it's been... fantastic. Settling in here, in London."

He nods and gives the others a charming smile. The top button of his dress shirt is undone, and the cut of his suit looks tailored. Every inch, the man I've always known him to be. Indecently rich and unfairly handsome.

"Harper has regularly advised me about art back in New York. I have her to thank for some of my best purchases."

What?

I blink up at him from behind the desk.

"Is that so?" Aadhya says in a warm purr.

Eitan lifts an eyebrow and looks at me like he's reevaluating everything he thought about his gallery's brand-new American employee. "Well, well," he says. "What a lovely surprise, indeed."

I put the coffee table book down with as much grace as I can, considering it weighs more than any book ever should.

"I didn't know you were moving on to this gallery, or I would have reached out," Nate says.

He's laying it on thick. I don't know why, either, but judging by the looks on my coworkers' faces, it's working. I clear my throat. "It was a rather quick career decision, that's true."

He nods, and there's a flicker of acknowledgment in his eyes. Quick is an understatement for what I'd done. Pulled the rug out from under Dean, got on a flight, and left everything I've ever known behind.

Only weeks before the wedding.

"But a great one. I've bought a fair number of works from this gallery. Wouldn't you say, Eitan?" Nate gives the Englishman a wide grin.

Eitan's lips curve slightly. "Indeed you have, Mr. Connovan. A most fruitful association."

"For us both," he says. "Say, would you mind if Harper shows me around for a bit? I would love to hear her take on some pieces, and then I'll meet back up with you to finalize a few things."

Aadhya stares at Eitan. I stare at Eitan. It's a blatant snub, even wrapped up in the determined charm Nate Connovan has always exuded.

"But of course," Eitan says. "You two must have a lot of catching up to do. Aadhya will be here if you need anything, and, please, come see me on the third floor when you're done."

Mr. White handles it gracefully, I have to give him that.

Nate looks at me with a raised brow. "Let's."

Okay then.

Rising from my seat, I don't dare look in Aadhya's direction. I can already hear the hundred-and-one questions I'll have to answer when I return. Likely from each of them.

I fall into step beside Nate. He's tall, towering nearly a head over me. His long strides are measured next to mine. I try to focus on the art around us and not on his presence, but it's nearly impossible.

Here it comes, I think. *The admonition. The questions.*

Telling me how upset Dean is.

What a giant mistake I've made.

"How have you been?" he asks.

I glance his way. "Good. It's been a lot."

"Yeah. I can imagine."

I match his tone of voice, keeping mine low, too. Lord knows galleries are great for making sound carry. I steer us toward the adjacent room, bypassing all of the Vesper pieces Eitan had been determined to show Nate.

"Did you know… Did you know that I work here?"

Nate is quiet for a beat, and my stomach sinks. *Shit.*

"I did," he says. "But I'm also a regular customer. We would've met eventually."

So Dean had told him. A week and a half since I let Dean know it was over. Since I blew up my life. Since I did everything I could to get as far away as possible… but, apparently, I can't escape him. Even here. At my new job, in my new city.

I wonder if I'll ever be able to wash his stain away.

"Don't say whatever you came here to say," I urge. My voice is fiercer than I expected, but I still hate how it wavers. "Please, Nate. I know you're his friend, but… *don't.*"

He stops in the middle of the Blue Room. We're surrounded by light fixtures in here, and the window blinds are kept permanently drawn, allowing the soft illumination from lamps to play across the walls.

He looks serious. He's never looked serious. Not once in the four years since I met him as Dean's friend, that night at the bar.

"I won't say a thing," he says. But then his lips curve and the seriousness breaks. "Except that I'm looking for this painting by an up-and-coming artist… I believe you said her artist name is Nova D'Arc when I asked you for new recommendations last time we spoke. Could you or this gallery facilitate a purchase?"

I want to sag into a heap on the floor in relief. Dean had expressed his feelings and thoughts clearly enough; I couldn't handle it if Nate had come at me, too. If he laid on me all the reasons why I was terrible for changing my mind.

"Yes," I say. "Of course. It's what we're here for."

Nate runs a hand through the thick, brown mass of his hair. There's a cut to his jaw that's always been severe, stronger than Dean's, and an air of intimidation I've never been able to get past. I know he is Dean's friend, but Nate is also well-known in New York, and Dean had never stopped gushing about him. About Nate's family, about their company, about the billions in assets.

"Perfect," he says.

"You've really been buying art? On my recommendation?"

Nate looks away, toward the dancing light on the walls. "I have."

"That's insane," I say. The words just slip out.

He chuckles in surprise. "Is it? I was under the impression that you majored in curating and art history."

"Yes, but an education doesn't make me an expert!"

"Tell that to hopeful college applicants," he says.

"You've *really* been buying art," I say softly. I had never realized our sporadic conversations at parties or over the dinner table had resulted in action. That he had acted on any of my whims.

"I have a small collection," he responds. "It's a good investment and keeps my portfolio diversified."

Right. I shouldn't have assumed… "Yes, that makes sense. Art is often used in that way."

His eyes snap back to mine. "You disapprove."

I shake my head. Remembering who I'm talking to and *where* I'm doing it. Who might be overhearing. "I don't. Art's value is in the eye of the beholder, but it's also in the market. And the art world thrives on high evaluations."

That curve to his lips returns. "That was very diplomatic."

"Thank you."

"You're welcome."

I look at him, and he gazes back at me. The silence stretches out a few seconds too long. The easy friendship I've always had with Nate has always been circumstantial. Rooted in his history with Dean.

And that history feels heavy now. While Dean's presence in this room might be unseen, it's far more tangible than the displays of dancing light around us.

He clears his throat. "So, are you settling in okay? In the city?"

"Yes, I've found a place, and I have my work visa. Still trying to sort out the whole phone number thing." I shake my head and look through the large arch toward the rest of the gallery.

"Where are you staying?"

I don't answer him, not right away. It's all too much. Him, here.

I wonder if he'll call Dean immediately after this.

If he'll tell him everything.

"Harper," Nate says, his voice hushed.

"Did he ask you to come here? To check up on me?" I cross my arms over my chest and tilt my head to look him in the eye. "I'm sorry, Nate, but I can't… I don't want him to be informed about my life. I don't want you to—"

"I won't," he says.

It's really hard to believe that. Maybe he sees that on my face, because his normally easy-going expression tightens into something more intense. "Harper," he says again. "If you'll let me, I would very much—"

"I hope you don't mind," a cultured British voice says, "but I poured us all a glass of champagne." Aadhya comes to a stop under the arch, with three flutes on a tray and a bright smile on her lips. "Finding everything all right?"

I accept the glass of champagne. "Absolutely. I think Mr. Connovan would love the ethnographic sketches we keep in the Garden Room. Why don't we all go there together?"

It's a narrow escape, and judging by the heavy weight of his gaze, not a very subtle one. But my escape from New York hadn't been very subtle, either.

Nate takes a glass too. "Lead the way, Harper," he says in a smooth, authoritative tone, and it's clear the conversation isn't over.

Yeah. The escape will only be temporary.

Chapter 2

Nate

Harper is in London.

The knowledge feels sharp, wedged beneath my skin like a splinter I can't pull out and can't stop returning to. My thoughts have been running over the fact again and again in the past two days.

Harper is now in London. And she's no longer with Dean.

Dean had called me, clearly shocked, telling me I no longer needed to fly to New York for the wedding. *She got cold feet. Spoke of some internship, about her dreams, and how she'd felt something was off for a long time but didn't have the guts to tell me… It's such bullshit.*

I'd asked him why he thought she hadn't been able to tell him before then, and what had happened to set this off, but he'd hissed that he didn't fucking know. Maybe he'll be more self-reflecting later on, but then again, I'd known the guy since college. He had many strengths, but that had never been one.

"The meeting with the Ridley team is in ten minutes," my assistant says. She's standing in the doorway to my office at Contron's European HQ, a furrow between her brows. "Are you okay?"

"Yeah, I'm fine."

"Looks like you need another coffee."

I shake my head. That's the last thing I need. "Thanks, but I'm good."

"All right," Trish says in a tone of voice that makes it clear she doesn't believe me. She's never been shy about giving her opinion, and I've always liked that about her. Much better than my brother's robot-like assistants.

"I won't be back at the office afterward," I tell her. "Field all emails and calls, and let whoever wants me know that I'll be back tomorrow morning."

Her eyebrows rise. "There's nothing in your diary."

"No," I agree smoothly.

Trish nods again and smiles. "All right then, sir. I understand. Have fun."

"Thanks," I say.

But I'm not sure if fun is exactly the thing I'll have. Not if Harper's mood the other day is anything to go by. I'll have to play my hand well, but that's what I've been trained for. That's what I do day in and day out here. Handling our European subsidiaries and liaising with the executives back in New York.

The Ridley meeting goes smoothly, and I leave the office a few minutes after it concludes. London is gray. Contrary to what most people believe, it's not *always* gloomy, but right now it is. The historic buildings with their gray stone around my Regent Street office mirrors the overcast skies, turning everything into one color palette.

I make it to the gallery by Duke of Kent Square five minutes before it closes. It's a beautiful structure from the Victorian period and includes columns and large windows. There's a small square in front with a fountain that hasn't been turned on, yet. It's mid-April, and the space is already ringed by elaborately planted tulips and spring flowers.

I lean against the fountain and wait with my arms crossed over my chest.

Her coworker, the black-haired woman who loves to flirt, emerges first. I've always flirted back in the past. After all, game respects game. But now I look down at my shoes and run a hand over my face. She doesn't notice me. Two men I don't recognize follow. And, finally, ten minutes past the gallery's official closing time, Harper exits.

Her blonde curls are pulled up into a ponytail today. It's messy, with a few tendrils loose around her face. She's in a pair of thigh-high boots and an oversized gray coat, a hint of a green turtleneck peeking out from beneath the collar.

She's always looked so uniquely herself. Artistic and effortless, like she doesn't have a care in the world for what others might think when they see her.

I take a step forward.

She stops in her tracks when she notices me. Her green eyes widen, and she blinks rapidly.

"Nate?"

"Hey," I say. "We didn't get to finish our discussion the other day."

"No, but you purchased two art pieces," she says curtly. She starts walking again, her heels making small clicking sounds against the cobblestones. I fall in step beside her. "What were you thinking, waiting for me outside of my work? What if someone saw you?"

"They didn't."

"But what if they did? This would look… look… so weird."

I raise an eyebrow. "That you're meeting with a client you have an established relationship with? I'd say that looks very diligent. As a boss, I appreciate employees who take initiative."

She shoots me a glare. "Yes, but that would be giving a false impression."

"Is it? Am I not a client of the gallery? Are you not in the business of selling art and maintaining client relations? Fake it till you make it, Harper."

"You know what I mean," she snipes. Her steps speed up, taking us in the direction of the King's Road and the crosswalk. "Look, I really don't want to be rude, and we've had fun in the past, but I don't want to be in any kind of contact with Dean. I don't want to talk about it, and I don't want to talk to *you*, and have it relayed to—"

She steps out onto the street and straight into oncoming traffic. I react on instinct, grabbing the back of her coat and pulling her sharply toward me. The double-decker bus honks loudly. She stumbles into my arms, and I move us a few extra steps to the safety of the sidewalk.

"Are you okay?"

She sweeps a few strands of hair off her face and looks over her shoulder. "Oh my God, that was… he just came out of nowhere."

"Yes," I say, "he came from your right. They drive on the opposite side of the road here. Did you get hurt?"

Harper shakes her head. "No, no, but that was so close. Holy shit."

"It takes getting used to. You have to look both ways. See that?" I lift a hand off her waist and point to the street, where *look left* is emblazoned with white letters on the asphalt. My voice comes out sharp. "Don't do that again."

"I don't intend to." She blinks up at me, and that's when I realize that my right palm is still pressed to the small of her back… with my arm wrapped around her middle.

She's closer than she's ever been before. Looking up at me with her wide eyes, a few freckles sprinkled over her nose, and I could look at her forever. I've always been able to do that. Look at her without needing to breathe, all to see the nuances of her expressions and the depth of her gaze.

But she's never been mine to look at.

I retract my arm and take a step back. "Sure you're okay?"

"Yes. Thanks for reacting so quickly."

"Been in the city for a while," I say. There's strain in her eyes, and it makes me frown. "Let's sit down. Get something to drink."

She slowly shakes her head. "I really shouldn't."

"Yes, you really should." I put a light hand on her shoulder and turn so we face the little café at the corner of the street. My hand is only resting on the wool fabric of her coat, but I feel keenly aware of the touch regardless.

This attraction has always been inconvenient. Stupid. Annoying.

Inescapable. I've tried, but I can't make it stop.

She looks at the café and then up at me. There's a clear conflict in her eyes. "You're Dean's best friend," she says. But she's smiling, just a bit.

I run a hand along my jaw and make my voice surprised. "Aw, so that's why you've been acting strange around me?"

She gives a tiny chuckle. *"Nate."*

My name from her lips shouldn't sound that good. It really shouldn't. "Well, how about this," I say. "Let's take that fact and put it in a box, and we'll put that box away. For now, I'm just your friend... and the only person you know in London. Let me buy you a coffee or a glass of wine and hear how you're settling in."

A small smile curves her lips, and her dimples make a quick appearance. "In a box, huh?"

"A very tightly shut box."

"As long as it's stuffed deep in a closet, and the closet door is locked... okay. And you won't tell Dean about this?"

"I won't say a word." And I mean it, too. He's my friend, and he had asked me to keep an eye on her. But that doesn't mean I'll be reporting to him.

Harper walks ahead of me to the café. I follow, leisurely. It's hard to wrap my head around seeing her *here,* in the city I've lived in for the past two years.

Pausing by the entrance, she glances at me. "You coming?"

I step past her to pull the door open. "Of course. Ladies first."

"I'll never get over your chivalry," Harper says. Her voice has warmed from when she first saw me, but there's a guardedness to her that hadn't been there before. Not when I'd been Dean's friend, not during the dinners or parties we'd occasionally attended together.

But I understand.

I'd been a friend, too... and now I'm a potential foe. I'll have to prove her wrong on that count.

We grab a table by the windows, overlooking the square, with its flowers and the fountain. In the distance, the gallery is visible. Harper orders a large lemonade, and I ask for a black coffee.

She takes a deep breath. Her green eyes are curious on mine, and a bit cautious.

"Will you tell me now?" I ask. "Where do you live? How have you been settling in?"

She looks down at her hands that are resting on the table. "It's okay. I found temporary housing, about twenty-five minutes away."

"By Tube? Or walking?"

"Tube," she says.

I frown. "Okay. Looking for something more permanent?"

"Yes," she says. "I haven't been here for long. And I hadn't exactly planned out my trip here, either."

"Right."

"I mean, I did, because I applied for the internship and the visa... but I never thought I'd *actually* end up going." She smiles crookedly and shrugs. "Sorry. I know that belongs in the box."

"You're in control of the box," I tell her.

"Okay. Thanks. And thanks for saving my life back there. That was way too close for comfort, and, to be honest, it's not even the first time it happened."

Fuck. "It isn't?"

"No. I really have to brand it into my head to switch directions when I check to cross the road." She shakes her head, smiling ruefully. "A lot of adjustments. But I like the city. There's nice energy here. It's almost like New York, but… calmer, somehow. I don't know how to define it. Not yet."

I nod, still hung up on the admission about her nearly dying *several times* since she's arrived. "Yeah. Different areas have unique feels, too, more so than in Manhattan. You'll explore it all, I'm sure."

"I'll try to," she says. The waitress brings our drinks, and Harper grips her lemonade with both hands, looking out the window.

I don't like the silence. Not with her, not when it's a contrast to the lively discussions we've had in the past. The discussions where her personality came out, when I got her perspective on things. I've never met anyone with quite the same opinions as Harper. She surprised me constantly.

Why'd you leave Dean?

The question burns and has since I found out the news. But I can't ask it. It belongs in the box, and as far as I'm concerned, that box serves us both just fine.

"What's your plan while you're in London?" I ask instead. "See all the sights? Go to every gallery and museum?"

Her face lights up. "Yes. I have a long list of the things I want to see."

"Give me your top picks."

She does, running through everything from the Tower and the Buckingham Palace to obscure museums and galleries I've never heard of.

"Well," I say. "I think you might need more than six months."

"Maybe. I'm not thinking too far ahead right now. All I want is… to explore a new place. To discover a new me." But then she shakes her head like she shouldn't have said that.

"I think that makes perfect sense."

Her eyes widen. "You do?"

"Of course. You think I didn't do the same when I first came here?"

Now her smile is curled with interest. "No, I don't. You've

always seemed… What did you change? I can't imagine you wanting to change a thing about your life."

That makes me chuckle. I use the pause to reach for my coffee and take a sip. The main reason I lobbied my brother for the London position isn't one I can share. Not with her… since *she* was the main reason.

"What does that mean? You think my life is perfect?" I ask. It's easy to play this role with her. To lean back in my chair and give her a lazy smile.

Harper rolls her eyes. "I mean, kinda? You're a jet-setting bachelor. You work in this hugely successful company that I never understood. You're handsome, rich, and you buy art on a regular basis… I've heard a ton of things, Nate, and I bet it's a pretty nice life."

I grin at her. She thinks I'm handsome? "Well, I think that might be one of the nicest things you've ever said to me."

"Did you just trick me into giving you a compliment, just to win a point?"

"Maybe I did," I say. She's halfway through her lemonade, and I don't want to leave without… *something.* Without knowing I'll get to see her again. I shouldn't try to. Shouldn't ask. But there's no self-control, not when she's here in front of me. When she just laughed because of me.

"Do you know anyone else in London?"

"Not a single person," she says. But then she smiles. "Just you."

I reach into the inner pocket of my suit jacket and find my phone. "I have a suggestion for you."

"A suggestion?"

"Yes. Two, in fact, and I want you to consider them before giving an answer."

Her eyebrows knit together, but she's intrigued. I can tell. "All right, this sounds… interesting. It has nothing to do with the box?"

"Nothing at all. I will never open that box, it will have to be you," I say. "Trust me on that."

She nods, a bit hesitantly. "Okay. I appreciate that. So, what are these suggestions?"

"There's an exhibition at the London Modern tomorrow night." I click open the email and flip my phone to display the invitation to her. "A new group of artists is being showcased."

Her eyes grow wide as saucers as she reads the invite. "And you were *invited* to this?"

"Yes."

Her gaze shifts to mine. "*How?*"

I shrug. Invitations like this regularly end up in my inbox or are filtered through my assistant, and most of them, I decline. I have no doubt this one came courtesy of her boss at the Sterling Gallery. I'd become a big art buyer, and big art buyers are always welcome at events like this.

"Like you said, I'm very handsome."

She giggles, a bit breathlessly. "Right, of course. Well, you have to go, of course. Are you asking if these artists are someones you should look into? To make a purchase?" She furrows her brow and looks back at my phone, and I see her eyes reading. "I know two of them… the third I'll have to investigate. Off the cuff, I think you should consider acquiring a piece or two by the first one. She's starting to get quite a lot of traction, so her works won't be bargain finds, but I still think it's a wise investment."

"Mm-hmm. And how do you feel about advising me on the night?"

"Like… in person?"

"Yes. This invitation includes a plus-one."

Her eyes, already large, spark with excitement. "Really?"

"I joke about many things, Harper, but never about art."

"Oh my God. And the entire museum would be closed to the public?"

"Yes. I think… scroll down a bit. They have private tours going on during the event."

"I would love to. Oh my God, this is…" But then conflict

blooms in her gaze. "But I'm not sure it would be appropriate."

I raise an eyebrow. "You—the art adviser. Me—the art buyer. This is already an established pattern."

"You can't keep doing that."

"Doing what?"

"Twisting the truth."

"I'm not," I say. "It is the truth."

She looks back at the invitation, and I see the war waging in her eyes. She wants to go. I knew she would. My assistant had called London Modern earlier today and asked if my RSVP could be changed from not attending to confirmed at the last minute.

And, originally, it didn't include a plus-one. Trish had asked to rectify that, as well.

"Harper," I say, and her eyes flicker back to mine. They look greener than usual under the interior lighting. "I'm the only person in London you know, and I've got connections. Use me. It's okay."

She blinks. "Really?"

"Yes. You and I were on good terms before there was a box, and I hope we can still be so. Besides," I say and give her a crooked smile, "I could really use some company. Most of those art exhibitions bore me to death."

Harper laughs, and the sound sends a rush of heat down my spine. I'm going to get addicted to that sound. To hearing her make it again.

"Okay," she says. "I'll go. Thank you very much."

I'm playing with fire here. Always have been when I'm with her. But I know this fire can only burn me. Because despite the use of the word "handsome" earlier, I've never been a choice for her. It was always Dean.

Pining for this woman has been the bane of my existence these past four years. But I can't seem to make myself stop, either… and now, I'm getting ready to pine up close.

Chapter 3

Harper

The knowledge that I know Nate, beyond the basic degree of acquaintanceship, has changed something at the gallery. I felt it immediately after our first encounter, but it became more noticeable in the following days, with both Aadhya, Eitan, as well as Brett—another sales associate—asking me circumspect questions about my life back in New York.

Any other big clients? Aadhya inquired with a smile, before popping chewing gum into her mouth. She always smells brightly of mint. Eitan had been slightly more casual about it all. He'd joined me one morning when I was adjusting the signs for the new exhibition in the North Room, and spoken about the importance of client relations. But there was a tone to his voice that hadn't been present before.

Nate had helped me impress my coworkers.

It feels unearned, but I try to ignore the impostor syndrome that loves to rear its ugly head. Nate had said that their impressions can't be false, since they are technically true. He had bought art on my recommendation, therefore…

I suppose, he is my client, in a roundabout, white lie kind of way.

The work is fun, at least, and every single morning, I walk into the gallery with a feeling of *this is exactly where I should be.* I haven't felt that in a very long time.

"What were you doing before this?" Aadhya asks. It's Friday afternoon, and we're both sitting in the back office, working on our laptops. Sorting through the orders and the deliveries coming in next week.

I look at her over my screen. Her hair is in a beautiful sleek bun today, the kind of style I can never get my curls into. "I was a research assistant at a museum in New York."

Her eyebrows rise. "Wow, that sounds amazing."

"It was interesting, yeah," I say. But I shrug a little. "It did get tiring after a while. It was a small museum, with almost no visitors, and the exhibition coordinator wasn't interested in any kind of innovation."

Aadhya's eyes soften. "Oh, no."

"Yeah."

"So, what were you researching?"

"I put together all kinds of suggested purchases, and each one was rejected."

"Goodness," she says matter-of-factly. "That sounds like a nightmare. I'm glad you got out of there."

That makes me smile. *Thank you,* I think. It's a throwaway comment for her, but it's the first time someone has validated my decision to leave the job I'd been tied to for years, and all the rest that came with it.

"So am I," I say.

She wiggles her eyebrows. "And is that little museum where you bumped into the billionaire clients?"

Oh no. I thought we were done talking about Nate. I lift a single shoulder in a noncommittal shrug. "He was a friend of a friend when we were introduced."

This makes her nod, and I see interest flash in her eyes. "I love that. You must have some great friends."

"Thanks. But I'm sure you do, too, right? How long have you been working at Sterling Gallery?" She's also infinitely more glamorous than me and hasn't been sitting in the equivalent of a dusty broom closet for the past four years, focusing on research tasks that went nowhere.

At 5 p.m., I head into the restroom to freshen up. There's considerably better water pressure here than in the hovel I'm renting, and I take the opportunity to quickly wash up.

I leave my hair down, but add a headband to keep it from being too unruly. Swipe on a touch of lip gloss and add dramatic eyeliner. It's not ideal as far as touch-ups go, but at least I'm in a great outfit—a long, blue silk dress and an oversized men's blazer thrown over it.

Aadhya is packing up her bag when I return to the office. She throws me a knowing smile. "Off to a night on the town?"

I grab my own bag. "Yeah, kinda."

"Of course you are." She grabs her own lipstick and applies it carefully while looking in the small mirror she keeps at her desk. "Where are you headed?"

I hate lying. I avoid it as much as I can.

But saying where I'm going, and *who* I'm going with, would spark the wrong kind of assumptions. False impressions and all that be damned.

"He's picking me up," I say instead.

Now Aadhya nods. "So, you're going on a date, and you've been in London less than a fortnight?"

"Yes."

"Okay," she says, nodding once again. "I might have underestimated you, Harper from New York."

I smile at her. "And you're not going on a date tonight?"

"Oh no, I absolutely am," she says. "Compare notes tomorrow?"

Hand me a shovel and I'll dig this hole even deeper, I think. "Sounds great. Enjoy your night."

"You, too," she says with a wink.

I head out of the gallery. It's a beautiful spring day, still a bit chilly but the evening sunlight counteracts it. Spring used to be my favorite season. Still is, actually. Dean had been a summer-lover, wanting to spend every day outdoors during the hot months. The Hamptons, Montauk, Connecticut. For the past two summers, he had us scheduled to the nines. *A week here, a weekend there, we have to make this party…*

He hasn't called me this past week. I know better than to think it's done, that he's accepted my decision. We'll speak soon enough again. But with each day that passes without an angry text or call from him, the calmer I feel about the choices I've made.

My mom is a different matter. My phone is practically burning in my bag with the six texts from her I haven't answered in the last twenty-four hours. She doesn't understand my decision.

Neither can my big brother, my stepdad, nor my two younger half sisters who hoped to be flower girls at the wedding. My cousin Ashley, who's not only family but also my best friend, is the only one who told me to go when I said I'd been having panic attacks in the bathroom every night for a week straight at the thought of marrying Dean.

The second I walked out of our apartment, out of *his* apartment, that anxiety had settled. It hadn't disappeared, but it had lessened, diminished, as if my body realized it was no longer in danger.

I was finally free.

I walk down the sunbathed London street and feel like everything around me is brand new… because it is. Nothing gives quite the same adrenaline shot straight to the soul as traveling. I wish I had done more of it before. But at least I can do a ton of it now.

I can make up for lost time, and I can become the person I always dreamed of being. And maybe I can get to know myself in the process.

Nate is waiting at the corner of Cadogan Square, a few blocks away from the gallery. He's leaning against a black car, parked neatly in front of one of the white townhouses. I'd fallen in love with all of them on my very first walk in this neighborhood. Tall, beautifully built stone structures with glossy black doors. Each windowsill on the first floor has flower boxes, filled with ivy and white cyclamen.

He's wearing a suit and a pair of sunglasses, his brown hair swept back over a square forehead. In a navy suit without a tie, the top button undone. He looks cool. Unapproachable. Rich. A couple walking a dog send him several long glances.

Nerves swirl in my stomach.

He has always been so closely associated with Dean in my mind. But he's also been funny, and kind, and nothing but good to me as his best friend's girlfriend. Welcoming even, and genuinely interested in my work.

Use me, he'd said.

And there's no doubt that the event he's taking us both to is an opportunity for me. I've been excited ever since he mentioned it. The London Modern is an internationally renowned gallery. But a private tour? The unveiling of new artists?

He could be Dean himself, and I might have said *yes* for this opportunity alone.

Nate spots me. He pushes off the side of the car and reaches up to take off his sunglasses.

"Harper," he says. His voice is deep, and a little amused.

"Hey. Sorry if you've had to wait awhile." I don't know much about his job, but I know enough to realize that he's one of those people who is perpetually busy. Frequently traveling for work, stopping over in New York for a day at most sometimes before jetting off again. At thirty-eight, he's ten years older than me; the same age as Dean. And that difference has been blatant for as long as I've known them both.

Their careers are established, their bank accounts full.

"Not at all," he says. "Now, are you ashamed of me?"

I chuckle. "No, I'm not."

"Well, having to park around the corner to pick up a girl is *mildly* embarrassing."

I glance at the car behind him. I know nothing about vehicles, but recognize an expensive model when I see one. "Can you imagine if you pulled up in that outside my work?"

"I can," he says. "Your boss might have had a heart attack out of sheer joy."

"Because he would have thought you were there for him?"

"He should be so lucky," Nate says easily.

"It's just that I want to make a name for myself at this gallery," I say. "And I don't want anyone to get the wrong impression. You know, about us."

His eyebrows shoot up toward his hairline. "And what might that impression be?"

"Nate," I say with a groan. He's never serious, not for a second, and it helps settle the nerves in my stomach. Being around him is easy. It always has been. "Don't make me say it."

He chuckles and opens the passenger door. "I'll take pity on you. Now, if you're ready..."

I slide into the car. It sits low to the ground and the interior smells like leather. A glance at the center console tells me more than enough of what the vehicle might be worth. Dean would have been all over a car like this. He's always liked swanky wheels, while they have never interested me. This is, clearly, a car with a capital C.

Nate gets into the driver's seat.

"You're driving in London," I comment.

He revs up the engine. "I am," he says. "Your tone is disapproving. Think I'll crash, Harper?"

"No, but they drive on the left side, and the traffic is..." I shake my head. "I'm just surprised, is all. And then there's parking."

"Parking is a bitch," he acknowledges. He pulls away from the curb and onto the calm Chelsea side street. "But I need to drive."

"You *need* to?"

"Yeah." He glances at me, flashing me a quick grin. "I don't do it a lot, it's true, but I'd go crazy if I couldn't at all. Besides, I've been here for two years now. Driving on the left side isn't so hard."

"But everything is in… reverse."

"Yeah, you have to adjust your thinking." He stops the car at a red light and looks over at me again. "Want to try it some time?"

"Drive? In London?"

"Yes," he says. "This car is an easy one to handle. I have another that's a stick shift, but we can start with baby steps."

My instinct is to say no. *Absolutely not.* I haven't driven in years, considering I was living in New York, and my first time getting back behind the wheel shouldn't be in London.

But I've said *no* for too long. Remained within the gilded lines until they started to feel like a cage. And the reason I'm here now—the reason I left the engagement ring behind and moved to a new country—is to experience new things.

I wrote out a list on the plane. *Thirty things to do before I turn thirty.* I tried to outdo myself with each new entry, to think big, to think back to what I wanted before I became a responsible adult. Visiting Europe's biggest art museums—the Louvre, the Prado, the Rijksmuseum—is on the list. So is buying the first piece of art myself. And…

Start saying *yes* to things.

"Maybe," I say instead. I run my hand over the leather interior. "If you have great insurance."

Nate chuckles. "Consider it covered."

He drives through crowded streets. I'm grateful for the tinted windows, for the privacy they allow as I look out at the cityscape. The people on the sidewalks, the bus stops, the old stone buildings. Neighborhoods change subtly here from one borough to the next. And as we leave the royal borough where I work, the buildings become more modern. Nate drives us over the Thames. The water is a deep gray, almost hovering on blue.

I love this view. The river snakes through the city, and from our vantage point on Lambeth Bridge, I can see Parliament and Big Ben, and the London Eye on the opposite shore.

Nate pulls up to the museum, housed in the giant building that was once a factory. The parking lot is full, but there are a few vacant spots marked *reserved,* and Nate confidently swings into one as if it's ours.

I peer out. "Uh, can we park here?

"My team called ahead. It's all good," he says with a smile. "Ready to look at some art?"

The staggering privilege of that move momentarily takes my breath away. Not only is he invited to these kinds of events, but he must also be considered a VIP.

"I'm ready."

And I am. But it doesn't stop the excited nerves from making my stomach turn.

Nate locks the car, nods at a lot valet, and then we walk up the steps to the museum. It's closed to the general public during the event, and suited attendants line the entrance.

After Nate gives his name to a woman with a clipboard, she smiles warmly at us. "You're both so welcome. Come on in. There's a cloakroom to the left and complimentary drinks right up ahead. My coworker by reception can get you started with a private tour if you'd like."

"Thank you," I tell her. "This is amazing."

She smiles at me. "I hope you enjoy it."

We check our coats, get a glass of champagne each, and then I head off toward the reception. Excitement is thrumming through me like a low-level electrical current. This place is astonishing, and I can't wait to look around.

Nate's voice is amused. "You want to start with the private tour?"

"Yes. Or shouldn't we?" I glance at him. "I think that sounds incredible, but if you'd rather mingle or look—"

"No, no, let's do it," he says. "Art waits for no man or woman."

"I just want to ensure we get a spot."

His lip curves. "Of course. Lead the way."

The woman behind the counter beams at us when we come up. She's wearing a name badge with the museum's logo and looks directly at Nate.

"Mr. Connovan," she says. "It's an honor to have you here with us tonight."

I glance at Nate from the corner of my eye. *An honor?* Just how much art does he buy?

"I wouldn't miss it," he says. "Harper here is my art adviser from New York."

The attendant's attention shifts to me, she smiles warmly. "How wonderful. Welcome to London, Harper…?"

"Elliot."

"I'm very glad you're here, too. I'm Susan Ritchie. I'm in charge of the new exhibition here tonight. We would love to show you both around, if you're available?"

"Yes," I say immediately. "We'd love that. I've heard so much about Soren's art, and the interplay with light. It's amazing to get to see his pieces showcased here."

Her eyes sparkle. "We think so, too. Tell me, what art agency are you with, Ms. Elliot?"

"Oh, I'm… I work at a gallery. Just started here in London."

Nate is a steady presence beside me, and his voice is steadfast when he speaks. "Harper has been a freelance art adviser for years. She's helped inform most of the purchases I've made for my own collection."

Susan nods. "Marvelous. Let's see if a Soren might be something to add to it, then, shall we?"

"Let's," I say. "And perhaps we could drop by the permanent collections?"

"But of course," she says smoothly and starts to lead the way. We follow a few feet behind.

I elbow Nate and quietly say, "You have to stop hyping me up in front of these people."

"And why would I do that?" he asks. "Every word is true."

Chapter 4

Nate

"I can't believe this," Harper says while buzzing by my side and enjoying her second glass of champagne. A curl has escaped the headband and has fallen in a whirl over her temple.

She's admiring a giant abstract. It has whorls of green and blue, and, to my eye, it's nice but not unique.

"Believe what?" I ask. "It's the fortieth abstract we've seen tonight."

She shakes her head. "Not at all. This might be our twentieth, but it's not a true abstract at any rate because… see those black lines along there? They're interspersed and represent walls. It's a recurring theme in his pieces. And you have the chance to buy it."

"Mm-hmm." I raise an eyebrow at her. Tonight, she's been happier than I've seen her in a long time, listening to everything Susan Ritchie said during the tour with rapt fascination. They ended up discussing the merits of Soren's art until I think they both forgot I was in the room.

It's wonderful to see.

Selfishly, I'm glad I could give her this evening. That despite the Dean-shaped box hidden in the back of a metaphorical closet, she said yes. I want to give her more experiences like this.

"You know what," she says, her tone teasing. "I don't think you deserve to own this painting. Not if you won't admire it the way it should be. This should be hung on its own wall and given ample space to be admired. There should be a chair in front of it just to sit on and observe it."

"I would love to see how you live, if that's your decorating ethos."

"Oh, I don't have any art like this," Harper says. "But if I did, that's what I'd do."

I run a hand along my jaw. "And you said this was for sale?"

"Yes."

"And you're recommending I purchase it."

She looks up at me, and her eyes are trepidatious. "Well, I don't know if I would… it's a big thing, to recommend for you to buy it."

"You've done it plenty of times before."

"No, I didn't know you actually *acted* on my words before," she says. "That was different. I was just expressing my opinions."

"So express it again about this. Don't think about me or my wallet. If *you* were building an art collection, would this piece be something you include?"

Her eyes light up, and she waits only a second before answering. "Yes. It would be."

"Great. I'll buy it."

"Jesus, Nate, you can't… Oh my God. Will you really?"

"Of course. I have it on great authority that this is a wise investment."

"That's not what I said," she retorts.

I turn, intending to find Susan and tell her to reserve the painting when Harper's hand grips the sleeve of my suit jacket. "Nate. It's terribly expensive."

"I know."

"No, it's like… this is the kind of painting *galleries* buy. Not private individuals."

I raise an eyebrow. "Let's pretend I'm starting a gallery, then."

Harper lets out a nervous laugh. "Okay. Okay, yeah. It's just... God, you're rich."

That makes me chuckle. "Hate to break it to you, but yes, I am. Thought you knew that already, though."

"I knew. But I haven't actually, like, *seen* it before." She shrugs and looks away from my gaze. "The sports car, the gallery invite... the art purchasing. It's big leagues stuff."

Her tone of voice makes me want to ask what she thinks of it. I'm not sure if it's a good thing.

"I suppose it is," I say instead.

Dean's well-off, but she's never seemed interested in glitzy or glamorous things. I know they've done some traveling, and I suspect he spoiled her when they were together. But I've also always had this feeling that she didn't appreciate being indulged, at least not the way he did it.

Should've taken her to art galleries.

The thought feels sour in my mind. Dean is hurting. I know he is. And so is Harper. I shouldn't be taking any joy from their breakup.

It probably makes me an asshole for feeling relief when Dean first told me about it.

I know I'm terrible for bringing her here.

"Nate," she says. She glances from the painting I intend to buy back to me, and there's a nervous glint in her eye. "I truly appreciate us being here tonight, and that you invited me."

"I sense there's a but coming." I raise my champagne glass in her direction. "Let's hear it."

"But, I'm confused why you're not angry with me." Her eyes narrow, her eyebrows furrow. "I'm not telling you to be angry if you're not. I've just been trying to figure out why you're doing this for me. Why you have agreed to put... to put *him* in a box, agreeing not to discuss everything? Why aren't you furious?"

"It sounds a lot like you want me to be angry with you."

"No, no, that's not what I mean."

My brow rises in disbelief. "Isn't it? Because I feel aggression coming from your side of this argument."

Harper rolls her eyes, and a smile tugs at her lips. "Can you be serious for five minutes?"

"I can, if you force me to be. Let me think, why am I not angry with you..." I take a long sip of my champagne and focus on the whirls of paint on the canvas in front of us.

What answer can I give that she'll accept?

"Back home, everyone is angry," she says.

My eyes dart to her again. The furrow is still there, creasing her forehead, and there's a look in her eyes that I don't like. Not at all. "Not everyone," I say.

"Well, Dean sure is. Dean's parents and his sister. Even my parents are... concerned. I feel like I set off a bomb and then got on a plane." Her gaze shifts to own glass of champagne, and she chuckles a little. "Sorry. Maybe I shouldn't have had a second one of these."

"Champagne tastes best when it's free," I say. I feel numb, hearing her words, her question, and seeing the look of sadness on her face. Sadness about the end of a relationship while I felt nothing but joy at the same.

It's a punch to the gut, knowing how fruitless my feelings for her are, and how wrong they've always been. How unwanted, unneeded, and unwise.

And how I've never been able to turn them off regardless.

"Maybe you did," I say. "Set off a bomb. But maybe you needed to. And the people in your life will realize that with time."

"Will they?" she asks. But she's smiling a bit. "Because I don't think Dean's parents or his sister will ever come around."

"Maybe they won't," I admit. "But maybe that's not... a huge loss."

Her eyes widen, and then she chuckles. "No, you've met them, too. I don't think it might be." Then, she covers her face with a hand. "God, what am I saying? Please don't tell—"

"Of course not. Never."

Harper nods, and her hand slides down to the side of her neck. She cocks her head. "So? Why aren't you angry?"

I thought I escaped that question.

"Because you broke up with Dean?" I ask. Like clarification is necessary.

And it's really, really not.

But she nods anyway. "Yeah. So close to the... the wedding."

"If that was the right path for you," I say, "then it was the right path for him, too. You shouldn't be together unless both of you are fully in. In time, I'm certain he will realize that as well."

She digs her teeth into her lower lip. "Yeah."

"And besides, we're friends. Always were." I incline my head toward the painting we're standing by. "Not to mention, you're invaluable to my private interests. I couldn't possibly lose that kind of asset just because of a breakup."

Harper laughs a little. "Of course. Right."

"Now come on. I think the artist himself is here somewhere."

"What? Really?"

"I heard he might show up around... yeah, around eight to give a speech."

She smiles. It's wide and happy, and her eyes dance with excitement. "I can't believe I'm doing this. That I'm here. This is incredible."

"Believe it," I say quietly. I want to make her smile like that again.

Harper turns, and her curls brush against my shoulder. I catch a scent of her perfume, of something floral with just a hint of spice.

Her voice is soft. "Look, see those people over there? By the sculpture? The woman in red is a legend in the British art scene. I've heard such cool things about her."

"Go say hi."

"I can't."

I nod. "Yes, you can. Go. Say hi."

"She would—"

"What do you have to lose?"

Harper digs her teeth into her lower lip again, but then she nods. Resolve enters her eyes. "You're right. I have every right to be here."

"Of course you do."

"Okay. Let's do this."

My phone buzzes in my suit pocket. I wish I could chuck it across the room. It's the second call tonight, and there was a reason I didn't pick up the first one. But I also know that I can't let it go too long without a response, or he'll keep calling, and at the worst possible moments.

"Go ahead. I'll join you in a bit."

She nods and walks in a straight line toward the art legend she wants to speak with. I watch her go, taking in her familiar form.

I answer my phone without looking away. "Hey."

"Nate," Dean says. "How's London?"

"It's good. Same as always."

"Great. Look, I know I've been... Did you do what I asked you to do?"

I look at Harper. She's made contact with the lady in red. She nods a few times, her curls bouncing. "Yes. I spoke to her at her work."

"And?"

"She's fine. She's doing well here."

He sighs on the other end. "Good. It's so fucking frustrating that she won't... anyway. Good. Thanks for checking up on her."

"Yeah," I say. It's the one thing I agreed to do when he called and told me the wedding was off, and that she was heading to London.

And now that's done.

"So, ah… I've been thinking," he says. "She needs time to cool off. To come to her senses and get over this whole rebellious idea of hers. I figure I'll give it a month or two and then I'll fly over there. See if I can make her see reason once she had a few weeks to consider her actions."

"Dean, I'm not sure—"

"It'll work. It has to work," he says. "But I need another favor, man. Can you keep an eye on her? Make sure she's not getting into trouble?"

In the distance, Harper's hands are moving animatedly as she describes something. I see the lady in red smile.

"Mm-hmm. Sure."

"Thanks, man. That's all I need, to know she's doing okay."

"Right. Look, what really happened between you two?" I ask. I know I shouldn't, but the question slips out, disappearing into my phone, and off across the Atlantic.

"Fuck if I know. One day everything was fine, and the next, it's over. Her explanations made no fucking sense, and I—"

"I have to go," I cut in, spotting Harper's excited smile and frantic wave, calling me over.

"Nate?"

I'm already walking her way. "Talk to you later, Dean."

I hang up and slide the phone into my pocket. My insides churn, a bitter taste sitting on my tongue. A feeling I am familiar with. Lived with for years.

Guilt.

Guilt for wanting my best friend's girlfriend.

Guilt for accepting dinner invitations that I should have declined.

Guilt for looking Dean in the eye and telling him that they make a great couple.

And now… *Keep an eye on her.*

That's never been a problem.

Keeping my eyes off Harper was always the issue.

Chapter 5

Harper

I'm on cloud nine when we leave the museum.

"Did you see the man in the striped navy suit? In the far corner?" I ask Nate as we walk out of London Modern. "He's one of the world's largest art buyers. Renowned in the business. *Renowned.*"

"He should have put that on his name card," Nate says, "so I would have known."

"And the way they'd arranged the art in the South Gallery… I know we weren't supposed to take pictures but I did it anyway."

"I saw. What a rebel."

I elbow him again. I feel like I'm floating. It's the excitement and champagne and the glittering view of London. Across the river, the St. Paul's Cathedral is lit up, towering over the surrounding buildings. "You mock, but I just had the best night in… I can't even remember how long."

"You know, I think you should change that," Nate says. His voice is easy. Comfortable to listen to. I've always liked talking to him. "New city, new opportunities… you could have plenty of best nights."

"I think I should. At least try to, you know? Do you have any more exclusive art events to go to?"

Nate runs a hand along his jaw. "Well…" he says.

I shake my head. "No, don't worry about it. I know this was a one-off. And I greatly appreciate it, too. Also, I promise not to impose on you while I'm in London."

"Mm-hmm. Thank God," he says dryly.

"Besides, you're likely very busy. What hot date did you have to cancel tonight to take me here instead?"

He rolls his eyes. "Harper."

"Come on. There must be someone. Or many someones?" I wiggle my eyebrows. "I've heard stories from Dean, about your dating life."

"All exaggerations, I'm sure."

"I think he was underplaying it." I nudge Nate's shoulder as we come to a stop next to his car. It's safe and sound in the VIP parking spot beside the museum, surrounded by taxis and people, but I still think it's crazy to drive in London.

Crazy… and very him.

"I didn't have a date for tonight," he says. "You saved me from looking humiliatingly, embarrassingly alone."

"Oh, because you're never seen alone?"

"I avoid it at all costs." He unlocks the car and opens the passenger door for me. "At your service."

"I bet ladies love this car," I tell him.

He shakes his head, but he's smiling as he shuts the door.

I lean back in the seat and buckle up. Happiness is a beautiful lingering feeling in my stomach. *What a night.* And as I look around the vehicle's interior, it's easy to imagine Nate impressing his dates with it. I bet they *would be* impressed. Dean had mentioned some of the women Nate had gone out with. One was a model, I recall. And then there was a struggling actress, and I believe there was a singer at another time, too.

I know he was engaged. Once. Long before I met him and Dean. Nate was in his midtwenties then, and it didn't result in a marriage. But more than that, I don't know.

Nate slides into the driver's seat. He reverses one-handed, turning around to look over his shoulder at the pedestrians. His jacket sleeve rides up to showcase a thick silver watch around his wrist.

I cross my legs. "I can't believe you spent… I can't even say the amount. *That* much money in one evening."

"Mm-hmn. On the painting?"

"Yes? What else could I possibly mean?"

"Oh, parking here is outrageously expensive," he says. "I drop a fortune on that alone each week."

"The Tube isn't that bad, you know."

"I'm sure. That's why I don't go on it. Leaves room for other people to enjoy."

"You're such a philanthropist."

He smiles, eyes still on the road. It's a small, genuine smile, as if he's enjoying this. Not like he's trying to charm or impress. I hadn't noticed there was a difference before.

"That's me," he says. "So come on. Tell me where I'm driving you to."

"Uh, it's a bit far."

"I can do far. I prefer far." He runs a large hand along the leather of his steering wheel, almost lovingly. "So where to?"

I tell him the name of the area first. He nods, but a faint frown invades his profile. "Right. A rental?"

"Yeah, short-term. It was all I could find, considering I decided to move so… so quickly.

"I've never been to Fairwood."

"I can bring it up on the GPS," I say.

"That's all right. Give me directions instead," Nate says. He sounds nonplussed by all the activity going on outside the windows. The road follows along the Thames, passing bridge after bridge, curving along with the river.

I do as he's asked, guiding his route, and glance at him out of the corner of my eye. I hadn't planned on him driving me home. It's definitely appreciated, considering the late hour and the long Tube ride, but I'm not prepared for him to see where I live.

I don't even like where I live.

It was the best I could find on such short notice and within my budget, without completely exhausting all of my savings. It sucks. That's the nicest thing I can say about it. When I protested about the deposit being twice as high as noted in our agreement, the landlady told me to accept it or move on. I should have left. I know that. But I had just flown overnight. I was tired from lugging my giant suitcase, and my eyes stung from so much crying, so I accepted the terms.

The buildings start to change the further out we get. The Shard and the business area around it are long gone and are replaced with half-maintained brick structures. Fewer vehicles are on the road, and those that are, are certainly not sports cars.

I glance at him again. He's quiet, one hand on the wheel and the other resting lightly on the center console between us. But I can almost feel his mind turning.

"It's good for now," I tell him, almost preemptively. "But I might move later, if I find something else I like better. And that I can afford."

He makes a humming sound. Not quite a yes or a no.

We approach a small roundabout with a liquor store beside it. A group of guys is hanging outside it. One of them shoves the other, and the fellow shoves back. Their loud voices reach us despite the closed car windows.

Nate's frown deepens into a scowl.

"Take the first left," I say. "There's a park down the street, actually. It's pretty in the daylight."

"Mm-hmm," he responds.

"Third house on the right here… yes, this is it." He pulls the car to a stop at the curb, and I start unbuckling my seatbelt. "Thanks for tonight. I had a terrific time."

But he's leaning over, looking past me and up at the house

to our left. The scent of his cologne is dark and spicy, with a hint of smoke. "This is where you live?"

His words drip with disapproval.

"Yes, but it's only temporary." I grip my bag tight and put a hand on the door handle. "Thanks again. Get home safe, okay?"

"I'm not worried about me," he says. Then, he unbuckles his seatbelt and gets out of the car.

I scramble to follow him. "Nate?"

"I'm coming in," he says. His face is set in drawn lines, that playful smile is missing from his face this time. He locks the car and throws a glance down the street, to the roundabout and the youngsters we'd seen. "Let's hope the car is still here in ten minutes."

"Nate," I say. Now I'm the one following him to my own front door. "What are you doing?"

"This place looks like it's one bad storm away from collapsing. This intercom… it's broken, isn't it?"

"Yes, but they're gonna fix it."

He pushes on the front door. It gives way easily under his touch, and we both stare as it slowly opens. The silence grows tense. "The front door doesn't even lock," he says darkly. "Come on. Show me the rest."

"I don't think that's necessary."

"I think it most definitely is." He shuts the door behind us but mutters something about it being useless.

I head to the stairs, and he follows. His presence feels heavy and judgmental, and I hate that he is seeing this.

Hate the idea of him telling Dean, who, in turn, might tell our mutual friends… I shove my hands in the pockets of my jacket and try to hide how my breathing grows laborious with every step.

"Look," I say, stopping outside the scratched-up blue door that's mine. "I haven't exactly cleaned. I didn't know I'd be having an impromptu house inspection after a lovely night at the gallery."

Nate is staring at the scratches on the door with a dark expression. "What made those?"

"They were here when I moved in."

"Charming," he says. "Come on, Harp. Open the door."

"You're being very domineering right now. And hypercritical," I say. But I put the key into the lock anyway. "I can hear it in your tone."

"Good. I'm not doing anything to hide it."

"No, that's patently clear," I mutter. I push open the door to my tiny, horrible room. I've hated it since I moved in. It's furnished, but that's a generous word for the things my landlady had left behind. The bed is a squeaky metal mess. The small desk that functions as a dining table sits crooked. Although fully functioning, the kitchenette is minuscule, and it also has a mildew issue that makes it less than enticing to use.

Nate stands in the doorway, taking it all in.

"Don't look at it like that," I tell him. "Don't make me defend this place because I really don't want to. But like I said, it's temporary."

"Temporary," he repeats. "You've been living here since you moved to London?"

"Yes."

His expression darkens further. "Why haven't you unpacked?"

I look at my suitcase, zipped up and lying on top of a small bench in the corner. Away from walls and cushioned furniture.

"Because," I say, and this one hurts to get out, "I'm worried there might be bed bugs here." I glance at him and spot a horrified expression on his face. "Don't look at me like that. I'm only concerned that it's a possibility. And I'm looking for another place to live."

"Harper," he says.

"Look, not everyone can drive sports cars and live in… in… whatever trillion-dollar apartment you have. This works!

It's not great, but it's just until I land on my feet. Housing in London isn't cheap." My cheeks are flaming with color.

Just as in New York, the housing here is scarce and expensive. Except in New York, I was a master's student and lived in a dorm. Later, I moved in with Dean, and at his place, my rent was nominal.

Things are different now. I *want* them to be different now, but that has come with some adjustments.

"I live in a townhouse, not an apartment." His tone comes across as distracted as his gaze travels around the tiny studio. Outside the window, police sirens start to wail. The sound makes me wince.

"Very pretty park," I remind him, "and it's *right* down the street."

"Harper, I don't—"

"Okay, it's not that pretty. But it has a pond and plenty of ducks," I say quickly. "Please, just stop looking at this place like you're judging me."

"I will. If you pack your things."

"What?"

"Get packed. I'm taking you to my place."

"You can't be serious." I stare at him, and he stares right back at me, eyes steady. There's not a trace of humor on his normally smiling face. "I'm not spending the night at your townhouse."

"No," he agrees, "because it won't be just one night. This place is dingy, unsanitary, and unsafe in about fourteen different ways. You're not staying here."

"This is my home," I say. The statement falls flat in this shithole of a room. I definitely don't think of this place as home. But I'll be damned if he's the one who gets to decide where I live. I'm the one who does.

"Harper, I have a townhouse in Kensington. It's a short walk from your gallery," he says in a firm voice. "There's a guest room. You'll have your own space, your own bathroom. Shower with no mildew. Certainly no bed bugs."

"I can't *live* with you."

"Why not?" he asks. His gaze falls to the window, and a frown appears on his face again. "This place isn't safe. And I have the room."

"You're being crazy. That would never work. How would…? Come on, Nate. You don't really mean this."

"I'm dead serious," he says. Then, he sighs and runs a hand through his hair. "You've known me for four, almost five years. I have a huge house. You'll have a key and your own floor. It's free, it's comfortable, and closer to your work."

"I need to live on my own," I say. My voice wavers, but only slightly. "That's what I've been doing most evenings; trying to find other options."

"You can keep looking for an alternative place to live while crashing at mine," he says.

"Nate, I can't."

"Because I'm Dean's friend?" His eyes soften, but creases still line his forehead, letting me know he's feeling frustrated. "That's in the box. It will stay in the box. I told you, I'll never be the one to open it."

I shake my head, but I can't find the words. The idea is outrageous. "You're being so overbearing right now."

"I know I am. But I also doubt I'll be able to stop."

"Nate," I say with a sigh.

"Look, if you need more time to think about it, I'll get you a hotel for tonight. For the rest of the week, somewhere in Chelsea, close to your job. But here… I can't have you stay here."

The corners of his lips tip up, and it's the first time in an hour I see the Nate I recognize. Ever charming, ever self-deprecating. "For my own peace of mind, Harp. There's no way I can live with myself, knowing you were being eaten alive by bugs in a room with no lock."

"My studio has a lock. It's just the building's front door." But I sink onto the single chair and prop my head on my hand. Looking around at the place, the decision almost makes itself. This place sucks. I know it. He knows it.

But I want autonomy, and moving in with Nate isn't the way to get it.

At the same time… cohabiting with *potential* bed bugs and obvious mildew isn't exactly living it up, either.

He probably has great water pressure.

A bed with a mattress that isn't trying to kill me.

Neighbors that don't argue or have loud sex.

"Okay," I say. "But only for a week, until I find something else."

"However long you need," he says.

"Which will only be a week."

His lip curves. "Okay. A week. You'll have the place to yourself most of the time. I work almost every day, often late."

"Of course you do." I run a hand along the back of my neck and look at my suitcase. Already packed and ready to go. "Doing whatever it is you do for a living. Four years, and I've never been able to figure it out."

"It's not as interesting as your job."

"Now you're just being modest." I sigh and head over to grab the few things I have next to the bed. There isn't so much a nightstand as a small stool placed beside the metal frame. I throw everything into my backpack. It doesn't take long.

"Modest," he repeats softly. He takes down my stuffed suitcase and rolls it to the door. "Not something I've ever been accused of."

"How surprising," I say.

He chuckles. "I like you sarcastic. Do you have everything?"

"Yes."

"Nothing in the mini fridge?"

"No," I say. When he raises an eyebrow, I'm forced to admit the truth. "It doesn't work. Hasn't for a week."

Nate shakes his head. "You'll tell me the name of the landlord or agency later," he says, "so I can shut this whole place down."

"Sounds like a great way to get my security deposit back," I say dryly.

He mutters something I can't catch and picks up my bag. "Let's go, Harp, we're headed home."

Chapter 6

Harper

"These," I say, "are all yours?"

Nate runs a hand over his jaw. He doesn't look at me as he closes the car door behind him, and heads to the trunk to unload my bags. "Two of them are."

"These two… to the right?"

"Mm-hmm."

"Shit," I say, looking at a small vintage sports car. Aston Martin? It has to be it. Parked beside it is a towering SUV—a Land Rover. Its paint sparkles under the overhead lights. "I didn't know places in London had garages like these."

"This square does," he says. He'd pulled into an underground garage in Kensington. We're off on one of the quiet streets bordering Chelsea, close to the area where he picked me up mere hours ago.

It feels like it's been days.

I grab my backpack as Nate takes my large suitcase and starts heading to the exit. Five minutes and two locked doors later, we emerge onto the quiet sidewalk of the Kensington square. There's a small fenced garden at the center, with high trees that reach far above the surrounding townhouses.

And what townhouses they are. They look impeccably maintained, white brick construction with beige stucco around the windows and stoops. Glossy black doors beckon, their numbers emblazoned in gold.

"Number eight," he says. "That's mine."

His code unlocks the gate, and I walk up to the front entrance. The townhouse is two… no, three stories tall. I've never been inside one of these. Just walked by them to and from my way to work, wondering about the people who have twenty million pounds to own one.

People like Nate.

"I'll get you a set of keys and the code," he says, unlocking the door. It swings open, revealing an interior bathed in soft light. "Come on in, Harper. Welcome."

I step into the entryway. "Oh."

"Yeah. It's bigger than it needs to be, for one person, at least." He rolls my bag to a stop at the bottom of a narrow staircase. "Want the tour?"

"Mm-hmm. Yeah, that would be… good."

"All right." Nate's voice sounds amused. "Well, here's the living room… the kitchen. It was renovated just before I bought it, and I kept it as it was." My eyes dance over the light oak cabinetry, the expanse of stone countertops, and the giant island. The large kitchen table is next to the windows that must open to a garden.

"Here's the study… and the den. I guess the Brits call it a sitting room. Or a drawing room? I'm not entirely sure." He stops by a door closest to the entryway. "This is the first guest room. You can choose but, personally, I think the ones on the second floor are better."

"Better," I repeat. The guest room I'm looking at looks like a suite in a five-star hotel.

"Yes. Larger." Back out of the room, he grabs my suitcase and pauses on the first stair, looking at me over his shoulder. There's a crease between his eyebrows. "You okay, Harp?"

I swallow. "Yes, absolutely. I'm just overwhelmed."

"Overwhelmed," he echoes.

"Yeah. You know, for a bachelor, you have a beautiful taste in interior design."

His lip quirks, and then he turns, starting up the stairs with my giant bag in hand. "I didn't decorate it."

"Right. Of course." Because he'd paid someone or bought it furnished. I knew. *I knew* he was a Connovan and worked for his family's giant company. Knew he had more money than God himself. Heard it all from Dean. Had even seen it on occasion, when our paths crossed at parties. But the reality hits me anew. The magnitude of it all.

Dean's occasional jealous comments ring in my head. How uncharitable they had seemed to me. I often thought he was silly, considering how rich Dean was himself. In my eyes, both men were unbelievably lucky and successful.

But now I see the difference. This isn't rich. This is wealth.

Halfway up the stairs, I freeze. And just stare.

On the landing, Nate notices my stunned state. "Ah," he says. "Yeah, I bought that one."

On the wall of the stairwell is a large oil painting. Across the primarily black canvas, an abstract white piece of fabric has been painted, fluttering on an invisible breeze.

"You bought the J. Quinton I spoke about," I say.

"Yeah. I did."

"When? Three years ago?"

"Mm-hmm. You told me it was a great investment."

I feel a bit breathless as I say, "I think I mentioned that she's breaking new ground and will probably continue to get more recognition."

"Yes. A sound investment." His tone is dry and a little bit hesitant. As if he's expecting me to contradict myself now.

"I can't believe it. You have a Girardi in your house. God, it's beautiful. Don't you think?"

"It is."

I take a few cautious steps up the stairs. It's hard to tear my eyes away from the artwork, but when I do, it's to look at Nate. Standing with his hands in his pockets at the top of the staircase. Somewhere between the event and this, he's undone the first two buttons of his white shirt.

"Your room is through here," he says.

I follow him. "Do you have more art here?"

"A bit more, yeah. This is your bedroom. There's a bathroom through that door there, and these closets are all empty. Use them. I promise I don't have any bed bugs."

"I don't know if I'd care if you did," I say. Walking into the room is like… oh my God. I can't wait to sleep in the giant fluffy bed or walk barefoot across the plush carpet.

I turn, taking in the space. The light oak closets, the inlaid lighting in the ceiling.

The three art prints along the left wall.

I stare at them. "Nate."

"Yes," he says.

"You bought the Asher & Wren prints? From the auction I worked at?"

He runs a hand over his nape. "Yes. I told you, you've been advising my art collection for years."

"But… I… wow." I sit down on the bed and just stare at the black-and-white prints. This day has been long. Too long, and it's all crashing down on me. "I never knew."

"No. I don't know if I told you." He chuckles and leans on the doorframe. "I suppose I owe you a good deal of commission now."

I shake my head. "No, no. You letting me stay here for the week is more than enough. Thank you. It hurts my pride to admit it, but that place wasn't… very nice."

Both of his eyebrows rise. "That description *was* nice, though. Because that place was an utter dump."

"Compared to this? Absolutely."

"Compared to anywhere."

I reach down and undo the zipper of my leather boots. It feels amazing, freeing my feet after a long day. "So you work most days?"

"Yes. Cleaners come on Mondays, around noon. They'll do

any laundry you leave in the hamper. Help yourself to anything in the kitchen and feel free to cook." He crosses one ankle over the other, his gaze s from my stockinged feet to the windows of my bedroom. "You have my number if you need anything."

"Yeah." I look at him, hesitating only a moment before saying what I need to. What has been burning in my chest the entire drive here. "Nate? You know the box?"

His focus shifts back to me. "Yes?"

"Please don't tell Dean I'm staying with you for the upcoming week. I get it if you feel that you have to, but I… I don't want him to know about my life now."

Nate's quiet for a moment, but then he nods once. "Got it. Won't tell anyone you're crashing here."

"Thank you. I just… I want a clean break. That's what this is all about."

"Yeah. You got it." He takes a step out of the room, his mouth shaping into a smile. "I'll let you—oh. Did you drop this?" He bends just on the other side of the threshold and picks up a folded piece of paper.

As he unfolds it, I see the familiar crumpled edge, and I'm off the bed in a split second. Shit.

"It must have fallen out of my backpack," I say. It was in the front pocket, and I must have forgotten to shut it last night after I read through the list for the fifteenth time since writing it.

30 Under 30

I nab it out of his hand. Nate lets it go easily, his eyes moving to mine. Amusement dances there. "I see."

"Did you?" I ask.

"Almost nothing. Looked intriguing, though."

I fold it and put my hands behind my back, locking them tightly together. The paper crumbles slightly in my hold. "Just something I wrote on the plane ride over."

"Fascinating."

"Not really," I say. The idea of him, with his freedom and power and money, seeing my ridiculous little list… of maybe even making fun of it the way I know that Dean would have. Nope.

Not having that.

"All right then," he says.

"Thanks again for tonight."

"Anytime. I'll be gone early tomorrow."

"Me too. I'm on the early shift at the gallery."

His lips curve. "And how early is early?"

"I need to be there by eight."

"Good time. Shouldn't take you long to walk from here."

"No, I'm looking forward to that." I shift my weight to my left leg and don't look away from him. Standing right outside my door. "How about you? Where's Contron's office?"

"In Mayfair."

"Ah. That's east of here."

"It is, yes."

I find myself smiling, too. "I'm learning."

"'Course you are. Won't be long until you're the one driving around London, not me."

"Well, don't hold your breath for that."

He nods again. "Maybe I will. I think you're going to surprise even yourself here, Harp."

I have to swallow again. "That's the plan, at least."

"I'm looking forward to seeing it come to fruition," he says. Then he looks back, at the stairs leading up to the next floor. "I'll be up around seven. Breakfast will be downstairs if you want any."

"Thanks. I appreciate that. All of this, I truly do."

His lips curve, and then he nods. "Night, Harper."

"Good night, Nate." I watch him walk up the stairs and then slowly, quietly, shut my bedroom door.

The water pressure is excellent. The blowdryer in the bathroom is powerful. When I crawl into bed an hour later, between pressed sheets and on a mattress that's never heard the term *metal springs,* I fall asleep before my head even hits the pillow.

And when I dream, it's about art on walls, art I've seen and loved over the years all gathered in one place.

Chapter 7

Nate

I have one week.

One week to convince her to stay. For her to realize that she doesn't need to spend money on another shitty place out in the suburbs. And a whole week of restless nights, knowing she's sleeping under the same roof as me.

Sleep hadn't come easy. I'd laid awake in the deafening silence for hours, waiting for a sound to puncture it. Any sound at all. Footfalls as she moved around downstairs, running the shower, creaking doors. But Harper's been soundless from the moment she closed her bedroom door and disappeared into the guest wing that's hers.

Will I ever be able to think of it as anything but hers now?

Maybe she has been making sounds, but my townhouse is soundproof. I've never listened to sounds this intently before.

I'm up and ready to head out before she's awake in the morning. I've got an early meeting with our contractors in Japan. It's a fourteen-hour time difference between Tokyo and New York, but it's only nine with me being in London, so my brother likes to delegate these calls to me.

Before I leave, however, I make sure to order breakfast. I don't usually eat it myself, but I promised Harper it'll be here. It's delivered while I'm still on the doorstep. A large box of pastries and smoothies, and freshly squeezed orange juice. I bring it in and leave it on the kitchen island for Harper to find.

The workday moves the way it typically does, which is fast, and I'm grateful for it. It's easy to sink into a million things that constantly need to be done. I have a feeling I'm going to need to do more of that in the coming week than I ever have before.

One week. That's all I have.

One week to savor… and one week to survive.

My phone is usually on silent while I'm in meetings, but I keep it on the entire day in case Harper calls. In case she can't find the key I left for her, or something breaks, or anything else. Anything at all.

In the few quiet moments I get during the day, my mind mulls over the place I'd seen yesterday.

The studio apartment from hell. *Apartment* is too generous of a label. It was a room with a nonfunctioning mini fridge.

In the area where I wouldn't let anyone I care about walk home alone at night.

Getting her out of there was the only thing that mattered. Making sure she is safe. And now she is… for a week.

"Nate," my assistant says. She's standing in front of my desk, her brows drawn low. Like she's studying me. "Hey. Do you still want me to sort out the car for tonight?"

"Tonight?" I repeat.

"Yes. The ribbon cutting at the new library up by Hampstead Heath. You mentioned how going would be strategic, seeing as the main benefactor is Mads Knudsen."

"Right," I say blandly. Knudsen is a major stakeholder of a European company Contron has been trying to partner with for months, with no luck. It's one of my several key priorities as a Connovan and the Contron's representative in Europe.

We have lawyers. We have strategists. We have one hell of an executive team. But we only have three Connovans, as my brother Alec loves to say, and sending one of us in is the equivalent of the nuclear option.

"Cancel the car," I say. "Tell them I won't make it."

Her eyes flare in surprise. "All right. Shall I make alternate plans?"

"No. Actually, yes. Send flowers to the event—tell them I wasn't feeling well. Make a donation to the library. Something for one of their programs for underprivileged youth."

"Got it. Delivered directly to Novus Tech's board members?"

"That's too direct. Send it to the opening itself, but make it excessive. A giant bouquet. Something that won't be missed."

She nods briskly. "Right."

It's Harper's first night at the townhouse. I don't… I *should…* but I don't want to leave her there alone.

Maybe she has plans. Tons of them.

Maybe she would rather I wasn't home.

But still, I can't bring myself to attend the function, to smile and network, knowing that, at the same time, Harper might be sitting in my home and looking up new places to live.

Or exploring the townhouse on her own… I showed her most of it. Everywhere except the gym in the basement and the third floor.

My floor.

It doesn't have much—a small library, my bedroom, and an ensuite. A large wardrobe.

But it does have plenty of art on the walls. Even more of the kind that reveals too much.

If she looks into it more.

Thinks about it further.

About why I bought everything she'd ever said she liked.

I'd need to play up the investment angle more. Strictly speaking, it's not untrue. *False impressions,* her voice echoes through my mind. Chidingly. But I've built a career out of giving people exactly the kind of impression they want.

I leave the office and drive home earlier than I have in months. My assistant hasn't left her desk yet, and I rarely walk out before her. But now I'm the one telling her to have a good evening.

The commute home is calming. It always is, even amid the London bustle, the traffic, the pedestrians. There's something about all of it that sets my nerves at ease. The vehicle under my control, the solid feel of the steering wheel in my grip, the power of the gas pedal beneath my foot. It's like mediation.

One week with Harper.

I can do that.

That's not the problem, I think. Because I might enjoy it too much… and then she'll move out, get on with her life, and disappear from mine.

At least, as Dean's girlfriend—and later fiancée—she was still in my social circle. Even while she was across the ocean and in love with my friend.

One week to make her see *we* can still be friends.

Or one week to make peace with letting her go for good.

I park the SUV next to the McLaren 720S I drove yesterday to take Harper to the London Modern and head up to the townhouse.

The look in her eyes last night had been… The word escapes me. Disconcerting, maybe? She looked at my cars, my home, and then at me like she saw a different man.

I don't know if it's in my favor or a strike against me.

"You shouldn't care either way," I mutter. Sticking my hands in my pockets, I walk up the stoop to my familiar black door. I bought this place two and a half years ago. An investment property, and the Connovan base in London. Odds are, I'll never sell it. When my tenure here is done, it'll be maintained as a residence for whenever Alec or Connie need to pop over. Or I'll rent it out if we don't need it for a while.

When I unlock the front door, I'm greeted by the sharp shrill of a fire alarm blaring at the highest volume. It echoes off the hallway walls as the light sheen of smoke hangs in the air. As if it's a living entity, it sees a way to escape and billows out through the still-open door behind me.

Shit.

"Harper!" I holler. I drop my briefcase and rush through the living room. "Harper?"

The beeping is coming from the kitchen. It's almost impossible to hear anything over the piercing sound. Where is she? What's happened?

I find her in the kitchen. She's standing with her back to me—the oven door is down, and smoke rises in a thick column from the inside—while she's waving a towel in the direction of the gaping back door.

"Harper!" I yell. She doesn't hear me, so I walk around the counter. "Harper?"

She jumps back with a shriek, her eyes wide. "Shit! Nate?"

"What's happened?"

"I tried to bake!" There's frantic energy in her movements. I can barely hear her over the incessant alarm, and it's starting to make my ears ring.

I grab one of the dining room chairs and scan the ceiling. *There.* Climbing up, I reach until I can grab the damn thing and twist it off, then press the button.

Everything goes mercifully quiet.

"Nate. I'm so sorry."

"Are you all right?"

"Yes, yes, there's no fire or anything. Just a lot of smoke." She coughs and keeps fanning the oven. The cloud of black has started to dissipate. Rushing toward the open door to the garden and freedom.

"What were you doing?"

"I was trying to bake. It didn't go… great."

The tame use of words makes me laugh. I lean against the kitchen island and just watch her, standing in an apron I didn't know I owned, waving a beige towel. Her blonde hair is secured in a giant hair clip but small curls have fallen out, framing her face.

"Glad you're finding this funny," she says, but she's smiling, too.

"How could I not?" The inside of the oven is marked by sooty stains. "What were you trying to make?"

"Scones."

"Scones," I repeat. Then, I chuckle again. "Aren't they very simple?"

"Okay, do you know how to make them?"

"No," I admit. "But if eating them counts, I have my fair share of experience."

"Yes, well, the butter... melted. I don't think I used the right tray. It dripped onto the bottom of the oven, and when I opened the door..." She stops waving the towel, standing up straight. "It billowed out."

"Mm-hmm. Trying to burn down my house on day one?" I cross my arms over my chest and try to hide my amusement. "You're making me think you *want* to go back to the bug-infested hellhole."

Harper rolls her eyes. I love it when she does that. "At least there's no oven there, so I'm safe from my own stupid ideas." She cradles her right hand, absently touching a finger. "And I managed to burn myself. Fantastic."

I step closer, putting a hand on her shoulder. "Come on. Let's get some cold water on it."

"Yeah, that's a good idea..." She steps to the sink and my hand falls away, where it belongs at my side. "I feel so stupid. I'm sorry Nate, this isn't what I intended for you to come home to. I didn't know if you'd be home at all, and I thought... I just wanted to try making scones." She blows out a heavy sigh. "Guess trial batch number one didn't go so well."

I look at the small golden lumps lined up on a tray left on the counter. "They look good."

"They look awful."

"Edible, though."

She gives me a withering look. "Barely."

I lean against the island, resting my hands on the edge of

the stone surface. "Why did you decide to bake scones right after work?"

There's a tiny suspicion in my mind, and it has to do with the list I'd seen yesterday. The one that had fallen out of her bag.

30 Under 30 list.

Sometimes it pays off to have a photographic memory. I only scanned half the entries in the second before she grabbed it out of my hand, but it had been more than enough to understand what I saw.

She's made herself a list of things to experience.

And number seven had been *try a new recipe.*

Was this it? Scones?

Harper sighs. "It's stupid."

"Tell me anyway."

"You'll laugh," she warns, but her voice is dryly amused, too. "Okay, so I watched a lot of The Great British Bake Off in the last few weeks."

"Wherever you were going, I didn't expect that," I say.

"It's a comfort show. And I rarely bake, so I wanted to try. Make something British." She looks over at the scones. "Well, I guess trial batch number one is a bust."

"Mm-hmm. You're welcome to try again."

"Even though I almost burned down your kitchen?"

"Even if you do end up burning it down." I nod toward her hand. "Need a Band-Aid?"

"No."

"Medical attention?"

She chuckles. "No."

"A scone, ordered from the nearby bakery?"

She rolls her eyes. "Insulting. And no."

"All right then." I close the oven; the smoke is gone now. The cleaners will handle the disaster zone when they swing by next time.

Harper turns off the faucet and gently dries her finger. The burn looks small. Thankfully.

I shut the back door to the small garden, blocking out the lingering evening chill of the early spring.

"I didn't think you'd be home," she says.

Right. "Hoped to have the entire house for yourself?" I drawl.

"No, no, it's your place." She leans against the counter, much like I had earlier. "I just figured you'd have plans. Considering you're, you know… you."

"Because I'm… me?"

"Yeah." Her lips turn into a smile. "No event to go to? No ribbons to cut, no investors to woo?"

"Contron doesn't have investors," I say. "We invest."

She smiles. "Sorry, my bad. What a faux pas."

"Quite horrendous, actually."

"So sorry," she says again. "Does that mean you're the one being wooed?"

I raise an eyebrow. "Usually, yes."

"Wow. What a life you must lead," she says. There's teasing in her tone, and I love it. It's so much better than the stilted awkwardness of our first meeting in London, when Dean was a shadow between us, and her eyes held distrust. "But there must be someone, no? Are you dating anyone? Tell me when I need to be out of the house."

"Harper," I say.

She rubs her hands together. "Because I can leave for an evening or be out of here all weekend if you need. Is there a girlfriend coming over? Or someone who spends the nights?"

Fuck.

False impressions, I think again, reminding myself that I've always been great at delivering. "Not this week," I say. "Have to give them some time off."

She chuckles. "Of course. How generous of you."

"I try."

Her fingers tap against the stone counter, and her lips purse in thought. "Maybe that's how I can repay you for letting me stay here. I can be your wingwoman."

"Harper," I say again.

"No, no, think about it. Let me buy you dinner and a few drinks this weekend. I'm great at this."

"Have you ever been someone's wingwoman?"

"Yes! I was a wingwoman all the time in college. Of course, I wasn't always successful, but I don't think I was to blame. Except for the time I made a guy think *I* was into him instead of my friend, but really, I was just buttering him up by speaking about—anyway. Not important." She gives me a bright smile. "Let's do that. Tomorrow night, if you don't have any plans."

I make a mental note to cancel my attendance at the fundraising gala for the Sustainable Technologies Foundation, too.

"Sure. But I don't need a wingwoman, Harper."

She nods, and her smile turns a bit embarrassed. "I don't doubt that for a bit. I'm just... trying to repay the favor. Somehow."

Right. I nod and glance down to her hand, at the burn on her left index finger. *You're the one doing me a favor,* I think.

"Throw in some freshly baked scones and we have a deal."

She flashes me a truly beaming smile. "Okay. Awesome. Tomorrow, then."

"Tomorrow."

Chapter 8

Harper

For the second night in a row, I sleep like a princess on the giant bed. And when I'm showered and ready for the day, and walk downstairs, he's already gone. Just like the day prior.

And just like the day prior, there's a large spread of breakfast foods on the kitchen island.

Scones included.

I frown at the pastries. Does he do this every day? Get someone to deliver things? I'd put the leftovers in the freezer yesterday, but it was almost full. I'll struggle to do the same today.

If I was staying longer, and if I knew him better, I'd talk to him about food waste.

It's a beautiful day in London as I walk to my work. The sun is shining, and everywhere around me, the trees and shrubbery have started to explode with leaves. The cherry blossoms are in bloom, weighing down the branches of the trees I pass, their pink petals beautiful against the blue sky.

Try a new recipe was not a success.

But at least I attempted to do one of the things on my list. A few of the others, such as *stay out all night* or *get a tarot card reading*, still seem too daunting, but researching last night in bed made them feel more real. Made the possibilities of all kinds feel more real.

Aadhya is upbeat at work. The gallery is throwing a giant start of summer cocktail party in a few months, and she walks me through all the things we need to do before then.

Finally, I think. A job with actual stakes—a job that requires me to think, and act, and be creative. We spend half the day planning out the organization of the space, and the rest of the time entertaining buyers.

A call comes in while I'm walking home.

I stare at the name on my screen for long seconds. Panic unfurls in my stomach, grips my chest, making it hard to breathe. The instinct is to shut my phone off entirely. To drop it on the ground and watch it crack and shatter.

But I had seen the emails, too. The cancellation of our venue so close to the wedding is… well. We won't get our deposit back. Not for the venue and not for the caterers.

And we need to deal with it.

I take a deep breath and lift the phone to my ear. "Hello."

"Harper," he says. Dean's voice isn't angry, and my fight or flight response slowly drains away. "How are you?"

"I'm good. How are you?"

"Great, yeah. Calling from the office. It's your… afternoon now, right?"

"Yes. It's 5 p.m. my time."

"Awesome." There's a pause, and it's not entirely comfortable. "I'm guessing you've seen the emails."

"Yes. I told you, I'll pay my half. Just give me a few months—"

"Harper," he says. "We don't have to cancel."

I close my eyes and lean against the wrought iron fence beside the sidewalk. Not this. Not again. I can't have this discussion again, can't handle the cajoling, the guilting, the anger. He has many tactics, and all of them are grating.

"We've spoken about this."

"You've spoken, but I don't agree," he says. This time his voice is harder. "I say we keep the reservations—"

"I've already told the venue to cancel. I've made all the arrangements, and I'll pay my half as soon as I can, Dean." My voice is firm. It's easier to be firm over the phone than when he's in front of me, his eyes turning hard, and his temper rising.

"I don't care about the money," he says, and I know it's a lie. Because he's always cared. When it mattered, he was happy to throw it in my face, that it was *his* apartment we were living in, that it was *his* family's beach house. But when I tried to contribute, he always turned me down, too.

I'll never live like that again.

"Look, will you at least call my mom? To explain yourself? She's heartbroken," Dean says. "She doesn't understand why you just left. She thinks of you like a daughter, you know. Gave you those family diamonds last Christmas."

"I gave them back," I whisper. Of all the tactics, guilt is the one I find the hardest. I have no defense against it.

"Harper," he says. His voice is coaxing, but there's anger beneath it. "New York is your home. What are you doing, running off to a different country? Doing a traineeship at twenty-eight? You would be—"

"In the future, just text me about the wedding logistics," I say. My hand is shaking around the phone. "Bye, Dean."

"Ha—"

I hang up and immediately turn my phone on airplane mode. I don't want another call or a text—nothing. My breathing is hard. I keep walking. Focusing on one step after the other, and not on the panic still squeezing my chest tight.

When will it end? Being reminded of him, the barrage of emails about the canceled wedding arrangements, my friends and family asking me what happened…?

Guilt makes my stomach churn. His mother had been wonderful. She will never realize, never will see that her son is anything other than a prize. In many ways, he's a great man. Until I understood he wasn't—not for me.

The mold he expected me to fit into was too tight.

It had shrunk around me until it was like Saran Wrap, invisible but swathed tightly like a noose. And he hadn't listened to any of it. Any of my concerns, my thoughts…

I didn't think you could be alone in a relationship until I started dating Dean. Until I woke up one day and looked across the bed, realizing that he knew nothing about my inner thoughts. And worse… didn't care.

The final blow had been a conversation I overheard. He was up earlier than me, and on the phone. He'd always been a loud speaker. I don't think he was even trying to be quiet this morning; didn't care whether I heard or not.

He'd been speaking to his brother, I'd later figured out.

He'd said that he was planning on my career being over after the wedding. *When we have kids, for sure.* There had been a pause, and I'd felt my stomach sink, because this was a conversation we'd had before. He wanted me to stay at home. I was adamant I wanted to work when possible.

And then he said the thing that broke something inside of me. *It's not like she has much of a career to begin with. An art degree is pretty much decorative.*

It was not the worst he'd ever said. But piled on top of my own misgivings, the panic I'd been feeling as the days edged closer to the wedding, and the application I'd sent into the London gallery without his knowledge…

It had become painfully clear that he didn't think I was capable. That I was someone to be controlled, guided, escorted. More of a pet than a true partner.

I'd packed my bags right away.

I remind myself of all of that as I walk the final blocks to Nate's home. Remind myself of where I am, that I got out, that I'm better now. That I made the right decision. That I don't have to feel guilty for my choices. Hurting him wasn't great, but marrying him in the state I was in would have been far worse.

I hope he sees that someday.

I stop outside Nate's enormous townhouse. The key is heavy in my coat pocket, and I turn it over once, twice.

Then, I walk up to the gates of the small courtyard park instead. If Nate's already home, I'm not ready to talk to him. Not ready to talk to anyone until the ball of knots inside my chest has started to untangle. Or at least not ache the way it does right now.

I stop at the wrought iron gate and try to push it open. It won't budge. There's a lock on it.

Beyond the gate, I can see the winding path, leading to a small grassy square that's surrounded by hedges. There's a fountain behind them.

Locked.

I didn't see that coming. For a few long seconds, I just stand and stare at the nearby garden. So close, yet locked away.

A moment later, a dog barks, and then there's activity around my feet. I look down to see a spotted dachshund at my feet—dancing around, the ears flopping.

"Well hello there," I say.

The dog is quickly joined by another, all-brown dachshund. Their leashes are held by a man, probably in his seventies, standing beside me. He looks dignified in a small cap, a tweed jacket, and a pair of green chinos.

"Hello there," he says. His accent is all British upper crust. "Were you trying to get in?"

"Yes, I'm sorry, I was. I didn't realize you needed a special key. I'll get out of the way for you." I reach down and pat the spotted dog on the head. His front paws are on my shin, his tail wagging rapidly. "Beautiful dogs."

"They are, aren't they," the man says. "Tell me, where do you live?"

"Number eight."

"Ah," he says. There seems to be a whole world in that single word. "I live in nine."

"Really? Then, we're neighbors," I say.

He nods. "It would seem so. You're living with that American man, with all the cars."

A blush creeps up my cheeks. "Yes. We're friends, and he's letting me stay at his place for a while."

"Hmm. Well, in that case…" He holds out his key demonstratively and uses it to unlock the gate. "The house keys all go to the gate."

"Oh, really?"

"Yes, reserved for those who live here on Clarence Square." The dogs race ahead, sniffing at the grass inside the garden. "Which is you at the moment, love."

I smile at him. "Thank you. I'm Harper Elliot."

"Richard Edwards," he says.

There's something so wonderfully formal about him, his entire demeanor, and the two dachshunds. Each has a beautiful collar with a tartan print.

"Nice meeting you, dear. And please tell my neighbor that he has a most wonderful Aston Martin."

"I will, definitely."

He nods at me again, like a gentleman bidding adieu to a lady, and walks into the garden with the dogs trotting along beside him. The gate swings shut behind him, and I search for my own key in my coat pocket.

It fits perfectly.

A locked garden. I've never heard of that before. I sit on a bench and breathe in the scent of trees and grass, listening to the water in the fountain gurgle until I feel like myself again.

Nate isn't home. I called out for him as I walked up the stairs, but there was no reply. I focus on getting ready for our dinner. When it's almost seven, I shoot him a text.

It feels weird.

All of it, when I think about it too much, feels weird. Staying in Dean's friend's house. Going to dinner with said friend. Having drinks. But when I stop myself from overthinking it… it's fun.

Exciting.

I'm comfortable around him, for the most part, in a way I didn't expect to be. He's easy to tease, and he gives as good as he gets. And something about the light way we communicate brings me peace.

My phone vibrates with a text.

"I'm downstairs. Ready when you are."

What? When did he get in?

This is the problem with living in a home this big. You can't hear a thing happening.

I give myself a final glance in the mirror. The silk skirt, the camisole, and an oversized blazer in hand. The reflection staring back at me looks good. I've always loved this, the art of getting dressed. Mixing up the things I find in vintage stores. My hair is a curly mess, but at least it's *somewhat* under control, and I throw on a headband to keep the mass of it in place.

Nate is lounging in the armchair in the entryway, set at the bottom of the stairs. One arm is thrown over the back, long legs stretched out while he's leaning against the cushion. He's looking at his phone with a faint frown.

The sharp suit from the other night is nowhere to be seen. He's in a pair of gray slacks and a linen button-down, the top two buttons undone again.

He looks up when he hears me.

The frown disappears, replaced by the slight curve to his lips. "Hello."

"Hi. Have you been waiting long?"

His eyes glide down over my outfit for a long moment. "Forever," he says.

Something in his tone makes me blush.

We leave the house on foot. He asks me where we're going, but I tell him it's a secret.

"And we're walking?" he asks.

That makes me chuckle. "Yes and no. One of your cars would *not* have helped. Not if we're having drinks later. This place is close."

"How do you know restaurants to go to already? You've been in London for five minutes."

"Almost two weeks at this point."

His eyebrows wiggle. "My point exactly."

"Come on, don't be skeptical. The place I'm taking you looks cool."

"I'm sure it is," he says. But he's smiling, just a bit, and excitement makes my steps lighter. I didn't realize how much I'd missed having a friend in the past few weeks. Since I made the decision, since I packed up my life, since there was no time for anything but logistics and guilt.

We come to a stop outside the Mediterranean Grill restaurant. Large windows give ample view of the interior, the low-standing tables, surrounded by pillows instead of chairs. The middle of each table is inlaid with a firepit, allowing diners to grill their own meat.

"Here?" Nate asks. But his voice is amused.

"Yes. Doesn't it look cool?"

"It does. It also looks like fire hazards are your thing, Harp."

I chuckle and reach for the door. "Good thing you're here then. You can turn off the fire alarm. Let's go."

We get a table in the corner. The lighting is dim, and we sink onto the pillows across from each other. Nate grumbles a bit. But it's easy to see in his expression that he's inwardly amused, and something inside me softens. Good. This isn't the sort of place I could have ever convinced Dean to go to.

We order and are soon presented with a spread of food. I ask Nate about his job. He details it slowly, reluctantly, and dryly. The third time he says that he's a glorified errand boy, I roll my eyes.

"That's not true, though. I know it's not."

He reaches for his glass of wine. "And how would you know?"

"I've heard things. About what you do. Expanding the company in Europe."

"Yes. Among other things. But mostly, I just do what New York tells me to do." There's a glint in his eyes, though.

"Why does that make me think you *never* do exactly what you're told?"

"No, it happens sometimes. If it's the right person asking." He holds his wine glass casually—the stem dangling through his fingers—and leans back against the pillows. "What about you, Harper?"

"What about me?"

"Do you ever do exactly what you're told," he says. In the dim lighting, his face is half in shadow, but I can still see the spark in his eyes.

I swallow. "Sometimes. But I'm trying to shake the habit."

"Mm-hmm. Becoming a rebel."

"Well, trying to, at any rate."

He nods. Takes a sip of his wine. "Which is why you've made a list of things to do. Like trying a new recipe or staying out all night."

My eyes widen. "You bastard!"

He breaks into a grin. "I'm not blind, Harp."

"How much did you read?"

"Not much. Not at the time, anyway."

"What?"

He shakes his head, still smiling, and taps his temple. "I have a photographic memory. Your list is stored in here."

"You're kidding me." I bury my face in my hands and wonder if I can sink through these beautifully-patterned pillows. "Okay. If you're gonna judge me, judge me in silence."

"Why would I?" he says with an easy drawl. "It looked like fun. Some of the points, anyway. *Staying out all night* was cute. You've never pulled an all-nighter?"

I bring down my hands and find him taking another long sip of his wine. "No, I haven't."

"Well, that one could be easily arranged." He reaches for the pita bread that's been set between us and tugs off a piece. The rest of our meal is massacred on the table, grilled and half-eaten. Delicious. "Number thirteen is especially intriguing."

"Number thirteen," I repeat, and my blood turns to ice. "Is that the one..."

"It is," he says. *"Sleep with someone who is wrong for you."*

Another blush creeps up my cheeks, but I just level a finger at him. "That list was not meant to be read by anyone."

"Mm-hmm. Want it to go in the box, too?" he asks casually, like it's no big deal if I tell him off for teasing. If I set a boundary that he'll keep without a care.

But I just reach for my glass of wine. "No. It's okay. It's a pretty outrageous list, after all. I just want to... do things outside of my comfort zone."

"Mm-hmm. Like, trying to burn down my kitchen."

"Definitely outside of my comfort zone."

He watches me with heavy-lidded eyes. There's a calculation in them I recognize, though I've only seen him look like that a few times in the past. When he and Dean used to talk about business or investments.

"Do you feel like you were firmly in your comfort zone before?"

"In a way," I say, digging my teeth into my lower lip. "I just felt like I woke up one day and realized... I hadn't made any decisions for myself in years. You know? I turned twenty-eight. Only two years left to thirty... and, somehow, I skipped having all of those wild experiences that people talk about enjoying in their twenties. Or, I stopped having them at some point." I shake my head as if I can shake off the feeling. "I never interned at a great museum. Never lived abroad. I just slotted right into Dean's life and let him... Sorry. That's in the box."

"Don't apologize," Nate says. "It's your choice, that box."

"My choice?"

"Yes. Whether or not we open it."

I nod and run a finger along the wooden edge of the low-rise table between us. "I just want to be in charge of my future, I guess. Take back control of it. But the problem is, I don't really *know* what I want my future to hold. Ergo… the list."

"Ergo," he says, a smile lurking in the corner of his mouth. "I get it. It makes sense."

"I'm glad you think that, because it barely makes sense to me. But it's the best thing I could think of," I say.

He nods. Shifts against the pillows and looks at me like he's holding back a secret. I narrow my eyes at him. "What are you thinking now?"

"Nothing," he says. "Just that I think you should dress in athletic gear on Sunday and meet me at noon in the living room."

My heart rate ratchets up. He's not judging me for the list. He's… participating in it? And I don't know if it's a sign of how starved I've been for company, for approval, for someone who genuinely listens to me, but I can't help smiling at him. And teasing him.

"Hey, while number thirteen might *technically* apply to us, that's not happening."

He chuckles. "If that's what I was aiming for, would I ask you to wear workout clothes?"

"I don't know what a rich playboy prefers in bed. Maybe athleticism is required."

"Oh, it is," he says, looking down at his glass of wine. "But clothes most definitely are not."

Something tightens in my chest. "What are we doing, then?"

"If we're not having sex?" He says the word in such a nonchalant drawl, that it makes me look away. Down to my own wine glass. "We're checking another item off your list."

"Which one?"

"That's a surprise," he says.

I roll my eyes. *"Really?"*

"Yes. Live adventurously, right?"

"You're right." I look down at our empty plates and then out the window. Beyond, London and the thing I'd promised Nate beckon. The thing we'd gone out for. I look back up at Nate and give him my widest smile. "And speaking of adventures… Ready to have the best wingwoman in all of London at your side?"

His voice turns dry, and his eyes stay on mine. "Can't wait."

Chapter 9

Harper

He paid for dinner while I used the restroom.

"No, Nate," I say when I return and find the check handled. "This was supposed to be my treat. As a thank you for letting me stay with you."

"I thought being my wingwoman was supposed to be my treat," he says.

"Well, that too. You can have two treats."

He shakes his head. "No, I can't. Besides… if you're that set on taking me out for dinner, Harp, I'll let you in the future."

We leave the restaurant and cross a busy street. It's a Friday in Chelsea, and the energy is high. So is mine. I feel buzzed on life, and on a glass of wine, and the abundance of opportunities.

The people-watching here is something else.

The bar is an upscale sort of place, with hedges trimming the terrace and the bouncer keeping a tight control over who's let in. We find a spot in the corner, looking out onto the busy locale. Music plays softly from speakers hidden around us.

Nate orders a gin and tonic, and I ask for a glass of white wine. This time, he lets me put down my card. But he's grumbling when the waiter walks away.

I nudge his leg under the table. "Come on, surely your ego isn't that fragile."

"Fragile?" His eyebrows rise, and that faint smile curves his lips again. The one that feels the most genuine. "Didn't know you saw me that way, Harp."

"I didn't, at least not before I learned that letting a woman pay for dinner and drinks makes you uncomfortable." I'm smiling over the rim of my wine glass. "I already know you're rich. I've seen it. You got nothing to prove to me."

"Maybe," he says, leaning forward on the table, "that's not why I'm unhappy about this little idea of yours."

"Oh? Then what is it?"

He runs a finger along the thick edge of his tumbler. "Maybe I'm uncomfortable with you spending money on me when it's worth more being spent on yourself."

I narrow my eyes at him, and a flush creeps up my cheeks. It feels like an insult. Compared to him, I'm poverty itself. And he'd seen where I stayed before he swooped in and offered me a non-bug-infested room and a shower with excellent water pressure.

My conversation with Dean weighs heavily on me. It always takes me a while to shake off his comments.

"Harper," he says with a sigh. "I'm always uncomfortable when a friend spends money on me."

The admission makes me nod and lessens the pang of embarrassment. "Is that a part of having so much?"

"I don't want people to spend their hard-earned cash on things I could take care of myself."

"Maybe you just don't like people taking care of you."

His brows draw together, and there's no hint of a smile on his face. Only intense focus. I thought he'd smile at my remark. Return to the playfulness we'd had all evening.

"Maybe," he finally says. And then he smiles, a broad, charming smile, and leans back in his seat. "But you've finally done it. I'll suffer through this drink to make you happy."

"You're very generous."

He inclines his head and raises his glass. "I know, I know."

It only takes me a few minutes to glance around the room in search of potential partners. There are several beautiful women here—plenty of them around my age, a few younger, and some perhaps older. Nate is in his late thirties. But he could pass for a thirty-year-old rather than thirty-eight, and I wonder…

"Okay," I tell him.

He huffs a quiet laugh. "Okay? What's happening now?"

"I've done some reconnaissance. The hostess was definitely checking you out on the way in."

Nate's voice turns into a drawl. "Was she now?"

"Yes. And there are at least three women here I think would be interested in you. The one a few tables down, with the large drink? She's glanced at you twice in ten minutes."

"Damning evidence," he says.

"Oh, laugh all you want, but I know women."

"Mm-hmm," he says again. Twisting slightly in his chair, he surveys the bar. The place is pretty packed. It feels like the kind of place Nate would frequent regularly. Or Aadhya from work. A place to see and be seen.

A tenuous silence falls between us.

And I feel just a tiny bit stupid. He has always been kind to me. We've gotten along well. But now, we're sitting here, at my behest, just so I could thank him for his generosity. Lord knows he probably has ten other things to do rather than sit here with me.

His home is beautiful. I couldn't be more grateful… and a part of me wonders, looking at him in my peripheral view, if he kept his promise. Or if Dean knows exactly where I am.

I take another long sip of my wine. "So what kind of women are you interested in? Or men, perhaps? Both? That would give me twice the options."

His eyes glint with amused patience. "I'm attracted to women."

"Okay then, I suspected that, but one shouldn't assume." I tap a finger along the rim of my wine glass. "And what are you looking for?"

"What makes you think that I'm looking at all?" he asks.

I swallow. "Maybe you're not. That's totally fine, too."

His lips curve. "Tell you what, I'll let you know the type of women I'm interested in dating if you spill about the kind of guy you're looking for."

My eyebrows shoot up. "Me?"

"Yes. Only fair," he says. "If you're to be my wingwoman, I'll need to return the favor one day."

I shake my head. "I'm not looking to date."

"Maybe not right now," he says offhandedly and takes another long drink of his gin and tonic. "But you will be in the future."

The thought is... true. Even if it feels very distant right now. Way in the future.

I dig my teeth into my lower lip. "Okay. You describe your ideal woman, and I'll do the same."

His eyes glow. "And I'm supposed to go first?"

"Yes! We're talking about *you* dating."

Nate chuckles. "Why don't you tell me what you *think* I want. If you're that great of a wingwoman."

I roll my eyes. "You know, you can be really frustrating sometimes."

He grins crookedly. "I know. Now come on, lay it on me."

I cross my legs. Look at him thoroughly, assessing. Take my time. "This feels like a trap," I finally say. "But okay. Judging from what I know about you... and what I've heard... you date a lot of beautiful women. I believe there were at least two models and one C-list actress."

His lips twitch. "Right."

"Sorry. B-list?"

He lifts his hands, palms out as if in surrender. "Hey, don't let me interrupt. Go on."

"Right. So, beauty is important." But then I frown, because

I realize I don't know much more than that. Dean had spoken occasionally about Nate's dating life, shared stories from their fifteen-year friendship before I entered the picture. His failed engagement, and the real estate heiress he was briefly connected to.

"So far I seem somewhat superficial," he comments.

"Yes, well, I'm thinking. I guess you'd want someone who has a flexible schedule."

Nate's eyes widen. "Wasn't expecting that one. Okay."

"Yeah, that way she could join you when you travel or move countries. I also think you'd like a woman with her own career. Not too much of one, of course," I say with a smile, "so it wouldn't take her away from you. Just the right amount of non-threatening ambition."

His eyes darken, but the crooked smile is still in place. Even if it looks a bit frozen. "I see," is the only thing he says.

I shrug. "Just what I've observed about men like… well, like you. I think you also want a woman who is great at socializing and knows what to say and who to invite. You know, who can go with you to the gallery events and things like that."

"Mm-hmm," he says. "Her personality sounds nonexistent."

That makes me laugh. "Okay, but see, that's where I need your answers! I just gave you the basics, the essentials. Now tell me what you like."

"Right. Well, aside from a woman needing to be beautiful, constantly available, unambitious, and good at making small talk… I suppose I like women who can surprise me."

That makes me sit up straighter. "Who *surprise* you?"

"Yeah." His lips curve, crookedly. "I like the unexpected."

"Okay. That's a good metric… even if it's kinda hard to define."

"It is, and that's the point. I like them funny, too."

I chuckle. "Of course, they'd have to laugh at your jokes."

He shakes his head, but amusement glints in his eyes. "I don't need an audience."

"Right, right. Men always say that." I wave my hand, brushing that away, still smiling. "I think you like your women clever, too."

"Of course I do," he says.

My appraisal of him rises. I've seen enough rich men who rate that particular quality about a woman low on their list of demands. Who consider it a nice bonus rather than a necessity.

He leans toward me, bracing his hands on the table between us. "I think your questions are far more telling than my answers."

Something flips over in my stomach. "Are they?"

Nate just stares back at me. "Who's your ideal man, Harper?"

"I don't know. Why don't you tell me? Return the favor?"

His lips twitch with dry amusement. "I'm willing to bet it's someone who wants you for more than an arm candy to events."

I take a sip of my wine and motion for him to carry on.

His smile flashes again. It looks more dangerous this time. "You asked for it, so you ready to hear what I really think? I think that the man your questions allude to me being is someone you never want to date. *Again*. You're done. For good this time."

Everything inside of me stills. Goes cold, and then boils hot. Heat races up to my cheeks. *Did he just imply…?*

Judging from the way his eyes glimmer dangerously, he did.

Because the man I'd assumed he was, based on his wealth, his job, his history… is pretty much what Dean had been. And that shallow woman I pictured Nate being attracted to, was who Dean wanted me to be.

And what had smothered me until I couldn't take a proper breath.

"Maybe," he continues, voice dark, "you want a man who *doesn't* see your ambition as a problem or a threat. Someone who doesn't want a palatable partner for social events, who expects your schedule to effortlessly fit his."

I can't look away from his gaze, even though it feels like it's burning through me. On its imaginary shelf, I can hear the box rattle.

"Maybe," I say quietly. "I agree with you about that."

He takes another sip of his drink. Leans back in his chair, like he has noticed that I need space and gives it to me. But my heart is still beating fast. Nate's more perceptive than I had thought.

"You still want a man who appreciates beauty, though." The words are easy, light. He's looking out the window as he says it, at the line of people now trying to get into the upscale bar.

The return to his charming self makes me chuckle, and the tension in the air bleeds out. This is the Nate I'm familiar with.

"Describe him to me," he says with an amused drawl. "Your perfect man. Would he be a painter? An artist? Someone you could talk with about art history?"

My smile feels easier now. We're on safer ground. "Using that logic, your perfect woman is someone who understands… whatever it is you do at Contron."

He huffs a laugh. "If that's one of the criteria, I'll be single for life."

"Maybe that's not so bad. I've thought about that lately. Maybe I'll join you in glorious singlehood. Focus on my career and my friendships, and on the art collection." I hold up my drink with a smile.

He looks at it dubiously, but then lifts his own with a small shake of his head. "This," he says, "is the stupidest thing I've ever toasted to."

We clink our glasses together.

"Why?"

"Because you're obviously not going to be single for the rest of your life. You mentioned the hostess checking me out? Well, there's a group of guys across the room, and at least two of them have been looking at you longer than they should have if they weren't interested."

On reflex, I glance over to where his gaze has shifted. "Really?"

He snorts. "Single for life, my ass."

I grab my drink and move over to his side of the table, sitting next to him on the lounge sofa. "I need a better view," I tell him.

"You're a woman on a mission."

"Of course I am. Okay… see the woman at the bar, talking to her friend? The brunette with a glittery handbag. She looked at you while we were walking in."

"Wow," he says. "I'm flattered."

I roll my eyes. "What should I do? I'm thinking I go up and order, and while I'm waiting for a drink, I'll talk to her. Start up a friendly conversation, and then you join us." Adrenaline is already flowing through my veins at the notion. I used to do things like this often when I was a college student. Cared less about what people thought.

Nate's thigh rests against mine. "I've never seen you like this before."

"Like what?"

"So hellbent on a stupid idea." There's reluctant amusement in his tone. "I'm almost enjoying it."

"Almost?"

"Nearly all the way there," he says. "Could be convinced if you went just a bit crazier."

My heart speeds up. "Maybe that's what I need. To get crazier. Even if my family already thinks I've gone insane."

"They do?" he asks. "You seem perfectly rational to me."

I look at him out of the corner of my eye. "I can't tell if that's sarcasm or not."

"I told you, I like women who surprise me," he says. "You

certainly do, Harp. All the time. Now come on. Let's get out of here."

"Already?"

He downs the last of his drink. "I'm not going to flirt with a random woman tonight, Harper. Not even to make you happy."

A flush creeps over my cheeks. "I'm sorry, I didn't mean to—"

"Don't apologize," he says, and that wide smile is back. "It's just, I'm enjoying your company far too much to make small talk with a stranger."

The compliment makes me blink a few times before I smile back at him. "You do?"

Something glitters in his eyes. "Oh yes," he says. "Now tell me about this recent madness of yours."

Chapter 10

Nate

The threat of rain hangs in the air on Sunday. It casts London into grayness that feels far too familiar by now and leaves the air humid. The streets are calm and quiet without the weekday traffic, and I let my foot hit the gas harder than I'm usually able to. Something inside of me relaxes as the speed increases.

Harper is silent in the passenger seat.

She's dressed in an athletic getup—tights and an insulated jacket—but her hair is down. It falls in soft golden waves over her shoulders and is pushed back with a black headband.

A black headband that looks like the one she wore the first time I saw her at that college bar.

I glance over at her. In so many ways, she looks just like she had that night. Curious. Pensive. Gazing out the windshield, her mouth just slightly parted, hands clasped in her lap.

In other ways… everything has changed since then.

I tap my thumb against the steering wheel. I hadn't seen her yesterday. Work had occupied most of my day, and she'd been doing errands. By the time I got home from an event I couldn't get out of, the living room was dark and the door to her bedroom shut.

I walked right by it on my way up to my floor. Ignored the slight tingle in my hands, clasping them into fists at my side.

What she'd said at the bar…

It confirmed the suspicions I'd harbored since the night she, wearing her black headband, met Dean and their love story began. Suspicions that I could never discern from my own jealousy, but ones I couldn't dismiss, either.

That she was wasted on him.

And then, she'd described the kind of woman she thought I wanted.

Harper looks out her window. "We're not going very far?"

"No," I say. "It's close by."

Her voice turns amused. "And I'm still not allowed to know what we're doing?"

"You know it's something off your list," I say.

"Yes, but there are thirty things on it," she says. "I still haven't decided whether I'm okay with you having memorized everything on it in a span of a second."

That makes me grin. "How long do you think it'll take to make your decision?"

"I'm not sure. I think it depends on what we're going to do today."

I nod and hide my smile. "Of course." The list had been a jumbled mess of highs and lows. From archery to staying out all night, to going to a tarot card reading, to having a threesome.

I slow the car to a stop at a red light next to Kensington Gardens, and the silence in the car feels thick with tension.

We both know that I'd seen it.

And what it means.

"It belongs in the box," I say. My words don't ease the strain enveloping us. If anything, it makes it worse, but the words had slipped out regardless. They sounded harsher than they should have.

Because it says something about Dean, too.

"How does it work, having a photographic memory?"

Harper's voice comes out a bit higher than usual. When I glance over, her cheeks are pink.

I wonder if they go that shade when she comes? What does she sound like? How does she look? Would her curls be wild around her face and her mouth half-open?

My hand tightens around the leather. "I can recall images in great clarity."

She chuckles. "Yes, well, I think that's the gist of it. But have you always had it? When did you realize it was something you could do that others couldn't? And was school a breeze?"

Amusement tugs on my lips. "Didn't know you were so interested in getting to know me better, Harp."

"Come on. This is super cool. I've never met anyone with a photographic memory."

"It's not very common. It's not even very well-studied." I tap my fingers against the steering wheel again and glance at her out of the corner of my eye. "For me, it's visual. For some reason, I can effortlessly, and very vividly, recall details from memory."

"How was school for you?"

I chuckle. "Studying for tests was pretty easy, if that's what you're thinking."

She's angled toward me in the car, her lips stretched into a smile. "And when did you realize? How did you figure it out? I mean, you must have assumed everyone could do it."

"Yeah. I thought it was normal." The road ahead curves, and I move the car into the left lane. We're almost there. "I realized it when I was nine."

"That's pretty young."

"Mm-hmm."

"How'd you figure it out?"

The image flashes in my mind, even after all this time. The five bottles of pills Alec and I saw on Mom's vanity before she came in and ushered us out. The labels with miniature text warnings that looked like essays.

Realizing I could remember the names of each one when my brother couldn't.

He made me write them down for him. The next day, after school, he went to the pharmacy to ask what they were. And that's how we realized Mom was sick.

She passed away shortly after.

I turn the car into the parking lot. "My brother and I were playing around, and I realized I could remember more than he could."

Harper's voice is soft. "Oh. Was he jealous?"

"He's not the jealous type," I say. At least not of me. He's too ambitious, too perfect, and too disciplined for that.

Pulling into a spot, I turn off the engine, and cautious silence settles in the car. For a moment I wonder if I should tell her the real answer. The pill bottles. The death sentence.

But I don't want to detract from this moment. *One week,* I think again, *and half of it has already passed.*

"Is this... oh my God. We're trying archery?" Harper's voice is cheery with surprise. "That's why I needed to dress like we're hitting the track?"

"Yes."

She opens the car door, rushing out to the parking lot. There's color on her cheeks and a wide smile on her face. For a moment, I just lean against the side of the car and look at her.

"You like surprises," I say out loud.

Harper's smile turns to me. "Of course I do. I know some people struggle with them, but I never have. Come on. Let's try this. Did you call ahead?"

"Yes. An instructor is waiting for us."

She's already halfway to the field where targets are lined up at equal distances. A small wooden building stands at the edge of it, and a few people are milling about. One of them is getting into a shooting stance.

"Nate," Harper calls. Her voice is impatient and excited. "Come on."

I lock the car and try to hide my smile. "Coming."

Our instructor's name is Calvin. He's forty-eight and loves archery. All of this he makes explicitly clear in his little introduction, showing us how to hold the bow and explaining the physics of the draw. The bows are made out of light metal, and mine weighs almost nothing in my hand.

Harper is like a sponge beside me. I can feel it, her soaking up everything the instructor says.

When it's finally our turn, Calvin comes up beside us, pointing out the individual targets for us to hit.

Above us, the sky has turned an even darker shade of gray.

"You go first," I tell Harper

She looks at me over her shoulder with a small smile. The black headband she's wearing is pushing her wild curls away from her face, but one has escaped, falling over her forehead.

She's gripping the bow tight. "Watch me be victorious," she says.

I grin. "Go for it."

She releases the arrow. It flies straight, hitting the outer ring of the target that's been pinned to a large bale of hay.

"I hit it!"

"Sure did," I say.

She's grinning at Calvin, too, and quickly nocks another arrow. Calvin corrects her form a few times, and then she's shooting at a steady pace for a beginner.

I shoot a few times while Harper's back is turned and she's focused on her target. Calvin gives me an approving nod and moves off to the side.

"I shall be just there should you need me," he says.

Harper looks at me over her shoulder. "Wanna make a bet?"

"Oh, you're feeling that confident now, are you?"

"This is so much more fun than I imagined. Look, I've only missed the circle twice."

"Very impressive."

She looks over at my target and sees the three arrows embedded in a semicircle at the outer edge. "You're not looking so bad yourself, Connovan."

"High praise."

She gets into position again, her feet shoulder-width apart, her shoulders down, arms taut. Firing, she hits another arrow in the outermost circle.

We're alone on the range now, and, in the background, I hear Calvin chatting to someone in low tones. I take a small step closer to her. "Yes, let's make a bet, Harp."

She nods, her curls bouncing. "I already know what I want if I win."

"And what's that?"

"I want you to answer a question honestly."

The stab of fear is instant. As if she reached into my heart and squeezed. But it recedes with a few rational thoughts. There's no way she knows.

I haven't shown any signs of it.

I raise my bow and aim deliberately off-center. My arrow misses the target entirely. "You want me to accept the odds when I don't even know what the question will be?"

"Yes." Her tone is still excited, energy drumming beneath the surface. "Or are you scared?"

"You're baiting me, but I'll admit that I'm intrigued." I line up another shot and deliberately put this one on the bottom of the target. Just barely hitting the outer circle. "All right. You'll have your honest answer if you win... but if *I win,*" I say, lowering my bow, "you don't move out at the end of the week."

Harper lowers her own bow in surprise. "What?"

I reach for another arrow with calmness I don't feel. "If I win, you won't rush to move out."

"Nate... I can't impose on you indefinitely."

"It's not an imposition." I raise my bow again and focus on the target, and not on the green eyes I know are resting on me. This time, I hit the upper edge of the target. Still far away from the bullseye. "If I win, you give yourself a month instead of a week."

"A month," she breathes.

"Yes. No stressing about moving out."

Harper digs her teeth into her bottom lip. A small furrow lies between her pulled-down brows, and a shadow falls over her thoughtful eyes. I feel them trying to figure me out.

"Why?"

"Why not?" I ask in response. My fingers grip another arrow, holding the feather-light weight up in the air. "I'm out of the house most days. It's good to have someone there to take care of it."

"Like, water the plants?" Her voice is so incredulous that it makes me chuckle.

I spin the arrow around in my hand. Meet her gaze with a steady one of my own. I've been in plenty of negotiations. I'm more than capable of smoothing over awkward situations and convincing people to do what I need. What the company needs…what the family needs.

"I don't want you rushing into another dumpster of an apartment, in an area known for its crime rate, with an hour-long commute." I nock the arrow in the bow, aim, and take a deep breath. Shoot.

"Darn," she murmurs.

Yeah. I hit it right where I intended… on the edge of the paper. Not even on the target.

"I can't be responsible for your premature death," I say with a drawl and lower the bow. "If I win, you take a month, and you search for something that's safe and comfortable."

Her eyes are narrowed, but then she glances at my abysmal performance with the bow and nods. "All right. It's a bet."

"Good."

"Great."

I smile behind her back. "Three shots, highest combined points wins?"

"Sounds good," she says.

We retrieve the arrows we've already shot and head back to our starting positions. There's an undercurrent of energy I can't quite shake. It makes my skin feel tense, and my fingers fist tightly around the light handle of my bow.

"Ladies first," I say.

She hits the middle ring and grins in surprise at her own success. It's infectious, seeing this zeal. It's the same intensity she'd had at the exhibition event at London Modern a few nights ago.

Happy.

"Go on," she tells me.

I line up my shot. Breathe out, focus... and let the arrow fly. It hits the bullseye with a dull twang.

She inhales sharply. "Holy shit."

"Lucky," I say, and lower my bow. "Your turn."

This time she hits the outer ring and curses softly as she tallies up the points. I feel her heavy eyes on me when I draw my second shot, too. It lands next to the first, right at the edge of the bullseye. But it counts.

Adrenaline makes me grin.

"Nate," she says. "How did you just do that twice in a row?"

I rest both hands on the top of my bow, leaning the tip of it on the ground. "When I was a kid, my brother and I were regularly shipped off to various summer schools and summer camps."

Anything to get us out of the city and out of Dad's care. He'd had enough to handle with my little sister and the company that he'd dedicated his entire life to those first few years after Mom died.

Not to mention his grief.

"And you did archery."

"Four summers in a row, yeah."

"I hate you." She breathes. "So the shots you made earlier, they were... what? *Decoys?*"

"It might have been a deliberate misdirection on my part." Her look of outrage makes me laugh. "You already know I don't mind false impressions."

"Clearly." She glares at her target and then at mine with obvious dismay. "You need to miss the target, and I need to hit a bullseye for me to have any chance of winning."

I look around. Calvin is nearly out of sight, standing by the far edge with a thermos in hand, chatting with a bearded man.

Moving closer to Harper, I say, "Your stance is good. You're doing exactly what he said… but lower this arm. Draw the bow."

She does exactly that, holding it taught. Her left elbow is too high. I step in behind her and put a hand on top of her left biceps. Gently push it down until her shoulders are in a straight line.

"That's it," I say. A lock of her hair is teasing my cheek, and I try to ignore it. Fail to. "Pull it back, nock by your mouth… look at the bullseye, and take a deep breath…"

She inhales deeply, softly, and I let my other hand hold her right shoulder steady. Touching her like this is a bad idea.

But all of this is a bad idea.

"Aim… and let go."

She holds a second longer before letting it fly.

The arrow hits the bullseye with a sharp sound, vibrating where it's stuck.

Harper lets her bow drop and turns in my arms. "Oh my God!"

"You did it," I say.

She glances at the target, blush coloring her cheeks. And I realize I'm still holding her shoulders. Slowly, reluctantly, my hands drop. Fall to my sides, where I let them fist tightly.

"I don't know what magic you just performed, but thank you," she says, looking back up at me. Her green irises have small flecks of gold in them. I never noticed that before, and I notice everything. It feels like an oversight.

Her smile softens. "You know, you just helped an opponent."

"Mm-hmm. I know. Bad idea."

"Terrible. If you miss the target now, I'll know you don't *really* want me to live with you any longer," she teases.

I lift an eyebrow. "Moment of truth."

"Yup."

"What's the question you want to ask me?"

"I can't tell you unless I win," she says.

I take a step back and reach for my bow. Weigh it in my hand, and with it, my options.

But as curious as I am, her safety sways the balancing act. And living with me is safe. Driving her back to some godforsaken-cardboard-box of an apartment, in the same city but light years away, isn't an option.

So I walk to the target and pull out the arrows already embedded in my bullseye. "Got to make room," I throw out to her over my shoulder.

She chuckles. "You're that confident?"

I am. Because for the first time in what feels like forever, I'm playing to win with stakes that actually matter.

I line up. Pull my shoulders back, draw the bow. Breathe in… release.

The arrow hits the bullseye.

I exhale softly. "Look at that. You're my roommate for a while longer, Harper."

That's when the first raindrops fall. The sky opens up, and the soft drizzle quickly turns into a downpour.

Harper laughs. "I can't believe you made that shot. When did you do this last?"

"I was fifteen, I think, so… twenty-three years ago."

"I hate you," she says again. But she's already lifting her bow to shoot again. "Teach me how to hold it steady again."

I look at her determination, at the gentle smile on her lips, and the way her hair is already darkening from the rain. And she doesn't care at all.

Grinning at her, I step in closer. "All right. Like this..."

She shoots a few arrows in a row, hitting the middle ring most times, and once, the outer circle. But her shots are steadier now.

The rain is pelting my face, dripping off my jaw. Rivulets run down her forehead and across her cheeks.

"It's raining," I finally inform her.

Harper turns to look at me. Her smile is wide, and it hurts to look at. "Are you afraid of a bit of water?"

"No. But I think everyone else is." I glance around meaningfully at the now completely deserted shooting range.

"They must think we're crazy," Harper says.

I retrieve all of my arrows and glance at her, where she's doing the same. My hands still tingle from when I touched her just a few minutes earlier. "Upset?" I ask her.

She looks at me and gives a tiny shrug. "No. I'm not too proud to admit that you have a beautiful home. The bed is divine, the water pressure... It won't be hard to live there for a full month."

The words make my lips twitch. "Good."

"But I am puzzled." She pulls out the final arrow from where it was embedded deep in the hay bale. "I wish I'd won the right to ask that question."

I lean against my target. The scent of wet straw hangs lightly in the air, and the rain is cold, but I ignore all of it. "Ask the question, and I'll decide if it's something I can answer."

Harper steps closer, gripping a trio of arrows in her left hand. The points leveled straight at me.

Her eyes narrow. "All right. Nate Connovan... why are you being so nice to me?"

It's not the question I expected.

But it's definitely not one I can answer.

I run a hand over my jaw, raising an eyebrow. Give her a pointed look and try to calm my racing heart. "That's what you want to know?"

"Yes. I have a suspicion, but I don't want it to be true." She shakes her head slowly. "So I want you to tell me the truth."

Her eyes are piercing. Demanding. And I should look away, swallow the damning truth, and make a joke. *I don't want it to be true.* Surely she can't suspect. Can't know, couldn't have guessed.

Dean never did.

But she's so much more observant than Dean has ever been.

"You don't want it to be true," I say instead. The words come out more softly than they should, hanging in the humid air between us.

Harper gives a single nod. "If it's because Dean told you to, because you think you can help the two of us get back together, I don't want this friendship."

Relief makes me momentarily lightheaded. It sweeps through me so fast that I smile and watch the corresponding frown on her face.

"It's not," I say. "I don't think I can help you guys get back together."

Trust me, I want to add, even as the guilt tastes like acid in my guts. *It's the last thing I want.*

She nods, but the furrow between her eyebrows doesn't completely disappear. "Okay. As long as that's the case."

"You have nothing to worry about." I lift an arrow and spin it around. "Except winning against me."

She smiles again. "Bring it on."

It isn't until I'm back in the car half an hour later, soaked from the rain and listening to Harper's happy thoughts about the experience, that I realize I hadn't, strictly speaking, told her the truth.

Dean did ask me to keep an eye on her.

But the reason I agreed had nothing to do with him.

Chapter 11

Harper

It's Thursday, almost a full week of living at Nate's, and I've finally found a routine that works. A large part of it is predicated on the comfort that his house provides. The bed that feels like heaven, the plush carpeting in my room, the small desk I've set up as my own little home office. I bought a new journal in a small stationery shop in central London. It's leatherbound and has wide-lined pages, and I started to write in it that very same evening.

Journaling is something I've done since I was twelve.

The act itself was comforting, and keeping up the routine felt like self-care. Maintaining the habit was like coming back to myself and hearing myself think out loud. Putting thoughts down was often the first step to me really understanding them… or changing them.

I love my two windows that look out onto the square and the garden that we share with all of Nate's neighbors. The walk to work is beautiful, winding past houses that I'm starting to use as mileposts. *The house with the blue door—that means I'm only six minutes out…* The work itself, with Aadhya warming up to me, the influx of new art coming into the gallery, and the event planning, is exciting and challenging.

It's all starting to feel good. Right. The hyperactivity of my first time in London, when my nerves were frayed and I'd been living in a state of constant vigilance, is slowly draining away.

Slowly.

My mother's remarks on the phone while I'm doing my grocery shopping seem to confirm that.

"You sound calmer," she says in her brisk Boston accent. "The job is good, then?"

"It is. It's much more exciting than the position I had in New York."

"Mm-hmm." Her voice is laden with unspoken thoughts, but I know them all, and I don't want to hear them. My mother is amazing. She's supportive. She also shows her love through actions rather than words, and right now, there's no action she can take. So she's left with no way to express her caring nature.

It's taken me years to understand that tendency in her.

"I'm fine. I promise. The only thing I'm sorry about is how fast the change happened." I reach the dairy section in the store and search for the new kind of yogurt I'd discovered last week. It goes straight into my basket. "I know it took you and Greg by surprise."

"Surprise," she repeats. "Yes, well, it certainly did. We had no idea you were anything but set on Dean."

"I didn't know myself for a long time, not consciously."

"Mm-hmm," she says again. It's more thoughtful this time. "And is your apartment still good? The landlord fixed the window issue?"

"They did, yes. The place is turning out really nice," I say. It's a total lie. The second I walked into the place where I lived before, I knew I couldn't show it to my parents. They'd never understand.

"Good, good. You know Greg and I would love to come visit you."

I smile. It warms my heart, even if it's predictable. Showing support by actions. "Maybe in a month or two, when I'm fully settled."

"Let us know when, and we'll book," she says. There's a brief silence on the line. I reach for a box of basmati rice and await the words that will come.

"Dean called this weekend."

Her words shock me, even though I braced myself for *something* in that span of dead air.

I close my eyes. "He did?"

"Yes. I think he just wanted to check in, to be honest. But he did mention one thing… Honey, you won't let him handle the cancellation fees?"

"No. I'm going to pay my half."

"He was the one who insisted on a big wedding," Mom says. "It's only fair if he—"

"I'm paying my half," I say. My voice sounds firm, and I know I'm being stubborn, too, but I can't imagine owing Dean anything. Not anymore. I won't have him using that as an excuse to call, to pester, to nag, to guilt. I want to remove myself entirely from his influence.

And now that I told him *no*… he's gone to my mom instead. He knows, just as well as I do, that the cancellation charges for the wedding are the last screws he has in me.

"Okay," Mom says with a sigh. "I won't pretend to understand, but I don't want you to overexert yourself, either. All right?"

"I know, Mom. I'm not."

She sighs again. It's a softer sound. "Doesn't his friend live in London, too? That rich heir Dean spoke about; the one who came to your Christmas party, once? What was his name…? Greg searched his family on the internet when we got back home, after the party."

I grab a package of chicken breasts. Look down at the price tag and give Mom what she's looking for. "Nate Connovan."

"That's it. Isn't he in London?"

"I think he is, yes."

Mom chuckles. "Maybe you'll bump into him. Think he'd

recognize you on the street?"

"Considering I dated one of his closest college friends for four years, I suspect the answer is yes."

"Yes, well, you know the sort. Dean was like that, too. But that guy, he had an even bigger bank account to back up that kind of arrogance. No, I think you need to leave that type of men behind."

"I think I need to be single for a while."

"Of course, honey. That might be a great idea right now. But when you're not... you know, I have plenty of teaching assistants who are—"

"Mom."

She chuckles. "All right, I'll stop. I just want you back home."

"I know," I say. It's definitely a part of my guilt trip, my parents' clear reluctance with my entire London adventure. Knowing I was letting down more than just one person with my sudden decision.

"I have to go, sweetheart, I'm sorry. Lunch break is over, and I have class in five."

I grab a package of linguine. Look down at the overflowing basket and realize I'll struggle to carry it all home. "That's okay. What are you lecturing on today?" I ask. Mom is an English literature professor, and I always love hearing what's on her schedule.

"We're doing Victorian literature for a few weeks. You know—Dickens, Hardy, Tennyson. Today, I'm lecturing on... let's see here. Social norms and gender roles, and how the authors reflected the rapidly changing society of the nineteenth century."

"That sounds riveting," I say, and I mean it.

Mom's voice is pleased. "Thanks, honey. Have a good evening."

"Have a good day," I tell her.

"Love you."

"Love you, too."

I pay for my large grocery haul and add it to the two other bags I'm already carrying. Working in the center of it all as I do is dangerous. There are too many fun shops to pop into on my lunch break or on my way home.

The walk to Nate's townhouse isn't long, but the heavy bags make it feel endless. I have to stop twice to rest, and when I finally make it home, I've gone from slightly annoyed to pissed off.

He has no right calling my parents.

No right to tell them about our private business, my choice with regard to the money, or to make the case to my parents in hopes of getting them to sway my decision.

My stomach is tied in a tight knot. One that has slowly been loosening over the past week, but now is back to its vise-like hold on me and my tattered nerves. Uncertainty hangs over me like a question mark.

I unlock the door to Nate's townhouse. "Hello?" I call. But the place is empty, the lights are off, and it looks just as it did when I left this morning.

He's been out of the house more than he's been in since the archery and the rain. When I felt like we started to become friends. The last three mornings he's been gone before I came down to the kitchen, and he hasn't returned home until after I've already gone to my bedroom, shut my door, and either watched reruns of my favorite show on my laptop or wrote in my journal. I've heard him walk by. Up the next flight of stairs to the top floor, the one I've never been to.

It almost feels like I'm living here alone.

I put the grocery bags on the large kitchen island. One of them tips over, and two oranges roll out onto the stone countertop.

It's time to get real.

If I'm living here for another month, I need to start cooking real food for myself. Stock up the pantry with stuff, do a bit of meal prep, and maybe make some lunch wraps to bring to work.

A month.

That's what he'd wagered. And I can't pretend like the lump that seems to be stuck in my throat doesn't have anything to do with the *why* behind his bet. I'd asked Nate, and he was adamant. This isn't something he's doing *for* Dean, and this isn't at Dean's behest, and…

I think I believe him.

I want to believe him.

Which leads to other questions. Mainly…

Then why?

I open the fridge and start unpacking one of the four grocery bags I've brought home. Onions, carrots, a large zucchini… The fridge was almost entirely empty. It's also enormous, and my purchases hardly fill the vastness.

That's when I hear the front door open.

Nate's voice is muffled, but I hear the tension bleeding out in his tone. I stick my head over the threshold, looking out at the entryway. He's on the phone.

He sees me. Nods once, his face tight.

I pop back into the kitchen. Despite his hushed speech, it's hard not to catch snippets.

I thought you told him that was a nonstarter… What? We've never celebrated Easter together… Yes. It's an option… I'll consider it.

And then, much closer to the kitchen, the final words. *Talk soon.*

I quickly turn back to the open fridge and the bag of potatoes I'm holding. Behind me, footsteps echo down the hall, and then a surprised scoff.

"Did you empty Tesco?"

I close the fridge door. "Almost. I decided that if I'm going to… stay here longer, I should commit. And I'm tired of living off takeout."

It's expensive, too.

Nate nods and looks over the bags spread across his kitchen island. He's in a suit, like always, but sans tie. His hair looks messier than usual, and there's a tightness in his jaw, around his mouth, that I haven't often seen.

"I promise I won't burn down your kitchen. Again."

"Go ahead. Torch it all."

I reach for a bag of rice and frown at the bitterness in his voice. "Are you okay?"

He runs a hand through his hair. "Yeah. Of course."

"You've been busy," I say with a shrug. Opening one of the cabinets, I find the lower shelf completely empty. Great. "Out of the house a lot."

"Yeah. Things have been intense at work."

"Want to talk about it?"

"No," he says simply. But it doesn't sound like a refusal. More like honesty. "You bought… what's this?"

I look over to where Nate Connovan is standing, in the beautiful luxury kitchen, holding up a turnip. Looking nothing like his normal charming self.

I can't help but laugh.

"What," he says. "Is it obvious?"

"Let's just say, I think it's pretty clear you don't cook a lot."

"If that only struck you now, you haven't seen how empty my fridge is." He turns the root over. "A confused carrot?"

"A turnip," I clarify. "Throw it here."

He lifts an eyebrow but does what I've asked, tossing the turnip over the counter. I catch it and smile at him. "I'm going to roast veggies and chicken for dinner tonight. Want some?"

Now both his eyebrows rise. There's a short pause where I'm sure he'll say no, but then he nods. "Yes. Thank you."

"Of course."

He leans both hands against the island. "Are you planning on feeding an army I don't know about?"

"No, but I am planning on meal prepping." I hold the turnip up in his direction, like the world's non-pointiest weapon. "Speaking of meal prepping. Do you use some kind of delivery service for those breakfast spreads?"

His eyes narrow. "Yes. Would you like more of something?"

"No, I would like less." I open the freezer and show him the mountain of pastries I've squeezed in over the past few days. "We'll never eat them all!"

That finally gets a smile out of him. "I guess I didn't think of that."

"And it's always untouched when I come down. Do you even eat any of it?"

He runs a hand along the back of his neck. "Some days."

"Wasteful," I say with a soft tsk.

He nods and reaches for another bag, pulling out the package of flour. "So you're, what? A professional chef on the side?"

"Not at all. I'm just a regular person who tries to feed herself and picked up a few skills along the way."

"I've been alive for… thirty-eight years, and I haven't picked up any cooking skills," he says. I listen to him rummage around in one of the bags. "Crackers. Cheese. Apples. This is…"

"Domestic?" I ask.

"Yeah."

I open the freezer and find a spot for the giant bag of frozen broccoli I bought. "I don't mean to pry, but you sounded a bit annoyed on the phone when you came home. Everything all right?"

There's complete silence behind me.

I open a drawer in the freezer and put in the chicken breasts. "Don't mean to overstep, you know. You're allowed to say *no comment*. Just wanted to ask how you're doing."

"Harper," he says.

I look over my shoulder with a smile. "If it's—oh my God."

He's holding the slim, purple box in hand. It's luxurious cardboard, with gold typeface printed along the top. It had set me back almost one hundred and twenty pounds, and I've yet to know if it's worth it. The attendant in the little sex shop in Chelsea had assured me that it is.

"I don't think this goes in the fridge or the freezer," he says calmly, eyes still on the packaging. *Reading.*

A furious blush spreads across my cheek.

"Maybe the pantry?" he asks.

"Nate, that wasn't… shoot. I'm sorry you had to see that."

"I'm not," he says. There's something very controlled about his face, and his eyes slowly lift from the vibrator to meet mine. "I didn't know they sold this at Tesco."

"No, I went to a shop during lunch." I look back down at the intricate package, still in his hand, his large fingers curving over the box. Embarrassment makes my voice higher than usual. "Are you inspecting that?"

The corners of Nate's mouth finally tip up into a small, true smile. He holds up the box and starts to read. "Double the fun, double the orgasms. The extended tip is designed for internal stimulation of the G-spot."

"Nate!"

His voice deepens. "The flexible second arm is ideal for clitoral stimulation and adapts to every body type."

I bury my face in my hands. "Yes. That's what a sex toy does."

"Mm-hmm. The Sensation Siren 3.0. Oh, and look at this. It's made from medical grade silicone."

I spread two of my fingers to peek at him. He's still turning the sex toy over in its box. He's smiling, even if his eyebrows are drawn tight. "You don't even have to look at it anymore. You've probably already memorized the entire packaging text."

"Of course I have." He sets the box down with a soft thud and looks at me. "It has twelve vibration settings to appeal to every woman's personal needs. Who knew? *Twelve.*"

I finally crack and laugh weakly. "Yeah. There was one that had twenty-four but that felt like overkill."

"Twenty-four," he repeats softly. Then, he cocks his head.

"One wonders how mortal men will be able to compete."

"Mm-hmm. Maybe it's dangerous for me to get used to it," I say. The comment slips out before my brain catches on that I'm not talking with one of my girlfriends back home.

I'm rewarded with another raised eyebrow. "Or you'll just have to date better men. Vibrating ones," Nate says.

"Have you ever met one?"

"Those with great imagination can do anything," he says. There's a curve to his lips now and a glittering in his eyes. It makes something in my stomach tighten. "Toys don't have to be just for solo play."

I reach for another grocery bag because his gaze on me is too much. My fingers graze a cardboard package of eggs. "Interesting. I didn't look around in that section of the store too much. The couple's… section."

Out of the corner of my eye, Nate looks large. Tall. He's turning an eggplant in his hands, much like he did my vibrator. "That's a shame. It's the most fun section."

"Is it? Maybe I should explore it. In the future."

"In the future," he repeats. "When I've successfully been your wingman."

I run a hand over my hair and push back the loose tendrils. "You're talking like someone who's… familiar with that side of the store."

He shrugs and tosses the eggplant into his other hand. "That vibrator wouldn't have been my first sex toy purchase."

"Are you implying that this was mine?"

He grins, crookedly and a bit wolfishly. "Wasn't it?"

I reach forward and grab the vegetable from his large hands. "Yes, but I don't like that it's so obvious."

Nate chuckles. "It was a lucky guess."

"Sure, sure," I say. But I feel too hot; blush is spreading across my cheeks.

And while I cook dinner, and as the conversation flows, on the kitchen island between us, is the incriminating purple box.

Chapter 12

Nate

I can't fall asleep.

The moment I turned off the lights and closed my eyes, the conversation we had earlier started replaying in my head.

The discussion over dinner. The easy chit-chat and her curious questions. She asked me things I can't remember having ever been asked before. Did I like living in London? What do I miss most about New York? My favorite way to eat potatoes.

She'd asked the last question while stabbing her fork into an oven-roasted potato, and with the full intensity of someone who's clearly given it a lot of thought.

But the talk about her vibrator that preceded it all… It had set off emotions I'd tried hard to keep under wraps.

So I'm lying on my back in this large bed, staring at the ceiling, and thinking about her vibrator. The length. The breadth. The girth.

The damn vibrations.

And I'm wondering if she's using it right now.

Just a floor below me, separated by a single flight of stairs, in the guest bedroom I passed a million times and a million mornings before she moved in.

I squeeze my eyes shut, but that doesn't do a thing to dissolve a mental image. My imagination lingers on Harper, her messy curls spread across a pillow, her full lips parted on a soft sigh.

Naked.

Her knees bent, slightly splayed, and her hand working between her thighs. Maybe she'd warm herself up first without the vibrator. And then turn it on, slide the device over the soft skin of her stomach, and press it to her clit…

I blow out a frustrated breath and put an arm under my head. I shouldn't imagine this.

Not that it's the first time my mind has wandered in that direction.

I used to feel guilty. Guilty because I knew she wouldn't want me to picture her that way, and guilty because it was the ultimate betrayal of Dean. That guilt was stronger than my anger, frustration, and the wasted fucking need for her.

The need I've always felt for her.

And now she's in my house. Just downstairs. She cooked me dinner tonight, and she smiled and laughed with me. We're friends now. *Becoming* friends, at any rate, outside of her relationship with Dean.

But my traitorous self can't seem to be content with that.

I want her to like me. That's the truth of it. I can admit it, at least.

So, I'm trying. Doing whatever I can to make it happen.

But I also know it's not the right move. She's not looking for anything. She's been hurt by Dean, and they *just* broke up. Of course, she still has feelings for him. The thought makes my stomach turn.

She's single. She's not attached to him any longer. But that still doesn't make her mine.

And yet, knowing that does nothing to make the vision in my mind go away, because it never does, does it? I've also never had to contend with her presence before like this.

Is she using the vibrator right now?

I can't believe she never used a sex toy before. If I'd been her boyfriend, if I'd been Dean, I would've spoiled her with orgasms. Discovered every single way to make her come.

Make play essential in the bedroom.

But maybe Dean and Harper didn't need to spice it up. Maybe they—

I stomp out the thought and smother the familiar jealousy. It was always the ugliest of my emotions attached to Harper, and I knew it was entirely undeserved. I released most of it when I moved to London. Once I saw Dean far less often, and by extension, the two of them together.

My need for her won't go away, however. Has been coursing through my body since I found that vibrator among her purchases, tempered only by our conversation and her food and the obligation to act normal around Harper. But now that I'm alone and in bed, the *need* is all I feel.

I'm hard.

Have been since she said goodnight at her landing, one hand on her bedroom door while the other held her large bag.

I knew what was in that bag.

The silence around me is absolute. I haven't heard a sound from her room below, but I strain to listen anyway. As if I'd be able to hear her soft moans through wood and brick, and mortar.

I reach down with my right arm and surrender.

My cock has been resting against my stomach with angry urgency, but I don't give it what it wants. I stroke it leisurely. Give in to the temptation and let my imagination run wild.

Harper's familiar form blooms in front of my shuttered eyelids. How she might look beneath her clothes.

The soft swell of her tits, her rosy nipples. Her stomach. Her hand at the apex of her legs. The vibrator pressed against her clit, or inside her… I imagine her pushing it all the way in, the length disappearing into her pussy, and the little vibrating nub coming to rest on her throbbing bud.

Her breathing turns heavy. A moan escapes as the vibrator settles inside her heat.

I imagine her sweating. Skin flushed and glistening.

And I imagine her eyes on me, as my hand controls that vibrator.

She trusts me. Wants me. Begs me to let her come.

I tighten my hand around my shaft. Stop all movement for a few seconds to prolong what's already been going on far too long.

For years.

Imagine myself turning the vibrator around, releasing her center from the constant onslaught of a throbbing pulse. She mewls in my mind, and I replace the vibrator with my fingers. Dance them lightly over her swollen clit.

I throw back the covers, and the air feels cool against my heated skin. Using my thumb, I trace light circles on the sensitive underside of my head, right where the vein connects. Mimicking the sensations I want to give Harper.

She's arching, her eyes drifting shut… her mouth parting slightly. I wish to God the hard flesh my hand would be the soft, wet folds of her pussy instead. She'd say my name. Beg for release.

I grit my teeth and speed up my strokes. The pleasure builds until it's almost painful, so strong it makes me hiss. My cock glides smoothly through my grip, and then I erupt, shooting across my stomach in spurts that leave me groaning.

Fuck.

I lie in stunned silence, broken only by the pounding of my heart, before I get up and clean up. Fatigue finally settles in my limbs, and I think sleep will come easier now.

But it doesn't.

I'm left lying in the darkness, body sated but mind racing, wondering who Harper is thinking of while she uses her new vibrator.

I wake up to the blaring sound of my ringing phone. The familiar ringtone cuts through the fog of sleep.

My room is still pitch black.

But a quick glance at the screen of the still-buzzing phone shows the time. It's an hour later than I normally get up. My assistant is calling, probably wondering where the hell I am. I've asked her to call if I ever deviate from the schedule.

I answer, barking out a short *I'll be in soon,* and toss the covers off. Hit the controls to open the black-out curtains, and the room starts to fill with light. My shower is done in record time, and I pull on the first pair of slacks and a white button-down I find.

There's a meeting in thirty minutes I can't miss. The deal with our Japanese contractor is too crucial, and my brother has been working on it for almost a year. I need to be in the video conferencing room on time.

I'm racing down the stairs. Phone in the pocket of my pants. I'll need to grab a jacket from the entryway…

… Someone walks out onto the second-floor landing.

I catch a glimpse of wet blonde curls cascading over bare shoulders and a lush towel wrapped around her body.

Harper.

She scrambles back with a shriek. The corner of the towel comes untucked and the edges part. Gravity takes over. Stars collide. I forget how to breathe.

An expanse of rosy, pale skin.

The swells of her tits. Pink, pert nipples.

Soft stomach, the curve of her waistline, and the beginning of her—

She snatches the towel back up before it falls past her hips. "Nate?!"

My feet are glued to the last tread of the staircase. "Yes. Good morning."

"Holy shit, you scared me." Her eyes are wide, hands tight around the towel. "You're never home at this time!"

"Overslept." My voice comes out gruffer than I intended,

and I run a hand over the back of my neck. *Focus, Connovan.* "Didn't mean to scare you."

She shakes her head. I've never seen her hair wet before. The curls are thoroughly damp, dark enough to make her appear to be brunette. Her face is flushed. "It's your house. I shouldn't have… I don't usually walk around in a towel."

"That's okay," I say woodenly.

"Yes, well, that was a lie. I usually do. See, I like to go downstairs and put the coffee on after my shower, that way it's done by the time I've gotten dressed."

"Smart."

She nods quickly. Gives me a tentative smile. "I'm sorry about that. Didn't mean to flash you, I promise."

"I know. It's okay."

"Forget you ever saw anything, all right?"

I clear my throat. "Already forgotten."

It's the second lie I've told her in the past two weeks. Because try as I may, try as I should, I won't be able to forget the sight.

She smiles at me again. "Thanks. Um, there's yogurt in the fridge if you want breakfast. Let me change… I'll come down."

I head down the stairs. "Take your time," I say over my shoulder.

It isn't until I'm alone in the kitchen, out of her presence, that I release the breath I've been holding. Grabbing a hold of the counter, my knuckles turn white.

I shouldn't have seen that. Shouldn't have scared her.

There are so many boundaries already crossed in my imagination, but now that I've actually seen her… it's going to be impossible to stop traversing over more invisible lines.

I push the thought away. Bury it deep inside like I've done so many times before. Focus on Harper instead.

She'd been embarrassed.

Even though she had nothing to be embarrassed about.

The woman is perfection. I've always known it, and seeing her now, well…

Perfection was too mild a word.

I head to the giant coffee machine in the corner. The elaborate, gleaming metal contraption that can make everything from a flat white to a latte to espresso. A purchase I made last summer and seldom use. It's quicker to have coffee delivered to my office.

I don't know what she likes.

But I turn it on and make both a cappuccino and espresso. Opening the fridge, I find a container of orange juice. After draining a full glass, I roll my neck. Reach for my phone.

I need to leave.

But I should say something first. Tell her that it's okay. That I'm sorry. That she shouldn't be embarrassed. But the words feel stilted, uncomfortable in my mind, and I'm halfway out of the kitchen when her hurried footsteps echo on the stairs.

She's dressed now. An oversized printed dress, a tweed jacket, and a pair of ballet flats.

Her hair is pulled back in a low bun.

"Hey," she says.

I smile back. It's automatic. "Hi."

"Smells like coffee. Did you…?"

I shove my hands in my pockets. "Yeah."

"Oooh, you're using the cappuccino function. I haven't tried that one, yet. Is that what you normally drink?"

"Yeah," I say. A second lie of the morning, and it's not even eight. I take a step closer and open my mouth to apologize.

"I've never even seen it being used." She cuts me off before I could get the words out. "Do you make coffee in the morning? If so, you must clean it thoroughly once you're done."

"I rarely use it." There. Some truth.

Her eyes widen. "You should! This is like… the Rolls-Royce of coffee machines."

"I know. I bought it."

She chuckles and reaches for the espresso. "Can I drink this?"

"I made it for you."

I stand there in my bright kitchen, sunlight streaming in through the French doors that lead to the garden. Sipping on a cappuccino while silence stretches the minutes but the clock doesn't stop ticking. I'm going to be late and…

I can't leave.

She looks at me over the rim of her cup. "Sorry about what happened upstairs. Truly."

"Don't apologize," I say. "Really. Don't."

She smiles a little. "Okay. I won't."

"Good."

Her gaze drops to my shirt, and then she looks back at her coffee cup. "Slow day today?"

"No. Not really. I overslept, and I have back-to-back meetings most of the day. And tonight…" I blow out a sigh. "A charity event. I'm obligated to go."

"Oh. What for?"

"I honestly have no idea. I'm sure my assistant will brief me beforehand so I can avoid making an ass out of myself."

She giggles. It's a soft, happy sound. "I hope she does."

"What are you doing tonight?"

"I'm going out with two friends, actually. Aadhya, who works at my gallery. Remember her? And one of her flatmates. It should be fun."

"Stay safe, all right?"

"Of course. I'm always safe."

"I saw where you lived before. That wasn't— Harper?" She's put down her cup and is coming closer, *much closer,* her eyes locked on my shirt. I set aside my cappuccino.

"You've buttoned this all wrong." Her hands find the fabric of my shirt and start undoing the tiny fasteners. Her fingers brush my chest once, twice, as she correctly does up the shirt.

"There," she says softly.

My hand finds the edge of the counter. Caging her in on one side. I'll be really late for this meeting, and Alec will be annoyed.

So be it. He often is.

"Thanks," I say.

She dips her chin in a slight nod. We stand there for a few long seconds, neither of us saying a word. The only sound is the slow drip from the coffee machine.

My phone rings, breaking the moment. Harper blinks and looks down, and I take a step back to look at the device. Trish's name flashes on the screen. I hit *decline.*

"The office?" she asks.

"Yeah. I have to go."

"Have a good day at work," she says, gripping her cup of espresso. She looks rosy-cheeked and bright-eyed, her hair still damp, her face free of makeup.

"You too, Harper," I say.

And just like that, I'm making morning coffees together our new routine.

Chapter 13

Harper

"You didn't," Aadhya says. She's wearing the same excited expression as her friend Tamsin, sitting side by side in the upscale bar in Mayfair.

I nod. "Oh, I certainly did. Dropped the towel and everything."

Tamsin covers her face with her hands, while Aadhya leans back. Her mouth is shaped like an *O*. "That's mortifying."

"Thanks!" I say, but I'm giggling. "I know. His face was horrified, you should have seen it."

"Okay, I bet it wasn't actually *horrified*," Tamsin says.

"No, it was. Legitimately." I shrug, feeling warm and happy from the glasses of wine we've shared. I'm so glad I asked Aadhya to come out for a drink after work tonight. And through her, I've now met her flatmate, Tamsin, an upbeat girl studying fashion design in the city.

The bar is vibrant, the area is buzzing, and I feel like the energy has seeped beneath my skin. This is why I moved. This is what I want.

New experiences. New people. A new chance.

"No bloke has ever been horrified at seeing a fit girl nude," Aadhya says. She's wearing a tiny glittery cardigan and waist-high pants. Her long, black hair is in a side braid.

She's fierce, as always. "And you're *positive* he doesn't fancy you?"

I shake my head. "No, no, it's not like that between us."

"Right," Tamsin says. "He just offered you to stay in his house."

"It's what friends do," I say. They don't know that my new roommate is... well, *Nate.* Aadhya knows him as a gallery patron. The last thing I want is for her to realize that he and I are friends and not "the client and the art dealer."

But I also didn't want to lie when they asked me where I'm living. So I fudged the truth a little.

My roommate is now an unnamed old friend from New York.

"Look, I love you," Aadhya tells her flatmate, "but if you moved in without paying rent, I'd be like... *Mate, come on.*"

"Me, too," Tamsin says. But then her face turns thoughtful. "Is he gay?"

I shake my head. "No. Just not interested in me that way. Well... I don't *think* he's gay. I've heard plenty about him and women before, so he might be bi, I suppose."

"Hmm," Aadhya hums. "Is he fit? You didn't drop your towel on purpose, did you?"

"No! He surprised me."

"Right. Because that's a classic trick. Give them a peek at what they're missing," she says and waggles her eyebrows.

"Tried that often, have you?" I ask.

Tamsin gives a dramatic sigh. "She does it every morning. You're hot, but it's getting tiring staring at your perfect tits and arse each day, Aads."

We all laugh. The girls are easy to talk to, far easier than the first time I met Aadhya and thought her intimidation itself. She is, in some ways. Fierce and cool but also entirely human, the way we all are, and I'm glad we're becoming friends.

We finish our drinks by midnight and head out. My Tube stop is in the opposite direction from theirs, so I wave goodbye to Tamsin and Aadhya outside the bar when they leave.

I dig through my bag for my headphones, my fingers brushing past my wallet and a package of gum… but there's a conspicuous absence of jingling.

My keys.

Searching the depths of my purse reveals what I already know. *Shit.* I forgot them in my work bag at the gallery before we left for the bar. I'd brought the clutch for this specific purpose and only thrown in the most important things for my night out. Wallet. Headphones. Gum.

But no keys.

I start walking to my Tube stop, but my steps are slow. How long will Nate be out tonight?

My fingers move over the phone before I think better of it. Finding his name, I press call. I'm right next to a rowdy pub, across from the movie theater and a Michelin-star restaurant.

I love this city and its dualities.

"Harper," Nate says. His voice is businesslike. "Is everything okay?"

"Yes, yes, I'm fine. I just wanted to know… are you home?"

There's a slight pause before he replies. "No. Why?"

"I think I forgot my keys."

"You think?"

"Well, I know. Sorry, I don't mean to bother you. When are you gonna be home? Or if you're not planning on coming home at all, that's fine, too. I don't want to stop you from… from… having fun or seeing where the night takes you."

"Harper," he says. There's amusement in his voice, and I like hearing it. Like his deep drawl. "I'm wrapping up now. The concert just ended."

"Oh, that's perfect."

"Where are you?"

"Mayfair. Outside… The Black Swan."

"That's the name of every pub."

"No," I say. "Some are also called The White Horse, or The King's Head, or The *Queen's* Head, or sometimes The Red Lion."

He chuckles. "You've been drinking."

"Of course I have. Haven't you?"

"I might have had a sip or two"

Someone shouts beside me, and a group of men laugh. I take a few steps away from the noise of the pub.

"Where are you?" Nate asks again.

"I told you. By The Black Swan."

"I don't know every pub in London," he replies, "despite living here for two years. A shocker, I know."

"No worries. I'll just head home, and we'll—"

"I'll come find you. We'll go home together," he says. "Send me your location."

"Okay, sure. If you're happy with that?"

"Yeah, I'm close by. Are you somewhere safe?"

That makes me laugh. "Nate, I'm in central London, on a Friday night. There are people everywhere."

"That's what I'm afraid of."

"I'm fine. Perfectly fine. I might even enjoy a pint here while I'm waiting. I learned about the perfect amount of head tonight."

Silence takes over the line. A heartbeat passes. Another. "*What?*" he finally asks in an incredulous voice.

"Head! It's the foam part on top of the beer. Honestly, Nate, haven't you learned *anything* British in these two years?"

"Why don't you enlighten me when I—" Someone interrupts him in the background, a feminine voice, but I can't make out words. "Sorry about that," he says once he's back. "I'm leaving the concert hall now, walking over to you."

"Sounds good. Pip pip!" I say.

"You're crazy," he says. But then he mutters "cheerio" under his breath and hangs up the phone.

I lean against the brick wall with a smile on my face. The

people-watching is excellent. Those coming in and out of the movie theater are so different from the ones exiting the prestigious restaurant next door, and the atmosphere is buzzing with energy. It's Friday night and the start of a brand-new weekend. Full of possibilities and options.

By the time Nate arrives, strolling up the street in a tuxedo, I know what I want to do.

And it doesn't involve going home.

He glares at the unruly guys outside the pub with a disapproving frown, as if they'd done more than just be loud a few feet away from where I'm standing. But when he reaches me, his mouth tips into a crooked smile.

"Forgot your keys, did you?"

"Yes. At work. I won't be able to get them back until Monday."

"That's fine, you won't need them over the weekend. I have spares." He looks around the street. "Had a good night?"

"Yes, it was great. I think I made a new friend."

"You did?"

"Yes." I tilt my head to the side, excitement pouring through me. "Tell me, are you in the mood to go home? Be honest."

He lifts an eyebrow. "I don't know, Harper. Are you?"

I point to the marquee sign across the street. *Midnight showing,* it says, and beside it the name of the latest action-adventure movie.

"The movie started five minutes ago. I bet we can still get tickets."

Nate looks at it for a long moment. His profile—the sharp cut of his jaw, his brown hair falling over a high forehead—stands out against the brightness of a nearby streetlight. I've never seen him in a tux before.

Only suits.

It makes him look distinguished. *Different.*

I wonder if he's been to a movie in years. If he even goes

to pubs, or diners, or *walks* places like he just did. When we go home later, will he take the Tube? I can't imagine he would.

He looks back at me. "You want to go to a movie, Harper."

There's something in that sentence that feels heavier than it should. Something in his eyes…

But then he grins. "Let's do it."

Seven minutes later, we're seated at the very back of the theater, a giant popcorn box between us, and sodas in our hands. The previews had already started, but no one seemed to mind when we made our way to our seats.

Nate sits beside me. I glance at him a few times until he asks *what* under his breath without looking away from the screen.

"You're wearing a tux," I whisper back, "in *a movie theater*."

He reaches for the popcorn. "That's what happens when you don't give a man enough time to choose his outfit."

I laugh into the back of my hand. It's a quarter after midnight, I don't have keys on me, and I'm watching a movie in a foreign city.

And I know, without a shadow of a doubt, that it's not something I would have done six months ago. Not something Dean would have ever thought was a good idea. And over the months, then years with him, those thoughts seeped into me. Became my own.

Even though they never really were.

Nate eats more popcorn than I would have expected. When I reach in for another handful, right when the hero on screen is jumping out of an airplane, Nate's hand brushes mine.

We both pull back.

"Sorry," I whisper.

He shakes his head. Tilts the bucket toward me. "Ladies first."

I reach in, and he murmurs something close to my ear. I

can barely make it out. "I can't remember when I was at the movies last," he repeats.

That makes me smile. "Maybe you should go more often," I whisper back.

I curl up, tucking my legs under me. I rarely sit in the back row. It's surprisingly nice up here, and private, with the seats on either side of us empty.

I glance down at Nate's hand a few times. It rests on the armrest between us, palm curved over the edge. No ring on his left ring finger. Only a wrist watch, peeking out beneath the sleeve of his jacket.

He has nice hands.

Broad across the backs. Long fingers. Blunt nails.

When the movie ends, we walk out of the theater along with the two dozen other people who showed up for the midnight showing. I yawn but stifle it quickly.

Nate catches it anyway. "I hope you're not tired."

"I'm not. Well, a little. But it's worth it. I've never gone to a midnight movie before." I nudge him. "Have you?"

He runs a hand through his hair. "No."

"So, when was the last time you were in a movie theater? Let's get numbers on this."

He lifts both eyebrows. "You want to embarrass me."

I nudge him again. "Answer the question, Connovan."

"Probably… five years ago. I do go to the movies. Just not very often."

"Once every five years."

He tweaks my nose. It's so surprising that I blink at him. "Yes, wiseass, once every five years. Now come on. I have an idea."

"We're not going home?"

He holds up the building door for me. The streets of Mayfair are calmer than before, but by no means quiet. London is like New York. It never sleeps.

The early May weather is warm, and despite the lateness

of the hour, I don't feel cold. Not as I watch Nate walk out backward onto the sidewalk.

"What do you have planned?" I ask.

A crooked smile spreads across his face, making his eyes crinkle. "What's item number twelve on your list?"

It takes me a moment, but only one, before I realize what he's asking. The same energy from earlier, of possibility and excitement, spreads through my limbs.

"Stay out all night."

Chapter 14

Nate

London isn't asleep, not yet, but it's starting to snooze. It's almost 3 a.m., and the streets are scattered with a variety of people you wouldn't find anywhere else. Drunk tourists. Partygoers. A random group of cyclists dressed in sports gear and racing down the street.

Harper is walking beside me, step in step. Her energy is high. Has been since we left the movie theater.

"What are we going to do?" she asks. "Are you hungry? Oh, we could go to one of those chicken shops. Or maybe that's not your thing?"

"And why not?"

"You're in a tux."

I glance down at my clothes. "Yeah. So what?"

Harper giggles. The sound is heartwarming and washes over me like a gentle wave. "I didn't think you'd be this… chill."

"Mm-hmm. Because I always seemed uptight?"

"No, no, you never have." She shrugs lightly. Her dress falls around her form, the glittery fabric catching the streetlights in subtle play. "It's just that I always saw you as slightly *above* things like this."

"It's not making any more sense the second time."

"Okay. Remember the time you came to… to Dean's thirty-fifth birthday party?"

Of course, I do.

He rented out an Asian Fusion restaurant on the forty-second floor of a skyscraper in Manhattan, filled it with people he knew and plenty he didn't. Harper had been wearing a gold dress and a smokey eye shadow, and her curls were piled high atop her head.

One wrong move, I'd realized that night, and I might blow this whole thing. Blow my cover, reveal too much, and be cut off from them both forever.

One wrong move, and my attraction to her would be blatant, to both of them.

"What about it?"

"Nate," she says meaningfully. "You arrived by *helicopter.*"

That makes me chuckle. "Yeah. I think that makes me pretty chill."

"No, that's insane! Normal people don't do that."

"And I normally don't. That was a special occasion." Besides, I'd been forced to, or I wouldn't have made it on time. The chopper dropped me off and continued on with my brother inside. Basically a rideshare.

"Have you been in a helicopter?" I ask.

She shakes her head. "No. I'm afraid of heights."

"Really?"

"Deathly. It's my one flaw. The only chink in my armor."

"That explains why there's nothing on your list about bungee jumping, skydiving, or any of the usual bucket list items."

She blows out a breath. "That's because I do want to *make it* to thirty and beyond."

I chuckle again. "Helicopters are safe."

"There's ample evidence to the contrary."

"How did you fly here?"

"Planes are different."

I look up at the sky. "Make it make sense."

She giggles and nudges my shoulder with hers. It brings us back into close contact, and damn it, I shouldn't like that she does that so casually now, so effortlessly, but I do.

I really do.

"That's *different*. I always grab an aisle seat and don't look out the window. When I get a bit anxious, I distract myself. Watch bad movies or read a book."

"Mm-hmm." We stop at a red light. Across the intersection is the edge of Hyde Park, and beyond it, Green Park. Wellington Arch towers over everything. Trees, pedestrians, cars. "This is excellent information."

"Why?" she asks. "And where are we going? Oh, can we go into the park at night?" Then, her excited voice turns suspicious, and she nudges me again. "You're not trying to murder me or anything, are you?"

"I am, actually, thanks for asking. Any final words?"

"Yes. Um… just give me a few minutes to think about them."

I nod. "Take your time. I'm not in a rush. Look over there?"

She follows my pointing finger to a building rising in the distance. "We're close to Buckingham Palace," she says slowly. "Right?"

"Yes. Thought we'd walk by."

"I've never been here at night before." Her steps speed up, and I smile at how her curls bounce. Harper smothers a yawn with the back of her hand, but she's not slowing down. "This is so cool. There are almost no cars out."

"We should go for walks more often at… three-twenty."

We make it to the palace and stand outside the wrought iron fence that keeps the public out. The giant, rectangular building dominates the background. The ornate facade is illuminated by soft lighting.

"I only see a few guards patrolling," she says quietly. "That's all?"

"I'm willing to bet there are cameras, infrared sensors, and plenty of heavily armed soldiers within those side buildings, ready to pounce if we so much as put our hand through the fence."

She grins at me. "Wanna try?"

I put my hands on her shoulders and pull her away from the fence. "No, I very much do not. We're here on visas."

Harper chuckles. "I thought you were the wild one. I've heard stories about you, you know. From college."

I roll my eyes. "Much exaggerated, no doubt."

"Really? I seem to remember one about an unplanned road trip in your dad's Rolls-Royce, where you and Dean wound up in New Mexico, with your wallets stolen, and apparently, with a case of bad—"

"Don't say it."

"—rashes."

I groan. Run a hand over my face. But I can't look away from the teasing smile on her lips. "Not my proudest moment. In my defense, I was nineteen."

"Oh, of course. I also did that when I was nineteen," she says in a deadpan voice. "What did your dad say? Dean never told that part of the story."

He'd been furious.

But he'd been furious in a disappointed kind of way. Like he didn't expect anything else from me, and as if it was all an excuse to get out of the finals.

And then he'd made me buy him a brand new Rolls-Royce with money taken from my trust fund. Which, in hindsight, was absolutely the right call. If someone dented my vintage Aston Martin, I don't know what I would—

"Nate," Harper prompts.

I meet her curious gaze. "He wasn't particularly pleased with me."

She smiles. "I imagine not."

"That was a long time ago. I was…"

"Young?"

"An idiot," I say. "For a large part of my early twenties, that's exactly what I was. You, on the other hand, are very impressive."

She rolls her eyes. "I'm twenty-eight."

"But you were twenty-four when I first met you, and you were certainly not accidentally setting fire to books in the college library or having all-night benders."

My mind is still thinking about what else Dean might have told her. How much of her impression of me is filtered through his words.

"How would you know that?" she asks with a wide smile. "Those are assumptions."

I raise an eyebrow. "Oh, I know you were wild in other ways. You always have been. But not in stupid ways."

"I think there's a compliment in there somewhere."

"There is." I glance down at my watch, and away from her too bright eyes. They draw me in like nothing else. "Come on. We have a ways to go still and only forty minutes to make it."

"Where are we heading?"

"You chose the movie," I say. "Let me choose this. I'm willing to bet you'll enjoy it."

"Lead the way, then. As long as I don't end up in New Mexico in a stolen Rolls-Royce…"

I laugh. "Not this time, Harper."

We walk down to the river and cross it into Battersea. The city grows increasingly quiet around us, the stillness punctuated only by the occasional car or a rowdy yell. More than one taxi stops beside us, but I decline them all.

Harper's earlier energetic, wine-assisted chattiness has settled into something more mellow. She tells me about her coworker and that coworker's friend, and about the new exhibition the gallery is planning, and mentions the restaurant a block from her work that she wants to try.

And then she asks me the same types of things.

If I like my coworkers, which of my cars is my favorite, and what I do at the office.

"Just explain what you did today. Like, step-by-step, from when you arrived at work. What were the actual tasks?"

I hide my smile with the back of my hand. But I do what she's asked, and she listens like she actually cares.

Like she honestly wants to know.

So I detail how I led the regional team meeting, sat in the two meetings with key clients, double-checked my financial team's reports before forwarding the files to New York, and had a strategy session with my brother about our future growth opportunities.

She listens to all of it. Asks follow-up questions.

"It's interesting," she finally says.

I smirk. "You don't have to lie."

"No, it is. I mean, I don't understand everything you said, at least not yet, but I think I'm getting there."

"You don't have to," I say, and look at the maps app on my phone. It says we've arrived. "We're here."

Harper looks at the unassuming metal building in front of us.

"And this is…?"

I reach for the door and pray that I've done my research correctly. "Come on, Harp. Get inside."

"Harp," she repeats and walks toward me. "I've always wondered why you call me that. Like the instrument."

"What nicknames do people usually call you?"

"I've never had a nickname. My name doesn't really— oh. *Wow.*"

I follow her inside, and the cool, thickly scented air is the first thing that hits me. Describing it as *floral* would be an understatement. It smells of plants—cut stems and leaves, and blooming flowers.

Vendors have set up their stalls, with bunches upon bunches of cut flowers displayed in the large hall. It's a mélange of bright colors and deep greens, creating a beautiful tapestry.

"Oh my God," Harper breathes. "A flower market?"

"Yes. They open at 4 a.m."

I glance down at her. She appears stunned, and I can't help but wonder what her expression means. *Good idea?*

Her face slowly breaks into a wide smile, and she walks forward in awe; hydrangeas in various colors on either side of her. "This is incredible. I didn't know this existed!"

"It's a wholesale market, I believe. Selling primarily to other retailers, to hotels, movie sets, that sort of thing." I follow her and notice the curious eyes of a few vendors. Right.

I *am* in a tux.

Harper stops at the stall selling giant palms and runs her hand over the glossy green fronds. "I want them all," she says.

I slowly undo my bowtie, leaving it hanging around my neck. Unfasten the top two buttons of my shirt. "Then, we'll get all of them."

She giggles and moves on to a large fern. "Your house is big, Connovan, but not that big. Oh, look!"

She moves on to a stall with tulips in every possible shade. I trail her through the market. When she's distracted by a large selection of hydrangeas, I approach a vendor who sells peonies.

"Give me the largest bunch you have," I say.

"How many hours till you get them into some water?"

Shit. I glance at my watch. "At least four."

He nods and wraps the flowers up tightly. Glances behind me at Harper and smiles at me. "Good job, mate. Taking your girl to a flower market after a night out."

I glance back at Harper. She's out of earshot, talking animatedly to a woman running another stall. She looks happy.

My girl.

"Thanks," I tell the vendor. I don't correct him, even if pretending like she's mine is the sweetest form of torture.

Harper's eyes widen when I hand her the bouquet. Her gaze darts from the flowers to me and back again in rapid succession.

"Really?"

"Really," I say. Run a hand through my hair and look away, like this is nothing at all.

She takes a deep breath, inhaling the scent. Her sparkling eyes meet mine. "These are my favorite flowers."

"I know," I say. The words escape, revealing far more than I'd planned. But they are there. Hanging in the fragrant air between us.

She glances back down at the bouquet. "You do?"

I swallow. "You mentioned it once. At Josh's wedding."

"Oh. That's right."

She'd been on Dean's arm at our college buddy's wedding three years ago. It was shortly after she moved in with Dean, and she looked at him like he was her entire world. Like it would be the two of them standing next at that altar.

I saw them hold hands during the ceremony, saw Harper brush away the tears from her eyes. And that's when I decided to start pushing my brother. Whenever I could, I told him over and over that we needed a person we could trust in London. And then I conveniently volunteered for the position.

But she doesn't know any of that.

"They're just flowers," I say gruffly. But we're still standing too close, her hands tight around the stems, and her eyes on mine.

"Nate," she murmurs. "I feel like I have to—"

The vendor beside us shouts at another, breaking the moment, and we both take a step back. She clears her throat. "Thank you. For all of this."

I give her a broad smile, the one that gets me past lines at venues and events and charms our clients. "Anytime, Harp."

She smiles back, but there's a thoughtfulness in her eyes

that makes me wonder if she's disappointed somehow. Like my response was the wrong one.

But still, she clutches the peonies tight for the rest of our visit.

Chapter 15

Harper

I've started noticing it. The mask he puts on to be what he thinks other people expect of him. The smile he makes to charm his way. I used to find it easy to be around. That wide smile used to put me at ease. But now…

I question if that's his true smile.

Because I've seen how he smiles when he's unguarded. The small, crooked ones when he's amused despite himself. How those smiles reach his eyes and make them look warm. Those are the smiles I want.

He gave me peonies. Beautiful, giant buds that will open fully in the coming days. Become bold, showy blooms.

Odd. That's the word. It feels odd to have—through some kind of magic—gotten to know Nate Connovan this way. Unexpectedly.

To want to get to know him even better.

The sun hasn't yet begun to rise when we leave the flower market. It's hovering just below the horizon, but the sky is already brighter than it was an hour ago. The dark has given way to a deep blue tone that will only keep brightening.

There isn't a cloud over our heads.

"Are you hungry?" I turn to him, where he's leaning against a lamppost. "I am. It would be the perfect end to this all-night adventure if we can go home and order in, and—"

"We're not ordering in." He runs a hand along his jaw and looks out at the Thames. "How do you feel about watching the sunrise?"

"I feel like that's an infinitely better suggestion than mine."

His eyes gleam with a smile. "Don't beat yourself too bad about it."

"I'll try not to. Where should we go?"

"Oh, I know a perfect place." He pulls up his phone, and his fingers fly across the screen. "I'm getting us a cab. This one's too far to walk."

A car arrives a few minutes later, and then we're on the road again. Tiredness makes my eyelids heavy, and it takes effort to avoid falling asleep in the backseat of a London cab. The rocking motion makes it nearly impossible, until a hand brushes against my arm.

"Harper?"

"I'm awake."

"Good," he says. His deep voice is amused. "We're here."

We emerge onto the nearly deserted sidewalk in front of a skyscraper. The exterior is practically all-glass exterior, tinted and clean. A bouncer is at the entrance, and a few people mill around beside him; a couple of them having a smoke.

Everyone is dressed to the nines.

"Okay, you won't look weird being in a tux here," I tell Nate.

He puts his hand on the small of my back. It hovers there, barely touching. "We have an elevator ride left, and then there will be food."

"What is this place?"

"Duck and Waffle. Open twenty-four seven," he says. He nods at the bouncer, and then we're through.

It's on the top floor, an elegant blend of a restaurant and bar. All around us are glass windows with views of London. The first rays of light are kissing the horizon, ushering the break of dawn.

"Wow," I breathe. "This is unreal."

Nate's voice is amused again. "Come on. Let's grab a table with a view. The sun should rise… right over there. We'll get a good view of Tower Bridge too." He leads the way to a small table right against the glass. The waiter is at our side in minutes. She smiles, handing us the menus. "Finishing off a long night?"

"Something like that," Nate says. "But mostly we're beginning a new day in style."

We end up ordering the drinks along with the food. This place is famous for its cocktails, and it takes me one glance at the list of signature beverages to realize getting anything else would be a waste. The drinks arrive quickly, and Nate leans back in the chair with his gin and tonic. With his bowtie undone, his thick hair, and that glint in his eyes, he looks almost dangerous.

It's easy to forget just who Nate is when he's helping me air the smoke out from his kitchen after a culinary mishap, or making coffee in the morning. But it's just as easy for me to be struck by the realization again.

And right now, I'm struck.

On a regular day, Nate doesn't seem that much older than me, but at the moment, those ten years are apparent; the faint lines across his forehead make him look distinguished.

The things Dean has told me wind through my mind. Now, though, they are enhanced, changed with the firsthand knowledge of Nate himself. Of his beautifully renovated Kensington townhouse. Of his attachment to cars. His job and family, and the way he carries himself.

I've met other men through Dean, but no one quite like Nate. No one else whom Dean admired so much, and no one else whom Dean envied more.

No one more richer and no one more powerful.

"You're looking at me." Nate's voice holds no trace of amusement now, just a quiet observation. "Like you're trying to solve a riddle."

"Maybe I am. Maybe you are a very fascinating person."

One of his eyebrows rises. "I think you're vastly overestimating me."

"No, I don't think I am." I shake my head slowly. "There are a ton of things I would ask you. If I could."

Nate looks out of the window. I follow his gaze to where the golden sun is slowly rising. "Ask then," he says. His voice is a bit gruff.

I take a sip of my drink. It tastes like passionfruit and vanilla, and if there's alcohol in it, it's cleverly disguised. "It might offend you."

"Have I ever given you the impression that I'm easily offended?" He shakes his head, looking over at me, and puts a large hand directly over his heart. "That hurts more than any words you might say."

I roll my eyes. "I'm going to hold you to that if you ever get upset."

"Please do. I'm a man of my word." He inclines his head in my direction, his eyes still gleaming. "Give it your best shot."

Alcohol, adrenaline, and tiredness blend together in my system into a heady cocktail. Nothing about reality feels quite *real*. Not the bar, not the view of the city, not the sunrise. Not the early hour after a late night or the man sitting in front of me.

"You were… I… how did you turn out *normal*?"

Both his eyebrows rise. "What?"

"You were raised wealthy, right? You had these kinds of experiences all the time. Archery camp and, and… beautiful cars. International travel and amazing schools. How did you grow up and not become absolutely unbearable? You could be arrogant, belittling, entitled. I've met plenty of people who are."

He runs a hand along his jaw. It takes me a second to realize it's to hide his smile.

That makes me chuckle. "It's not that weird of a question!"

"No. It's just very you," he says.

"Very me?"

"Mm-hmm. It's also flattering. How do you know I'm not arrogant, belittling, and entitled when you're not watching?"

I tilt my head. Examine him. "I suppose you might be. Yes, it's possible, especially at work. I have a very small sample size to work with. But I think that if you're arrogant, it's in a joking way. That if you're belittling, it's unintended. And if you're entitled, it's… well. An accident of your birth."

"You're giving me a lot of grace right now."

"And you're avoiding answering my question," I say. "I only know what I've… what I've heard about your family. Is it true that you used to go on family holidays on a private jet?"

He runs a hand over his face. "That little tidbit made its way to your ears, huh?"

"Yes. Sorry."

"It happened a few times, yeah. But we didn't go on family trips very often." He takes a sip of his drink, and when he sees me still watching, he blows out a breath. "You really want an answer."

"I want to know more about you."

"Demanding," he chides. But he leans back in his chair like he's settling in. "We were raised in comfort, my siblings and I. I'll be the first to admit that. We were given every opportunity. Summer camps, tutors, internships… It was a paved road. But my mother didn't come from the same world as Dad. She was very insistent on us learning good manners, empathy, and how to have fun."

My voice comes out hesitant. "I heard about her. I'm really sorry, Nate."

His lips tilt up in a half smile that's not all too amused. "Thanks, but it was a long time ago."

"Still. Time doesn't really matter when it comes to that sort of thing."

His eyes sharpen. "Of course. You lost your father."

"Yes, when I was three. I don't have any memories of him. My stepdad, Greg, is the only dad I've ever known." I shake my head. "This isn't about me."

"No, because it couldn't be that easy." He looks down at his glass again. "Dad raised us alone after she died, and the lessons changed. He's always been more achievement focused. It's hard to feel entitled when you have to work for everything. Not the material things or opportunities, perhaps, but all the other things that matter to a kid. Attention. Affection. Approval."

"All the A's," I murmur.

He huffs out a laugh. "Yes. All the A's."

"You have a big brother, too," I say. "Competitive?"

"Terribly," he says easily, the word falling from half-smiling lips. "Until I decided to give up the fight. I'd rather lose on walkover than on merit."

"Clever."

"Well, that's the one thing I have going for me. Or at least I did." He lifts his drink and drains it entirely. "I *usually* make good decisions."

I smile at him. "Usually? What have you— oh!"

The food arrives. Two large plates, two sides, and a small bowl of bread. It's a veritable spread, and I know the bill will be just as large, but this is an adventure. The scent of waffles, truffle fries, and beef sliders wafts in the air between us.

"This is the way life should be lived." I reach for a few fries, and they taste like magic. We both dig in, and for a few minutes there's no conversation at all.

"Tell me about your parents," he says. "Your mom and stepdad."

I shake my head again. "This is supposed to be my time to ask you invasive questions that you won't remember later."

That makes him laugh. "I'm not that drunk, and neither are you, not anymore. Come on. Tell me."

"My mom is a professor of English literature. Greg works as an accountant. They're very ordinary, boring people, and they gave me a very stable upbringing."

"English literature?"

"Yes. She raised me on Jane Austen, the Brontë sisters, Dickens… Actually, it's partly why I was so excited about this job being in London. I love period dramas, the history, the beautiful architecture. My mom might come for a visit later, and we're looking at doing one of those tours. You know, the one that stops at Shakespeare's birthplace and Jane Austen's home and stuff?"

"There are tours like that?"

"Nate," I tell him seriously, "there are tours for *everything*."

He smiles into his glass. "Of course there are."

"So, I'm going to try to do that. Mom's been… well." The recent conversation, about how Dean had spoken to her and tried to influence her to change my mind, dampens my excitement a bit. She's been supportive. Mostly. She just doesn't understand, and that was hard in the beginning, when I was still doubting my own decision.

The food disappears at the speed of the rising sun outside our window. The golden rays illuminate London and make the serpentine Thames glitter wherever it's glimpsed between the buildings.

For a few long minutes, we just sit and take it all in. It isn't until we leave that I realize I never took a picture. But forgetting to photograph beautiful moments is the best of signs.

It's six thirty when we emerge back onto the sidewalk. The tiredness is like a blanket around me, heavy and welcoming, and even Nate looks like he could do with a nap. He runs his hand through his hair several times while we wait for our cab.

Some people throw us curious glances. It's fairly deserted

since it's Saturday, but a few who walk by are in suits. Working, despite the weekend, here in the financial district.

With Nate in his tux and an undone bow tie, and me in my golden dress, it looks like we've been partying until dawn. A couple that's stayed out all night.

That thought makes me giggle.

Nate brushes his shoulder with mine. "What are you thinking of now, Harpy?"

"Harpy?"

"You said you'd never had a nickname, so I'm testing some out."

I giggle again. "Well, *harpy* is terrible. And I was thinking what the people walking by must be thinking of us right now."

Nate leans in, his breath by my ear. "About how much they want to be us."

I roll my eyes. "No, they're not."

"Of course they are. You think I can't be arrogant, or belittling, or entitled?" His gaze makes my stomach tighten. "I will tell you exactly what they see. They see two people who've had the night of their lives. They see frivolity and excess, the result of a night of partying. And if they're male, well..." His lips curve into that crooked smile, the real one. "They very much want to be in my shoes right now."

My throat feels dry. "Because they think you're going home with me?"

"They do." He chuckles, and the tension in my stomach breaks. "And I am. Just not that way."

My smile widens. "Don't get any ideas."

"Don't worry," he says dryly. "I won't."

It's a miracle that I manage to stay awake in the cab. We walk in muted silence up the steps to the townhouse. The sun is high over the rooftops now, and birds chirp happily from behind the garden walls.

"What time did you wake up yesterday morning?" he asks.

"Seven-fifteen." I glance at my watch. "Shit. I have another twenty minutes for this to be considered an all-nighter."

"Then we'll just need to keep you awake for the next twenty minutes." Nate locks the door behind us, and I wander into the living room, an area I haven't used as much as I would have liked, mindful of his space.

Now I throw myself on the giant couch.

He chuckles. "TV?"

"Please, or I won't be able to keep my eyes open. And make it really, really loud."

He turns it on. Sits down on the couch next to where I'm sprawled, melting into the soft cushion from sheer exhaustion. Any second now, I feel like I'm going to topple into the blissful void.

"My eyelids are heavy," I say.

Nate's hand lands on my upper arm. "Don't fall asleep."

"I won't," I mumble. His touch feels good. Warm. I curl closer until my head is touching the side of his thigh. "This couch is... nice."

He chuckles. "I won't let you fall asleep."

"Good," I murmur.

"Tell me about your favorite... artist."

"Do I have to?"

"Yes," he says. "You have sixteen more minutes."

I yawn and search my mind for a painter or a sculptor who can be called my favorite. Which is hard. No one has a *favorite,* and I open my mouth to tell him just that.

He chuckles halfway through my rambling. "I get it. Favorite is hard."

"It's impossible. But there's one... It's a bit stupid." I yawn, my jaw cracking. "When I was... I don't know, eight maybe? I saw this painting of a Tuscan landscape at my grandmother's house. And I couldn't look away from it."

"A Tuscan landscape?" he says.

"Yes. Landscape paintings are an old staple of art history,

but you won't see them in any of the high-end galleries today. Still. The sunlight over the hills… It told a story."

"Does your grandmother still have it?"

I nod, and stifle another yawn. "It's my dream one day to buy… to buy another painting from that same artist. She's still active, I've checked. My friends from art school would be horrified." I chuckle a bit into my throw pillow. There are plenty of artists whose works I would love to have on my walls. Artists whose paintings are in this very house. But that one, the Tuscan landscape… It's what started it all for me.

"What do you love most about it? That painting?" Nate asks. His hand moves in a circle over my arm.

"I think it made me realize that art had a purpose. A story. That it was a window into new worlds… new perspectives. You know?" A shiver runs through me, and I draw my knees up to my chest.

Nate notices. He reaches behind him, jostling my head, and grabs the blanket. "I know," he says and unfurls a thousand pounds of some kind of soft wool over me. Then his hand returns to my shoulder.

"I like your hand there," I mumble into the pillow beneath my head.

"What was that?" Nate asks. He slid down on the couch, his long legs stretched out in front with his feet resting on top of the coffee table.

"I like this."

"Mm-hmm," he says. "Staying out all night? Going to make it a habit, Harp?"

I chuckle. That's not what I meant. "Maybe."

"Not to be dramatic, but you'll give me a heart attack if this becomes your regular thing."

I close my eyes. It hurts too much to keep them open. "We should hang out here more often. On the couch. I've never seen your giant TV turned on."

Gentle glides across my shoulder, on top of the fabric. It feels like his hand.

I'm almost asleep when he finally answers. "We should. I'd suggest this week, but I'm traveling most of it." His voice is low. A bit resigned.

The news makes me frown. "You are? Where to?"

"I have to be in Stockholm on Tuesday, and Berlin on Thursday."

"Business?"

"Business," he repeats. His hand is still moving up my arm. "You'll have the entire house to yourself."

"It's too big for one person."

His exhale is audible. "Yeah. I'm learning that, too."

"When do you get back?"

"On Friday," he says. "I haven't told you this, either, but I'm hosting a party here next Saturday night."

"You are? Here?"

"Yes. The plans were set before… before this."

"Before me," I murmur.

"Yes."

I yawn, so wide that there's a pop in my jaw. "Well, I can be out of the house if—"

"Of course not. This is your home," he says. "Come to the party."

I nod into the pillow. My tongue feels too heavy to speak, just as heavy as the rest of me, and I hear Nate's breathing. It's steady and deep, and it could easily lull me to sleep if I let it.

And I so want to let it.

"What time is it now?" I ask.

Nate's voice is the last thing I hear. "You can sleep now."

And sleep I do.

Chapter 16

Harper

Harper: What are you doing right now?

It only takes a few minutes before I receive a picture back. It's of a half-drunk coffee cup, a closed laptop, and a large conference table with a basket of pastries in the middle. In the background, a cityscape of a European city is visible through a window.

Nate: Meetings.

Harper: Don't text during your meetings! Pay attention.

Nate: I'm trying, but someone won't stop texting me.

I smile down at my phone and pop it back into my pocket. It's day three of Nate's traveling week, and, somehow, that first *have a safe flight* text has morphed into an entire conversation that never ends.

It's hard to forget, too, what happened on Saturday morning. When I'd woken up at noon to a bright living room… with Nate's arm around me.

He'd been slumped against me, his face serene and

relaxed in sleep. I was reluctant to move, but my left arm felt numb. One minor shift, and he was awake, too.

I looked away from his warm gaze and messy hair, toward the coffee table and the forgotten flowers lying there. A blush had spread furiously up my cheeks, and I said the first thing I could think of.

My peonies! I forgot to put them in the water.

Nate's voice had been hoarse with sleep and a bit husky. *Don't worry, Harp. I'll buy you more.*

Now, days later, and with Nate as a constant presence on my phone… through the grocery shopping and the long work hours, and the evening walks around the neighborhood, I've finally figured out the right word on the tip of my tongue.

I'm *happy*.

That's the word, and that's how I felt with him that night. I experienced happiness in a profound, deep way. Brought on by adrenaline, possibilities, and Nate.

I find myself wanting to ask him more things, all kinds of things, but he's not here to answer any of them. He doesn't really talk about himself a lot. Not beyond the surface level.

It makes me wonder what lies beneath it. Who hides beneath the mask he puts on.

A few hours go by before my phone buzzes again. It's another picture; this time, of a beautiful summertime city near the water. He had sent me several photos of Stockholm so far, each one prettier than the last.

Nate: People are swimming right in the city. It's wild. It's only May!

Harper: Jump in.

Nate: I'm in a suit. Also. No.

Harper: You're the one who was telling me to embrace adventure.

Nate: What do I get if I do it?

I dig my teeth into my lower lip and look over at Aadhya. She's focused on the computer screen, working hard on the summer event the gallery is hosting in two months. Under Eitan's supervision, we've been given a lot of leeway with the planning. Hostesses, catering, the open bar. This work is unlike anything I was allowed to do in my old job.

I should get back to doing it. But first…

Harper: It's either there or in the Thames when you least expect it. I'm a good shover.

Nate: Threats? From Harper Elliot? You really are becoming a new person.

I smile down at my phone. At least I'm trying to. I've put my "30 Under 30" list up above the desk in the beautiful guest room that's now mine. Now the goal to *stay out all night* is ticked off with a bright blue highlighter. So is *try archery.*

Harper: I have a friend who's a cutthroat in business. Has no problem lying to get what he wants. So I'm learning, yeah.

Nate: I think what I said was "false impressions."

Harper: Why did you assume I was talking about you?

The phone goes silent, and I imagine Nate getting into a booked car. Grumbling about not being allowed to drive himself, and zipping through streets I'd love to walk one day. It remains silent when I go to an evening Pilates class I found in the neighborhood. I even try befriending, albeit somewhat awkwardly, the woman exercising next to me. She doesn't seem offended by my chatter, which is a great start with Brits, I've learned.

When the class concludes, I sit down on the mat and take a picture of my legs and the distant mirror. Nate had teased me just a few days ago that I'd probably buy a gym membership and then never use it.

Harper: Made it to class for the second time, for your information. Definitely a solid investment.

His response is immediate.

Nate: Those are your workout tights?

Harper: No, this is my prom dress, actually.

Nate: Very funny.

Nate: I should come with you to Pilates sometime.

That makes me chuckle.

Harper: I would love to see you struggling at something, for once.

Nate: I struggle with things all the time. I'm just very good at hiding it. Case in point.

He sends a photo of an upscale restaurant and a large menu where nothing is written in English.

Harper: How are you gonna solve that?

Nate: I'm going to order whatever chef recommends and then eat it with a smile on my face. Even if it's pickled herring.

Harper: Send me a pic of the food when it arrives.

Nate: Absolutely not. This is a business dinner. Can you imagine if I tell people to wait before eating because I need to take a pic?

That makes me laugh again.

Harper: Are you with them now? You should talk to them! Not me!

Nate: Don't worry. You're helping me to appear aloof and busy. I just referred to you as my brother in New York, by the way, the CEO of Contron. They're very impressed.

Harper: Go eat some fish.

The next few days fly by in a flurry of back-and-forth texts. Nate sends occasional pictures from his trip—he's in Berlin now—little updates and jokes.

I didn't think I would miss him.

But I do.

The giant townhouse is quiet and I have it all to myself, but the luxury doesn't feel the same without him in it. It feels empty, a shell that's waiting for him to return.

I leave work in a hurry on Friday, excited to finally see Nate again. But when I arrive home… he's not here. The empty rooms continue to mock me and the silence is deafening.

I pause on my landing and look up at the narrow stairs leading to his floor. The top level is the last place in this giant, elegant place I haven't been to.

But I valiantly stop myself from snooping.

Harper: Where are you?

Nate: Have to stay another night in Berlin. There was a fuckup with a supplier. I'm annoyed.

I bite my bottom lip and struggle with the same feeling. I thought I would see him tonight. Had hoped… thought we could order in, watch a movie perhaps…

Harper: Oh. Hope it gets resolved!

Nate: It better.

So I head out instead… and go to a bar in Chelsea.

Grab a drink by myself is on my list. Although everything inside me screams at how *weird* it is to sit in the bar with a single glass of wine and no one to talk to, I force myself through the profound awkwardness of the first fifteen minutes.

Once I get over my self-consciousness, something amazing happens.

It becomes enjoyable.

Watching the people, feeling the pulse of the night, and drinking my white wine. I don't let myself be distracted by my phone, either. I am simply present in the moment, in a way I haven't been for a very long time.

As I walk home with another thing checked off my list, I feel a newfound sense of empowerment.

Ridiculous, Dean would have said. I can hear the tone he would have used, too, like my ideas were fanciful and childish, and had no place in an adult's life.

I'm reclaiming that sense of wonder one step at a time, and with it, myself. Who I used to be when I indulged my whims, when I focused on *fun* instead of stability. Tiny movements toward the woman I want to be. Toward the life I want to live.

I walk aimlessly through the kitchen and run my hand over the stone countertop. Look outside the windows at the dark garden I've still never really sat in. I'll have to change that, soon.

Maybe he needs to stay in Berlin for another reason. One he didn't want to share. It would be unreasonable of me to expect a single, wealthy man in his late thirties to spend every weekend at home or work.

He probably doesn't need a wingwoman anyway. He might already have someone.

The more I think about it, the more it feels obvious. Of course he does. Which leads me to wonder why he hasn't just said so.

Maybe he keeps that close to his vest, too. Another thing that he doesn't share easily or at all.

I turn in feeling more dejected than I have in weeks. However, even the comfort of my glorious bed isn't enough for restful sleep.

I wake up early on Saturday morning, the day Nate is supposed to host a party at the townhouse.

Yet he's still not home. The place is still empty.

I go out for a walk in the neighborhood. The spring weather is beautiful, the sky is blue, and I love the architecture in Kensington. It's almost noon by the time I get a text from Nate.

> Nate: Finally got a flight out. It's been a shitshow here. My assistant and the party planners should be at the house soon to start setting everything up. Don't worry, they'll stay on the first floor.

Damn. Does that mean I won't see him until the party? I'm typing a question about when he'll be arriving when I'm interrupted by two energetic barks.

Stanley and Quincy, the two dachshunds, and Richard are headed my way. He's wearing another flat cap but no jacket this time, just a dress shirt with a down vest.

"Good morning," he tells me. Quincy sits politely at his feet while Stanley nips around mine. "Isn't it a fine day?"

We end up walking together in the garden. Now that I know how to access it, I'm here more often, in this beautiful and serene space reserved for local residents. The fountain in the middle bubbles happily, and Stanley revels in my pets, his little tail wagging. His floppy ears are like silk.

"I have a ball in here somewhere," Richard mutters and reaches into the pockets of his vest. He holds up the ball to me with a knotted hand. "If you want to keep him entertained."

I spend a solid hour chatting with Richard and playing with the dogs. He's British, almost aggressively so, but he doesn't seem to mind my small talk and aimless hovering. Quite the opposite.

When I finally head home, the townhouse's glossy black door is wide open. Two men walk up the steps, carrying a giant cooler between them.

Preparations have begun.

I wave hello to the middle-aged woman standing in my living room—in *Nate's* living room—and giving orders to caterers, porters, and all kinds of other personnel.

I sneak past everyone up to my room. Nerves keep me there for most of the afternoon. I read a book, search for a potential new apartment, and select what two art museums I want to go to the next day.

As the afternoon drags on, I choose a dress to wear tonight, only to change my mind and pick out another, and then another. I finally settle on a black dress that goes down to my ankles. It covers a lot... but it's formfitting, and that makes it revealing all the same. I usually wear an oversized blazer with it, but standing in front of my huge bathroom mirror, I decide to skip the blazer.

The old me would cover up. Not the new me. Not London me.

Downstairs, the music starts to play, and I hear a pair of hurried feet descending the stairs outside my room.

Nate.

He's home.

I don't know anyone but him at this party.

I barely know what kind of party it is.

Cracking open my bedroom door, I peek through the gap. There are voices downstairs. Plenty of them, and for a moment, I consider closing the door and hiding. And maybe the old me would have done that.

Retreated with a book.

But that's not the person I want to be. The person I'm working really hard to become, to inhabit, who embraces opportunities when they strike.

I walk down the stairs.

The first floor of Nate's townhouse has been transformed into an elegant bar. People mill about, glasses of champagne in hand. The front door is open, and a man is standing just outside. Is that a bouncer? At a *house party*? Music is playing from speakers I can't see. They must be hidden.

My steps slow as I approach the bottom of the stairs. I'm scanning the room, looking from person to person. I don't recognize anyone. Most look about my age, some are older, and a few younger.

It's a good thing I didn't throw on my blazer. But perhaps I should have worn heels instead of my ballet flats. People are dressed to the nines.

I run my hand down the banister. So far I can't see him. Not in the living room, nor in the adjoining kitchen…

But then I spot him.

Standing in the doorway to the study, hands in his pockets, talking to the two men whose faces I cannot see. He's nodding to whatever they're saying, but his eyes are locked on me.

Watching me descend the stairs.

I smile at him, excitement rushing through my veins. It's been a long week without him.

His lips curve in response. It's a tiny reaction, but it's there. A silent hello.

I wind my way toward the kitchen island where I usually have my breakfast. Right now, the space is teeming with people. A woman in an apron is pouring more glasses of champagne, and the expensive stone countertop is laden with canapés and snacks.

As house parties go, this is a far cry from the small dinner parties Dean and I used to host.

I grab a flute of the bubbly and a small cracker with some kind of pâté on it. Catch the snippets of conversations around me. Something about *the investing season is almost over* and *stocks are a winter sport* drift my way, and I wander to the back door that leads to the garden.

I don't know how to introduce myself. *Hi, I'm Nate's... live-in friend?*

His art adviser. That's what said he called me at the gallery, and it's not incorrect. False impressions and all that. Maybe it's time I learn to use them to my advantage, too.

"You came," Nate says.

I turn to find him beside me, with his own glass of champagne in hand. He looks calm, serene even, his face pleasantly neutral.

Like he knows he's being watched.

"You're back," I say. "And considering all I had to do was walk down the stairs, it wasn't hard."

He looks down at my dress, and a smile plays on his lips. "You look gorgeous."

"Thank you. Um, who are all these people?"

"I have no idea," he says.

I roll my eyes. "Okay, that can't be true. Who put the guest list together?"

"My assistant, the party planner, and my brother," he says. "I made a few additions."

"Really?" I look over my shoulder, eyes halting on a group of beautiful women standing by the dining room table. "Who?"

"You, among a few others."

I nudge his shoulder. "Thanks for that, by the way."

"I wasn't going to confine you to your bedroom."

My gaze meets his. "Haven't seen you all week."

"No. I'm sorry about that. The trip had to be extended." He sighs, eyebrows scrunching together. "Our supplier in Berlin was delayed getting to the meeting, and we couldn't come to a... solution. I had to stay longer to hammer it out."

Despite the otherwise pleasant expression on his face, there are faint circles under his eyes and tenseness to his jaw.

He's wearing a mask.

"Well, it was very quiet around here without you."

"Was it? I'm sorry."

"You should be. I was forced to tackle several of my goals on my own."

His eyes darken. "Which ones?"

"Um, going out to a bar by myself. I also went to the movies alone after work on Thursday."

"All right. Good job," he says. "If you did number seventeen, don't tell me about it. I'll never be able to see the guest bedroom in the same light again."

A laugh escapes me, but I can't look at him. "It's still so embarrassing that you saw that."

The *threesome* I had impulsively put on the list.

"I don't think *embarrassing* is the word I'd use," he mutters. He takes a long sip of his drink, his eyes thoughtful. "Two men? A man and a woman?" His eyebrow lifts. "Or two other women?"

I look over my shoulder. "We can't discuss that *here*."

"Why not?" he asks. "It's a party, isn't it?"

"It's not that kind of party." But then I look around—at the beautiful people in elegant dresses and suits. Take in the crooning music playing from the hidden speakers. Scrutinize the flowing bar. "Wait. It's *not,* right?"

He snorts. "You think I'd throw an orgy and invite you?"

"You'd throw an orgy and *not* invite me?"

"If I did," he says calmly, like this isn't the stupidest conversation I've ever had, "I'd warn you first. Now come on." He leans closer, his eyes on mine. "Which threesome is it that you want?"

"Nate!"

"What? Want me to go first?"

My eyes flare. "You want to have a threesome?"

"I've tried it." The words roll off his tongue ever so casually, smoothly, his eyes not leaving mine. Like that's a perfectly normal thing to say.

"You have," I breathe. "What kind?"

"I'll tell you mine if you tell me yours."

"That's not fair."

"It's entirely fair," he says. "You just don't like it."

That makes me grin. "I was trying to give a false impression."

"Good try, but I'm the master of them," he states. His eyes drop briefly to my lips, then flit away.

"Is that what you're doing tonight?" I ask. "Giving a false impression?"

His wandering gaze freezes for an instant. But then he looks at me and smiles, just a teeny twitch of his lips. "There is an ulterior motive for having this party."

"Tell me what it is so I can help."

"I wish you could, Harp."

"What's the deal?"

"A few of the invited people are more important than others, that's all."

I step closer, our shoulders brushing… and look over at the crowd. Give them all a quick glance. "Who?"

"They're impossible to describe."

"Why?"

"Because they all look alike," he says dryly.

My gaze snags on the group of women standing by the dining room table. They all look beautiful, but fairly similar, indeed. Dresses, heels, blow-dried hair.

"I see." A frown pulls on the corners of my mouth. Maybe he'll let me help this time? It's definitely an easier environment here, less risky, easier to introduce myself. "Anyone in particular you're interested in?"

"What?" Nate turns, follows my line of sight. There's a quiet sigh when he sees where I'm looking. "Ah. You're still determined to be my wingwoman."

"Isn't that what you meant?" I ask.

His eyes narrow into slits. "Would you like me to return the favor? There are plenty of eligible men here. Single. With stable jobs. *Available*."

I take a long, slow sip of my drink. It's a terrible idea. I'm not ready to date yet... but I feel like being wild, and drinking more than I should, and embracing the new me.

Making bad decisions has never felt more fun.

"It's a deal," I say.

"A deal," he murmurs, voice close to my ear. "May the best wingman win."

Chapter 17

Nate

Harper took my breath away as she walked down the stairs.

She does it regularly but in ways I'd gotten used to, like feeling the pinpricks of pain rather than an outright punch to the gut. Tonight had been another gut punch. Just as the first time I saw her at that college bar, sitting alone but not lonely, looking at her surroundings like she was analyzing them.

She descended those stairs in a floor-length, curve-hugging dress, with her wild curls draping over her shoulders. A soft smile on her lips and a dreamy expression in her eyes as she looked out over the living room.

For the briefest of seconds, it felt as if she was coming from upstairs—*our upstairs*—to our party. The hostess to my host.

I take another deep sip of the Negroni I'm drinking. It's my third, and I should slow down. This isn't a party like the ones I once used to throw. With friends, and poker, and the ultimate goal of getting hammered and laughing our asses off. There's a purpose to this party.

Harper finding me a date was not it.

And it sure as hell wasn't finding one for her, either.

But here I am, drawn in by the smile in her eyes and the teasing in her voice, doing it anyway. It feels like a repeating pattern.

Across the room, I spot her talking to a brunette standing by the fireplace. They're both smiling. Cautious, tentative, *hello-we-just-met* smiles.

I turn away. Roll my neck and try to find the person I was supposed to impress with this whole shindig. Plenty of people here are acquaintances, yes, and a few are friends. But there's one person here I need to connect with. Mads Knudsen.

I spot him in the garden, having a smoke. The cigarette casually dangles from his fingers, his gaze fully locked on the young man he's talking to. Mads's mistress-turned-second-wife should be somewhere around here, too. It had taken a lot of work to get an invite sent to them; even more to ensure they'd accept.

I drain my Negroni and step out into my backyard. Knudsen is the major stakeholder in one of Northern Europe's largest energy companies, and it's a stake my brother wants to acquire. It would give us an excellent infrastructure and a corporate foothold for future Contron expansions in the region.

Problem is, the man doesn't want to sell.

People with a lot of money fall into two camps. Those who want nothing but *more* money, in a never-ending cycle of greed. They're easy to work with.

But then there are the rich people who can't be bought with money alone. You have to finesse them with experiences, with promises, with status. With things they can't just use their no-limit credit cards to get themselves.

It's a slower game, that one.

Knudsen greets me when I arrive. Introduces me to the man he's been talking to, someone who is a good ten years younger than me. This guy is good-looking in that swoopy-haired, clean-shaven, preppy-boy sort of way. I know the type well. Once upon a time, that was me.

Before I joined Contron and aged a decade.

I hate this guy on sight.

I hate that he is the sort of guy I *should* be introducing Harper to—if I was playing her game, if we were the kind of friends she thinks we are, the kind of friends we should be.

"This is my nephew," Knudsen says and slaps the pop-star-wannabe on the shoulder. "Willard."

"It's a pleasure," I say. "Hope you're enjoying yourself."

"I certainly am."

"Tell me," Knudsen continues, "didn't you mention a few weeks back that you had a sizable art collection?"

"I might have, yes." I give him a wide smile. "Did you come by to purchase it from me?"

"No, no, I don't have a great eye, but this guy does." He points at his nephew. "One of London's greatest up-and-coming art dealers, he is."

"Is that so?" I raise an eyebrow at the nephew. "Freelancer?"

"I'm attached to the Robert Asher chain of galleries, but I do a fair bit of freelance work, as well." He has a narrow chin, thick eyebrows, and a mouth that looks just a bit too smug. "What kind of art do you collect?"

"Modern, mostly, and a few of the abstract expressionists."

Willard runs a hand along his jaw. "Fascinating. I would love to take a look at your collection when time permits."

Knudsen gives me a pointed stare. *You'll take care of my nephew, won't you, Connovan?*

A slow game.

A long one, too.

I smile at the pip-squeak. "It would be my pleasure. My art adviser is here tonight, as it happens."

His eyebrows shoot up. "They are? What's their name?"

"Harper Elliot."

"I'm not familiar with that name," he says, "but I'd be happy to speak with her."

Mads Knudsen takes another puff of his cigarette. "It's

fantastic, isn't it," he says in my direction, "how well-connected people can be."

"You mean how well-connected people like us are."

He chuckles. I'd learned early on that Knudsen has a good sense of humor, occasionally quite dark, and I leaned into it fully. It suits me better to use cynicism, anyway.

"Right you are," he says easily. "So, which of these pretty women here tonight is your date?"

"I'd say Kathleen, but I know she's taken."

He chuckles again. "Stay far away from my wife, Connovan."

"I will, but it will pain me to do so."

"Say that when she can hear you if you want bonus points," he says easily. "A man like you can't be single. I know this. Willard knows this. It's one of the laws of the universe. Come now, tell me."

He's trying to connect. And I need to tell him what he wants to hear. That's the part I'm expected to play, the way I always have.

I give him a sly smile. "I didn't *come* with a date today."

He grins. "Ah, but you might leave with one. Good, good. That is— oh?"

Both Mads and Willard turn to the two women standing beside us. One of them is Harper, and a jolt passes through me at the sight.

She's looking at me with a smile in her eyes. "Sorry to interrupt, gentlemen. I was just wondering if I could steal Nate for a moment?"

"Of course," Mads says with his own sly look in my direction.

That's when I notice the brunette standing next to Harper. I clear my throat. "As a matter-of-fact, why don't you two join us?"

It doesn't take long to introduce Harper to the two men as my art adviser. Willard's eyes light up, and he corners her immediately. Leaving me nodding goodbye to a smiling Mads Knudsen and standing next to a very chatty brunette.

Fantastic.

Mads is happy. I've been a wingman to Harper in the loosest sense of the word. Everyone must be thrilled.

Everyone but me.

The brunette's name is Lucy Simmons. She had mentioned to Harper wanting to meet the host of this beautiful party. Apparently, the friend who invited Ms. Simmons here didn't know who was throwing it, and she's thrilled to discover it's me.

Her eyes are fringed with long, artfully curled lashes. She's pretty. A few years ago, I would have been interested in talking to her, in finding common ground and sharing a few laughs. I wouldn't have thought twice about asking for her number or inviting her to stay for a nightcap and whatever else might, and often did, follow.

I would have enjoyed Lucy Simmons, and she would have enjoyed me.

But something happened a few years ago that changed the game for me.

Still… this is how Harper decided to play.

There's a dark and angry part of me, spurred by the fresh drink I'm holding, that wonders if she really cares so little. If she truly wants to see this… *Me* and this woman she's picked out for me.

I glance across the backyard. Harper is sitting next to Willard, both of them talking animatedly. She's holding a glass of champagne nodding.

She must catch me watching because she looks over.

Our gazes collide.

She's the first to smile. But then Lucy asks me to sit down, and I look away. Refocusing on the woman talking to me.

So I sit down with her. Offer her a drink and ask about her job, her background, her hobbies. She is quick to laugh and is a good storyteller, and I nod along, shifting closer on the lounge seat.

Nursing another Negroni and stealing glances at Harper and Willard.

They seem engrossed in their discussion. She's pushed her hair back and is nodding vigorously at whatever he's saying, and when she laughs, I hear it across the backyard. Over the sounds of other people talking and the music playing.

My chest feels tight with something ugly.

Lucy puts a hand on my arm. "How are you liking London?"

And so the night drags on. But I can only make it an hour before the ugly thing inside me needs an escape.

"I have to be honest," I tell Lucy. Her eyebrows shoot up but she nods. She's been surprisingly easy to talk to. "My friend, Harper, introduced us in the hopes of playing a matchmaker."

Lucy smiles. "I figured, yeah."

"It was nice of her. Problem is, I'm hopelessly in love with her."

There's a brief silence, and then Lucy lets out a small *oooh.* Her eyes light up. "Really?"

I chuckle at her reaction. "Yes. Is that a good thing? Because it's felt fucking awful for four years."

"It's exciting. She clearly fancies you. She gushed about you earlier."

"Well, that was because she wants to win a little game we're playing. It's called 'who's the best wingman.'"

"I see. And you don't want to win?"

"I definitely don't," I mutter, shooting a look across the yard to where Willard has draped his arm along the back of the couch. It disappears behind Harper's shoulder.

They're still talking.

"I see," Lucy says, and then she nods. "Okay. I'm enjoying our conversation. Why don't we keep playing the game? No strings."

I raise an eyebrow. "You'd do that?"

"It's more exciting than listening to some moneyman drone on, which is what I'd be doing while talking to other blokes here," she says and lifts a shoulder in a shrug. "So. Yes."

I actually laugh at that. "Okay, you may be right."

Lucy smiles, and puts a hand on my knee. "So. Tell me all about Harper and how you're finally going to win her over."

It's nearly one in the morning when we wrap up our chat. By then, we've spoken about almost everything under the sun, minus a few hard-to-solve political problems and the national debt, and I've kept an eye on Harper and Willard doing the same.

What could they possibly talk about for that long?

Most of the party guests have cleared out. I don't want to leave the backyard but I do it anyway, turning away from where Harper is giving all of her smiles to Knudsen's nephew. *One step forward in that relationship,* I think miserably. One step back in my own.

I don't have a fucking relationship with Harper, I remind myself. The bartender has left, but there's an array of drinks still artfully displayed on the counter, so I pour myself another gin and tonic. She doesn't owe me one. I've never ever once thought that.

But that doesn't mean that it doesn't hurt.

I drain half of the drink before ambling off to the hallway, heading to the study. Somewhere I can shut the door behind me and not watch any more of Harper's smiles wasted on another man.

I've seen enough of those already with Dean.

But someone stops me, a hand on my sleeve. I look down to see Harper. There's a distinct flush across her cheeks. She's been drinking, too. "How's it going?" she asks.

"With what?"

"With Lucy, of course." Her gaze flits to the kitchen where a few stragglers are pouring themselves drinks.

"Oh. Her."

"Yes, her," Harper says. Her eyes are piercing on mine. "I don't think you should ask her to stay over."

"And why is that?"

She shakes her head, and her hand is still tight on my wrist. "She… she… it would be too fast."

"I thought you wanted me to find someone. You've talked about it often." I lean in closer, that hideous thing in my chest unfurling its wings. "How's it going with Willard, the boy band imitator wunderkind art dealer?"

Her eyes narrow. "Fine. He's… fine."

"Well, Lucy is fine, too."

"I still think it's a bad idea."

"So I ask again…" I say in a low voice. "Why is that?"

"We haven't tested the acoustics," she says. Her eyes are piercing on mine, her voice just shy of shaky. "I don't want to hear the two of you all night. It would keep me up."

"Do you think I want to hear you and *Willard*?"

"Right. We haven't thought this through," she says, as if that's perfectly sensible. Her hand tightens around my wrist. "We need to run sound experiments first."

"Sound experiments," I mutter.

She's looking down at my wrist trapped between our bodies. Still locked in her grip. *Sound experiments.* I use my free hand to lift her chin, forcing her eyes to meet mine.

There's irritation in her gaze, twin to the emotion roiling in me. "You came here to tell me not to sleep with Lucy," I say. "Are you jealous, Harp?"

Her eyes flare. "Don't be ridiculous."

"Am I being ridiculous? You're the one who introduced her to me, who pushed this whole idea in the first place. And now, you're concerned over *potentially* hearing us fuck?"

She stiffens, swallowing hard. I'd used the term deliberately, and it hit its mark. "Excuse me for valuing my sleep," she nearly growls.

"Are you sure it's not that you're upset about me spending the entire evening talking to Lucy?"

There's anger in her eyes. "If I have to admit it, then you have to admit to not liking Willard. You stared at us all night."

"Fine." I lean in closer. My fingers are still holding her chin, her hand still gripping my wrist. "I *hate* him."

"You're jealous," she breathes.

"Of course, I'm fucking jealous. If you decide to take him up those stairs and into your bedroom…"

"What?" she asks. Her breath is warm against my lips. "What would you do?"

My hand moves from her chin to the back of her neck, fingers sliding into the silky curls. The air between us is hot, and it grows electric when I draw closer.

Too close.

All of my pent-up frustrations tonight unleash at that moment. In that fragile, tense moment when my lips hover just a hairsbreadth from hers. A tiny static spark ignites a supernova. I don't know if it's my anger, jealousy, or the incessant need for her, but something pushes me over the edge.

I kiss her.

Her lips are soft and pliant against mine, and a small sound escapes her. A faint sigh of surprise. Then, she's kissing me back. Her mouth slants against mine, lips parts, and it's everything.

Everything.

She tastes like warm champagne. I brush my tongue against her lower lip. Sweep it into the warmth of her mouth. Glide against her sensuous tongue.

For a split second, her grip on my wrist disappears, only to reappear on the labels of my shirt. She sways into me, tugging me closer, and my freed arm wraps around her waist.

I feel high.

Having Harper in my arms, melting under my lips,

hearing the soft sounds that she makes, tasting her kisses… It's better than any drug I'd tried in my twenties. Better than the elation of winning a multimillion-dollar contract at work. Better than all of my previous sexual experiences combined.

Her hand slides up from my lapel to my nape. Fingers thread through the strands of my hair. And then, she runs her nails over my scalp, and red-hot fire races down my spine.

Blood rushes with it. I harden in an instant. Fuck. This is everything I ever imagined and more. *She* is everything.

Harper presses herself to my chest, and I pull her tight, crushing her curves against me. Somewhere in the fractured, kaleidoscopic mess of my mind, where only she exists, I realize I'm kissing her too hard.

I try to ease up. To slow down. To use more finesse.

But with another tug of her hand on my hair, those intentions fracture, too. She pulls me down the hall until I have her pinned against the wall, our lips never breaking contact.

I want to know what she likes. I want to know what her skin tastes like, so I tip her head back and slide my lips along her jaw. Down to the soft skin of her neck.

A soft exhale escapes her, and it sends another wave of desire racing through me. I'm so painfully hard against the metal buckle of my belt, I feel like my dick is going to explode at any moment. It doesn't matter, though. Not with Harper in my arms.

"Nate," she whispers as she once again rakes her nails over my scalp.

Fuck.

I bite lightly on her shoulder and shudder at the sensation that evoked. Harper giggles, and I kiss the spot where my teeth grazed her. Kiss up the soft column of her throat, making her giggles turn into another soft sigh.

"Nate," she whispers again. "Is… is… Lucy still here?"

"No," I mutter. "She left."

Harper swallows. I feel it against my lips, pressed to her

throat. "Good. Willard isn't here anymore, either. I sent him home."

My hand tightens around her waist. "Good girl."

A shiver passes through her, and then, she pulls my face down for another kiss. One turns into several, until she's once again pinned to the wall by my starving body. Her right hand slides into the collar of my shirt, fingers brushing my heated skin. Her touch feels cool compared to the fever raging inside me.

The crash of breaking glass makes us both flinch. It's loud and nearby, and is immediately followed by raised voices. The kitchen. The stragglers.

We pull apart, both of us breathing heavily.

"That didn't sound good," she whispers.

I let go of the curls I'd been holding on to. "No. It didn't."

She swallows hard and lets her hands drop, too. Once again, we're just two people standing far too close in a dark hallway.

"I should check on that," I say.

The corners of her mouth lift into a smile, and I can't help but notice her kiss-swollen lips and the thundering of my heart.

"Good idea," she murmurs. "Don't let them wreck the kitchen I've come to love, please."

I take a step back. It physically hurts to distance myself from her, to try to calm the pounding need inside me. "Of course not. It's yours."

She smiles a little and backs up toward the staircase. Heading to her room. That smile on her lips, I'll remember forever.

"Good night, Connovan," she says.

"Good night, Harp."

Chapter 18

Harper

"So you haven't spoken since last night," Richard says. He sounds contemplative, his gaze stays on Stanley rolling in the green spring grass, his British accent crisp.

"No, I was out most of the day, and he had a meeting that he took from his home office." I stroke my hands over Quincy's soft, floppy ears. The cute bugger was content with running around for all of fifteen minutes before wanting to be picked up, and he now sits between Richard and me on the park bench.

"Right. Interesting," Richard says. Despite the warmth, he's in a blazer and a necktie, although his usual flat cap has been exchanged for one with a longer brim to shade from the sunlight. "And now you're avoiding the chap by talking to me."

I chuckle. "I'm having a great time."

"No need to flatter an old man," he says, but his voice is soothing. "This is somewhat of a conundrum, I suppose. Your feelings are clearly divided on the matter."

"Yes. I don't regret it, but it's not something that should happen again."

"Because of your mutual friend," he says. "This ex-fiancé of yours, who, judging by what you've told me, seems deserving of the ex role."

"I agree. He's also the reason I was hesitant about hanging out with Nate in the first place. My plan has always been to get as far away from my ex as possible. But now…" I look down at the dog resting his head on my lap, eyes closed, soaking up affection along with the evening sunshine. "Now, we've become real friends, too."

"Of course you have," Richard says. "I think that's a knack of yours." He stretches out his legs with a muffled groan and looks at Stanley, who is lying supine at his feet. "In youth, friendship is easy to take for granted. It often comes by easily, but it can be gone just so. Plenty of opportunities to make new mates when your life is busy and your days are long. But as years pass, new friends are terribly hard to come by, and you realize you may have treated true friends far too cavalierly… and lost them."

I follow Richard's gaze to Stanley and his softly wagging tail. "I'm sorry if you've lost someone."

"We all lose friends," he says. "Just make sure you're okay with the reason you lose them. Not talking this out with your fine fellow would, I believe, be a mistake."

I nod slowly. "You're right. Of course, you're right. We can't live together and never address it."

"You can. But take it from someone who's lived seventy-eight years, if you don't handle things as you must, they never *truly* go away."

I smile. "Handsome *and* wise?"

Richard huffs a laugh. "You Americans and your compliments."

"What would be the more British thing for me to say?"

He frowns in thought. "'That's sage advice,' perhaps. Or nothing at all. Just a nod of approval."

"I'll do that next time." I bend down to press a kiss on Quincy's soft head. He smells like grass and dog, in the best of ways. "Thank you for listening, I greatly appreciated it."

"Quincy and Stanley are good listeners," Richard says. Even though I know, and he knows, who my compliment was actually meant for. We say our goodbyes, and I leave him and his dogs sitting on his favorite bench and reaching for the book he put down when I came.

The house is quiet when I walk through the door. The cleaners were still working diligently when I left for the day, but they're gone now, and with them, all the evidence of last night's party. The living room, the kitchen, the dining room—every area has been restored to the beautiful luxury I've gotten to know when I arrived here a few weeks ago.

Nerves make my stomach tight. I fight the impulse to escape to my room and, instead, walk into the kitchen. It's Sunday night, and my usual routine is meal prepping. So that's exactly what I start doing. Even as my mind is having a hard time focusing on cutting up the carrots and zucchini, stubbornly lingering on the previous night.

I had too much to drink. So did he, I think. That has to be the reason for what happened, and *I know* that, but it doesn't make the memory hold any less weight.

Footsteps echo in the living room, shoes against the hardwood floor. My hand squeezes around the knife I'm holding, the carrot forgotten beneath the blade.

Nate enters the kitchen.

He's in workout shorts and a black T-shirt, his hair ruffled and damp at the temples. There's high color on his cheeks. He must have come from the basement gym.

He stops when he sees me. Glances from me to the array of food and Tupperware in front of me on the kitchen island.

One second passes.

Another.

"Hey," I say. "Worked out?"

He nods and runs a hand through his hair. Gone is the easy, charming smile on his face, the one he had used to liberally last night. *The fake one,* I've started to call it.

"Yes." His voice is smooth, but it holds a careful note. "Haven't seen you around much today."

"I went to the British Museum, actually. Another check mark on my list, and then I took a walk in the park."

"Right. Enjoyed it?"

"Yeah, the museum was great. Really big. I'll have to go back," I say. The tension feels thick, like I could cut it with the knife I'm holding if I try hard enough. My pulse is racing. "The party last night was fun."

Nate takes a single step closer, but his face is unreadable. "Yes. It was."

"The caterers, they made those amazing cheese stuffed dates wrapped in prosciutto? They were so good, I've already googled recipes so I could try making them myself. Didn't you think they were awesome?"

"I don't think I tried them."

"Oh. That's a shame." I swallow hard and reach for the bag of bell peppers. My hands need something to do. "I think I had a bit too much to drink."

Nate's eyes are heavy on me. "Did you?"

"Yes, and so did plenty of others. I can't believe they dropped an entire bottle of Dom on the kitchen floor."

Something flickers in Nate's eyes. The Dom was the crash that had broken us apart while we were in that hallway just behind him. This morning, one of the cleaners told me what it had been.

I can't read him.

Beneath my thin white button-down, I feel too hot under his gaze. "I think we were saved by the bell," I say with a little laugh.

He raises an eyebrow and finally, *finally,* looks away. Reaches for one of the red apples I've bought and turns it over in his hands. "Yes, that's one way of looking at things," he says.

Maybe he feels guilty, too. As soon as the thought strikes me, I feel mortified that I hadn't thought of it sooner. *Of course.* Dean is his best friend, and Nate kissed me in a moment of drunken frustration. Even if he had wanted to… he must be feeling…

I quickly shake my head. "I'm very sorry. It was never my intention… I didn't think about the position I've put you in."

Nate's eyes snap back to mine. "The position I'm in," he repeats. "With regards to… Dean?"

"Yes." I lift my hand and mimic locking my lips. "I won't tell anyone about it, I promise. We can add that to the unspoken-about box, if you want?"

He nods, but his jaw clenches. "How much weight do you think that box can hold?"

"A lot, I hope." I press both of my hands flat to the stone countertop, the marble is cool beneath my sweaty palms. "We've become friends, haven't we? You and I? I don't want to risk that in any way."

Nate's lips curl into that crooked smile, the true smile, and something tight relaxes in my chest. "You haven't risked it."

I sigh in relief. "Thank God. So, can we… just forget about last night? Go back to the way things were?"

There's something tight in his eyes. But he nods. "Absolutely. Consider it forgotten."

I pretend to wipe my forehead. "I've been nervous all day about what you'd say."

"You never have to be nervous with me," he assures. But then he grins. "Unless it's about that list of yours. Because you know I have plans to make all of your wishes come true."

"All of them?"

"Well, minus the one, of course. I never did find out what kind of threesome you want." He takes a bite of the apple and leans against the doorjamb. "I need to take one of my cars for a spin next weekend."

I chuckle. "*Need to*?"

"Yes. They need to be regularly driven long distances to maintain the health of the engine. I was thinking about what you said the other day. About wanting to visit places where things were filmed or the story locations in books. Come with me, and we'll make it a day trip."

Relief and happiness rush through me so fast, that I'm almost left lightheaded. *Whew.* I hadn't ruined anything. *We* hadn't ruined this hard-won, uncomplicated, comfortable friendship. And we won't. As long as the hallway incident stays buried far, far inside that box, where it belongs.

No matter how amazing kissing Nate had felt.

Chapter 19

Nate

The British countryside and its roads are familiar to me now. There's a certain rhythm to the drive—to deal with occasional high-speed cars that pass while navigating through the narrow lanes with tall hedges on either side.

Once we leave the highway for a country road, we start counting tractors. But soon after, Harper insists on tallying muddy Land Rovers instead, and when we pass the fifth one in a row, she laughs.

"See?" she asks. "You should have chosen your Land Rover, not this sports car."

"This Aston Martin," I say and pat the wheel, "can handle these roads. And it was her turn."

"Her?"

"Yes. The engine needs a good run or she'll get rusty." I make a turn, and a long stretch of straight road lies before us. With wide-open skies overhead and only green fields all around.

I hit the gas.

Harper's gasp turns into a chuckle, and I relish the sound.

The burst of speed doesn't last too long. The next curve comes up soon enough, and I slow back down, taking it in stride. We're already an hour and a half outside of London.

"How much further?" I ask.

She looks down at her phone, our trusted GPS. "Um… not much. Seems like we'll be on these country roads until we arrive."

"Good," I say. Tearing myself away from the sight of her legs. She's in a white dress that ends just above her knees, and I keep getting distracted by the expanse of milky skin and the pale-pink toenails peeking out of her sandals.

"Why cars?" she asks. She's leaning back in the passenger seat, her legs stretched out. More than once I've had the impulse to reach out and put my hand on her bare knee.

As if that's my right, as if the move would be welcomed.

Each time, I've snuffed it out with the memory of her words on Sunday.

Can we just forget about last night?

I promised I would. That had been another lie. I'm racking them up, and each new one makes me feel like shit.

She mentioned Dean, and I'd known I was an asshole for not feeling more guilty, for being so focused on the taste of her lips and on the words she might say to not consider him at that moment.

This past week, I've thought it over.

Really thought it over.

Would I be okay with losing Dean's friendship if it came to that?

"Nate," Harper urges. There's a smile in her voice. "Are you okay?"

"Yeah. Sorry. Just thinking."

"You've been distracted the last few nights," she says. "You didn't even pay attention to the movie on Thursday night."

I grunt, not disagreeing with her. My lack of focus, though, had little to do with deep thoughts, and more with her sitting next to me on the giant couch in nothing but a pair of short shorts and a tight T-shirt.

"You're sure? I… well, I overheard you arguing yesterday," she says. "Please don't be mad, I was in my room, and you must have been walking up to the third floor."

I snort. "Well, I guess we now know just how soundproof the rooms are."

There's a brief pause, and then she snickers. "Yes. Not very."

"That's… good to know."

"Yes. But… *are* you okay?"

"Of course I am." I glance over at her, only to find her eyes earnest, yet warm and thoughtful, on mine. If I didn't have the road to focus on, they would have captured me entirely.

"You can tell me, you know. Even if it's not funny or exciting or charming." She reaches for her bottle of water in the cup holder between us. "You don't have to perform for me."

I don't know what to say to that.

It takes me a minute or two to find my bearings. I listen to her drink, swallowing softly, and try to wrap my head around her words.

"Why did you say that?"

"Mmm, it's just an observation I've made," she says, putting her water bottle back and stretches out again with a sigh. "You're good at charming people, at giving them the version of yourself they want to see. I bet that's good skill in negotiations and to persuade people at work, right?"

My fingers tighten around the steering wheel. "Yes. It can be."

"All I meant was, you don't need to do that with me." She shrugs, and I catch the movement out of the corner of my eye. "I like spending time with you even if we talk about heavy stuff. Or if we're silent."

I could brush this off with a joke. That's my immediate impulse, but I swallow it down. Nod instead. "Noted," I say. "You're… I don't think I've ever known anyone quite like you, Harp."

"I'm sure you haven't," she says easily.

The words are spoken with so much confidence that it makes me laugh. She starts laughing, too. "I didn't mean it like that!" she quickly protests.

"Sure you didn't."

"No, no really. More like you probably spend most of your time with people in your social circle, if that makes sense."

"Not particularly." I glance over at her again, and then back to the road. "I was arguing with my brother."

"Ah, the one you were competitive with."

"Yeah. We're not seeing eye to eye about my dad. Or rather, what to do about him."

She makes a small *ooh* sound. "I'm sorry about that."

"It's fine. It's par for the course these days." I shake my head, my voice turning bitter. "My brother's relationship with our dad was better than anyone else's, but it's been strained in the last few months. And Dad let things between him and my sister sour entirely. She married someone Dad doesn't approve of, and he is stubborn enough to think he deserves an apology for that. So that leaves just me."

"Is he very involved?" Harper asks carefully.

That makes me chuckle. "No, not in the way you mean. But he does love imparting his wisdom and advice."

"Overbearing?"

"Somehow overbearing *and* distant," I say. "A magical combination mastered by David Connovan alone."

"He demands a lot of you and your siblings?"

"He demands everything," I say evenly. "Only now we're not so quick to yield to his commands. We are his children, after all, and he's never listened to anyone in his life."

She makes a thoughtful sound. "I suppose that's why he's been so successful in business, maybe? But it does sound like a tough way to live. And a very harsh way to raise children."

I nod. Pass a tractor, zipping past it as fast as I can go on the gravel road. This was the last topic I thought we'd be discussing today. But with my eyes on the dusty road, words come easier than I could have predicted. "Now he's giving me the berating he usually saved for Alec. Funny, I once envied my brother for getting all of Dad's attention. Now I pity him, if it was always this intense."

"Maybe," Harper says, "he's being pushy because you're the only one of his children who is still speaking to him? Your dad may be clinging to you and hoping you'll solve his problems with your siblings."

I glance at her again. "Yes. That might be it. I hadn't thought of it quite like that before."

"I'm a genius sometimes."

"And modest, too."

"Mm-hmm. What's the use in staying modest? Someone told me to 'fake it till you make it' or something like that."

"Such a cliche statement. I hope you told him off."

She laughs. "Tried to, but he dodged the bullet. He has a way of doing just that."

After a curve, another stretch of open road unfurls ahead. It bisects the pastures and meadows dotted with spring flowers and gleaming that vibrant green color they only get mid-May. In the distance, a speck of gray is getting larger. We're drawing close to the estate Harper wanted to visit.

"I think it'll catch up with him eventually," I say and hit the gas. "But not today."

Harper lowers her window, and air comes rushing inside the car. It plays with her curls, tossing them around her face. I lean my head against the headrest and smile at the speed, the sun, and the sound of Harper's laugh.

All of this will catch up with me eventually, too. Bills always come due. When she leaves; when Dean finds out about our friendship; when her traineeship ends.

But not today.

I pull into the gravel parking lot a few minutes later. The house is large and imposing, rising at the end of a long walkway. Georgian architecture, with pillars lining the front of the estate. The surrounding grounds are pristine and manicured, complete with a pond glittering in the distance.

We walk up the front gate, and Harper chuckles. I look down at her. "What is it?"

She shakes her head with a smile. "Did you notice how *everyone* looked at your car?"

I glance back. "No. They did?"

"Yes, of course they did. God, I don't know if you're obnoxious or charming, being so oblivious sometimes."

"Charming," I say firmly. "The answer is always charming."

She laughs again.

We make our way into the estate, where we're handed a brochure and sent on our way. Harper's fascination is evident. I follow beside her, listening to her excited chatter about the people who must have lived here, about the things she's learned from her reading, and from the old BBC adaptations she clearly loves. She takes pictures of everything, in every room.

"For my mom," she tells me. "I promised to document as much as I could."

She stops at several works of art that I would have overlooked. When I ask her about them, she shines up in a giant smile and tells me stories behind each.

How one composition is typical for the seventeenth-century artists, but not for those from the eighteenth whose pieces we saw in the other rooms. What areas of the paintings were likely to have been completed by an apprentice and not the master.

She speaks passionately. About it all, and I love watching her as she does. The smiles, the flush, the excitement in her eyes.

It's far more engrossing than the little text printed on the placards.

We finish the tour in the vast garden outside the house. The sun is warm, and somewhere in the distance, birds sing.

I hold out my hand. "Give me your phone, and stand…

here." When she glances at me quizzically, I add, "For your mom."

She smiles wide as I take her picture, and, for a split second, I wonder if I can send it to myself. A keepsake of this day and her happiness.

But then she takes the phone back and our fingers brush against each other's, and the moment is gone.

"They filmed one of the adaptations of *Pride and Prejudice* here," she says dreamily. "Look over there, outside that entrance… I can almost see the scene taking place."

"You'll have to show me that movie sometime."

"Really?" Her eyes light up. "Okay. Yeah, I would love that. We could do a marathon."

I wonder if Dean ever did this sort of thing with her. If they went on little day trips, if they laughed together, if they bonded over her interests. My stomach turns as jealousy squeezes my insides, quickly followed by the guilt, and, finally by a dark sort of satisfaction. Because even if they had… she's here now.

Doing it with me and not with him.

We walk around the gardens with the sun shining down on us from a mostly cloudless sky. Her hand brushes against mine, just once, and it makes my fingers tighten into a fist. Electric current dances along my arm. Since that night, since we kissed, being around her has become an excruciating torment.

The idea of *us* had always been my foolish hope. A dream. But now I know what she tastes like, what she feels like in my arms.

If my *need* for her was strong before…

We reach the pond. It's larger than it looked from the parking lot. A few swans glide around near the center and tall reeds grow along the edges. The water is dark and ripples softly from the movement of several rowboats tied up at the small dock, and the lone boat bobbing gently offshore as a gangly teenage boy navigates it amid the lilypads.

I look at the row of boats waiting patiently for new occupants.

"What do you think?" I ask Harper.

She's already walking to the dock. "I'm in if you are!"

Ten minutes later, sitting at the back of the rowboat, I'm maneuvering us to the middle of the pond. I lift the oars out of the water, and watch look around with that same dreamy, contemplative look she gets sometimes.

Like she's truly and completely present in the moment. Enjoying it to the fullest, and not thinking about work, or what to have for dinner, or reaching for her phone.

She just is, and I love watching her just be.

"I think," she says, "I'll add this to my thirty list."

"Add it retroactively?"

"Yes. It's my list, so my rules."

I chuckle. "I approve entirely." The sun is hot, and I reach for the sleeves of my white button-down, rolling them up, and feel sweat beading on my forehead.

"You look *just* as you should," she says.

I frown at her. "What does that mean?"

A flush creeps up her cheeks. "Well, in books and movies, the men wear these billowing white shirts. Although yours does have a bit less lace."

I chuckle. "A bit. Yeah."

"And you're not wearing Hessians."

"Hessian what?"

"Hessian boots. But the rest is pretty accurate." She looks around at the estate and tourists walking the grounds. "It's like we're in the middle of a historical romance or one of Jane Austen's stories."

"Mm-hmm. Except we drove a car to get here, paid entry, and we're not dressed appropriately…"

Harper scoops a handful of water and sends a few drops in my direction. "Don't ruin the moment."

I chuckle. "Fine. I'll be perfectly silent, then, like a gentleman of old."

"I'm not sure they were very silent. I'm probably supposed to be the silent one if we're playing by those rules."

I look at her, at the blush on her cheeks, and her warm eyes. Take the moment to appreciate the voice that I will never tire of hearing. "Then we're not."

She smiles at me. "Okay. Then we're not."

We're just floating out on the pond. Happiness fills my chest to the brim. Something I've missed for longer than I realized, when I was existing but hardly thriving.

The smile still hangs on Harper's face. She looks down at the sparkling surface and drags her fingers through the waning waves. "I don't think I could have handled living in a historical novel," she says. "As much as they're my comfort reads, I would miss running wa—"

Harper

My hand touches something smooth cutting through the water. A *snake,* swimming gracefully and almost imperceptibly along the surface. I shriek and scramble away from the edge of the boat, making it rock violently in the process.

"Harper!" Nate says.

I scramble to find purchase, which sends us into another rough sway from side to side.

Nate throws himself toward me, but it's too late. I'm already tipping too far back. His lunge for me obliterated the balance, making the rowboat seesaw worse than a drunken pirate on leave, and we both tumble overboard.

The water is cool and murky. Something slimy tangles around my legs, and my feet sink into the muddy bottom of the pond. I'm shoulder-deep in this muck and immediately kick off. It's instinct, to get away from the sliminess. More snakes?

Probably just *plants.* But still. There's a snake around here somewhere.

Someone shouts from the dock. Water splashes, and I realize it's me.

"Swim, Harper," Nate demands beside me. Right. We're in the pond. I make a few awkward strokes, aiming for the dock. I've never swam in clothes before, and it feels wrong, the fabric against my skin dragging in the water.

I'm the first to reach the dock. The wood is shockingly dry and warm under my wet hands when I grab a hold of the edge. There's no ladder. *Get away from the snake!* That's my only concern at the moment.

People aren't meant to go swimming in this little pond.

Something strong grips my waist, and then Nate's voice is by my ear. "I'll lift you. Ready?"

"Yes," I whimper back.

He hoists me halfway out of the water, and I scramble onto the dock. Dripping wet and shivering.

Someone chuckles behind me.

Nate.

I look at where he's standing in the water as it laps around his waist. His hair is plastered to his head, his white shirt clinging to his broad shoulders, but a smile is lighting up his face. "You all right?"

"Yes," I say. Something about that smile sets things at ease inside me, and I giggle. I'm high on adrenaline. "I can't believe that just happened."

"Me neither. Fuck." His gaze locks on someone behind me, and he raises a hand. "Don't worry! I'll get the boat."

He's off, setting across the pond in a crawl toward our rowboat. It's upside-down and bobbing serenely in the center of the pond. Like it hasn't just been the scene of a crime.

I stand up and watch him grab the small rope, and drag it back to shore. Trudging through waist-deep water. He uses his free hand to push his wet hair back and looks at me with a wry smile.

I laugh. It bubbles out of me, and soon enough, I'm laughing so hard that I have to put a hand over my mouth. I'm in shock and complete disbelief at the sheer absurdity of the situation.

"I'm glad you're enjoying this," Nate says. The teenager manning the dock steps past me and reaches out for the rope. Nate throws it to her, and she quickly ties the rowboat up, now right side up again.

But my giggle dies when Nate braces his hands on the edge of the dock. With strong arms, he lifts himself out of the water and comes to stand in front of me.

He's dripping wet. His white shirt clings to the contours of his body, and a few tendrils of hair have stuck to his forehead. His lightly tan skin stands out strongly against the fabric.

He looks like the lord of the manor after a summer swim.

His eyes sweep down my body, and the smile disappears off his face. His gaze quickly fixes somewhere over my left shoulder.

I look down. *Shit.* My white dress is pasted to my body, and my nipples are clearly visible. Hard even through the bra and dress.

I wrap my arms around my chest. "Whoops."

He glances at me for a second again before reaching for the buttons of his shirt. He undoes them with quick movements, one after another.

"What are you doing?"

"Here," he says gruffly and hands me his soaked shirt.

I take it. "What am I supposed to do with this?"

"It's something, at least, if you want to cover yourself." His voice is light, but his jaw is visibly tense. I wrap the wet garment around my body, and despite the cold and drenched state of me, heat races up my cheeks.

He's now shirtless.

Broad chest—lightly smattered with brown hair—and a taut stomach. Not lined with showy abs that speak of vanity, but hard and flat muscle achieved through regular exercise and an active life. His shoulders look strong. His arms, too. And his biceps. Standing just a few feet away from me beneath the warm sun, with shimmering water in the background.

I have to look away.

And now we're both not looking at each other.

"My phone," I say. "Shit, I just realized."

He huffs a laugh and pushes his hair back. "Yeah, mine, too. We need to find a bowl of rice or something."

"Do you see any around?"

"No," he says. But there's dry humor in his voice. "What happened?"

"I'm so sorry, I saw a snake. Touched it, even! In the water. I freaked out and..."

"And that happened," he says, his smile still in place. "Well, it made for a more interesting afternoon, for sure."

"That's one way to look at it."

"That's the only way to look at it," he says firmly. "Now come, we should probably try to get some dry clothes."

"Maybe they'll have some period costumes in the gift shop," I say.

He half chuckles and puts a hand on my shoulder. "I think the best we can hope for is an apron or tea towels," he says. "But let's go and see if we can patchwork them together into something we can wear."

Chapter 20

Nate

The gift shop doesn't have period clothing. In fact, they have no clothing at all, not even an apron. They do have tea towels, but we forgo them for the giant bath towels instead that match the rustic blue-and-white pattern of the wallpapers we saw in the great sitting room. Probably meant to be treasured… and not soiled by pond scum.

The staff and other tourists throw us curious looks. I give everyone a wide smile and move closer to Harper. Even with my shirt around her shoulders, the dress sticks to *everything.* I try very hard not to look and yet, of course, I notice everything, her curves, the indentation of her ass, her underwear transparent through the see-through wet dress.

I pay for the towels and drop a fifty-pound note into the donation jar next to the cash register. The sales clerk is staring wide-eyed at my shirtless and drenched form.

"Had an accident on the pond," I say loud enough for everyone in the store to hear. Shove another fifty into the jar. "The water quality is excellent, by the way. Good job on that."

The cashier dips her head in a tiny nod. "Uh-huh."

Harper's hand curls around mine, and she tugs me out of the store. "Come on," she says with a chuckle. "We were *dripping* on the centuries-old stone floor."

"It's probably seen worse," I say. "Actually, it's *definitely* seen worse."

"Yes, but those people in there haven't."

"I doubt we'll be allowed back here," I say.

She wraps one of the towels around herself. It covers her soaked dress entirely. Her hair is wet, too, the curls just starting to dry around her face. There's a light smudge of black under one of the eyes from her makeup, and I want to reach out and wipe it away.

"What a shame," she says happily. "The weird Americans who came in a sports car, fell into the pond, and destroyed the gift shop."

"We donated to the continuation of this beautiful estate," I correct her. "Tested the pond's pH levels, and left a memorable impression on these beautiful folks."

Harper rolls her eyes. "Come on. Let's drip all over your Italian leather seats."

"Well, I don't like *that* idea."

She laughs. "Do you have a better option?"

"No," I say and nudge her shoulder with mine. It's safer to look at her now, when the shape of her body isn't so brilliantly on display and making my brain short-circuit. "Let's go find some rice."

At the local supermarket, people stare at us, too. A little girl comments about us walking around in towels and is quickly hushed by her parents. We find rice, and then Harper stumbles on a small clothing section. I pick up a pair of striped pajama pants, sold in a cardboard box. "Did you know stores sell both food and clothes?"

Harper chuckles from where she's digging through a bin of T-shirts. "Yes, I did. Big stores like this usually do."

"Huh."

"I'm not surprised you don't know that," she says. Her voice is teasing again, and she tugs on the towel to keep it in place. "How often do you grocery shop?"

"Never."

"Mm-hmm, not surprised." She fishes out a small package with a grin. "Awesome. This fleece sweater is even on sale."

"Planning on wearing it to the gallery?"

"Yes, I think it'll look great paired with heels." She looks over at the pajama pants in my hands. "Is that what you're getting?"

"There are no normal pants."

"There aren't?"

"No." I grab a pack of dry underwear and a gray T-shirt. "Come on, let's get out of here. You must be cold by now."

She shrugs a little and doesn't look too bothered. There's a bright glow in her eyes. "Looking forward to seeing you drive a sports car in tartan-print pajama pants."

Fifteen minutes later, we've both changed in the small restroom by the entrance. Our cell phones are shut off and buried deep inside the bag of rice in hopes of pulling out the moisture. Damned fucking inconvenient, considering our phones were also our maps. This little diversion certainly made the time pass, and although it's still bright outside, my watch reads almost seven, and May daylight won't last forever. It's a two-and-a-half-hour drive back to London.

Harper chews on a granola bar she bought at the store. She looks… Well, it's hard to look away. She's sitting on one of the metal chairs by the entrance, her hair damp and wild around her face, drowning in a too-large sweatshirt and munching on a chocolaty snack.

She looks adorable.

"Sure you don't want one?" She reaches into the package for another bar.

"I'm sure," I say. "We can stop somewhere on the way home and eat. It's a long drive."

"Does your car have GPS?"

"It's a vintage Aston Martin," I say dryly.

She raises an eyebrow. "I have no clue if that means a yes or no."

"It means no. But the roadsigns should be pretty self-explanatory. All roads lead to Rome, and all that."

She stands, and we head out to the parking lot. It's sheer impulse that has me wrapping my arm around her shoulders. "Not how you expected the day trip to go, huh?"

Harper shrugs. The movement sends shivers up my arm. "No. But… this was infinitely more memorable."

"Too bad we didn't get a picture of the moment the boat tipped. Would your mom have liked that?"

She laughs. "Probably! I would have, that's for sure. Honestly, a water snake? In an idyllic pond? That's just rude."

"We probably bothered *it.*"

"You might be right about that. But I still feel like it was unnecessary to come so close to the boat." She shivers again. "I can't believe I touched it."

"Lucky it didn't bite," I say.

She pushes me away with a laugh. "Don't even bring that up, or I won't be able to sleep."

We get in the car and hit the road, and Harper plays around with the radio dial. There's a bag of chips on her lap, and she hands me a few every now and then. It's surprisingly…

Domestic.

Somehow we fall into that often, her and I. *Friends*. That's what she wants. But there's something about the calm, comfortable domesticity of us two that shimmers with so much more than that.

With something I haven't had in a very long time.

Harper settles on a station that plays old rock music. The road takes a sharp turn, and I follow along, zipping past low hedges. The sun has started to set. It's painting the sky an amazing shade of orange, and it'll be at least another forty minutes before true darkness sets in.

I hope we make it to the highway by then.

But my hopes are quickly deflated.

"I don't think this is the right road," Harper says carefully.

We're driving through a small village, cute enough, but without any signs pointing us back to the main highway or London.

I slow the car to a crawl and look out for any passersby. There are none.

The hamlet is picturesque, like so much of the English countryside. Crumbling brick hedges, ivy, oak trees. White limewashed houses with black wooden framings. A tiny church at the center of the village, so small that it couldn't have accommodated a person over the exact population of this place. Maybe it never needed to.

"We might be lost," I admit.

Harper chuckles. "Dean would never have said that, even if we were."

The casual comparison to Dean throws me off. I glance at Harper, but she looks perfectly calm, leaning forward to try to read any roadsigns.

"My ego isn't that fragile," I say cautiously.

She chuckles. "No, it's not fragile at all. We could *try* to turn on a phone to check Google Maps?"

"We could. But I'm not sure it's worth the risk, not yet. This village looks empty."

"It's probably dinner time. Everybody inside."

"Or there's nothing to do. It's abandoned."

"It's not. Look, there are flower pots over there."

That makes me chuckle. "Right. Well, we should probably go back to the main road, where we started."

I turn around near the small town square and backtrack to the country road. The gravel makes the tires spin, just slightly, before they find their grip.

As I accelerate around a curve, there's a sharp, violent jolt through the car. I hit the brakes immediately. Harper gives a small shriek, her hands reaching out to brace against the dashboard.

"What the fuck was that?" I ask. The car is in top condition. I hire someone just to maintain my cars. He comes every other week and checks over everything. Tops up the fluids and gas, washes and polishes exteriors, details the insides. The engine of each vehicle always runs smoothly—my maintenance guy is meticulous about oil changes—and I know for a fact my tires are in good shape.

"That didn't sound good," Harper breathes.

"That was a tire," I say with a sinking suspicion. Fucking pothole.

I just know it. But we're stopped in the middle of the road, so I carefully give it a bit of gas and pull the car to a grassy patch on the side. Right next to the houses we were keen to leave behind.

The car protests.

My soul hurts.

And it's all confirmed as soon as I get out of my seat. The front right tire, once in mint condition, is deflated. The black rubber is torn, and along the jagged seam, the fibers are flayed.

"Harper," I call out. My voice is calm, despite the frustration burning in my gut. My poor baby. I should have chosen the Land Rover after all. "Did you see an inn in this little village? Because we're going to have to spend the night."

There is an inn.

Harper saw it on our drive through, and after locking the car and grabbing our stuff, we trudge toward it. It's located right next to the tiny church.

The Crown Bed and Breakfast.

It's an old stone structure with a single car parked outside. So *someone* should be inside. And indeed… someone is. She doesn't look up when we come in through the door, despite the little bell that gladly announces our arrival.

"Percy, is that you?" the woman asks and flips another page of the newspaper. Short gray hair curls around her head, and a pair of red frame glasses rest on her nose. Her rolling accent is stronger than I've heard down in London. "I think the Harcourts are dropping by tomorrow with the new bed. Did you clear out the yellow room?"

"Sorry, ma'am," Harper says, "but we're not Percy."

The woman looks up from her spot behind the wooden counter. The decor is all English countryside, with floral wallpaper and carpeted floors.

Her eyes widen. "Oh my! I can see that you're not. My apologies. Have you come for a room?" There's an almost hopeful note in her voice.

"Yes," I say. "We had an accident just around the corner, blew out a tire on the car. We won't be able to get it replaced until tomorrow."

"Oh, dear," the old lady says with a shake of her head. "That's a shame. Well, we've got room for you. And hot food if you'd like, though you'd have to pop down to Ethan's two streets over to pick something up. Unless he's closed the kitchen early tonight. He does that sometimes if there's a good program on telly."

I blink at her. What a way to run a business. "We might attempt that later. Could we check in? I think we're both in need of a shower. If you have a phone, too, I'd love to borrow it and make the calls for the car."

"Of course! Come, come, let's get you sorted."

I lay my credit card flat on the counter. Harper looks around with those bottomless eyes, taking in the reception space, peering through the doorway to a room beside it. It's traditionally decorated… but there's an industrial table saw in the middle instead of the dining room table.

Renos?

The lady grabs a key from behind the counter. "We have the largest room available for you."

I clear my throat. "We need two rooms, please."

She pauses, and a frown mars her face. "Oh. I'm so sorry, dearies, but we only have one available."

"Is the place fully booked?" Harper asks. It's a wonder she can keep the disbelief out of her voice.

This place is deserted.

"No, no," the innkeeper says with a little laugh. "We're renovating. We have five rooms, you see, but there was some water leakage a few years back, and then, well...." She waves a hand in a dismissive gesture. "Permits, building companies, you know. Things take time. Right now, there's just one that's fully ready. I'm Edith, and my husband is Percy. We run this place." She blinks at us from behind her red frame, smile back in place. "Would you like to see the room, at least? It's quite lovely and spacious."

My brain is short-circuiting again.

It happens so quickly and so frequently around Harper that I haven't gotten a proper handle on it, yet. I should have, after all these years, but now it's disintegrating.

Spending the night together.

She won't want that. I look down at her, needing to see her eyes. But she's looking right at the lady. "Thank you," Harper says warmly. "We'd love to see it, and if there's only one room available, that's what we'll take."

Something reaches inside my chest and grips tightly. It makes it hard to breathe.

Harper follows the woman, and I trail after them both through the claustrophobically narrow hallway. Paintings hang on the walls—canvas after canvas of men and women on horseback and English landscapes.

The room *isn't* large.

There's a four-poster bed in the center with a paisley pattern on the cover, a window overlooking surrounding fields and the setting sun, and a door to what must be a bathroom.

And a single chair in the corner.

"This is it," the lady says warmly. "Please make yourself at home. I'll be in the lobby for at least another two hours, come down whenever you like to borrow the phone. We don't have a mechanic around here, or I'd be ringing a repair shop right this minute."

"Thank you," I say woodenly. My eyes can't seem to look away from the bed.

"Really, thank you so much," Harper says sweetly. "For the help. We'll be down in a bit."

The innkeeper steps out and closes the door in her wake. It shuts with a soft, near-silent click, but I hear it like it was a gunshot.

"Well," Harper says. She takes a few steps forward and sets down the small bag from the grocery store. "I guess this is home for tonight."

Chapter 21

Harper

I shower first. Standing in the bathtub, using a handheld showerhead to wash away the remnants of pond grime. Despite the poor water pressure and the awkward position, it's the best thing I've experienced all day. Right next to seeing Nate shirtless on the dock with water running over his tanned skin.

Which is incredibly confusing.

I use half of the complimentary sample-size shampoo bottle and nearly all of the miniature soap before remembering that Nate needs to hop in the shower later. I rinse my hair and scrub my skin until there are no traces of the pond left.

It's not *quite* as satisfying to put on the grocery store clothes again, but I do it. A pair of clean underwear and the camisole I'd bought. And then, I wrap the bathrobe I found hanging in the room around myself. The pants and the sweatshirt I was wearing earlier smell faintly like the pond, and I leave them folded beside the sink.

When I crack open the bathroom door to the room, I notice Nate sitting on the corner chair. There's a plate of food beside him.

"You went to the restaurant?" I ask.

His eyes are unreadable, and his smile is nowhere to be

seen. "I tried, but they were closed. Edith made us some toast and tea."

"Oh, that was nice of her."

He stands and runs a hand through his hair. The frown is immediate, like he realized just how dirty he is. "Yeah. Have at it. I'll grab a shower."

The bathroom door closes behind him, and I'm left in the comfortable silence of the cozy hotel room. This place is beautifully decorated, with a fireplace across from the four-poster bed. The pretty bedspread and matching ornamental pillows draw my eye, and I grab the plate with toast and sink cross-legged onto the softness of the mattress.

Nerves have been somersaulting my stomach since Edith led us to this room. And now, hearing the water in the shower, knowing Nate is washing off… naked… and he's going to come out here after…

To sleep in the same bed as me.

I shouldn't like the idea quite as much as I do. I have no right to, no claim to, no decency to.

On the small side table is a bag of rice. Our phones are still submerged in the grains. I chew on a piece of toast and consider turning mine back on. But if it's still wet, that might fry it completely… and what would I do with the phone anyway?

We're not getting out of here until the morning.

I drink chamomile tea and focus on taking regular breaths. Last weekend's kisses had been easy enough to ignore today. We focused on the estate, on having fun, then on the drive. Now, I feel like they are all I can think about.

The door to the bathroom opens. Nate walks out with only a towel wrapped around his waist. My throat turns dry when I'm presented with that magnificent broad chest. And then he turns around. Faces the dresser. I spot the droplets of water along his spine and across the muscles of his shoulder blades. Rivulets trickle from his damp hair; this wet, his brown stands look almost black.

Nate glances over his shoulder. "Eat all of that. I finished my piece already."

I swallow. Barely. "You're sure?"

"Yes." He rummages through one of the plastic bags. Pulls out another T-shirt from the two-pack he bought and puts it on. Grabs a clean pair of boxer briefs and disappears back into the bathroom.

I chew mechanically. Put the plate away.

Then, he returns, wearing nothing but that T-shirt and a pair of boxer briefs. A navy-colored set, as if they are meant to be.

His legs look muscled.

Of course, they'd be. I've seen his upper body.

I reach for the bedcover and focus on that single action rather than looking at Nate.

"I'll grab the chair," he says.

I look up at where he's lowering the window shades. "What? That looks so uncomfortable."

"It'll be fine."

I shake my head. "That's ridiculous, come on. I can't sleep comfortably knowing you're… not. There's enough room here for us both."

He pauses, hands stilling on the half-lowered blinds. "Are you sure?"

"Yes. It's only for a few hours, anyway."

I slip beneath the covers and chuck my robe across the room. The bed is a bit too soft, but it's warm, and the pillow is wonderfully fluffy behind my head. It's been almost a full minute of me situating myself, and the silence in the room grows more apparent.

"All right, then," he finally says.

I look up at the ceiling as Nate climbs in bed. With no TV, no phone, no book, I don't know what to do. Other than lie here and feel the undulations of the mattress as he settles into place.

We both lie there without saying anything as the moment stretches.

"I like this place," I manage after a while.

He runs a hand over his face. "Only you could say that and sound sincere."

"You don't? It's so cute, and historical, and the lady was so nice to us. Look at the crown molding."

"This place is ready to fall apart."

"No it's not," I say. "Isn't the decor in here nice?"

"It looks about seventy years behind the times."

"But that's the point." I turn on my side, facing him. "It's meant to evoke memories of a different era."

"No one who stays here can *remember* the eighteen-fifties."

I roll my eyes. "You know what I mean."

"I like when you do that," he says. "And yes. I know what you mean."

His eyes are unreadable again, in this dimly lit room, but there's a slight tilt to his lips.

"Like what when I do it?"

"Roll your eyes at me."

I blink. "I do that?"

"Yes, quite frequently, actually, when you're exasperated." His smile widens at my expression. "Don't stop doing it."

"Wow. I didn't realize I was."

"Makes it even better," he says. He turns onto his side, too, and now we're facing each other over the expanse of the pillow between us.

I wet my lips. Let the silence stretch and envelop us. "I'm sorry about your car. I know she means a lot to you."

His eyes narrow. "Yeah. It was my mistake. But we'll get her fixed up."

"Does everyone in your family like cars?"

"Not really." His voice is questioning. "Where did that come from?"

"Nowhere. I'm just trying to figure you out," I say.

"Maybe you like cars because it's something you do only for yourself. Something only you like?"

"Maybe," he says easily, "or maybe it's because they go really, really fast."

I laugh. It cuts through some of the tension that's keeping my body taut, lying here so close to him. If I move just a foot or two, I could touch him.

"Yeah, you're right. I'm sorry."

"Don't be," he says. "I like it when you try to understand me."

The words are quiet in the near-darkness. They fill my chest with warmth, and that feeling once again settles deep inside. That bone-deep knowledge—he hasn't had much of that in his life.

"Perhaps there's a small part of what you said that's also true," he says. "Dad likes cars well enough, but never *fully*. Not wholeheartedly. I like to actually drive them. My father, my brother, and now my sister, too... They all use car services. That makes sense in New York, to a certain degree, of course. But I don't think I could give up my independence."

"Oh," I breathe. That makes so much sense. What he's told me, what I've heard of his family. He wants as much control as he can get.

Nate's smile slants. "Yeah, I just realized how out of touch that sounded."

"That's not what... oh, about your family using personal drivers?"

"Yes."

"I already know you're rich, Connovan," I say teasingly. "The cat is out of the bag."

He chuckles softly. "Damn. Here I thought I've been good at pretending."

"I think you gave it away within the first... two minutes."

"Of meeting me?"

"Mm-hmm."

He's silent, and turns over to lie on his back. I look at the strong profile and the unblinking eyes looking at the ceiling. "You mean the very first time, in that college bar? Four years ago?"

"Yeah," I say.

"What do you remember about that night?" he asks.

I swallow. We're getting close to that box, the one locked and stashed on a shelf somewhere. But here, in the darkness, with him, it feels easier to talk. "I remember you joining us… Dean and I… after a few minutes. You were much more reserved than Dean."

He gives a dry laugh. "Yes. He was in a mood that night."

"You were more polite, too. But the rich thing… Your suits that gave it away," I say.

"Plenty of guys wear suits to New York bars."

"Not like yours and Dean's."

He turns his head to look at me. "You were captivating that night."

"I was?" My eyebrows rise. I'd been twenty-four, feeling alone in the big city, unsure about my next career move, and trying to enjoy a fun night out. Dean made certain it became one. He'd been a whirlwind, a hurricane, arriving into my life and sweeping me away with him.

"Yes," he says. "You were wearing a red sweater, and a black headband. You commented on the music. Said it didn't have the right beat for a bar environment. It was a curious thing to say."

"I can't believe you remember that."

"You know me," he says quietly. "I have a very good memory."

My mind flashes to the morning he'd seen me topless. To me urging him to forget about what he saw, while in the back of my mind, knowing that he has a photographic memory. Heat spreads from my chest and singes my cheeks.

He really does remember everything.

Silence settles over the darkened room. I don't know what time it is, but maybe going to sleep isn't a bad idea.

But I don't feel tired.

I feel too animated, like there's a live wire running straight through me.

Across the bed, I hear Nate's soft and steady breaths, and feel his unnatural stillness.

"Are you tired?" I whisper.

"Not particularly," he murmurs back. "Do you want to go to sleep?"

"I think it would be a good idea." I pull the cover higher up, almost to my chin. My hair is still damp from earlier, and now that the warmth of the shower has bled out, the cold is pressing against my scalp. "It's a bit chilly in here."

"Drafty. Just like it was in the eighteen-fifties."

"Hater," I whisper back.

He chuckles. "I could go look for more blankets."

"No, it's fine. The bed will heat up soon enough."

"Mm-hmm. It should."

"Aren't you cold?"

There's a beat of silence. "No. I'm really not."

"Oh."

Silence again, and then he sighs. Shifts closer until the body heat radiating from him is too delicious to avoid leaning into. "Come here. Get warm."

"You're sure?"

His reply is a hand on my shoulder, turning me on my side, and then the slide of his tall body as it fits neatly behind mine. That same hand then moves down to my hip, stopping there.

"Yes," he says against my neck. "Is this okay?"

He's warm and big next to me, and I wiggle closer until we're touching from calf to shoulder. "God yes. You're so warm."

"Told you."

His heated breath fans against my neck. I reach up and

push my wet hair to the top of the pillow, needing more of his warmth. His hand on my hip feels large and scorching, and with me not wearing pajama pants, just panties, his ring and pinky fingers rest directly on the bare skin of my thigh.

That tiny touch feels volcanic.

For a few long minutes, we lie like that. Touching everywhere, and neither of us any closer to relaxing. I wriggle a bit, trying to sink further onto the pillow and nearer to the body at my back.

"Still not tired?" Nate murmurs. His breath ghosts over the shell of my ear, and the pressure from the hand on my hip tightens. Just slightly.

"Trying to get there."

"What do you usually do at home?"

"Read a book," I say. "Or… sometimes…"

"Use the vibrator you bought," he states.

Heat pulses through me at the words. "I was going to say watch TV on my laptop." My whispered words sound breathless. I swallow hard. "But… yes. Sometimes, I do that."

The hand on my hip glides, just ever so slightly, across my skin. The sound is audible in the space between us. "I see."

"What do you do?" I ask.

"Read sometimes."

"But not usually."

"No," he says, fingers now feathering over my stomach. "Not usually."

"So what's the usual routine?"

His warm chuckle brushes over my neck, and I shiver at the pleasure of it. "Well, I don't need a vibrator, but…"

"Oh."

"Mm-hmm."

I arch deeper into his hold. The hand on my stomach is stroking slow, lazy circles. Setting every cell of my skin on edge, and I want him to touch more of me. I tip my head back, mouth close to his, and start tugging my camisole up.

"Your hands are warm."

"Yeah?" His hand follows the receding hemline of my cami, up my ribs, until fingers brush the underside of my breast. My breath whooshes out as those fingers brush once, twice, until his palm closes entirely over my left breast.

"Very warm," I confirm on an exhale.

"Glad to be of service." His voice is muffled against my head, and his thumb keeps stroking. The peak of my nipple. It hardens between two of his fingers, and liquid fire spreads from the touch, racing down to between my thighs. The darkness and heat envelop me completely, but I hear myself breathing, too loud in the quiet room.

"Nate," I whisper.

His lips brush along my neck, his hand still tweaking my nipple. "Harper," he whispers back.

I grind against him behind me. I want his hand to continue. To touch more of me.

Nate chuckles. "I see. You really do need me to play the vibrator part. Well…" His hand brushes over my breast once more before sliding in tight little circles down my ribcage and stomach to the elastic of my panties. Deft fingers play with the band for a second while my heart thuds a thunderous beat in my chest, and then he dives below the fabric.

His fingers stroke between my legs. All of my attention zeros in on that touch and the goosebumps rising in the wake of fingertips ghosting over my flesh.

"Oh," he mumbles. "I see."

See what? But I'm too focused on the feeling of his hand *there*, and I shift my top leg to give him better access. His fingers stroke along the full length of my folds, and I shiver when he brushes my clit.

"Turn onto your back," he tells me. His voice comes out raspy.

He shifts, and I move with him until I'm on my back with my legs bent and my feet flat against the mattress.

"That's it." His free arm slides under my neck and over, forearm resting on my chest. And through it all, he never stops touching me. Fingers beneath the fabric of my panties, mapping me. Teasing me.

"Is this what you do at home?" he asks. "In the guest bedroom..."

"Sometimes," I breathe. He's found the hard nub of my clit and is rubbing it in firm, tight circles. It sends heat pounding through me, and I arch into his touch.

"You like that."

"Mm-hmm."

He makes a deep, pleased sound and takes his hand away. I open my mouth to protest when I feel it at my hip instead, gripping the fabric. I help him push my panties down. They end up halfway over my thighs.

"There, baby. I need to be able to touch all of you." His voice is hoarse, and deeper somehow, here in the darkness where I can't quite make out his face.

His fingers circle for a long time. So long that I start to go boneless, floating on the waves of pleasure not quite intense enough to get me over the crest. I turn my face into his shoulder. His skin is warm and firm and smells like soap. The same soap I almost used up.

"I need to get inside you. I want to feel you squeezing around me," he murmurs, running his fingers down my sensitive skin. He slides one into me, curving it, and I sigh at the sensation. "Fuck, your pussy feels good."

Another fierce blush spreads across my cheeks. His voice, the voice I've come to know so well, saying those things... speaking them against my temple. He adds another finger to the first. It's the most delicious feeling, the faintest of burns, as he caresses me on the inside.

"I'm not vibrating, am I?" he asks.

It's so surprising that a small laugh bursts out of me. "No. But I like it anyway."

"Like it?" He uses his thumb to press on my clit, and a small yelp escapes me. "I want to do better than that. Tell me what you'd do."

"I'd do… I'd do… what you're doing."

"Yeah?"

It's hard to get the words out. Hard when he's fucking me slowly with his fingers, curving them inside in a way I've never really experienced before, and using his thumb on my clit. "Mm-hmm. I mainly focus… just on my…"

"Tell me, baby."

The word comes out in a hush. "My clit."

"Most effective way to make yourself come." His voice is in my ear, and it feels deliciously decadent to have it there. Guiding me through all of it.

The soles of my feet press down on the mattress. "Yes."

"When you just want to go to sleep."

"Oh… yes."

His curling fingers are working a part inside of me that hasn't been explored before. Never been focused on. It feels different and good, and utterly exotic. Deeper, somehow, than any pleasure I ever felt. The kind that always radiated from my clit.

"You're so soft here," he murmurs. His breath is coming fast, too, and I love the sound of that, and the raspiness in his voice. I close my eyes and focus on the sensations. "Soft like silk, and so warm. *Fuck,* you're warm. I love doing this… rubbing your clit. It's so swollen. I can't vibrate, baby, but I can do this, and I can—"

My orgasm takes us both by surprise. It starts with a small gasp, and then pleasure overtakes me, radiating from his touch, his fingers, from deep within me. Where he had stroked steadily.

I arch my back, and the arm around my chest tightens, holding me securely, and it's all I can do not to moan. I have to bite down on my tongue to keep it from coming out.

Nate strokes me through all of it. His fingers skilled and slick now, moving along my pussy, little shots of electric energy traveling in ripples along my skin. So sensitive.

"That was good. That was so good," he murmurs. Are

those his lips against my ear? I want to turn and look, to turn and meet them, but I can barely move. I feel boneless. "You came so beautifully. You squeezed tight around my fingers, too, when you did."

"Did I?"

"Oh yes." His hand slides along my inner thigh, until he finds my panties, tugging them up with gentle movements until I'm covered once again. "You did so good."

The praise makes me feel hot again. Dean never said things like that. No guy I'd ever been with said things like that.

There's something hard against my hip.

As soon as I become aware of it, it's impossible to notice anything but *that*. In the warm afterglow of my orgasm, he's the only thing I can think of. *It*.

"Nate," I breathe.

His hand is brushing slow circles around my hip bone again, the way he had in the beginning. Returned to its original position. "Yes?"

"You're hard."

He's quiet for a long, heated moment. Then he shifts away and the pressure against my hip is gone. "Yeah. That tends to happen."

"Let me help you, too."

"That's not necessary."

I turn to my side, back in his orbit. His body is warm where it touches mine. "Don't you want to come, as well?"

He gives a sharp exhale. "Harper."

"What?" I lift onto my elbow. "That can't be… comfortable. Does it ache to have a hard-on? I've always wondered."

"Harper," he repeats again, but this time he chuckles hoarsely. Drapes an arm over his face. "Only you would ask me that right now."

"I'm curious."

"Yes, it can ache. Right now it really fucking does." For a

second, I don't think he's breathing. I'm not sure I am, either. But then he speaks again. "If you truly want to..."

My hand is already resting on his shoulder. I slide it down over his chest, over the sliver of taut skin on his abdomen where his T-shirt has ridden up. To the elastic of his boxer briefs.

He helps fold the band down and out of the way, and then my fingers stroke his length. Resting thick and hot against his stomach.

A jolt shoots through me.

Curiosity, and the same warm, heavy feeling from earlier overwhelm me. I close my hand around him.

He hisses and pushes his head back on the pillow.

"You okay?" I breathe. My fingers are fisted around his cock, and I feel his pulse beneath the velvety skin.

"Yes," he bites out. "I'm fine."

"Sure?"

"Yes, Harp. *Please.* I need you to—" His words break off when I start to stroke. His breathing immediately hurries. The sound is harsh, and I revel in it. Revel in the strong length in my hand, in the silky softness of his head.

I can't see him. Hidden beneath the cover, in the room that's cast in darkness. But I feel him all the same.

And it's exhilarating.

I stroke him firmly and listen to his sharp breaths. "You have to tell me, too," I whisper. "What you like. What you normally do."

"This... you're doing great, Harp. You're perfect."

"Should I grip you harder?"

"You can," he grinds out, "but it might kill me."

I push up on an elbow. "What?"

He chuckles hoarsely. "Nothing. I'm going to come quickly tonight, baby."

The endearment rolls off his tongue as easily as it did when it was his hand between my thighs. It sends warmth through me just as it did then.

His cock is thick, and it feels long as I stroke up the shaft. Incredibly smooth over the head. I trail my fingers down, following the vein, before finding his balls.

The man at my side goes rigid.

Gently, I play with them and settle back against the pillow. His skin is soft and warm, and the breaths that were heavy earlier are coming out labored now.

"This okay?"

"Yes," he grinds out. "You're having fun with this."

I smile into the darkness. "I definitely am."

He swallows. The sound is audible. I tease him for a while longer before returning to his shaft, quivering against his stomach. It's such a delicious weight. Seductive. I didn't realize I would miss sex, or miss touching a man like this, but I have.

I stroke him harder this time. Firmer. Nate's breathing ratchets further, and I listen to it, to him, to the sound of my hand around him beneath the paisley-print bedcover. He sounds like he's dying; and he sounds like he never wants me to stop.

"Talk to me," I whisper.

He gives a low groan. "Harper, I don't even remember my own fucking name right now."

"Oh."

"I need to... *shit*. I'm so close. Don't stop, baby. Keep going... yes... Fuck." He grabs his T-shirt and pulls it up to his neck, the movement disrupting the cover, and it's just in time. He comes in pulses I can *feel;* his cock twitching, spurting up his stomach.

I continue to stroke him and listen to his pained groans until he goes listless beside me. His cock is still heavy in my hand, still shuddering slightly. I keep up my gentle caress, and Nate gives a hoarse laugh. Reaches down to pull my hand away, but softens the blow of rejection by twining his fingers with mine.

"Sensitive?" I ask.

"Like you wouldn't believe." He runs his free hand through his hair and sighs. "It's a miracle I remembered the fucking T-shirt in the last second. We're done with accidents for today. Stay here."

He disappears into the bathroom, and I hear water running. Seconds later, he returns, and the mattress undulates yet again as he slips into place.

Nate doesn't hesitate. Turns toward me immediately and settles behind me just as he had earlier, with his hand on my hip.

He's not wearing a T-shirt at all this time. His torso is hot against my cooled back.

"Warm now?" he murmurs against my ear.

I close my eyes. Relax into the warm curve of his body, touching me from calf to elbow, and don't think at all. "Yes," I say.

It doesn't take me long to fall asleep.

Chapter 22

Harper

I wake up to a soft beam of sunlight on my skin. It takes me a few minutes to fully realize where I am, and why the cotton beneath my chin is slightly scratchier than the one at home. Why the bed is softer… and why I'm so warm.

I'm being held tightly by the large shape behind me.

His leg is between mine, and his arm is draped over my waist. Steady breaths fan my temple, and I close my eyes for a few seconds. It feels good to be held. Warm. Safe. I don't know when it happened last… if it ever had. Not like this. Dean had never been a cuddler, and—

Dean.

Nate. It's Nate. Of course, it's Nate. And last night, we had…

I blink at the pheasant statue on the nightstand. It matches the colors of the drapes. Nate made me come, and then I'd done the same for him. Under the covers and in the darkness.

Heat and mortification rise to my cheeks. I'm glad he's asleep and I don't have to face him yet.

He touched me as if he wanted to for ages, and like he enjoyed doing it the entire time. Not like there was a finish line to race toward or an end goal in mind.

I screw my eyes tightly shut and settle deeper into the cradle of his arms. *Can we do that again?* He is a bachelor. Has been for as long as I've known him. He's also been linked to a few high-profile women, beautiful ones who have been on his arm at various events every once in a while. Of course he's good at sex. Would it be so bad of me to enjoy him, too? For us to enjoy each other?

Nate's breathing turns into a sigh, and he shifts, just slightly, bringing all of my focus to the distinct heaviness against my ass.

He's hard again.

While still asleep, in the morning light, and everything inside of me tightens at that realization. I didn't have a chance to see him yesterday.

A stuttering breath, and then he's flexing his arm around my waist, clearing his throat. Awake. Or about to be.

I hold still. Waiting.

What will he do when he wakes up?

Something warm nudges my neck, my shoulder. His lips? "Good morning" He sounds hoarse, rough from sleep.

"Morning," I whisper back.

He clears his throat again, and the arm around me tightens even more. A second later, the erection pressed against my back is gone. Like he'd realized it too and shifted his hips away.

"Slept well?"

"Better than I should've, in a new bed and all," I say.

His arm moves. Hand goes to my hip, and I don't feel any less tense. Looking at him would solve all kinds of problems. But it might also start new ones, and right now, I don't know what I want more.

I push into seating. His arm falls away entirely, and I swing my legs over the edge of the bed. Look at the alarm clock. "It's… nine o'clock."

"Nine?" he repeats. "Damn. Didn't expect that."

"Can I shower first?"

"Of course." His voice is still hoarse, but there's something calm about it, too. Maybe he knows it's what I need right now to still my racing mind. "It's all yours."

"Thanks. Um, do you think our phones work now?" I stand up and realize I'm just in my panties and camisole, and the room is bright with morning light. I run a hand over my wild hair, suddenly self-conscious. It dried overnight, and I don't know what it looks like.

Nate sits up against the headboard. His hair is mussed, his eyes heavy on mine. The cover has slid down to his waist, and there's not a stitch of clothing to hide the breadth of his chest from view. The chest I slept against all night.

One of his knees is bent.

I wonder if that's to hide his erection.

I wonder if he'll take care of it while I shower.

And I wonder if I can ask him about it or if we're going to pretend like nothing happened.

"Hopefully. I'll call my mechanic while you shower," he says. "I'll get us out of here in no time. I promise."

I nod. "Thank you so much."

And when I emerge from the bathroom fifteen minutes later, he's up. Fully dressed and standing with his back to me. The bed is made, both of our phones are charging nearby. Whatever Nate did or didn't do in the silence of the bedroom is impossible to know.

I've put my hair up into a ponytail. It's the best I can do with the wayward curls. When Nate hands me my phone, I try not to flinch at the bright screen. It had been sort of nice to go twelve hours without looking at it once.

"He's on his way. My mechanic," he says quietly. "I'll check us out."

"Can I go for a walk around the town?"

"Of course you can, Harper. You can do whatever you like." I feel his gaze on me, and the softness of his voice makes me think of things done in the dark. *Do whatever you like.*

I swallow hard. "See you in a bit."

The village of Ashcroft is tiny, but it's cute. I snap pictures of the thatched roof on one of the houses and of a group of deer in a meadow past the village's stone church. Stopping at a quaint grocery store, now open, I grab a loaf of bread and a bottle of juice. Something for the drive back.

I find Nate with two men by the Aston Martin when I return. The car has a new tire, but the three of them are deep in a discussion about the one that had blown. The wiry man at Nate's right is looking down at the frayed rubber and shaking his head.

I sit down on the nearby stone hedge and munch on some bread. Watch the men discuss.

Twenty minutes later, the car is back in full working order. We say goodbye to Ashcroft and get back on the road.

The silence in the car isn't oppressive. It isn't tense. But it isn't exactly quite as natural as it had been yesterday, either. The unsaid words hang between us. I watch Nate's hand on the stick shift as he accelerates and think of where it had been last night. How those long fingers stroked and entered and curved inside me, and how it had been so much better than it had any right to be.

I play around with the radio. We share a bottle of juice. I munch on another piece of bread, and, outside the window, the beautiful pastoral landscapes gradually change back into cityscapes. Villages turn into suburbs. Fields become overpasses.

"Harper," he says when we're driving into Kensington, just before we arrive home. From the tone of his voice, I know what he has to say will be different from the passing conversation we've had so far.

My stomach tightens. "Nate."

He chuckles. "Didn't mean for this to become so formal."

"Good. It doesn't have to be, I think."

"It doesn't," he agrees. "I think last night was… well. You might think it's a mistake, again, like you did after the party."

I shake my head. "That feels kind of pointless at this point. Don't you think?"

Nate glances at me. His expression is guarded, the look in his eyes is hard to read. "Yes. I suppose."

I take a deep breath. "We're friends who like to... to... do things. Who clearly find each other... attractive." I glance in his direction again. He's busy reversing into the underground parking garage, right next to his other two precious vehicles, but he seems to catch my nervous glance all the same. "I don't mean to speak for you, of course."

He finishes parking, turns the engine off, and looks me dead in the eyes. "Harp, of course I find you attractive."

My throat tightens. "Right. So... given that... I think it's okay that we're friends who sometimes like to do some not-so-friendly things."

"Or very friendly," he says, "depending on how you look at it."

Tension seeps out of me at his words. "Yes. Exactly."

"Don't worry, Harp. I'm never going to go weird on you." He reaches across the center console and brushes a few strands of my hair back, notching them behind my ear. "We can be whatever you want us to be."

"Oh," I breathe.

His gaze is locked on my hair, and his fingers tunnel through. There's something in his eyes. Something I can't really place, can't really figure out—

He looks back at me and smiles crookedly. "No pressure."

"No pressure," I repeat. "And no strings?"

"None."

"And the box stays shut."

He nods. "The box stays shut," he agrees. *Dean never has to know,* and I feel relief unfurl inside of me like a sunrise. "Now come on. Let's get home and out of these fucking awful clothes. I don't want to wear pajama pants ever again."

"Just because they're not tailor-made doesn't mean they're awful," I tease.

He locks the car behind us with one hand and wraps his other arm around my shoulders. "I only wear sweats from Savile Row," he says. "Haven't you learned that by now?"

Tranquil delight floods me at seeing the townhouse. *Home.* The strength of the sentiment takes me by surprise. Somewhere over the past weeks, I'd come to think of it like that.

The month Nate gambled and won is almost up. I should be looking for a new place. Should start the process again. But I'll miss this place when I leave.

Nate unlocks the front door and shuts off the alarm. Then, stares at the envelope lying in the hallway.

Tossed in through the mail slot in the door.

My name is written on it in large, scrawling letters. No stamps.

"Harper…" he says and bends to pick it up. "It's heavy. Whatever it is."

I reach for the envelope, and he hands it to me almost reluctantly, as if there might be some kind of hidden danger inside. I open it up and tip the contents out.

A key chain. And a note.

"'Harper,'" I read. "'I have to go to the emergency room after a little accident at home. I've given the paramedic this note to drop at yours. I don't know how long I'll be gone. Can you take care of Quincy and Stanley for me? I will forever be in your debt.' Oh, it's from Richard! This must be his key."

Nate's voice is dark. "Your neighbor friend?"

"Yes. God, I hope he's okay. I wish I could text him. We never exchanged phone numbers." It's easy to picture Richard and his formal manner, and how he'd been forced to ask the EMT to walk over here with the letter. The dogs would be barking excitedly with all the new people "The dogs! They might have been alone since yesterday, depending on when he left this. We have to go."

"Richard," Nate mutters. But he follows behind me. "Is he… do you think he's very ill?"

"He's always seemed healthy to me. But you know, at that

age, I suppose anything might happen. Oh, I hope he hasn't taken a fall at home…" I'm already up the next stoop, key in hand. "Let's get the boys."

Nate's voice is hollow behind me. "At his age?"

"Yes. He's in his late seventies."

"Oh," he says. "Right. I thought he was… younger."

"He's your next-door neighbor!"

"I don't know my neighbors."

"Well, he certainly knows you. And he told me that you have a very beautiful vintage Aston Martin." I get the door open and I'm greeted immediately by the two dachshunds. Quincy's tail wags slightly side-to-side, like the distinguished pup he is, compared to Stanley's helicopter movements.

"I'll leave a note with my phone number… we have to take them home."

"Right. Shit. Yeah… I can pick this one up." It takes us a few minutes to find their leashes hanging on a hook in the hallway and to make it back into Nate's house. The difference between the two hallways feels stark. One is expertly and modernly designed; the other felt lived in, with slightly yellowed wallpaper and an oriental carpet.

We're left standing in Nate's living room, with the two dogs sniffing the new place thoroughly, scoping out their surroundings.

"This is okay, isn't it?" I ask. "Richard is lovely, and I'm sure he will be home soon. Quincy and Stanley are very well-behaved gentlemen."

"I think the brown one just peed on my rug."

"Okay, so they have incontinence issues. Gentlemen over a certain age often do." I bend to scoop up Quincy. His floppy ears are silky, and his little body is surprisingly warm. "It's very ill-mannered of you to point that out."

"Harper," Nate says. "If we're going to… babysit these two hot dogs, we need supplies. I don't have a single thing for pets in this house."

"I know. I've already made a mental list."

He runs a hand through his hair. Chuckles dryly, but then he just shrugs. "You know, I used to live a very orderly life here before you moved in. The house was always quiet. No near-nude women on the second floor landing, no meal prep containers in the fridge, and definitely no dogs."

I smile sheepishly. "I know. Sorry about that. I could start looking for another place, you know, if you—"

"No," he says. Bends down to pet Stanley, who is fighting with the fringe of the living room rug. "Never, Harper."

Chapter 23

Nate

Hot water sluices over my head and down my back, and the steam is making my breathing heavier. Thank God for this shower. When I bought this place, installing overhead showerheads in every bathroom had been a priority. The bathtubs remain. Large. Luxurious. *Unused.* I've never gotten into that habit. Never understood the appeal of baths.

I brace a hand against the tiled wall and let the fantasies invade. Only they're not just fantasies these days.

Harper had been in my arms.

I touched her, kissed her neck, and listened to the sweet sounds of her labored breaths as she came around my fingers.

The memory had been replaying in my head since it happened. Yesterday morning, in the little B&B room after we woke up. In the car during our drive back to London. While I watched her cuddle the dogs last night, curled up on my couch, in my living room, in my home.

Sleep was impossible last night.

It was always torturous to know she was just a floor down. But now… *fuck,* I wanted to be in the same bed as her again.

I tossed and turned and wondered if she was using her vibrator, and it was the first time I'd been jealous of a piece of silicon and two batteries. I got up before dawn. Gone for a run. None of it helped, so here I am, abusing the water pressure and aching for Harper.

Her touch, her smile, her body, her lips.

I reach down and stroke my cock. Grip it tight and close my eyes, like I had to in that bed with her, to avoid going off too soon.

Having her hands on me after all these years…

It had been a different kind of torture. *Agony* comes to mind, but the kind you never want to end.

I stroke slowly. Picturing her with that towel dropped to her waist and her perfect bare tits. Rosy nipples, a flush on her cheeks, and the damp curls cascading over her shoulders.

The image I'd told her I would forget.

I'm a bastard. But right now, there isn't a smidge of morals left in me, not as my hand moves more urgently, and I see her in my mind's eye.

I want to make her orgasm again. It's a need as overwhelming as my urge to come, right now, and I bite down hard on my tongue. My breathing accelerates in rhythm with my quick strokes. The water isn't great for friction, and it's just a bit painful, my grip slightly too tight, and damn it if this isn't exactly what I need at this moment.

She'd been so wet and silky around my fingers, and squeezed me so tightly when she came. *Fuck.* Based on what she said, I wonder if she'd ever had someone focus on her G-spot like that. It feels like a goddamn crime if she hasn't.

It is a fucking crime that I hadn't tasted her.

I widen my stance and pump into my hand like it's her heat. With my need for Harper pounding through me, my palm is such a poor replacement for *her.* But it's something; something I have to do because I can't go through my day like this. I won't be able to focus on my work. Haven't since she moved in, but it hasn't been like *this* before.

And now I know what her pussy feels like around my fingers. And I know how it feels to hold her while she sleeps.

I groan as the pressure builds, coiling at the base of my spine. Relief is only seconds away, and—

"No, Stanley! Stop!" The voice cuts through the blinding haze of pleasure. Her voice. I break off with another groan as the rising pleasure morphs into the pain of no release. Look through the glass shower door to the bathroom…

At Harper, standing there in an oversized T-shirt.

She's holding one of the walking hot dogs in her arms, her eyes wide… and locked on me.

"Hello," she says quickly. "Good morning. I'm so sorry, I fed them, and then they went exploring, and he just raced up here. Your bedroom door was slightly ajar so he got in and, and… and… you're showering."

I turn to face her. Naked. My cock still painfully hard, jutting straight out, and her gaze drops to it.

And then quickly flits away.

"Yes."

Harper's cheeks are burning, her hair pulled back in a messy bun, and she looks so beautiful and so surprised that I have to swallow another moan.

She hasn't seen me naked before.

Let her look, I think, and take a step out of the shower and onto the plush bathmat. Water drips down my body, and my cock feels heavy, bobbing in the air. *And let her like what she sees.*

"One second," she says quickly, still averting her eyes, and drops Stanley behind her, in my bedroom. The next moment, she's closing the bathroom door.

With her inside the room.

Her gaze fixed on my sink.

"Sorry, again. I'll keep a better watch on—"

"Harper," I say. "You can look at me. If you want to."

Her eyes find mine. They glitter. And then, they sweep down, over my chest, my stomach, stopping right on my dick.

The pleasure-pain coursing through my system is making it hard to think straight. I hadn't meant to work myself up, but I had, and damn if my cock isn't protesting and my balls aren't aching.

"Wow," she breathes. "It was so dark at the inn, I didn't see…"

"No. Neither of us did," I say. "Next time, I want bright sunlight so I can see all of you."

Her breath catches, and she takes a step closer. "You were jerking off in the shower?" There's a hint of curiosity in her voice.

"Yes."

"I thought it was a 'before sleep' thing."

"Lately, it's become an 'all the time' thing," I say, watching her watch me. Her gaze flicks from my eyes to my cock. She is intoxicating.

I reach down and grip myself again. Give my hard-on a long, lazy stroke. "Sleep well?"

"Yes," she breathes. "Well, not really. But it's okay."

"Me neither."

"That looks…" She takes another step forward. "Will you let me?"

Everything inside of me tightens, and I have to reach out to grab the frame of the shower stall for support. Water is beating down my temple, dripping off my hair, and I can't think of a single thing to say.

Her smile is everything.

I never thought I'd get to see her looking like this. Eyes warm with desire, a teasing and sensual smile on her lips. But here she is.

My dream come to life.

"Nate." She draws another step closer. Then she drops to her knees, and I think I might pass out.

"Harper," I say, my voice comes out gruff. Seeing her here, kneeling before me, and feeling her hands grip my cock… "That's what I want to do to you."

"Later," she says. Her eyes are studying me like she's never seen a dick before, and I know that's not true. Know it far too well, but it still does something to me. Does something that she—

"You're big. It felt like that, the other night," she says. Her left hand is gripping my shaft tight, her other playing with the skin of my head.

I don't think I can breathe.

"But it's hard when you can't see properly," she continues. "I want to..."

And then she takes the tip into her mouth, and everything inside of me short-circuits.

I'd been so close before, and I'm even closer now, and oh my God, the heat of her mouth and the grip of her lips... and the *sight* —it's burned into my brain. Her beautiful face, her beautiful eyes looking up at me as her beautiful lips stretch around my cock.

She starts sucking, bobbing gently, using her hand where she can't reach, and I squeeze my eyes shut. Focus on breathing. Ignore my labored sounds—wheezing, punctuated by groans—that I can't seem to control.

I reach down and tunnel my fingers through her hair. But I do more damage than good, because that messy bun comes undone in my hand, and wild curls spread all around. Some of them tickle my thighs.

"Fucking hell, Harp... I can't... you're too good." I dare to look down again and nearly come from what I see. There's a smile in her eyes as she hastens her movements. I want to buck, my hips want to push deeper into that sweet mouth, but I resist the urge until my hand hurts from gripping the shower frame so hard.

This is about her. It *should* be about her. Her pleasure, what she wants, making her come. I need to put her first in all of this.

But that's damned hard to remember when it feels like I'm about to come apart at the seams.

She swirls her tongue around my head, and I groan at the sudden spike of heat shooting through me. My fingers tighten in her hair. "Shit. Harper, that was..." She does it again and my words dissolve.

I lose them all.

Until she flicks her tongue back and forth on the sensitive spot beneath my head.

The edges of my vision turn black. "I'm going to come, I can't—"

She doesn't stop. Doesn't pull back. Just flicks her tongue over and over, and I roar, my fingers tightening on her curls as pleasure overwhelms me. It pounds down my spine, my balls tighten, and I explode. Pulse after pulse, and she never takes her mouth off me.

Stares at me through all of it.

I'm worried I might black out. Maybe I already have. But when I return to my senses, pleasure is still making my limbs feel heavy, and Harper is sitting back on her heels with a Cheshire smile on her face.

I give a hoarse chuckle. "Fucking hell, baby. That was unreal."

Her smile widens. "Yeah? Better than your right hand?"

"Better is an understatement." My breath is still coming fast. "I can't believe you swallowed."

Harper looks a bit embarrassed, but far too smug to let it take over. She shrugs. "I felt like it. You taste good. Clean."

"You couldn't have gotten me any fresher out of the shower." I run a hand through my hair. "Shit, that was unexpected. You're so hot."

"Thank you very much, Connovan." The smile never leaves her face.

I glance down at my cock, now sated and half-hard, hanging between my legs. *Don't get used to it,* I want to say. Instead, I reach for a towel and start rubbing my hair to get the worst of the dripping gone. "You're talented in so many ways, Harp. You keep surprising me."

She leans against the sink. "Friends take care of friends,"

she says with that incredible smile. "Your shower is larger than mine. Oooh, so is your bathtub. Look at that."

I glance behind me. "Yeah. Not like I ever use it."

"What? I take a bath at least twice a week here. It's the best."

"It sucks," I say and grin at her. "And not in a good way."

Harper rolls her eyes and pushes off the vanity. "Wow. Height of wit."

"It's early, my mind was just blown. Give a man a few minutes." I reach out and grab a handful of her T-shirt. "And where do you think you're going?"

"To let the dogs out and have my coffee."

I slide my palms around her, pulling her back to my front. Play with the hem of her T-shirt. It brushes along the tops of her thighs, and I bet she's only wearing panties beneath it. "What about you? Don't friends... take care of friends?"

I hear her audible swallow. "I'm not fresh out of the shower."

"I'm never going to give a shit about that," I say against her ear. "But there's a very conveniently located shower here if you do."

She starts to turn in my arms. "Maybe it's not—"

A phone starts to ring in my bedroom, and a few seconds later, a dog barks. Stanley. Left alone in my room.

Harper breaks out of my arms and hurries to the bedroom. I wrap the towel around my waist and follow her.

The hot dog is bouncing around my nightstand where my phone is charging. Ringing loudly. I grab it and watch as Harper lifts the dog, who immediately quiets, now that he's so diligently brought our attention to the dangerous electronic device.

It's my assistant. "Hey," I say. "Did you get the tickets?"

Harper is watching me, holding the puppy close to her. "Yes," my assistant says. "They were surprised that you finally responded after all the invitations."

"And you got two?"

"Yes," she says.

I look at Harper. "Set up a few appointments with the department stores. I'll also need something from the jewelers. Send me the catalog."

Harper's eyebrows rise. *Oh la la,* she mouths, still smiling.

"On it," my assistant says. "Anything else?"

"Book a car for the night. I'll be in the office soon," I say and hang up.

Harper is giggling, trying to escape Stanley's kisses. "You're going somewhere extravagant?"

I raise an eyebrow. "I'm not. But we are. How do you feel about attending a movie premiere?"

Chapter 24

Harper

I turn around in front of the mirror, watching as the emerald silk shines under the overhead lights. The dress hugs my body like a second skin down to my lower thighs, where it flares out in a subtle mermaid skirt. The strapless bodice fits over my breasts surprisingly well and cinches at the waist like only an amazingly designed corset could.

I've never worn anything this intricate. Never attended such a lavish event. Nate hadn't been able to come with me to pick out the outfit, and I worried over whether I made the right decision or not, that is until the attendant told me in no uncertain terms that this was the one. It looks like a grown-up version of a fairytale dress.

Using his credit card that he gave me had been another thing to fret about.

But he had made the argument, and made it well, that it was only right for him to take care of the expenses. He invited me to this event because he didn't want to go alone. *You're doing me a favor,* he'd said.

So here I am, an hour before the premiere, standing in the bedroom that's become my own. Strapped into a dress that cost a small fortune, with my makeup done and my hair in a sleek ponytail down my bare back. I straightened the curls out for the occasion.

I look at the mirror. "A movie premiere," I say quietly and run my hands down my sides. Over the sleek fabric. "I can't believe this is my life."

"Talking to yourself, Harp?"

I glance over my shoulder. Nate is leaning against the doorframe to my bedroom, wearing a tux again. He looks good.

He always looks good in a tux, but now...

Seeing him makes me feel warm inside. I can't look away from the snug fit at his shoulders and how he seems to be even taller in that garb.

"You're admiring me," he says, and his own eyes drop over my body in a slow sweep that makes my cheeks blush.

My throat feels tight. "So are you."

"Oh," he says, lips curving up, "I certainly am. And I won't deny it. You're gorgeous."

I perform a tiny twirl. "Good choice of dress?"

"Fantastic. I'm just sad I couldn't be there to watch you try the rest of them on."

"Mm-hmm. Maybe it's good that you weren't," I say. "This wasn't exactly cheap."

He snorts, like that doesn't dignify a response, and comes closer. That's when I realize he's holding a navy box under his arm. "I have something else for you."

"You do?"

"Yes. An accessory." He holds up the box and unfastens the lock. Opens the lid facing in my direction...

My breath seizes inside my lungs.

"Nate," I whisper. Nestled on pearlescent velvet is a diamond necklace. The gems glitter in the light. Dangling off the brilliant stand are several pendants. At the center of each is an emerald, but it's surrounded by a small row of diamonds that enhance the deep green sparkle.

It's the kind of necklace classic movie stars would wear. Millionaire heiresses. Royalty.

"I called the store attendant after you left," Nate says.

"She mentioned you chose a green dress. So I picked out a matching necklace."

I reach out a tentative finger and run it over the stunning display. "You got it on loan?"

"It's not a loan. Turn around, Harp."

I do, and catch the sight of us in the mirror. Him in his tux, standing behind me. Me in my green silk dress.

Nate brushes my hair to the side, baring my back, and places the necklace around my neck. It's heavy and cold, and the green perfectly compliments my strapless gown.

I feel his fingers against my nape as he closes the clasp.

"Nate," I say again. "I've never worn anything this beautiful."

He runs a hand over my ponytail, pulling the strands back into position. His fingers wrap around the mass. "I've never seen your hair straight before," he murmurs.

I try to meet his gaze in the mirror. But he's not looking at me. His eyes are fixed on the ponytail in his hand. "I don't straighten it often. It's so much work."

"I can imagine," he says hoarsely. "Your curls are all gone. They're beautiful."

I chuckle weakly. "They'll be back. A shower or some inconvenient rain is all it takes."

"Mm-hmm." He clears his throat and lets the tresses fall. "Let's go, if you're ready."

"I am."

I keep touching the necklace the entire way down the stairs and out to the car he'd hired for the night. I don't want to ask how many carats it is. I don't want to know how much this is worth. I just want to live in this moment, as fully as I can, so I can continue to *relive* it later when it's over.

Nate opens the car door for me. "Not driving yourself tonight?" I ask.

He looks rueful. "No. I contemplated it, but… I do want to have a drink. Or two."

"Good," I say. "You're fun when you drink."

His eyes linger on mine, and the awareness sparks there at the same time I realize what happened the last time he'd been drinking. When I had, too.

Us, making out in the dark hallway of the house at our backs.

We haven't kissed since then. We'd done… other things… while stranded at the inn, and then in the luxurious heat of his bathroom.

But we haven't kissed.

"Get in the car," he nearly growls.

My lips tug into a smile. "Yes, sir."

We ride in silence to Leicester Square and the movie theater—the cinema—that's hosting the premiere. I glance at Nate out of the corner of my eye. I've seen him dressed to the nines before. I've also had breakfast atop a London skyscraper while he wore a rumpled tux and didn't give two shits about it. But something about seeing him in one again, now after… after so much has transpired between us, hammers home the point of just who he is. How different our worlds are.

I'd forgotten how imposing he really is. How wealthy. But here I am, wearing a necklace that's probably worth more than the combined GDP of several small nations, and heading to an event where more than money is needed to get through the door.

Nate's phone buzzes, and he offers a quiet *sorry* to me before answering. I listen to the tone of his voice and look out the window at the city as we pass by. He also sounds different with others than when he's just with me.

"No, not that week. The week after can work. … No, I'm not. … It's a good idea. … Are you taking the company plane?"

I swallow hard. *Company plane. Right.* Contron has its own jet. I wonder how much it gets reserved for the Connovans themselves.

My eyes drift back to him. Nate is ten years older than me.

That age gap has never been conspicuous between us, but hearing him talk as he is now, seeing him command respect just by entering the gallery where I work, or being able to simply drop two hundred pounds for a tip at the small inn on the weekend…

It highlights those differences between us.

I'm nowhere near where he is in life.

Age is one part of it, but he came from a different background than I did. Just like Dean did. Advantages I never had. Nate also has a clear direction in his life. Confidence, self-assuredness, maturity… in many ways, it feels like he has it all figured out. Like he's pleased with where he is.

I bet he's never written a *Thirty under Thirty* list in an attempt to find himself again.

He hangs up with a soft click. "Sorry about that."

"No worries. Work?"

"Partly. It's only early afternoon back in New York." His eyes rest on mine, and I get the sense that he's hesitating. "My family is considering coming to London."

"They are?"

"Yes," he says. "We'll see if it happens."

"That would be fun. Your siblings?"

"Yes, and their partners. My niece and nephew."

"Aw, they'll love London, I bet." But then I frown. "Although, they've probably been here before, right?"

"They haven't, at least not all together," he says. "With work, my brother flies out alone whenever needed."

I lean my head back against the seat. "He usually stays in my room, right?"

Nate's jaw tenses. "Yes. He does." His eyes shift away, towards the window. "We're almost there… remind me what this movie is about again?"

I roll my eyes. "You're the one who invited me!"

"Yes. But it's a Jane Austen adaptation, and I know you're the expert."

"The first big-screen adaptation of *Sense and Sensibility*

that's been made in almost thirty years," I say. Excitement, like a current, has flowed through my body all day, and it seeps into my voice. "Do you think we'll see the actors?"

"I could probably speak to them, if you'd like."

My eyes widen. "You're not serious."

"I am," he says with a crooked smile. Confident. "They'll be busy, but there's no harm in trying."

"You just go through the world like that, don't you?" I ask. "With completely unfounded confidence."

He raises an eyebrow. "I wouldn't say it's entirely unfounded."

A blush rises in my cheeks. It happens in an instant, my mind jumping directly to the way his long fingers had felt, stroking my insides.

His smile turns smug as he reads the thoughts on my face.

"Okay," I admit. "Maybe not entirely unfounded."

"Tell me about this movie," he says. "What's *Sense and Sensibility* about?"

"Okay, so Elinor and Marianne are sisters, and they're living with their mother and younger sibling at a beautiful estate. Their father has just died."

Nate's lips twitch. "I see we're starting at the beginning."

"It's important," I say. But then, the car pulls to a red light just a block from Leicester Square, and all it takes is a single glance out at the crowds of people and the erected metal barricades on the sidewalks to derail my thoughts. Is that a…

"Nate," I say. "We won't be walking a red carpet or anything, will we?"

"It wouldn't surprise me if that's the main entryway, yeah," he says. "But the paparazzi and throng of fans will be focused on spotting the celebs who show up. They won't care about us."

My chest tightens. "You think we'll have to walk the red carpet?"

"We might," he says, eyebrows drawn low. "Don't worry, Harp. It'll be okay."

"I didn't realize we'd be like... *that* close to the celebrities."

"They're just people." He puts a hand out on the middle seat between us, and I take it without thinking. His palm is warm as his fingers close over mine. "It'll be an adventure."

I nod. That's true. And that's what I want. The excitement isn't gone, it's just tinged with nerves and a hint of performance anxiety.

They're going to photograph us?

"Keep telling me about *Sense and Sensibility*," he says. His thumb moves in a slow circle around the back of my hand. "Tell me what happens. The father just died..."

I explain it to him as best I can. Linger on the four main players, leaving out as much about Willoughby as I can. I tell him about Marianne and the patient love of Colonel Brandon.

"My favorite is Edward and Elinor, though. I love how tormented he is, how he clearly wants her," I say. "But he can't be with her, and you can see how it eats at them both up until the very end."

Nate's forehead is furrowed. "And why can't he be with her? That makes no sense to me."

"Because he's already engaged to a woman he met years prior, but it's a secret."

"That's idiotic," Nate says. His deep voice is matter-of-fact. "If he truly loves Elinor, he would break that off."

"Yes, but that would mean forfeiting his honor. He'd given his word!"

"Then, he should at least tell her how he feels, so she isn't misled."

"But that would also ruin his honor. Don't you see? He *can't* confess his feelings, knowing there is no point in encouraging her to return them, because he can't offer marriage. That wouldn't be honorable, either."

Nate's brow is furrowed. "I don't like that."

"It does seem a bit old-fashioned," I say.

He shakes his head. "Doesn't seem old-fashioned to me. But I still don't like it."

"Don't worry," I say teasingly and tighten my fingers around his. "There's a happy ending."

"Well, thank God for that," he says bitterly. "We can't have fictional people suffering."

He looks ahead at the sprinter van in front of us. A pair of glamorously dressed women are getting out of it, and my heart rate skyrockets. It's our turn next. Our driver has already had to lower his window and give our names and invitation to security.

Something warm touches my skin, and I turn to see Nate kissing the back of my hand. His eyes are on mine. "We're making memories tonight," he tells me. "Have fun, Harp. *Enjoy* this moment."

I swallow my fears and focus on the excitement instead. He's right. This is a night I will remember forever. A night I can't wait to tell my mom about. I know she's been planning to take some of her students to see this adaptation.

"Let's kill it," I say.

His lips break into a wide smile. "That's my girl."

My heart skips at his words and the emotion in his eyes. But then, my car door opens, and I'm waved out onto a deep red carpet and to the surrounding commotion.

Nate is at my side a second later and offers me his arm. We walk on the red carpet together and into the dazzling sea of celebrities, photographers, and elegantly dressed as if we do this every night.

Chapter 25

Harper

"Am I dreaming?" I whisper. Nate is standing beside me in the magnificent lobby of this theater, both of us holding a flute of champagne. Around us are such glamorous and fashionable people that I'm trying to take mental snapshots from every angle.

One of my favorite period actresses is standing just thirty measly feet away. Talking, smiling, hair in a messy bun, and wearing a slinky yellow dress. Her skin looks like it could have been airbrushed. I wonder if she's wearing the body makeup I've heard about on social media.

"I think I'm dreaming," I state. "Yes, I am."

Nate chuckles softly. "You're not."

"I'm going to have to add *attend a movie premiere* to my list of things, just so I can tick this off. This undeniably qualifies as an insane new experience."

"I'm glad," he says, and his voice sounds smug. "Figured you'd like this night. And the main event hasn't even begun."

"Were you planning on bringing someone else here?" I ask hesitantly. "And things fell through?"

His eyebrows furrow. "Well… No."

"How'd you get tickets to this?"

"I pulled a few strings," he says.

"Did you… did it… you were going here anyway," I guess. "And you had an extra ticket?"

Nate's eyes are steady on mine. "No."

I have to swallow. "Oh."

"You love these stories so much, you wanted to visit their filming locations." He lifts one shoulder in a shrug. "Plus, I look damn good in a tux. It's a win-win."

That makes me giggle. "You do, actually. It's practically criminal."

"And we can't always be in a rowboat on a pond. Or *in* the pond. Sometimes, we do things like this." His lips curve. "Don't worry, Harp. Tomorrow, we'll be back in the townhouse with Quincy and Stanley. Did you hear from Richard?"

"Yes, he's coming home tomorrow. I'm looking forward to seeing him." But then I shake my head. If he hadn't been planning on going here, if he didn't have another date, if this was a last-minute thing… He did this just for me? "Wait, how *did* you get these tickets, then?"

"There are strings. I pulled on them."

"Do I even want to know?"

"I'm not entirely sure," he drawls and takes a slow sip of his champagne. "It would mean implicating you in some criminal secrets, and I—"

"What?"

He grins. "I made a phone call and donated some money to a charity. It wasn't hard, Harper. Getting access never is."

"Not when you're Nate Connovan," I say.

He holds out his arm. "There has to be some perks to my miserable existence. Come on. Let's try to mingle our way to the most famous person in the room."

By the time the bells ring, and everyone enters the theater to take their seats, I feel almost giddy. I've spoken to three actors, two of whom I've loved for years. Each of them was both shorter and skinnier in person. I guess there's some truth to that saying about the camera adding a few pounds.

Practically vibrating with excitement, I settle into the seat with Nate on my right. The director of the film is here, and he and the actors speak on stage for a solid ten minutes before the movie starts to roll.

Someone regularly tops up our champagne as we watch. Offers us various snacks and hors d'oeuvres.

I'll never be able to go to a normal movie theater again.

When the movie ends, everyone applauds. People rise, and I quickly do the same. I brush my palm over my cheek to wipe away the tear that slipped out during the conclusion. Elinor's response to Edward at the end of the story always makes me emotional.

"You loved it," Nate murmurs at my side.

I nod quickly. "Yes. They'd… they'd captured the essence so well. Cut some scenes of course, but they really got the two love stories down."

There's an after-party, held in an adjoining ballroom. The walls are beautifully ornate in a way that only old European buildings can be. Intricate chandeliers and soft candlelight set the room aglow, and the same smiling waiters come by, offering more refreshments. I spot a singer I regularly listen to during my workouts. And a director who made my mom's favorite movie.

We're chatting with a few other couples about the movie when Nate spots someone he knows and is drawn away. Even left on my own for a few minutes, I find myself enjoying the conversation with these fabulous unnamed people. I bask in all of it—the atmosphere, the company—and even as I'm doing it, I remind myself of what an incredible life I'm living. How happy I am to be here, in this city, and to have a friend as good as Nate.

How happy I am to be my own woman again.

"Oh, there you are," one of the women addresses the newcomer to our group. My eyes widen when I see who it is. I try to hide my shock, but it's hard, unexpectedly coming face-to-face with the world-renowned action movie star.

He's not some B-lister. Not "sort of famous." He's literally one of the world's biggest celebrities, and even if his movies aren't to my personal taste, I still feel awestruck by suddenly seeing him in person.

And somehow he ends up standing right next to me.

Talking to me. Asking me what I do for a living.

"So you're an art expert," he says in a voice familiar to me from countless movies and commercials I've seen since I was a little girl. "Tell me about your favorite painting."

The question makes me blink. *What?* But I do my best to answer, and he nods, listening to every word with a lazy smile on his lips. He looks older in person than he does on screen. Thinner, too, and shorter, just like the other actors here. It feels like I'm having an out of body experience.

He's so close, I smell his aftershave.

"I'm shooting at Pinewood for a few months."

"Oh, really?"

"Yeah. We should meet up. I could show you around," he says, and the wide smile gets even wider. His teeth are all perfectly even, and so white, they're dazzling. I wonder if he has veneers, and the real teeth hidden behind the custom-made shells are filed to sharp vampire points.

"Uh, yeah. Maybe," I say. "That might be fun."

I give him my number in a daze, and then he's off with another wide smile in my direction. I'm left with a glass of champagne and a feeling of *what just happened?* while watching Nate make his approach through the crowd. He looks tall and broad, just as I've always seen him, and not shrunken down like the others.

His eyebrows are drawn together. "Was that Austin Silver?"

"Yes."

"Jeez."

"Yeah, I know. He asked for my number, to hang out sometime," I say with a laugh. The entire thing still feels surreal. "Can you *imagine*?"

Nate's eyes sharpen. "He did what?"

"I think I just got hit on." I shake my head while giggling. "Wow. I don't know who he thinks he is, at his age... Well, to be fair, I know exactly who he is. And clearly he does, too."

"You're going out with Austin Silver?" Nate asks. His voice sounds tense.

I laugh. "Good God, no! Never. He's ancient, and he's my stepdad's favorite actor. I saw his first action movie when I was... what? Nine? Absolutely not."

Nate's mouth softens into a reluctant smirk. "He's ancient?"

"Yes."

His voice becomes dangerous. "I believe he's only seven years older than me."

Oh.

"Well, sorry to say it, but that practically makes him Crypt Keeper. *Ancient news.* Far, far too old for me to be interested in."

The corners of Nate's mouth tip up, and his eyes twinkle. "Is that so?"

"Yes. It would be like kissing a corpse."

"Kissing a corpse," he repeats and steps closer. I shiver at the nearness. "Funny you'd say that, Harp. What does that make you?"

"I've never kissed Austin Silver," I breathe.

"No. And you never will," he says. "But you have kissed me."

My breath catches. "Have I? I can barely remember."

His eyes flash in amusement, and then he grabs my hand. Pulls me through the crowd. I hurry to stay in step. My beautiful green dress is flared around my legs, but it only starts to widen at my thighs, and I can't keep up with his long strides.

"Where are we going?"

"I have one final accessory for you. To complete the outfit," he says. He weaves by a group of laughing people near the exit to a hallway leading to the restrooms. When we make our way through, he looks at the signage until he finds one that has a discreet *staff only* written on it.

He opens the door like he owns the place.

It's a janitorial closet, and Nate pulls me inside before shutting the door firmly behind us.

My heart is pounding in exhilaration. "I think we're going to get busted," I say. "In five, four, three…"

He shakes his head and turns so his back is to the door, blocking anyone from opening it. "We're not," he says. With nothing but a dim overhead light, his eyes glint. "So you don't remember kissing me, do you?"

Ever so slightly, I shake my head. "Almost not at all."

"I think you're lying," Nate says, his large hand finding my waist. He pulls me to him until the silk of my dress scrunches against his tux. "But I'll remind you, just in case."

His mouth hovers over mine for a single delicious second. Then, he makes contact, and my eyes flutter closed. *Oh.* He kisses me with warm lips, practiced movements, and his arms circle my waist.

Without the irrational anger that we both felt the night of his party…

I melt against him. He's good at this, at these slow, deep, powerful kisses that entirely rob me of my breath. Liquid heat pours down from the press of his lips, spreading through my limbs. Pooling in my stomach.

Nate moves a hand to cup my face. His tongue runs along my lower lip, and I open on instinct. He deepens the kiss, and I rake my fingers through his hair, twisting, tightening my grip.

He groans into my mouth.

"Harper," he murmurs against my lips. "Tell me you want an adventure tonight."

I rise up on my tiptoes. Brush my mouth over his jaw. "I want an adventure tonight."

He groans again and releases his hold on me. But his eyes tell me this is far from over. "Good," he mutters and reaches inside his tux jacket. "I have one final accessory for you, baby."

I stare at the small velvet pouch in his hand. My mind feels blank. *Matching earrings?* What is this?

But then, he empties the contents onto his palm, and everything inside me tightens. It's a small silicon toy.

Bulbous on one end, with a small elongated piece that curves…

"Oh my God," I whisper.

Nate's smile flashes, and there's pure heat in his eyes. He sinks to his knees before me and reaches for the hem of my dress, slowly pushing it up—baring my lower legs. My knees. My thighs.

"I'm going to punish you for calling me old," he says. I reach down and grab the thick mass of my dress, helping him pull it over my hips. A fierce blush is spreading over my chest and neck, and my breaths are coming out hard. Like I've been running.

"I can't believe you're doing this," I whisper. *But please don't stop.*

Nate braces one of his feet behind him, firmly holding it against the door to keep the entry shut. His hands are warm and slightly rough over my thighs, sliding up to grip the thong I'm wearing. Slowly, he pulls the garment halfway down my thighs.

I gasp when his hand slips between my legs.

"Look at this pussy," he murmurs, his gaze locked on my bareness. I don't know if I've ever felt quite this exposed before. "You're wet."

I swallow hard. "Yes."

He leans closer, like he intends to kiss me. There. But then, his shoulders tense, and he forces himself not to. Reaches for the toy instead.

"Spread your legs for me, baby… that's it." Then, his hand is there, stroking over my sensitive flesh before pressing the toy against my entrance. It slots into place, and the faint stretch makes me shiver.

"This will vibrate inside you," he murmurs, his thumb rubbing circles around my clit. His eyes on me, like he's crafting a masterpiece. He fits the elongated piece to rest right over my clit, and I have to look down, at that pink silicon resting at the top of my slit.

He pulls my thong up, sealing it all in place.

The pressure against my clit is already delicious, the weight inside of me heavy and not entirely uncomfortable.

Nate pulls my dress down and rises, drawing me in for another kiss.

This one takes my breath away—there's nothing controlled about it.

"I'll handle the vibrations," he says against my lips, "from my phone. No one will be able to hear them."

"You're sure?"

"Dead sure," he mutters. "So, next time some movie star asks for your number, you'll know exactly who will be making you almost orgasm in public."

A shiver races down my arms. "You're jealous again."

"No," he says, mouth trailing down my neck. "I know better than to be jealous of men like him. You don't want him anyway."

"No," I breathe. "I don't."

Nate kisses the pulse on my neck before straightening. Takes my hand again, and pulls open the door. Bright light floods in, the sounds of music and voices, and we emerge back into a party for the rich and famous.

Releasing my hand, he wraps his right arm around my waist instead. Uses his left to unlock his phone. "This is for calling me old," Nate says, and a second later, the toy begins to gently pulsate inside me… and against my clit. "Who says real men can't vibrate?"

The shock of it nearly makes my steps falter.

But Nate is there, holding me, and urging me forward. His

mouth by my ear. "There's an investor here I need to talk to. Can you help me charm her and her husband?"

"I hate you," I whisper. Sensations undulate through me with each soft vibration, surging with the memory of Nate's lips on mine and his hands between my legs.

"I think that's just the thing, baby. You don't at all," he says with a crooked smile. "Now come on. We're going to have some fun."

Chapter 26

Nate

Watching the flush creep up Harper's neck and up to her cheeks is more riveting than any blockbuster movie. Her hand grips mine tightly, like she wants me close for support. A tiny sound escapes her and her breath hitches slightly when I change the vibration pattern.

Fuck, but I've been half-hard since the closet, and there's no sign that my condition will be abating.

Sliding that toy into place, seeing Harper's glistening pussy in the dimness of the tiny room, and hearing her breathing hard and fast because of me…

"Yes," Harper says. "I love that neighborhood. We live in Kensington, and it's right nearby." She's talking to the husband of an investor I needed to schmooze tonight. Her voice is pleasant, calm. With just a hint of strain.

I reach into my pocket and adjust the intensity of the vibrations. Change the pattern to one of pulses.

Watch as her hand tightens around the glass of champagne.

"You live together?" Sarah Fulton says. She's good friends with Mads Knudsen, part of a semi-incestuous group of rich Europeans who frequent London, Paris, and Berlin. All potential important allies for Contron.

I incline my head. "Yes, Harper recently moved here from New York to work at the Sterling Gallery."

"We're friends," Harper clarifies.

I increase the intensity of the toy by two measures at that comment. A gasp escapes her, but she quickly tries to cover it with a cough and braces her free hand on the nearby tall table.

"Very good friends," she adds. "He's the best."

I smirk behind the phone in my hand. Slide it back into my pocket and give Sarah a wide smile. "I apologize. Urgent questions from the team in New York. You know how it is with the time difference."

She waves it away. "Of course, of course. Bane of our existence. Our youngest daughter is spending a semester in Sydney. Eleven-hour difference. It's inhumane."

"Sydney? Is she liking it?" Harper asks. She's good at this. Talking to people and taking a genuine interest… even if her expression is currently more pinched than normal.

"Yes, she certainly is. Do you know what—our oldest son is good friends with Mads's nephew, Willard. They went to school together," Fulton says.

Her husband nods rapidly. "Yes, Willard mentioned that he was introduced to a new arrival into the art world. Could that be you, Harper?"

"Must be," she says happily. "He actually dropped by the gallery two days ago, to admire the selection of American impressionists we have and to speak with my boss."

"He's a good boy," Sarah Fulton says warmly. "So clever. He brought a previously unknown Covey to the market just a few months ago. Did you know that?"

"He told me about that, yes," Harper says.

The fucker, I think. He had monopolized her time for an entire evening at my party. They have art in common. He's a handsome European man of her own age. And he visited her at the gallery?

I turn the intensity up by another degree.

Harper sways on her feet and turns to glare at me.

I smile serenely back.

It takes us another five minutes of small talk before she makes our excuses. I follow along, a smile threatening to break out.

It isn't until we're a few steps away that she grips my forearm like a vise. "Nate," she says. "Please. I can't… I can't talk to any more people."

"It's getting too much?"

"Yes. I feel like I'm about to explode."

I run my thumb along her jaw, stopping on her lower lip. "That's sort of the point, baby."

Her eyes narrow. "I can't come here!" she whisper-shouts. "Everyone will see."

"Mm-hmm," I say. The idea of taunting her with it some more is fun… but I don't want to risk that happening. The jealousy of earlier is still lingering in my system. It's not a noble emotion. But it's there, and right now, the idea of other people seeing her as she comes is out of the question.

I wrap my arm around her waist. "Let's get you out of here, then."

She nearly sags into my side. "Thank God. I feel like… like… I'm made out of electricity."

We walk toward the exit, past the playing band and the open bar that will keep flowing well into the morning hours. These kinds of events always have a high risk of getting very wet.

"Poor girl," I whisper against her temple. But on my phone, I change the vibration to one without oscillating pulses.

It's a steady throb.

Her body draws taut. "Nate," she moans. "What?"

"You didn't tell me Willard came to visit you."

"Not me," she breathes. "The art gallery. Didn't seem important."

"He's interested in you."

"He's not. He's interested in what I can offer him," she says. Her tongue peeks out, wetting her lips. She looks almost feverish, and I want nothing more than to be home, right at this instant, where I can slip this dress off her and watch her body bow as she comes.

"I think he is… he is… something is wrong with him," she whispers. "Is that our car?"

"Yes." André gets out of the driver's seat. I don't use the car service very often, but when I do, it's always him I hire. He opens the back door for us, and I help Harper into the vehicle before slipping in after her.

She sags against the cushions, stretching out her legs in the ample space. "Oh my God," she whispers. "Sitting down… affects it…"

I shift closer to her on the seat. "You're close?"

"Yes," she whispers. "I can't… Nate."

It's a split-second decision. To turn the vibration off… or to let her come.

I hit the button that raises the partition, and the barrier rolls up quickly, blocking out André in the front seat. He's a good man. He knows where we're going, and I'll tip him generously when we get there.

"Nate," Harper whispers again. Her hands are curved around the edge of the seat, her eyes half-closed. She's breathing hard. "I'm going to…"

I pull up her dress. It's more difficult in the car, but not impossible. As soon as she knows where I'm heading with it, she helps me. A second later, the gown is bunched at her waist, and I'm pulling her thong to the side. Bending over to get my mouth into position…

I push the end of the toy off her swollen clit and replace it with my lips.

The sound that escapes Harper is half shriek, half gasp.

Her skin is warm and fragrant. Soft. And I have wanted to do this for weeks. Months.

Years, if I'm being honest with myself.

The other morning, after she'd given me the best blow job of my life, this was the only thing I wanted to do. *Needed* to do. But the reality of the day and the racing clock had sent her away to shower and get dressed.

It's too tight in the car for me to get in a better pose, but damn, beggars can't be choosers. The toy is still vibrating inside her pussy, so I focus all my attention on her clit instead.

Where Harper said she usually focused while touching herself.

Her hand slides into my hair, gripping tight, and I love the sound of her soft moans. Her hips move beneath my touch as she rolls them on the seat, against my circling tongue.

"Nate," she breathes. A cry cuts off her next half-spoken word, and she arches off the seat, pressing her clit tight to my lips. I suck on the swollen bud and listen to the sound of her soft moans and heavy breaths as pleasure washes over her.

It's the hottest thing I've ever experienced.

Everything with her is the hottest damn thing I've ever experienced.

As her orgasm fades, she still trembles, her fingers still tangled in my hair. I have to fight in the confined space to reach into my pocket and turn off the vibrations.

"I can't believe," she whispers, "that just happened."

Her hands slip from my hair and cover her face, hiding her from my view. I kiss her pussy goodbye and put the toy back in place, but without turning it on now. Pull the thong to rights.

Then, I sit down next to her. The car is moving, has been the entire time, but the traffic makes the progress slow.

"Friends help friends come," I say with my hand on the bare skin of her thigh. Pulling her closer to my side.

She chuckles into her hands. "That must make you the best friend I've ever had."

Her words are sweet. But they sting, the way everything does that reminds me of the differences in our goals. How differently we view one another.

"Harper," I mutter, pulling gently on her wrist. "Don't be embarrassed."

Her hands slip down her face. There's a tiny smudge of black mascara under her left eye, and her skin is flushed and sweaty.

"Was I terribly loud?"

"You were amazing."

She shakes her head in tiny movements, eyes still pleasure-drunk and soft. "I know I can get loud. Oh my God. The driver!"

"He didn't hear a thing," I say. "That partition is soundproof."

"You're sure?"

"Yes. It's a privacy feature, so people can take calls back here."

She relaxes against me. "Oh, thank God."

"And you were not too loud. You were perfect," I say. "And this weekend, when you came, in bed, you didn't make a sound."

"I tried very hard not to," she admits, a soft smile on her lips.

But I'm frowning. "Why?"

Her eyes dip down to my lapels, and she reaches out to play with the satin of my bowtie. Looks at that instead of meeting my eyes. "I don't know if I should tell you," she admits.

An unsettling feeling unfurls inside me. "Does this have to do with the box?"

She nods.

I try hard not to show any reaction. "Tell me anyway. If you want."

"He would say," Harper murmurs, smiling ruefully at my bowtie, "that I was too loud. So I tried not to be."

I freeze like a goddamn statue. Forcing myself not to scowl, not to hiss, not to protest. But I can't help it. "That's the stupidest thing I've ever heard. Fucking Dean. Was that why you were quiet this weekend?"

She nods, and there's a shy look on her face that is so at odds with what we've just done, with my hand on her bare thigh, with her body against mine. "Yeah."

"Don't," I say. "Not with me. I want to hear you. Fuck, Harp, it turns me on."

"It does?"

"Of course it does, as it should any normal red-blooded man." I shake my head, trying to clear the image of Dean from in front of my eyes. The idea that he'd said that to her, that he'd ever implied… that *he* had been allowed to do this to her—to taste her, to feast between her legs—and had the audacity to tell her to be quiet when she came. "I thought Dean was a better man than that."

She chuckles. "Sorry. I don't want to ruin your impression—"

"Fuck that," I say. "Not your responsibility. Besides, if he lost you, then he must have done something wrong."

Her eyes are on mine, and I can't look away from those green depths. From the softness in them and the hesitant emotions swirling within. My fingers stroke along the satiny skin of her outer thigh. She's warm.

"I think everyone believes it's my fault," she says quietly. "Not his."

"Well, I'm guessing *everyone* doesn't know the full story, do they?" I ask. "They shouldn't blame you for things they don't know shit about."

Her lips tip into a smile. "You shouldn't say things like that."

"And why not?" I ask. "It's the honest truth."

Harper's swift fingers have undone the bow tie at my neck and have slipped inside the fabric, brushing against the skin of my throat. "I do like it when you're honest with me. I feel like you're not honest very often with… others."

I raise an eyebrow. "Is that a backhanded compliment?"

"No," she says with a small laugh. "Just an observation. I think you have a lot of acquaintances… people who would consider you their friend. But I don't think you're so quick to return the sentiment. I don't believe you consider many of those same people as friends in return."

Her words feel heavy, and I struggle under the weight of them for a few seconds before I nod once.

"Maybe not," I say. "But I consider you my friend."

A friend I'm hopelessly, painfully and irrevocably in love with.

Her entire face softens with the warmth I feel in my very bones. "I feel honored that you do."

The words are on the tip of my tongue. They feel hot, too pressurized, and I know they'll wreck everything. But looking at the softness in her face, the warmth in her eyes…

"I want—"

There's a knock on the privacy divider from André in the front seat. I glance outside to see the familiar townhouse. The glossy black front door, flanked by two planters of boxwood, and a gold number eight in the center.

"Home," she breathes and pushes open her car door. I follow her out and thank André before heading inside the residence.

I watch her play with the puppies, letting them into the garden, checking on their water bowls… In her silk dress and the diamond necklace, her hair still in that sleek ponytail.

It's so easy to imagine her always living here with me. That this is our home. Our hot dogs. Our life.

My wife.

The word comes unbidden. A fantasy I didn't realize I had until I saw her walking around my kitchen, looking like a movie star.

It's late, past midnight, and the house is mostly dark. It's a weeknight… or I would have suggested we stay up. Order in. Collapse on the couch.

I would pull her into the shower, take the toy out of her, and give her one final orgasm before we'd both fall asleep.

But it is a weeknight… and the tired smile on her face, as she carries Stanley back inside the house, tells me she needs something else right now. Rest.

We say goodnight on her landing, with the dogs pacing around her heels and her mascara still smudged under her left eye. I want to reach out and wipe it away.

I tip her head back, leaning close enough for our lips to almost touch… and whisper, "Take good care of the toy."

She blinks a few times. "I will. I promise."

Once I'm inside my room, I tear off the tux. My skin feels too hot beneath it. My morning is due to start way too early, but I get into the shower nevertheless and replay the memories of the last few hours.

Hottest thing I've ever experienced.

She is so game, so open, so willing… so happy. *Adventurous.* I've never met anyone who means it quite like she does. Who is as earnest about enjoying life as she is.

Who treasures the small moments like she does.

I lie in bed on my back and stare up at my ceiling. It feels familiar. What preceded it does not.

Old.

She'd meant it, when she said it about Austin Silver. Joked about it when I made the point, but… she *had* meant it earlier tonight.

Maybe that's exactly how she sees me. Dean is my age, though. So it hadn't bothered her before. Does it bother her now? I promised Harper never to open the box, the one with her past. But that doesn't mean I don't have questions about it.

What truly happened? What does Harper need out of a relationship? What does she *want?*

I run a hand over my face. Fucking hell, *Dean.* I can't believe the son of a bitch told her she was too loud during sex. The knowledge has settled like a brick in my stomach, and it lessens the guilt that I've been grappling with since Harper moved in.

Lessened it significantly.

He never deserved her.

I knew it the very first night he had decided to speak to her, had walked up and charmed her with his good looks, humor, money, and that all-American smile. His drunken confidence.

She's mine now, I think.

However she wants me, whatever kind of relationship she wants… friends, friends with benefits, or that elusive more. The elusive *all.*

My phone pings.

I hadn't meant to leave the sound on, but now that it's on…

I reach over with a sigh to shut it off entirely.

Until I see the name on the screen.

Harper: Want to sleep down here?

I close my eyes. Breathe in. Breathe out. And then, I'm tossing off the covers and heading down the steps. Knocking twice on the door. Hearing the soft sound of her voice.

Come in.

She's sitting up in bed, her straight hair loose around her shoulders. It's still a new and odd sight to see. She's wearing a camisole. And around her neck, the diamond necklace, shimmering in the soft light of her night lamp.

The two dogs are lying beside the bed. Both are staring at me. Stanley's stubby tail is wagging softly. Quincy is less enthusiastic. The older dog hasn't yet made up his mind about me.

"Hey," she murmurs. "I think I might get… cold."

I walk around to the far side of the bed and pull off my T-shirt. Just boxer briefs will have to do. "We can't have that."

"No, not really." She pulls her hair over one shoulder and gives me a sheepish smile. Her eyes are tired, but happy. "I couldn't unlock this clasp, either. I think it has some sort of safety mechanism to it?"

"Yeah, it's a double clasp. Here." She scoots close, and I get it off her in a few quick moments before laying it on the nightstand.

She burrows deeper under the covers. "Thank you," she murmurs and shuts off the light. "For… everything. I had the most amazing night."

After only a second of hesitation, I slide beneath the blanket, reaching for her in the darkness. She sighs and settles against my body. As if she likes it there.

"Thank you for coming," I murmur. "These sort of events were a lot more boring before you came along."

She chuckles weakly, and it breaks into a giant yawn. "I'm sure you give all your dates sex toys."

"Never have before," I say into her ear.

"I like that." There's a smile in the sound of her voice.

"Mm-hmm. I liked the taste of you."

Another soft sigh. "I liked your taste, too."

"How convenient, then."

"Friends help friends," she murmurs. Another yawn, and then she snuggles even closer. I wrap my arm tighter around her waist, my hand finding purchase on her stomach. My fingers just barely brush the underside of her breast. "Thank you for… lending me the necklace. I've never… worn anything that nice."

Her breathing evens out, and I draw a deep breath. She smells good. Warm and floral and all woman.

"It wasn't a loan," I say.

But she's already asleep.

Chapter 27

Harper

Richard takes a long sip of the tea I'd prepared. I wait, with bated breath.

He swallows. Nods once, and sets the teacup back on the small circular table in Nate's backyard. "Yes," he says. "Very good."

I exhale in relief. "I was worried I steeped it too long this time."

"No, just right," he says. "Jasmine?"

"Yes, from the shop a few streets down."

"I like that store." He leans back in the chair and stretches out his legs with a sigh. The garden is green around us, flowers in full bloom in the beautifully landscaped beds. The space isn't big, but it's luscious, with a single oak in the far left corner that reaches high above the wooden privacy fence.

"I can get you some of it," I say. "Anything you need in the coming weeks, just call and let me know."

Richard's left leg is bandaged from the calf to just below the knee. He looks down at Quincy lying on his lap. The distinguished dachshund with some silver along his snout, matching the distinguished gentleman with lots of silver in his hair. Despite the oppressive heatwave that had struck London in this second week of June, our neighbor is in a long-sleeved button-down and trousers, colorful socks and loafers on his feet.

And a small flat cap, ever-present.

"Thank you," he says and runs an aged hand over Quincy's silky ear. "And thank you for taking care of the boys. I didn't know what to do, when the ambulance people came."

"Anytime."

He shakes his head a tiny bit. "I appreciate it more than you know. Most people… I'm not certain what I would have done if you couldn't look after them."

I reach for my own teacup. "Does your family live nearby?"

"No," he says. Petting Quincy's back, matte compared to Stanley's happy spots. "I have a daughter. She lives in Rome with her family."

"Oh, that's wonderful."

"It is," he says. "But it's far."

"Of course. Does she visit?"

"At times, yes. But I can't say I was the best father while my wife was still alive. I let her… I let her handle most of the social interactions." He shrugs and gives me a sad smile. "Keeping up with what Helen did. That sort of thing."

"It's never too late to learn to do the same," I say.

He chuckles dryly. "Right. Well… maybe not. I also have a brother. In Brighton."

"Brighton? That's much closer," I say. "Are you two close?"

Richard glances toward the house and the wide-open French doors that lead into the modern kitchen. It's early evening, and Nate should be back from work soon. He said he wanted to meet Richard, too.

"Sorry, I had to do the math," Richard says finally. "We haven't spoken in almost seventeen years."

My eyes flare. "Oh. I'm so sorry."

"Another victim of time, I'm afraid. One argument got bigger than it needed to, and we're both stubborn men." He reaches for his tea and looks away, like he's said more than he intended to.

I reach down to pat Stanley. "Think it's something that can be fixed?"

"Maybe. But at this point… I don't know." He clears his throat. "How are things with you and the Aston Martin chap?"

A blush creeps over my cheeks. "We've gotten closer."

"Ah. I suspected you would."

"You did?"

"Of course. From what you told me last time, you two like each other."

I swallow. The concept feels… scary. And right. "Yes. I think we do. But I'm not sure if it's quite that simple."

"It is," Richard says. His voice is perfectly matter-of-fact. "I know it doesn't seem simple when you're in the midst of things. But when you look back at the important times, past them happening… The truth is always painfully clear. Hold on to that."

I smile at him. "You always know what to say."

He gives a surprised chuckle. "No, I most certainly do not. My daughter would laugh if she heard you say that."

"Maybe there's a chance for—"

Footsteps sound close by, and then Nate is approaching over the green grass of his small garden. He's in a suit, no jacket and no tie, and in a pair of sunglasses. Cast against the obvious luxury of his house, he appears like a stranger for a second. Handsome. Wealthy. An image in a glossy newspaper.

But then, he takes off his glasses and looks at me, and he's Nate again. My Nate.

"You must be Richard," he says and extends his hand to the sitting gentleman. "No, please don't get up, don't trouble yourself. Heard you had quite a tumble."

"The damn staircase," Richard says. "Thank you for letting my dogs stay here."

"No trouble at all. I think Harper would even enjoy one of her own." Nate takes a seat across from us. "I'm sorry we didn't get a chance to meet before."

Richard shrugs again. "I saw you once in a while, but I don't think you were home as often. Up until a month ago, that is."

I look at Nate. But he continues to look at Richard, a smile spreading on his face. "Yes. It wasn't a very fun place to be before Harper moved in," he says easily. "I hear you're a fan of my vintage Aston Martin."

"Vintage?" Richard says. "The model you have, I recall when it was brand new."

"Ever had one?"

"Lord, no," he says. "The prices were outrageous then, now they're positively criminal. No offense."

"None taken," Nate says. "Would you like to take a spin in it? When your leg is all healed."

For a long second, Richard doesn't respond at all. Did he hear? Has Nate's offer offended him somehow? I know his leg must be hurting, and Quincy is a small but significant weight on his lap.

"I would like that very much." Richard finally says, and his voice trembles just slightly with emotion.

"What's this?" Nate asks a few hours later, after we'd helped Richard and the dogs home, and I promised to come over tomorrow evening to walk them. Nate is holding up a giant parsnip.

I roll my eyes at him. "God, you're so uncultured."

"And you're a Michelin-star chef."

"I am not. I just have some very basic but useful skills."

He eyes the large wok pan I have going on the stove. "That is not basic. It is most definitely useful, though. Can you live here forever?"

I chuckle. "Maybe. If you're okay with learning some of this."

"I'll learn anything you want," he says.

I hand him a large knife and point to the center island. "Go crazy."

"All these vegetables?"

"All of them. In tiny cubes."

He hums but does exactly as I've asked. Soon, the steady sound of his chopping fills the room, and I set about measuring out the pasta. I feel too hot, still, even though the sun is mostly gone and the night is quickly approaching. My skin feels sticky to the touch.

"I can't believe," he says like he'd read my mind, "that the previous owner didn't put in AC when they renovated."

"It's not a big thing in the UK, as I understand."

"No. But I should have predicted this." He looks across at me, a crooked smile on his face. "You can cook in less clothes, you know. I wouldn't mind."

I hold up a long piece of dry linguine in his direction. "That would violate all kinds of health and safety regulations."

"It's private property. None exist." His eyes glitter. "Imagine how hot you'd look in nothing but an apron… and how much cooler you'd feel."

"I think that goes for you, too, buddy," I say.

Both eyebrows shoot up. "*Buddy*?"

"Yeah," I say, smiling now, also. "Got a problem with that? Buddy."

"Not at all, champ."

I chuckle. "Okay, that one was awful. Old sport."

Nate reaches for a zucchini and starts hacking away at it. His smile is lighting up his face, and my chest feels warm, my cheeks are aching. It's been this way for the past two days, since the movie premiere.

Since the night he slept in my bed… as he did again last night.

But that's it. Nothing more than sleeping in one bed. Even if the need for more is there, ever-present, like a fire smoldering beneath the surface. It punctuates every one of our interactions. Leaves me giddy and my heart racing.

I know what this is, I know exactly what this emotion is, and I can't find it in myself to regret it.

"Old sport," he repeats. "Okay, that was a good one. I'll raise you… pal."

I laugh in surprise as I put the pasta into the water. "Pal? I haven't heard that one in a long time, bro."

"Bro?" he repeats. "I hate—"

My phone rings, and the sound cuts through the kitchen. I turn the water for the linguine down and reach for the device lying on the kitchen island. My mom mentioned that she'd call again on her break, which would be my evening.

"One second," I tell Nate, and hit the answer button before checking who it is.

"Hey, Harper."

Everything in me freezes at the sound of Dean's voice on the other end of the line. It feels too close. Like he's standing right beside me.

"Glad I got a hold of you. Is it evening over there?"

I can't look at Nate. "Yes. I'm cooking dinner."

"Whatcha making?"

I swallow. "Linguine. What's happened?"

"Do I need a reason to call you?" he asks easily. "Don't answer that, actually. I spoke to the caterers today."

"You did? I've already worked out—"

"Some kind of payment plan. Yeah, they told me," he says. "But I don't want you to worry about it. I took care of it."

Dread sinks through me like a stone in a pond. "Don't tell me you paid it in full."

"I did," Dean says. "It's not right to keep them waiting, Harper."

"I wasn't going to keep them waiting. I was going to pay it

off in four months, with interest, and they said they were *fine* with—"

"I'm fine with handling it," he interrupts. "And who knows, we might even be able to get some kind of future credit if we hire them again. They're usually fully booked."

"Dean, I told you I wanted to pay my half. I've told you this over and over again." I run a hand over my face, struggling to keep my voice steady. Across the kitchen island Nate has gone very still.

Damn. He's hearing all of this. *Seeing* all of this. Embarrassment mixes with frustration within me.

"You don't have to," he says. "I got you, honey. I'll always have you."

"No, you won't. You *can't.* That's the whole point—we're not together anymore."

"No, we're not," he says. "And that was your decision. A decision I still don't understand. I thought we had it good. Didn't I treat you nice?"

"Yes, you… that's not what this is about. I have tried to explain this to you. I told you that night," I say, "exactly why I made this decision. And I will pay my half of the wedding expenses."

"Okay," Dean says, but it's his placating voice, the one I hate the most. It sounds like he's speaking to a child who doesn't understand any better. "I'm sure you will. In due time. There's no rush, Harper."

Only that he'll continue being wedged in my life until my debt is paid. And now, it's not the caterer or the venue that are my creditors. He is.

When all I want is to stand on my own two feet.

And Dean knows it, damn it. He knows that I'll want to pay back what I owe, and to do that, I'll have to keep in contact with him. Irritation strikes me so hot and fast that it brings tears to my eyes.

"Dean," I say. "You called my mom a few weeks back. I *never* want you to do that again."

His voice takes on a tone of feigned hurt. "We were almost family, Harper. I care about your mother. She and Greg don't understand what happened, either."

"Don't call them again. I mean it."

"I can't make that promise."

Frustration makes me groan into the phone. "Why are you doing this? Why can't you just let me go? What's the *point,* Dean?"

He's silent for a long moment.

Like I've actually stumped him for once.

"You left me," he says. "And that was the wrong move." His voice comes across as confident, but there's a hint of wobbliness to his words.

"Screw you," I whisper. "You know exactly what you're doing."

"Have a good night in London, Harper," he says. "Enjoy the food. I sure miss your cooking."

The line goes silent, and I put the phone down with a trembling hand. The exasperation feels so palpable in me that I need to scream, to cry, to thrash. Something. Anything.

I rub my eye, but tears have already overflowed. They race down my cheek, and I hurry to brush them away.

"Harper," Nate says. His voice is soft in the otherwise quiet kitchen, punctuated only by the sound of boiling water.

"I hate him," I say fiercely. More tears make it hard to see, I'm so angry. "I hate him, and I know he's your be— your *best* friend, but I hate him so much. Why can't he just listen to me? Why can't he leave me alone?"

I can't really make out Nate's expression. But his eyes are on mine, that I see, and rapidly approaching.

His hands are on my shoulders the next instant. "Are you okay?"

"No. I'm pissed off. I'm crying because I'm *angry,* not because I'm sad. Okay? Because I'm not sad."

"Okay," he repeats. His thumb smoothes over my cheek, brushing away a tear. "What did he say?"

"The usual bullshit. He paid off the entire cancellation fee for the caterer. And that's on top of the original deposit, the one we can't get back, that we put down with his money. A few weeks ago, I tried to make a payment for the venue, and I was told that they had already received it!" I shake my head and force my voice under control. It's trembling, and I hate how shaky everything is coming out, how weak. I'm *angry,* damn it.

"I see," Nate says. But he doesn't sound like he sees at all. "And you want to pay your half?"

"Yes! Because otherwise… otherwise, he is going to hold it over me forever."

"How can he?"

"Oh, he's sneaky. He'll find ways. Like calling my parents or guilting me about his family… He knows that I wanted to pay my portion, to be free of any kind of debt to him. But now, it means I'll have to pay *him* every month for the rest of my… well… until I've paid it off." I shake my head. "I've tried *so hard* to get away from him. And here he is! Making it impossible."

"He wants you back," Nate says. "And he wants to punish you."

"Yes." I reach for the paper towels on the kitchen island and use it to dry my cheeks. A humorless laugh escapes me. "God, I'm so sorry you heard all of that. I never meant to drag you into… that."

"To open the box," he says quietly. "You wanted it to remain untouched at the back of some shelf somewhere."

"Yeah." I blow out a breath, my tears slowing down. The burst of anger fades as quickly as it had come, simmering down to the low-level annoyance I've felt since I left Dean. "I know he means… a lot to you."

Nate shrugs. "We were college friends."

"You were going to be his best man. At the wedding."

"Yes," he says. But the corners of his mouth tip into a

crooked, not entirely happy smile. "I think we both know that Dean is a bit more calculating in his decisions, though."

I blink at him. I hadn't known that Nate noticed that.

"I'm not an idiot," he says. "I know when people want me for me, and when they want what my money or influence can get them."

"Oh," I say with a swallow. "He did always seem... jealous of you."

"More so in the past decade," Nate says. He runs a hand in his hair and looks away, toward the stove and the water still boiling there. "I don't think either of us has been a... loyal friend in the last few years."

I shake my head. "You haven't done anything."

"Mm-hmm," he says, but it doesn't sound like he believes me. His gaze turns concerned. "Is this part of the reason you called it off? The wedding?"

I wet my lips. Are we really going there?

But Nate is my friend. And I no longer suspect he'll go to Dean. "Part of it," I say. "But there was more..."

Nate nods and takes a few steps back. Toward the built-in wine fridge. "White or red?" he asks.

I smile at him in gratitude. "Yeah, I think I need that. White? It's too warm for red."

"You got it." He chooses a bottle and motions for me to continue. So I do, sinking down at the kitchen table. Watching as he pours us a glass each.

"It didn't start out that way. I mean, you saw us, right? We had a great time together," I say.

Nate's jaw tenses, eyes focused on the wine he's pouring. "Yeah."

"But somewhere over the past years, I realized... I had lost myself. And became what he wanted. We spent the summers the way he wanted, visiting people up and down the Eastern Seaboard who he wanted to see. I tried applying to two internships before this one, one in Boston and one in Paris...

and he discouraged me from both. Said it would be unwise. And I believed that."

Dean was never going to let me be myself. And it took me a long time to wake up to that, and also to realize that, somehow, I had accepted it to the point where I no longer knew exactly what or who I was.

What I actually wanted.

"You wanted to get out of your old job for a while?" Nate asks. He's leaning against one of the French doors, eyes on me.

"I think so. Yes. Even though, at the time, I wasn't aware of it myself. Dean used to say it wasn't the right time… that I should be happy to even have a job with something as useless as an art history degree." I shake my head, and mortification makes it hard to find the words. I'm still embarrassed over what Nate had just witnessed. What he understood. "Dean took care of so many things. It was *his* nice apartment I moved into. And his money that bought groceries. He loved to… throw that in my face. Sometimes. And I took it."

Nate's voice is soft. "He did *what*?"

I bury my face in my hands. "Oh God. It's so embarrassing to say it out loud, now that I'm away from it all."

"It's not embarrassing," Nate says. His voice is sharp. "It's a lot of things, but that word is very far off target."

"He made me feel like I owed him. All the time," I say. "Like his word was the final word, like it was either do it his way… or no way. Did you know that his mother picked out my wedding dress?"

Nate's eyes narrow. "You weren't allowed to choose your own dress?"

"Oh, I tried to. But in the end, it was *heavily* encouraged for me to go with a more traditional option." I laugh weakly. "That's the one thing I won't insist on paying half for. It wasn't my choice."

Nate crosses his arms over his chest, the wineglass in his left hand. His jaw clenched.

He looks angry.

I hadn't anticipated that.

"And Dean knew all of that," he says.

"Yeah. I think it all came *from* him. The last straw, the thing that told me I couldn't stay another day was… It's so awful to say."

"I'm listening," he says quietly.

"I overheard him saying something on the phone. He didn't even try to hide it, to be fair. Somehow that felt terrible? He thought I wouldn't *care* when he told someone that my career would be over after the wedding, or at the very least, when we had kids. He called my art degree *decorative."*

Nate makes a low, hoarse sound. "Fuck. I'm so sorry."

"Looking back on it, he'd made that position clear before, but he'd never *said* it. Not like that. And I realized he didn't think I was capable of anything, not of my job, or of earning my own money, and definitely didn't respect me. At all. That word, *decorative,* really pushed me over the limit, at any rate."

"Broke the camel's back," Nate says. He shakes his head slowly, his jaw tense. "You left that day?"

I nod. "Yes. I wanted out of his cage, and all the strings he attached to *everything,* every exchange between us. That's what—shoot!"

The water boils over.

I spring to my feet and race to the stove. Put my glass down. "The pasta won't be very al dente, I'm afraid!"

"It will be delicious," Nate says. He's followed me, his voice closer by. Anger still laced through his tone. But now it has a hesitant note in it. "You know that there aren't and never will be any strings with me, right?"

I look down at the pasta and feel another kind of blush creeping up my cheeks. *With me.* We haven't discussed… what we are. Not yet.

But the way he said it…

"I know," I say. "Trust me, you're nothing like Dean."

He brushes my hair away from the back of my neck, and

then there's a pair of lips against the hot skin at my nape. His hands glide over my hips.

"In one way," he murmurs, his lips trailing down my bare shoulder, "we are very much alike. He had great taste in women."

I close my eyes at the sensation. "Is that a compliment, Connovan?"

He pulls my hips against his. "Yes," he says. "So, you want to go to Paris?"

"One day," I say. Nate's nearness is chasing away the hurt from the past, and letting my frustration slowly wash away.

"One day," he repeats. He rests his head on top of mine, and we both watch as I stir the pasta and sauce together into one delicious, creamy mixture. "How does this Friday sound?"

Chapter 28

Nate

I choose the Land Rover. Spacious, less conspicuous, and significantly less valuable. It has our bags in the back and ample legroom in the front. Plus a radio, which is key for Harper, who is handling the music on the drive.

London to the Channel takes no time at all. The Channel itself is slightly more of a hassle, waiting in line at Folkestone for our turn to drive onto the train shuttle. Harper makes soft *oohing* sounds at all of it. "So we can't drive the tunnel ourselves?"

"Not allowed," I say, and can't help the rueful note in my voice.

She laughs at me. "Twenty minutes of darkness?"

"Give or take, yes."

"And then we'll be in France." She reaches for her phone and changes the song to something in French; something I don't know, and clearly she doesn't, either. She smiles wide and leans back in the seat. "Did you say you had a business dinner tomorrow?"

"Unfortunately, yes. I've been needing to meet them for a while now. They could only do dinner."

"That's fine," she says. "Who are they?"

"Thierry works for Contron and Janos is a consultant we're hiring for an expansion into Eastern Europe. They're spearheading a project my brother has put a lot of money behind."

"That sounds exciting."

I give her a crooked smile. "You don't have to pretend."

"I'm not, I promise."

"The only downside is that it takes away from one of our two evenings in Paris," I say.

"Yeah," she says. "Or I can come with you."

My eyebrows rise. "You'd do that?"

Her smile widens. "I think I'd enjoy watching you work. I never have before, not really."

I run a hand through my hair and find myself liking the idea far too much. The idea of her being next to me. It feels like she belongs there. "You're very welcome to join."

She pulls her legs up and wraps her arms around her knees. There's a spark in her green depths. "Okay. Looking forward to it."

I narrow my eyes at her. "You look like you're planning something."

"I'm the epitome of innocence," Harper says, blinking dramatically.

"Mm-hmm. Why do I find that hard to believe?"

"Because you're a deeply distrustful man," she says, but she's grinning. "Tell me about the hotel you've booked."

"What a seamless segue."

She rolls her eyes, but her smile widens. "Tell me."

So I do.

All in all, Calais to Paris takes us almost four hours. We stop at a tiny village, and then at another one at Harper's request, before rolling into the City of Light. I've done this trip a few times previously, but the drive on the ring road around Paris, seeing the glittering Eiffel Tower in the distance, is still magnificent. *Le dame de fer*—the Iron Lady—rises above all of the other buildings.

It's late by the time we get to our hotel. My assistant booked the usual—a luxurious historic hotel located by Place

Vendôme, only a stone's throw from the Tuileries Garden. A valet takes care of my Jeep.

That alone makes this hotel leaps and bounds more appealing than any other place in the city. I won't be taking any risks with street parking, which is always a concern, regardless of leaving my Aston Martin behind.

The heat wave that's holding London in its grip hasn't reached Paris yet, or maybe it came from here, I don't know. At any rate, the evening air is warm but comfortable, nowhere near the sweltering conditions we left across the Channel.

Harper marvels at everything as we walk to dinner. Even at this hour, the restaurant is packed. When she can't decide between a few dishes, I tell the waiter to bring them all.

"I can't believe," she says, dipping a piece of fluffy white bread into the sauce that surrounds a single large lamb shank, "that we're really here."

"I can. This place is decidedly French," I comment. "As it should be."

She looks at our neighbors—a group who's fashionably dressed and laughing loudly. They're on their fifth shared bottle of wine. "It is. I love it. I love all of this. Nate…"

"Don't thank me," I say and hold up my hand. "This is as much your trip as it is mine."

"We both know that's not true," she says, and a faint shadow crosses her features. It makes me frown.

She's still struggling. Dean and his fuckign domineering.

And although I'm paying for this trip… it doesn't mean that she isn't in control. That she doesn't have a say in it.

"It is. I've been here a few times and have never gone to the art museums, which is a travesty, I know. Don't say it too loud so the others can hear. Which ones are we visiting tomorrow?"

Her face lights up with a brilliant smile. "Really?"

"Really."

"Well, we have to go to the Louvre, of course. That might take quite a bit of the day."

"I'm game."

"And then, I really, really want to see the Musée d'Orsay. It's close, right nearby. So is the Musée de l'Orangerie. The most incredible Monet is there."

"I can't wait," I say.

She rolls her eyes. "Ha-ha, I know, but if you need to step out or take a phone call, please do. Don't feel like you have to follow me around."

"I'm serious. I want to go."

A small smile spreads across her face. "You do? You're interested?"

"Yes. What's more, I'm very interested in seeing you happy, and I have a feeling you'll explain things that I don't know. It's like, I'll be getting a private tour of some of the grandest museums in the world."

She giggles, and the sound feels like victory. "I don't know these places. I've never been before."

"No, but you have a degree in art history, and I don't know Michelangelo from Machiavelli."

"Yes, you do."

"Fine, I do," I admit. She smiles and reaches for another spoonful of the garlic mashed potatoes. We've got too much food. I'd known that when I ordered and done it anyway, but it's worth it just for the smile on her face.

I think I've become addicted to it.

Provoking it. Inspiring it. Being on the receiving end of it.

It's midnight when we finally walk back to the hotel. The streets are quiet for a Friday, but then again, we're not in the party district. A few taxis slow down for us, but I wave them off.

Our room is grand, decorated with ornate wallpaper, and with a beautiful view out of the Tuileries Gardens and, beyond, the effervescent glow of the Eiffel Tower. The focal point of the bedroom, though, is large and covered in fluffy white hotel linens. A lone bed. But this time… it's on purpose.

Harper changes in the bathroom and emerges wearing the same outfit she's slept in at home for the past few days. A camisole and shorts. Her hair is braided and hangs down her back, but small curls have managed to escape and frame her face in wispy ringlets. She's beautiful. And tired, trying to cover a yawn with her hand.

I'm lying on my back on top of the covers.

"Hey," she says, smiling.

"Hi."

She pads across the space to her side of the bed. *Her side.* I feel too light. Like I'm not living in this reality, but some kind of fantasy, a world where I get to do things like this.

We haven't spoken about it. About us.

Haven't said a word more than *friends help friends come* and *want to sleep down here?* Everything else has been unspoken, unsaid, the words too real to be uttered. We're still just mere friends who find each other attractive.

Bringing up this discussion might change things.

Might change everything.

Harper climbs into bed, and I head to the bathroom to brush my teeth. When I return, she's snuggled in the covers, and the room is silent apart from her soft breathing. It's also dark, lit only by the lights from beyond the window.

"Want me to close the blinds?" I ask.

Her voice is sleepy. "No. I can see the Eiffel Tower from where I'm lying. I want to see it all night long."

"While you're sleeping?"

"I want to know it's there," she says. "And I want to wake up to it. Is that okay?"

"Of course it's okay." I slide in behind her, not hesitating in the least now. She's already turned her back to me and is lying on her side, perfectly arched.

I've learned to spot her invitations.

Shifting nearer to her side, I wrap my arm around her

waist. I've skipped the T-shirt tonight, and the bare skin of her arms and upper back is silky against mine.

"You're right," I say into the fragrant mass of her hair. "You can see the Eiffel Tower from here."

"I don't want this weekend to ever end," she whispers.

I tighten my grip around her. "It won't."

There's a smile in her voice. "I added something to my list."

"Did you? This system of yours is very convenient."

She sighs. "This isn't something I've done, yet."

"Oh? What is it?"

I settle deeper into the softness of the bed, closer to Harper's warmth, and slide my leg between hers. Feel the rise and fall of this incredible woman's chest beneath my arm, and watch the distant lights of the city.

"I want to kiss someone in front of the Eiffel Tower."

My smile is hidden against her neck. "Someone?"

"Mm-hmm." Beneath the covers, her hand covers mine, pulling it up to her chin. "Someone like you."

Experiencing Paris with Harper is better than both of the previous times I'd been in the city for business. By miles. She's genuinely happy, authentically curious, and wondrously amazed at everything we see. I don't know if I've ever known such sincerity.

She cries in the Louvre.

"Happy tears, I promise," she says, standing in front of a giant wall of renaissance portraits. A tear tracks down her cheek. "It's just… I've read so much about this place and heard so much, and I just never…"

I press a kiss to her temple. "I get it."

"Do you cry at car shows?" she asks, brushing the back of her hand along the line of her jaw.

"Well, no. Not recently."

"When did you cry last?"

"How did this get turned around on me?"

She smiles and rests her head against my shoulder, her eyes on the giant painting. "Because you fascinate me. Almost as much as this magnificent example of renaissance chiaroscuro."

"*Almost* as much," I murmur.

"Mm-hmm. That's high praise."

I wrap an arm around her waist. "Oh, I know, coming from you."

The rest of the day is filled with more joy than I can remember feeling in a long time.

I've never identified as an unhappy man. The years had been good to me. I've made enjoyment a priority, once I stopped competing with Alec. Work hard. Play hard.

Buy expensive cars.

Drive expensive cars.

Travel, meet people, drink, travel some more, buy another watch, move into the townhouse, attend a conference in Japan. One thing after the other, and it's all been satisfying.

But the last few months have been so decidedly different that it's hard not to see the truth. That there was a before and an after. Before Harper moved in. After Harper moved in. And the difference is so stark I might as well have become an entirely different man.

Hollow.

That's the right word for how I lived before. And how I will live again, if she once again slips out of my grasp.

"Look at that," Harper says. We're walking along the Seine, toward where the Eiffel Tower rises in the distance. Harper stops and points across the river, at the row of stands. "They're selling… art. I think."

"Prints, most likely. Come on." We cross the bridge, and she peruses through various offerings of the tiny market. My gaze snags on a picture of a vintage car painted on a thin canvas. It looks like the Ferrari 250 GTO, one of the greatest cars ever built.

Harper notices my interest. "Buy it," she whispers. "I know that you want to."

"Is that your professional opinion, as my art adviser?"

"Yes. I think that artist is one to watch."

"Will his work appreciate in value?"

"Yes," she says. "Sentimental value."

We leave the stand with two rolled-up canvas prints in a tube. The walk is beautiful—as most things in Paris are—and chaotic, and all other things it tends to be. The riverside wall along the Seine is peppered with tourists and Parisians alike, enjoying the fine weather.

The Eiffel Tower disappears when we draw near, hidden behind the tall buildings around us. The seventh arrondissement is old and storied, and the stone structures here are imposing.

And then, we turn a corner, and *she* appears.

Grand, and forcing one to look so far up that it gives you a crick in the neck.

Harper grabs my hand and pulls me forward. I follow her, loving this side of her. The side that takes what she wants.

I want her to have everything she wants.

"Oh my God," she says. "Look at that. It's so much taller than I thought!"

"Used to be the tallest structure in the world," I say. "Before us New Yorkers ruined that with the Chrysler Building."

"How rude," she says softly.

"Well, the French sort of ruined it for us first, by building the Eiffel Tower and beating the Washington Monument."

We come to a stop on the lawn. Around us, people are picnicking, sitting on the grass, drinking wine. Laughing.

Enjoying a summer day in Paris.

I wait until she's looked her fill, until she turns back to me with excitement in her eyes. Then I pull her in close.

"Oh," she breathes. Understanding fills her eyes, and her eyelashes flutter close.

I kiss her. Right there, beneath the Eiffel Tower in the late afternoon sun and with hundreds of people around us.

My lips ache from the sweetness of her kiss. The ache I've missed since our last kiss at the movie premiere. Since that hidden closet.

This kiss is new. In the open. But still as sweet.

I want to kiss her every day. Morning, noon, and night.

Harper's hands glide up my shirt, finding the linen collar. She grabs a hold of it and tugs like she wants me even closer.

She tastes delicious. Like the white wine we shared at lunch and the mint from chewing gum. Her soft lips move over mine, and when I slide my tongue into the warmth of her mouth, she opens for me as if she's been waiting for it.

"Another couple in Paris," someone says nearby. It's a British voice, and an exasperated one at that.

"It's the city of love," another one comments. "Don't begrudge them."

"Yes, but snogging in public?"

"They're in love," the second voice says. "Don't be a grouch."

Harper pulls away, a laugh bubbling out of her. She buries her face against my neck, and her laughter tickles my skin.

I wrap my arms around her.

"Don't be a grouch," she murmurs against my neck.

The speakers in question are occupying a giant blanket a few feet away, enjoying the sunshine and a box of wine. Students, by looking at them.

They're in love.

I smooth a hand over Harper's back. "Don't be embarrassed."

"I'm not," she murmurs and pulls back to meet my gaze. Her hands are still holding on tightly to the collar of my button-down, and there's a beautiful flush spreading across her cheeks. She's gotten a few new freckles over her nose from the day in the sun. "And Nate?"

"Yes?"

"I'm going to pay you back tonight," she says, a smile curving her full lips. "For what you did to me at the movie premiere."

Chapter 29

Harper

I choose my outfit with care. A short red tweed skirt, a pair of loafers, and a silk dress shirt lazily tucked into my skirt.

Typically, I always wear this skirt with stockings. It's almost indecently short otherwise. But as I turn in front of the large mirror in the hotel room, listening to the sound of Nate showering in the en suite bathroom… the omission is perfect for what I've got planned.

I run some hair oil through my curls and put a black headband in place to keep them off my face. Do my makeup.

And when he emerges from the bathroom, I'm all done, sitting on the couch with a glass of wine from the minibar.

Nate has a towel wrapped around his waist as he exits and is using a smaller one to dry his hair. He does a double-take when he sees me, and his actions seem to fall completely still.

"You okay?" I ask sweetly.

His gaze feels hot as it runs down the length of my bare legs. "That's what you're wearing?"

"It is indeed. Like it? I found this skirt at a thrift store years ago. I know how you like vintage things."

"It… leaves little to the imagination."

I look down at the hemline, where it sits midthigh. "Hmm. Maybe I should be careful about not bending over."

"You better be," he says, but there's fire in his eyes and a hint of a smile. "I'll be ready in five. Don't bend over, or we might not make it out of here at all."

I make my eyes wide. "Oh? What would happen?"

He chuckles and tugs the towel from around his waist. Pulling it away.

The smirk is wiped off my face. He always seems so comfortable with this, being naked in front of me. Wasn't the least bit self-conscious when I walked in on him jerking off in the shower.

And why would he be?

My eyes linger on his flat stomach, the hint of a V, his chest hair. And the length of his cock, sizable even when he's not hard.

"I'd describe it to you," he says, reaching for a pair of boxer briefs, "but then we'd be late."

I swallow hard. "Yeah. We… can't have that."

He puts them on and tucks himself in neatly. Reaches into the closet for a starched white button-down. "It wouldn't be professional," he says, "to introduce you to my colleagues with your face still sweaty after an orgasm. Or two."

I push off the couch. "You're awfully confident."

"Competent," he says. "That's the word."

I walk past him but don't make it far. He wraps an arm around my waist and pulls me against him. He smells like soap and aftershave, and I take a deep breath.

"Feeling good?" he asks me, mouth hovering over mine.

"I feel amazing," I whisper back.

He smiles and kisses me again. It's warm and minty, and I crush the pristine collar of his pressed shirt in my hand. "Good," he says. "Did you like it when I hit your G-spot?"

I blink against him. "What?"

He chuckles and releases me, grinning widely. Puts on his cuff links like he didn't just say the most outrageous thing. "I need to plan what I'll do to you later."

"Tonight is about torturing you," I say.

His smile widens. "And I'm looking forward to it. But I still want your notes, Harp."

"What if I have no notes?"

"Everyone has notes," he says. Pulls on a pair of pressed gray pants and unrolls a leather belt. I watch his strong hands fasten it with quick precision. "I want to make you come a hundred different ways, and I want you to tell me exactly how you need it. Do you like G-spot orgasms?"

"I think so. I think… the one you gave me at the inn was my first."

He runs a hand along his stubbly jaw. "Mm-hmm. That shouldn't make me feel good, but it does."

I roll my eyes at him and grab my clutch. "You're such a man," I chide. But I'm blushing.

"Of course I am. Tell me, did you enjoy it?"

"Who doesn't enjoy an orgasm?"

"Maybe I just want to hear you say it." He puts on his shoes, and then we're heading out of the room. "Maybe I just need some words of affirmation."

Now it's my turn to chuckle. "As if!"

He grins and pushes the button for the elevator. "I enjoyed it. Enjoyed eating you out in the back of my car, too. But I'm really going to enjoy doing it somewhere I can spread your thighs properly wide."

My mouth goes dry, and I look around the corridor. There's no one else here… that I can see. "Nate!"

"What?" he asks, still grinning crookedly. Knowing exactly what he's doing.

"You can't say things like that," I say under my breath. The elevator doors open, and he gestures for me to enter.

I step ahead of him into the gilded cage.

"And why not?" he says. "It's the truth. And you told me you like my honesty."

I roll my eyes. "Someone could overhear you."

"Yes, they might," he says matter-of-factly. "And if they do, they'd hear a man burning with a need for you."

His words make my mouth dry again. I look at the numbers on the indicator. Sixth floor, fifth floor… almost at the bottom.

So I lean closer, rising on my tiptoes until our mouths nearly touch. "Want to burn even more?" I ask and wait a heart beat. "I'm not wearing panties underneath this skirt."

The grin vanishes off his face. "What?"

I take a few steps back and smile at him. "I guess I forgot. Whoops."

"Harper," he says, but then the elevator doors open. Several hotel guests await outside, and I walk by the group like I'm not at all feeling the breeze along my bare legs… or between them.

Nate is silent during our short walk to the restaurant where we're set to meet his business associates. It's not a calm, comfortable silence. It's the silence of a man who is trying very, very hard not to crack.

The reservation is under Connovan, and the two men with whom he is meeting are already there, or so the hostess says. She leads us through a dimly lit interior where the candles are burning on every surface. The decor is old-school, with a slight burlesque touch to it, and I love it.

I feel like someone else tonight. Someone powerful. Someone in control. Someone… desired.

We join Thierry and Janos in a booth at the back of the restaurant. Thierry is French, Janos is Hungarian, and they're both easy to get along with. They seem to have a natural rapport with Nate, and it's clear they've all worked together for years. Despite his corporate role likely being the men's superior, the conversation feels easy. He makes me feel included—effortlessly, easily, more than just a prop.

I order a glass of champagne and the steak tartare, and listen with interest as they talk about Contron. I'm learning more from this conversation than I've ever done while previously peppering Nate with all my questions.

Halfway through my meal, I accidentally drop my linen

napkin onto the floor. "Whoops," I say and slide my chair back. I glance at Nate, sitting across from me. "Guess I'll just have to bend—"

His chair makes a sharp screech on the tiles as he pushes it back. "Don't you dare," he mutters and reaches for the cloth. Hands it back to me, his eyes dark.

I smile at him sweetly. "Thank you, Nathaniel."

I never call him Nathaniel.

His nostrils flare. "You're welcome, Harper."

Thierry and Janos don't make any comments on this weird exchange. On the contrary, they take it in stride, shifting the discussion to ask me about my work.

The soft clank of cutlery against plates. Food quickly disappearing. And beneath the linen-clad table, I slip my foot out of my shoe and extend it across toward Nate.

I've never done this before.

I keep eye contact with Janos, nodding at whatever he says, and slide my toes up Nate's lower leg. Find his knee and then the inner thigh, wedging my foot closer to his groin.

Nate makes a choking sound and reaches for his wine.

"You okay?" Janos asks.

"Yeah. I'm fine. Just a bit hard," he says. "My lamb, that is. It's slightly tough."

"Oh, I'm sorry about that," Thierry says earnestly. "We should call the waiter. This place is known for—"

Nate waves his offers away. "No, no, that's all right," he says, putting his fork down.

While he asks Thierry about an upcoming conference in Copenhagen, Nate's hand disappears beneath the table and encircles my ankle in a steel grip.

Keeping it in place.

He shoots me a dark look.

I give him a wide smile. "Copenhagen? Will you be attending?"

"I might," he says. His voice sounds unusually strained.

At my side, Thierry nudges my shoulder. "You should go

with him, if you have the time. It's a beautiful city, Copenhagen. Very different from Paris or London. It's really like nowhere else."

"That's not a bad idea," I say and look back at Nate.

"Of course it's not," Janos says. "A beautiful lady is the best travel companion."

They're both smiling at us like we're a couple. The insinuation, the clear expectation in their eyes, makes my chest warm.

Nate's looking at me, while beneath the table, his thumb makes slow circles on my calf. "Indeed she is," he states. But then, he taps his thumb against my skin in a few quick movements, and I hear what he can't say out loud. *When she behaves herself.*

I smile into my napkin.

When everyone is done with the main course and another bottle of wine is ordered, I excuse myself from the table. Nate watches as I stand and tug the skirt down to make sure it's in place. I smile at him before walking away. It's not a vibrator I'm using on the delectable man, but it is definitely getting him rattled, and I've never loved teasing someone more.

It makes me feel amazing to know that he wants me like this.

And that he hasn't been shy about telling me or showing just how much.

I ask a waiter for the restroom, and he points me toward the back. Weaving around a few tables, I eventually step into a small hallway with two doors clearly marked as gents and ladies.

As I'm opening the door to the women's washroom, someone puts their hand beside mine on the wooden surface. "Get inside," Nate says.

We both end up in a small red room, and Nate locks the door behind us. It's a beautiful restroom, matching the decor outside, with dim lighting and a boudoir-esque wallpaper.

Nate's hands find my waist. "You're insane tonight."

"Am I? Or am I driving you insane?"

"Is there a difference?" he asks, his voice hoarse. "I feel like we're the same person sometimes." His hands glide over my shirt, my hips, down to my ass. His fingers find the hem of my skirt. "I need to check."

My breathing ratches up by about a billion degrees. "I told you the truth."

"Maybe you did," he says gruffly and starts tugging up my skirt. "Maybe you've been sitting out there with your pussy bare against the seat, ready to bend over for a napkin and show Thierry everything that's mine."

I grip his shoulders. Heat is already flowing through me, singeing my skin. "You're really going to check."

"I'm really going to check," he says against my lips, and his hand slides between my legs.

Chapter 30

Harper

His hand cups me entirely. "Fuck," he mutters. "You were telling the truth."

I stand on my tiptoes and put my mouth to his ear. "I would never lie to you."

He curses again, and his fingers move, stroking through my folds. He presses his thumb to my clit, and a pulse of pleasure spreads through my limbs.

"You know," he says, mouth ghosting over the shell of my ear and his hand on my pussy, "we haven't had sex, yet."

My breaths are fast and shallow. "I know."

"If you're pulling stuff like this... does that mean you want to? Because touching you like this…" he runs a long finger along my slit, stopping at my clit, "and learning just how sweet you can be…" his fingers start to circle, "has made me wonder what you'd feel like around my cock."

"Oh," I breathe. My hands grip Nate's shoulders tightly. Over his shoulder, I see the washroom door. Still shut and locked. Keeping everyone else out. The idea of that closed door makes my heart beat so hard, I hear it thundering behind my ribs. "Maybe you should… try it. Let's check off number… thirteen."

Sleep with someone who is wrong for me.

But everything I've done with him feels so right.

"Try it," he mutters. "There'll be no trying, Harp. Once we have sex…" His fingers leave my clit. Move downward, stroking, and then he pushes two inside me. My eyes flutter closed at the sweet sensation.

"Yes?" I whisper.

He curls them. "Us sleeping together won't be a one-time thing. You know that, right? Once I know just how good you feel around me, the way you're squeezing my fingers right now, I'll need you over and over again. And we live together, baby. So that'll be often. Every day. Every fucking day."

I've never been so turned on before as I feel when I'm with him. At the movie premiere. In the back of his car. On the hard-tiled floor of his shower.

It's like my body surrenders completely to him. Every impulse, craving, everything I'm feeling… My brain completely shuts off. And I'm simply in the moment.

"Can you handle that, Harper?" he asks. His voice is in my ear, his cheek against mine. I breathe in deeply, and it's only him—the man and cologne and soap. "Orgasm after orgasm after orgasm…"

"Sounds hard," I breathe.

"I will be, that's for sure," he mutters. "Fuck, I need you so bad."

My voice is faint. "Then have me."

"Not here," he says and curses again. His fingers are still inside me, deliciously thick yet still not thick enough, stroking slowly. "The first time I fuck you, I want to be able to see you. Completely."

"Then take me back to the hotel."

He kisses me for a hot second and then pulls his fingers out. The sudden loss makes the air catch in my lungs.

"I wish I had the toy for you," he mutters. Then, without breaking our locked stare, he puts the two fingers he just withdrew into his mouth.

"Oh," I breathe.

"I'm an addict." He grabs my hand, and his voice is rough. "Let's make our excuses and leave. I need you."

We make it to the door before he suddenly stops. "Are you on birth control?"

"Yes."

He closes his eyes and swallows, hard. I see his Adam's apple bob with the force of it. "Jesus," he grunts and pulls the door open.

Thierry and Janos are still at the table. They're engrossed in a conversation and give us wide smiles when we return.

"Harper!" Janos says. "We ordered the tiramisu for you."

Shit.

I open my mouth to say thank you, but Nate beats me to it. "I'm afraid we have to leave. But we appreciate the gesture, gentlemen."

Janos glances between us with another wide grin. "I understand. You really do make a beautiful couple."

"Better than you deserve," Thierry says to Nate and reaches over to shake his hand.

A blush creeps up my cheeks. It's his right hand. Same hand…

Nate shakes Thierry's firmly. "I know, but I'm not planning on letting her go."

"You'd be crazy to," the Frenchman says. He kisses my cheek, and then we're off, out into the warm Parisian evening air.

We barely make it into the hotel elevator before Nate kisses me. The cab is small and it moves slowly with creaking sounds toward the seventh floor.

Once inside our suite, the door shuts behind us with a sharp, determined click.

Leaving us alone in the luxurious, quiet space.

Looking at each other.

Nate's eyes… I haven't seen such intensity in them before. I'm not sure he can't look away. There's a glimpse of something tightly leashed in his gaze, threatening to escape at the slightest crack in his control.

I walk to the minibar. "Champagne?"

He nods, just a single dip of his chin. "Yes. Let's."

My hands tremble slightly as I uncork the chilled bottle. Pour us both a flute and turn to see him undoing his cufflinks. Folding up the sleeves of his shirt.

Outside the window, the Eiffel Tower is putting on another late-night light display.

I'm nervous.

Warm. Anxious. Excited.

He's Nate. My friend, Nate. And everything we've done together… things that I've never experienced before, none of them were *this.* Sex. Until now, we were just having "fun." *Friends helping friends.*

He walks closer, his eyes on mine. Accepts the glass of champagne. We both watch each other take a sip.

The bubbles are silk down my throat.

"Do you think the dinner went well? Businesswise?"

"Yes." He raises an eyebrow, and his gaze drops down. "I think you impressed. In that shirt… and that damned skirt."

"It was a risk."

"I like risks," he says. "And I spent the entire dinner wondering what would happen if slipped my hand under your hemline."

My throat feels tight. "That was the point."

"Remember when you dropped your bath towel?" he rasps and steps closer. So close that our bodies are separated by a mere inch. "Outside your room?"

"Yes," I whisper. "You promised to forget what you saw."

He bends his head, and I rise on my tiptoes, needing his lips. But he skirts past them. Trails his mouth toward my ear instead. "I've broken that promise every day since."

I sway against him, craving more… and then, I reel back as cold liquid splashes over the skin of my chest. It drips into my cleavage, beneath my silk dress shirt.

I forgot the glass of champagne in my hand.

"Shoot," I murmur.

Nate is staring at my chest, like the droplets sliding over my skin are the most fascinating thing he's ever seen.

"Here," he says and takes the now-empty flute from me. He sets it aside along with his own, then finds a button on my blouse.

He undoes it, and then another, widens the gap between the two pieces of fabric… and leans to kiss my neck. My collarbone. The swells of my breasts. His warm lips chase away the chills the cold champagne had elicited.

"Oh," I breathe again, but it's softer now. Nate kisses the exposed valley down my sternum, right at the edge of the silk… held together by only one measly button now.

He unfastens that, too.

Tepid hands spread the fabric aside.

"Fuck," he mutters. "You were telling the truth. No bra."

"It wouldn't have worked with the look," I whisper.

His hands are tight around my hips, his eyes roaming my naked flesh. My suddenly aching tits and my nipples. They hardened in response to the cold liquid.

"So beautiful," he rasps and leans down, kissing one of my breasts. His tongue is hot against my skin, and I slide a hand into his hair. He's licking the champagne off me. Kissing it away.

His mouth closes around my right nipple, and when he sucks hard, my knees threaten to give out. *Oh.* My fingers tighten around the silky strands of his hair.

I'm barely hanging on, but then he uses his teeth to lightly bite… and I…

I didn't know it could feel like that. Had always loved having my breasts played with, but no one had ever used their teeth.

Nate groans, his mouth feathering over my chest to the other nipple. The first isn't left alone, though, and his hand closes over my breast. He can fit all of it neatly in his palm.

"Harper," he whispers, his lips capturing my nipple.

He's already sinking. I buckle under a myriad of sensations, and we sail gracefully to our knees on the plush hotel carpet. Falling back, I pull him over me, and his mouth never stops working—kissing, nibbling, and then moving down my ribcage.

He pulls up my skirt in one swift movement and spreads my thighs with the next. I barely have time to catch my breath before I lose it again.

His mouth is on my clit.

The ceiling above us is beautiful. Carefully stuccoed and adorned. Gilded. There's a chandelier by the entryway, and all of it blurs in my vision.

He is so good at this.

He learned so quickly what I like, and he does just that, pressing open-mouthed kisses to my pussy. Finding my clit and teasing it with his tongue, over and over again, with a steady pressure that sends my arousal sky-high.

"Oh my God," I breathe.

It's too much.

It's not enough.

It's everything.

"Right there." I slide my hand over his head, raking through his tresses. "Yes… I can't…"

His left hand moves my thigh up and away, his right slides down to my entrance. Pushing a finger inside of me at the same time he closes his mouth around my clit and *sucks.*

I explode.

And I can't even think about being quiet, about swallowing my moans, because I can't think at all. Lying on this hotel floor with Nate between my legs and his mouth moving like he wants to make this his full-time job.

I'm left shaky and hungry, and his mouth is still there, his tongue still teasing in half circles around my clit, his finger caressing within me, and I *need* him.

"Nate," I say and reach down. I want him fully on top of

me, inside me, but he won't budge. He's still locked between my thighs, his mouth moving over sensitive skin.

"*Nate,*" I insist. "I want you inside me."

"Not until you come one more time."

"No, *now*." I'm panting with the effort to pull on his shoulders, but I make no progress at all. Then, he slowly swipes his flat tongue over my clit, and I fall back onto the luxurious thick carpet. "Damn it," I say to the ceiling. "Why is it so hard for you to take your own pleasure?"

The tongue against me falters. "What do you mean?"

"It's always about me." I rise up on my elbows and look down at him, nestled between my thighs. It's one of the hottest things I've ever seen. His eyes dark and fiery, his hands spreading me wide. "I want *you* to come hard, too. I loved making you climax in your bathroom."

"Because I need to control myself," he says with nearly black eyes locked on mine. His large hands tighten on my thighs. "Harper, I've thought about the different ways I'd like to have you for a very long time, and I don't plan on rushing things."

My eyebrows rise. "You have?"

"Yes," he utters roughly. "You think I don't want to fuck you hard on this floor? Bend you over that sofa, or press you up against the shower wall?"

I can't breathe. Can't speak.

He brushes his fingers over my pussy, stopping to sink one deep inside. "I told you. I'll be insatiable once we start."

"I'm okay with that," I whisper.

Words are difficult right now.

His mouth tips into the crooked smile I love the most. "Remember that you said that."

"I will. Nate, I want you to let loose."

He rests his forehead against my hip. His hot breath sends shivers over my skin. His shoulders are tense.

One second. Two…

And then, he looks up at me with an intensity that makes

my insides clench. "You're on birth control," he says. "And I never had sex without a condom. I'm clean."

"You haven't?" I breathe out.

He shakes his head again. "I'm going to come inside you tonight. As many times as I can. If that's not okay, tell—"

"That's okay," I say quickly. "Yes. *Please*."

Another one of those crooked smiles, and he pushes up on his knees. Sitting there between my spread thighs with his hair mussed and his white shirt half-undone. "Please," he repeats. "I think I like it when you say that."

I slip off my blouse and let it drop to the floor beneath me. "Please."

His eyes flare, and roam over my body. Spread out before him, and I don't feel an ounce of self-consciousness. The dimness in the room and the reverence in his eyes make that impossible.

He undoes the remaining buttons of his shirt and shrugs out of it. "We'll make it to the bed later," he assures and grips his belt. I watch him unfasten it while his chest heaves. While he pulls his zipper down and pushes his pants down.

His cock springs free. It looks red, the crown nearly purple and weeping. It seems like another of those painful, aching erections.

Nate grabs my thighs and pulls me closer. I'm still wearing my short skirt, now just a belt around my waist.

He grips himself and runs the head of his cock along my folds. We both watch the movement, and I shudder when he brushes against my clit.

"Harper." He fits the flared tip to my entrance. His voice is pained, and it comes out like a groan. "You'll be mine after tonight."

And then, he pushes in.

The sudden fullness makes my breathing hitch. He wedges deeper, inch after inch stretching me in the most delicious of ways. Sinking all the way to the hilt, he stills, his hands gripping my thighs.

Nate's eyes are closed, and a sharp color spreads across his cheekbones. He's kneeling between my thighs like he's praying.

Like he's worshiping.

I make a small mewling sound. *Move,* I think. I need you to *move.*

His eyes open, and then he does. He rolls his hips in a slow, punishing rhythm, and the angle makes my breaths shallow and rapid. It's like he's pushing against that spot inside with every thrust.

His thumb finds my clit and presses down, applying constant pressure.

All I can do is pant and hold on, my hands scrambling across the plush carpet for some kind of grip. And all the while, his eyes are fused on me. On my nipples, my stomach, my thighs, my eyes, my lips, and where he's entering me.

I feel drunk on his gaze.

The rocking of hips increases, and there's a sheen on his forehead. That's when I realize that he's still holding back.

Still trying to control the uncontrollable.

"Nate," I whisper and reach up to grip my breasts, arching my back. I've never done this before, never been so eager to put on a show, but it feels fun. Freeing, intuitive, and I'm not thinking. Just being.

Nate's movements stutter. It only takes a moment and then he's on top of me. His arms braced beside my head and his hips moving fast and hard, unbridled, with no careful planning.

He really does fuck me into the floor.

I wrap my leg around him, and his pistoning stutters once more, becoming jagged. His eyes close and his face tightens. The sharp thrusts mean he hits my clit, and I come again, completely surprised by this orgasm. My gasp turns into a moan and my hands into claws on his shoulders.

Nate roars, and then he's coming, too. He groans with

every pulse of his cock, with every snap of his hips, and when it's over, he collapses on top of me.

He's heavy, and the feeling is delicious, being anchored down to the earth. I wrap both of my legs around him and tighten my arms.

"Good," he finally mutters, pressing a kiss to my cheek. Raising himself up on an elbow. "You weren't the least bit quiet."

A flush spreads over my face. "Oh. Sorry."

He shakes his head, and the crooked smile is back. Inside of me, I already feel him growing hard again. "Never apologize for that. I want to make you scream louder next time," he says. "Let's scandalize Paris, Harp."

Chapter 31

Nate

I wake up to a sleepy Harper in my arms, her body wiggling as if she's trying to get out from under my arm.

I tighten my hold and nestle closer to the mass of her hair. "No," I grunt. "It's too early."

She giggles. "I have to pee!"

"No."

"You can't deny me that."

"I can't deny you anything," I say, "except personal space."

Harper chuckles again. Her ass is distractingly near, rubbing against my rapidly awaking cock. My right hand is resting against her ribs, fingers grazing her breast. She smells good. Like herself and sex and hotel linen.

"Nate," she says while managing a brisk escape. One moment she's here, and then she's gone, sliding out of the sheets. "I'll be right back!"

"I'm counting the seconds." I turn onto my back. The room is cast in partial sunlight from the drawn drapes, the glow entering through the narrow gaps. Despite the intensity of the night, I'm half-hard again.

I grin up at the ceiling.

And what a fucking night.

Sleeping with Harper had been a constant fantasy of mine. For the past four years, I've used my right hand while imagining us in various positions. Often feeling guilty. But that did not stop the visions from playing out in my mind.

Reality has been so much better than anything my mind had ever conjured up.

"Nate?" Harper's tentative voice comes from the bathroom.

I sit up in bed. "Yes?"

"I think I'm gonna jump straight into the shower," she calls.

I throw back the sheet. Lord knows I need one, too. "We can take one together," I say. "Let's save water."

"So climate-conscious," she retorts.

"Of course. It's one of Contron's core values for the upcoming decade." I'm grinning as I grip the handle. Open the bathroom door.

Harper is standing in front of the giant mirror, beneath the spotlights.

And she's fully naked.

Turning every which way to look at her reflection, a tiny smile on her lips. "I'm covered in your come," she says.

I freeze at the threshold. Possessiveness so strong it's like a tidal wave sweeps through me, and I harden in an instant, staring at the woman I've spent all night making mine.

It might not mean that. Not to her. But in an animalistic, primal part of my mind, that's exactly what I'd done. Every single time she came with my name on her lips… and every time I filled her up.

She looks at me, a blush creeping up her fair cheeks. "Sorry."

"Don't say sorry. I love it." I wrap my arms around her waist from behind. "Besides, I'm the one who left it there, wasn't I?"

"Mm-hmm. Yes, you are." She leans her head against my

shoulder and watches us in the mirror. She's so beautiful. Long legs, curved hips, pink nipples, and wild hair.

"And now, you want to wash away my pretty markings," I say in a tutting voice, brushing my hand over her hip, her thigh, between her legs.

She laughs. "I never pegged you as the possessive type," she says. Turns in my arms and pulls me toward the giant shower. "Happy, charming, easy-going Nate Connovan."

I reach past her and turn on the water. There's no other place on Earth I'd rather be at this moment than right here with her naked and smiling in my arms. "Maybe I'm only easygoing about things that don't matter," I say. I don't add the next thought that comes to mind.

Of course I'm possessive... when it's you.

We hit one more museum before driving back to London. It's a lengthy trip—four hours to the Channel and then almost two more back to the city. But I've never been one to mind driving long distances.

And when Harper is in the passenger seat, I could keep driving forever.

She's chatty. Happy. She spins through music, plays a lot of her favorites, talks about the weekend that passed. She's wearing the same short skirt from last night. And more than once I find myself resting my hand on her thigh while driving on the highway.

I don't know if that's *friendly*.

If we're still in that damn *friends help friends* mode, but I don't care. And she doesn't seem to either, her hand occasionally coming to rest on top of mine.

One of these days, I'm going to have to tell her.

All of it.

But not yet. The last thing I want to do is scare her off, to ruin this, or to put any kind of pressure on this situation. It's far too precious for that.

We stop at a fast-food restaurant, and she looks on in amusement when I eat a burger and fries. I have to tweak her nose and ask if she thinks I'm some kind of weirdo who's never had fast food.

She shakes her head. "No. It's just, this isn't a Michelin-starred cuisine. It's not fancy, or served by a waiter, or hand-cut and hand-seasoned, and it's not—"

I roll my eyes, taking a page from her book. "I can be a man of the people. For an hour or two."

Harper laughs, and I tweak her nose again. It's hard to not touch her. Now that I've begun, I'll never be able to stop.

We pull into London around eight thirty in the evening. Harper has kicked off her shoes and is curled up on the passenger seat, half-asleep, with my sweater covering her legs.

I park the SUV outside the house rather than pulling into the garage. Easier to unload our bags.

"Harp," I murmur, jostling her shoulder gently. "Baby, we're home."

She blinks her eyes open. "Huh?"

"We're home."

"Oh. Already?"

That makes me chuckle. "I'm glad it didn't feel long. Yes. Already."

She yawns and puts on her shoes. I get out of the vehicle and grab the bags from the back.

Harper exits—her braid is messy, her smile tired, but she looks happy. And something about this scene is so domestic that it makes my wrung-out heart tighten painfully.

"Home," she murmurs and stretches. "Finally."

I set the bags down on the sidewalk. I can't help it. I have to reach for her. "Home," I repeat and turn her smiling face up to mine.

My lips are barely brushing hers, and I shift to deepen—

"What the *fuck*?"

The voice is furious, close, and American.

I lift my head, but tighten my arms around Harper. Scan around... until my eyes land on a man sitting on my stoop, half-hidden behind the shrub. I hadn't seen him there. Had been so focused on our things and on Harper.

Dean stands, his face carved into angry incredulity. He looks from me to Harper, who has gone rigid in my arms, and then back to me.

A tense silence settles over us.

It lasts only a moment before Dean walks down the stairs, shoving his hands into the pockets of his jeans. There's a suitcase behind him, tucked next to my door.

"Dean," I say. My voice comes out remarkably calm. "You didn't tell me you'd be coming."

"Yes, I did." His voice is acidic. "I called you on Friday, and when you didn't answer, I texted you. But I guess you've been too busy to check your messages."

Harper's hand falls from mine. "What are you doing here?" she asks.

I hate how her voice sounds. Shocked. Hurt. And anxious.

Dean's eyes land on her. "Didn't waste any time, did you?"

"Dean," I say sharply. "I get that this is a surprise, but don't say things you'll regret."

"Things I'll regret?" he asks and shoots me a hateful glare. "You're the one doing things you'll regret. Harper, man?"

"You know just how amazing she is, or you wouldn't be here."

He shakes his head in disbelief and looks back at this ex-fiancée. Seeing them together again, standing here... it makes my stomach turn. I don't know how I managed it for so many years.

I hate how he glares at her.

"I came to London to see you," he says. His hands come out of his pockets, and form fists at his sides. "To convince you that your leaving was a mistake. I wanted to talk about the wedding cancellation fees and see if we could come to some kind of… settlement. I even have a goodie bag from your mom with me. She put together your favorite American foods, and *fuck you*, Harper. My best friend?!"

"He's not your best friend," Harper says with a vehemence that surprises me. Judging by the look in Dean's eyes, he's shocked, too. "Be honest about that for once, Dean. You think he's just a great contact to have and maintain."

Dean's lips turn into a snarl. "What do you know? He and I went to college together. And now he's done this… fuck. I had no idea you two were involved. Was this happening before, Harper? Is *this* the real reason you called off the wedding?"

"Cool it," I tell Dean.

He glares at me.

Harper takes a step forward, leaning in like she's ready to strike. "Nate had nothing to do with calling off the wedding. That was all me." Her voice is sharp, dripping with anger. "I *hated* the way you treated me the last two years we were together, and you refused to listen to me about it. The only one to blame for our breakup is you. Not Nate."

A flash of genuine hurt passes through Dean's eyes, there and gone again in a blink, his face returning to a sneer. "Right. I'm to blame? Our friends and families were just as surprised as me. That doesn't tell you something?"

"Yes," she says, voice fierce. "It tells me that we were great at putting up a facade."

Dean crosses his arms over his chest. "I had to talk to the wedding dress designer yesterday. She called my mother in tears, upset that the gown she worked on for months would go to waste."

"You're lying," Harper says. "I spoke to her myself weeks ago."

"Then, why did my mother tell me that? You're saying *she's* lying, too?"

"Because the wedding designer is her best friend's daughter! Because you control everything!" Harper's voice turns exasperated, and she shakes her head so sharply, making her curls bounce. "Dean, why did you really come to London? Don't tell me you came here to see me."

"Why the fuck else would I be here?" he says. "Now that I know my friend is a backstabbing snake."

"I never lied to you about Harper," I say.

Dean gives me a withering look. "Right. Just conveniently avoided mentioning… this, you two, when we spoke on the phone."

"You weren't ready to hear it," I say simply.

Harper's voice has steadied. "Did you come here to try to convince me to go back to New York? To coerce me with the wedding costs?"

"Coerce," Dean scoffs. "I came because this misguided little plan of yours has been going on for far too long. You're across the fucking ocean, doing an internship? At twenty-eight?"

"It's a junior trainee position," she says. "Not that you'd know. You never listened when I spoke about my goals and ambitions."

"So now it's my fault that you had a quarter-life crisis?" He shakes his head and looks over at me. "Where does Nate factor into this? Was he your little savior when you needed money? You traded me for him?"

Harper makes a tiny, pained sound, and it pierces through me like an arrow. I step forward. "Shut up, Dean," I order. "Just shut up about things you know nothing about."

"So I'm correct," he says.

"No, you're wrong, and hurt, and angry. And you're saying shit that's only going to make things worse. You won't be happy you reacted this way when you've calmed down."

"And you'd know that how?" he asks me, cocking his head with the sneer still in place. "Because you never do things you regret? No, you never do anything at all. The perfect Connovan boy—rich since birth, with everything handed to him."

"Don't make me repeat myself," I tell him.

"Stop it. *Stop.* Nate hasn't done anything wrong," Harper says. "We're friends. I'm single, he's single. It's not a crime."

Dean bores his eyes into her. "I'm going to enjoy creating a monthly payment plan for you. You said you wanted me to add interest, too, right?"

"Yes," Harper says, and I see her physically pull her shoulders back. Steel herself to stay resolute in her decision, despite his tone making it into something ugly and coercive.

I hate seeing it. Hate seeing her forced to be strong when she doesn't have to be. Hate that Dean has this hold over her. At this moment, it's hard to look at my friend and remember that I ever felt guilty about being in love with his fiancée.

He never deserved her.

I've felt that way for years. Felt guilty about feeling it. Now, the guilt is gone, washed away, and I'm left with a bone-deep certainty.

"Dean, grab your bag," I say. "You're not staying here."

"Fine." He reaches for the handle of his travel case. "Damn right I'm not."

He steps past Harper and opens his mouth, but I beat him to it. Put a hand on his shoulder. "You've said enough. Leave her alone. Harper, if you want to go inside, feel free."

Her eyes meet mine, and there's gratefulness there. Then, she's gone, walking up the steps and unlocking the door with her key. I can't imagine ever asking for it back.

"I don't even know what to say to you," Dean growls. His voice is low and furious. "I asked you to keep an eye on her. Not to start fucking her!"

I cross my arms over my chest. "Maybe you should have fucked her better, then, and she wouldn't have left."

His eyes widen. It's a low blow, and I shouldn't have said that. Shouldn't have gone there at all, I know that, but Harper's pained expression when she talks about his actions haunt me. I want to hit him where it counts. I want to knock the wind out of him and send him on his way.

"Fuck you," he spits. "You could have told me about it."

"I could've. And I would have, if you hadn't showed up unannounced here like this. Were you planning to stay with me?"

"Of course I was. You once said I had an open invitation." He crosses his arms over his chest. "Now, I wouldn't step foot in your place."

"Good. Because you're not welcome in any of them."

"What the hell happened, man? Why did you decide she was more important than this?" His eyes narrow, and his voice drops. "Why are *you* angry at me here?"

Oh.

Oh.

I level him with a stare I've seen my brother use more than once. A look my dad is an expert at, and my voice naturally slides into the same unforgiving tone they perfected. "Because I know better now. I know how you used your money to manipulate her. How you consistently ridiculed her dreams, and how you've continued to call and hound her about canceling the wedding. Enough, Dean. *Enough*."

"So you're on her side now?" He shakes his head, again. "You were just waiting in the wings, huh? Waiting to swoop in and scoop her up as soon as she was single."

I lean in closer. "Maybe I was, Dean. And maybe you should have realized what a catch she was when she was yours. But she's not anymore. And you will stop calling her."

"Not for you to decide," he sneers.

"Enlighten me. What's the plan? You're paying for wedding expenses, taking on the debts so that she will feel beholden to you. And then, you'll use that as your excuse to keep in constant contact with her as she repays you." I raise an eyebrow. "At some point, I'm guessing, you plan to tell her that it would be much easier if the two of you just got back together. Because then, she wouldn't have to make the payments anymore. Right?"

Dean's silence and the anger in his eyes tell me I'm spot-on.

"How much is it?"

He grits his teeth, but he answers. Spits out the number as if it hurts. And it's so much lower than my ballpark estimate that it makes me laugh.

I don't mean to. But to concoct all of this over that sum…

Dean's eyes flash with indignation. "As if you haven't done that and worse in business."

"Sure. In business. Not to a woman I love." I reach into my pocket and grab my phone. "Let's see. With interest, right?"

"What are you doing?"

"I'm setting up a wire transfer. I'll have that to you with… let's say I round it up for good measure, hmm?… By Tuesday at the latest. My assistant will call you to confirm."

"You can't do that," he says.

"Of course I can. And I just did." I slide my phone back into my pocket and gesture to the street. "Now, I suggest you get a cab. Check in to a hotel… and grab the first flight back to New York tomorrow."

He takes a step back, hand tightening around the handle of his suitcase. "You can't keep her locked up here," he seethes and looks toward my townhouse. "You can't keep her from me."

"If she wants to see you, Dean, she's more than welcome to. But last time I checked… she doesn't. Has asked you repeatedly to stop calling. Tried amicable ways to resolve the cancellation fees. So I'm telling you, not advising you, to leave London. Now."

Dean's eyes burn. "I always fucking hated you. You know that? You had it so easy in college. Got a multibillion-dollar company handed to you. Fuck you, Nate. You can have her."

I smile. "Jealousy doesn't look good on you."

"Screw you," he scoffs again, then he turns and walks

quickly down the sidewalk. Past the park and back to the main road.

I remain standing in the same spot long enough to make sure Dean is really gone before I grab our bags and head inside my home, where Harper is waiting for me.

Chapter 32

Harper

"Do I have to?" Nate asks. He's leaning against the doorframe to his bathroom—so much larger than mine—and stares at the tub as it fills like it's a snake poised to strike.

I dip my hand in the bath water. It's the perfect temperature. "Yes. And if you hate the experience, you'll get to gloat forever."

He looks at me, and that curved smile that transforms his face is back. I love seeing it. Along with the teasing glint in his eyes that is present more and more often when he looks at me.

Something about those stares of his makes my chest warm.

Nate reaches for the buttons of his shirt. He'd gotten in from work just twenty minutes ago, and I was quick to grab him for a bath. Dragging him up the two flights and stairs and through the bedroom I'd only briefly seen before.

"What's that?" he asks while shrugging out of his shirt. Broad chest on full display, and I almost drop the bottle of bubble bath liquid I'm pouring into the stream.

"Oh. It's soap. I love the scent, and it will make the water foamy."

He unfastens the buckle of his belt. "I'm an idiot," he says, "for not immediately realizing this would mean I'm naked around you."

"Did you take a bath fully clothed last time?" I tease. "That's why you didn't enjoy it. You weren't doing it right!"

He smiles. "Oh, that explains it."

"Stick to the Excel sheets and cars."

"I don't work in Excel," he says, "but I'll take the latter any day of the week."

I look down at the tub, the swirling soap, and the quickly forming bubbles. The water is almost halfway up by now, and the steamy air is getting heavy with the floral scent.

"You didn't… has he contacted you since Sunday?" I ask. It's Tuesday, and it's been two days since the showdown outside the townhouse. Guilt and fury has been swirling inside me ever since, my mind vacillating between the two.

Nate's hand comes under my chin, and he tilts my head up. I'm sitting on the edge of the tub, and with his height, he's looming over me, but his face is thoughtful. "Are you worried about him coming back?"

I swallow. "A little bit. He knows where I live now."

"I'll hire security."

That makes me chuckle. "No, no, I don't think that will be necessary. His ego is… well, it was always fairly fragile. He measured himself against you a lot. Now, knowing that you and I are…"

Nate's lips tip up at the corners, and his thumb strokes across my cheek. "We are…?"

"Well, you know. *Involved*."

"That's right. Involved," he says. "He won't bother you again. Let me know if he does, and I'll handle him."

"Yeah," I say, but guilt churns in my stomach. I try to shake it off and gesture at the water. "Come on. It's time."

Nate grumbles, but he does what I ask. Steps out of his boxers and sinks into the almost-too-hot water. A low groan escapes him, and I sit down by the head of the free-standing tub. I've already rolled up and placed a towel there for him to rest his head against.

I'm here to win an argument, after all.

Nate's eyes meet mine. "You're still worried about it."

He knows me too well. I sigh and look down at my hands on my lap. "No. Not really, more that… Well, I destroyed your friendship, didn't I? It does bother me how Dean spoke to you. I know he was jealous, but you two *have* been friends since college, and here I am—"

"Harper," Nate says. "Let me get this right. You're feeling guilty about being the reason Dean and I will likely never speak again?"

Spoken so starkly, it feels like a punch to the gut.

I nod.

"Don't be. Not even a bit. I will never feel bad about losing him as a friend."

"You won't?"

"No," Nate says. "He showed his true colors the other day. Besides, do you think I would want to be friends with him after hearing how he treated you?"

"Then I'm the one who turned you against him," I say.

Nate rests his head back on the towel and drapes his arms along the porcelain edges of the tub. "No. You just opened my eyes to a relationship I've already been feeling shaky about."

I blink a few times. "You were? Every time I saw you in New York before you moved, and then after… although it was less often… you seemed so happy. Like you liked Dean. I never noticed anything otherwise."

He closes his eyes, and I notice color seeping into his cheeks. It must be from the rising steam heating the air around us. "I was good at hiding it."

"Oh," I say.

"And I'd take having you over being friends with him every day of the week."

The words slide over my skin, slipping through my limbs.

Having me. Happiness unfurls, chasing away the guilt. Is that how he sees it? Does he have me? Do I have him?

We still haven't defined anything. Haven't spoken about us. I'm not sure if I can quite yet… but I'm getting there. All I know is, there's no one I want to spend my time with more than Nate.

"I'm going to wash your hair," I say instead and reach for the shampoo.

Nate cracks an eyelid open. "You're going to do *what*?"

"I promise you'll like it." I scoot closer to the tub and run a hand through his hair. "And if you still hate having a bath in thirty minutes, you'll win this debate forever. Remember?"

"Thirty minutes in this water," he mutters, but he dips his head obligingly under the surface for me.

"How you suffer for me," I tease and rest his head back against the edge of the tub.

His hair is a few inches in length, and I start lathering it with shampoo. Use both my hands to massage his scalp.

I've never done this for anyone. This whole idea started on a whim, something fun for us to do. But this feels almost meditative.

Nate keeps his eyes closed and forehead smooth—no furrows mar his serene expression—but there's no smile on his lips, either. He sighs softly.

"Not so bad, is it?" I whisper and slide my hands to the back of his head. Dig into the muscles of his neck.

"No." His deep voice is languid. "But I think that's less about the bath and more about you."

I smile. "Let's say it's a fifty-fifty effort."

By the time I'm done, he looks relaxed enough to be half-asleep, his hands gripping the edges of the tub. But he dips his head again for me when I ask.

"Nate," I ask, picking up the soap. "Can't you tell me something… something you don't usually tell other people?"

He slides his warm gaze to mine. "I am not particularly fond of pistachios."

I burst out laughing, and he smiles, pleased with himself. "That's not what I meant!"

"But that's something I usually keep under lock and key."

I dip my hand into the water, splashing him. "Can you be serious for a moment?"

"I can, if I must," he says. Leans back against the towel and looks at me with half-lidded eyes. "Okay… you want my secrets?"

I grab the loofah and pour soap onto it. "I want to get to know you better."

"Mm-hmm. I tell you something… and you take off another piece of clothing."

My eyes widen. "This is about you enjoying a bath."

"Of course it is," he says, face perfectly innocent. "And isn't having a beautiful view crucial for an enjoyable bath?"

"You're insatiable," I say, but I'm smiling.

"I warned you I would be, once we started this," he says. He lifts his hand off the tub's rim and wraps his fingers around one of my curls. "And you've already managed to get me naked. The bath was just an excuse, right?"

I roll my eyes. "You're such a guy. Okay. I'm game."

"Of course you are," he says warmly and leans his head back against the edge. "You're game for everything. Okay. You want me to bare my soul here, alongside my body? While I'm defenseless in soapy water?"

He looks up at the ceiling and thinks for a moment. The previously smooth forehead gets a new crease. "You know that my father has been giving me more attention in the last six months than he has in the past ten years, and all of it is because my sister and brother have shut him out."

I blink at him. "Yeah."

"I'm not upset about it. It's just a fact. But I think it's because he wants me to act as a mediator."

"That's not a role you should have to play."

He shrugs. "I'm the middle child. It's the role I was born to play."

My fingers find the buttons of my cardigan and undo them. I shrug out of the garment and throw it back toward the open door leading to his bedroom. Only the camisole and skirt left.

And my underwear and bra.

Nate smiles. "Good girl."

"I can't believe we're negotiating on this," I murmur, but I'm smiling, too.

"I can."

Picking up the loofah once again, I gesture for Nate to lean forward. Start soaping the broad muscles of his back. I know he runs and lifts weights, but he must have been doing that consistently for twenty years or more. His body is shaped like an athlete's. Taut skin and strong muscles.

My next question is easier to ask to his shoulder blades than to his face. "Dean… once mentioned that you had been engaged? Before I knew either of you, but that it didn't work out."

Nate shrugs. "Dean ran his mouth a lot, I'm learning."

"Was that a secret?"

"No," he says and braces his arms against his bent knees. Water sloshes softly against the edges of the tub. "It's just not something I talk about often."

"Is it sensitive?"

"Not particularly," he says, sounding genuine. Not bitter. "It was a long time ago. Yeah, I was engaged to a woman I met at work in my mid-twenties. We dated, moved in together, got engaged. It ended… What is it now? Seven years ago. I was thirty-one at the time."

"What happened?"

"She decided she wasn't in love with me anymore," he says.

My hand jerks across the expanse of his back. "Oh. I'm sorry."

He chuckles. "God, don't be. That wasn't meant to be. I don't regret it."

"That's a very healthy way of looking at things," I say softly and start kneading the muscles of his shoulders.

Nate groans, and his head falls forward. "Jesus, Harper. I don't know what I've done to deserve this."

"Maybe you don't need to do anything to deserve it. Maybe you just need to be you," I say.

He's quiet for a long moment, and then he chuckles dryly. "That goes against the entire Connovan ideology."

"Your dad didn't raise you like that?"

"I think," he says, "that's another question. And you still need to remove a piece of clothing for your last one."

"Demanding," I murmur, but I reach for the hem of my camisole. Whip it clean off, leaving me in only a skirt and panties.

Nate leans back against the tub and gestures for me to move so he can see me. I shuffle to the right, loofah in hand, and give a little *ta-da*.

His smile widens, eyes sweeping over my collarbones, breasts, and stomach.

"My favorite art piece," he murmurs, arms draping over the edges of the tub. "Perfection."

"You're biased."

"Entirely," he agrees.

I dip the loofah under the water and then run it across his chest. His eyes are warm on me. "Right. No, we weren't raised thinking that 'good was good enough.' Rest was wicked, failure was unacceptable, and the goal was always to make Contron the best it could be. I knew exactly where I would be working since I was ten."

I glance up at him. He doesn't sound bitter… but how can he not be? "That sounds hard."

He shrugs, and the surface of the water ripples. It's still mostly covered in bubbles. "It was. But I was very privileged. We all were. I can't complain that I got a chance at a career many people work their entire lives for."

"You're allowed to complain. It's your life."

"Mm-hmm. Well, complaining is another thing Connovans don't do. Unless you're my father, of course. He's allowed to complain about our performances as much as he wants."

"That's unfair."

"Life is unfair," he says. "Another of Dad's favorite slogans."

"Okay, I'm not liking this man," I say with a frown. Beneath the water, I'm using the loofah across his stomach and abs.

Nate looks content, his eyes lazy. "You're not the first. But he also instilled the value of hard work, education, perseverance."

"You work a lot, that's true."

"I worked even more before you moved in." He nods to my skirt, a smile on his face. "Off."

I grumble about him being so needy but wiggle out of the skirt happily. Having him so close, so naked, so large, and so distinctly male is intoxicating. So is getting to touch him wherever I want and however I want.

"Jesus," Nate says as I sink to my knees again beside the tub. "You're so pretty. Always have been."

"Always?" I ask. Find the loofah and start along his legs. "Even when we were just friends and I was Dean's girlfriend?"

His voice is surprisingly serious when he replies. "Always."

"Oh." I try not to get ahead of myself. Had he always…? I didn't know he'd been attracted to me before a few weeks ago.

Before we moved in together and became friends.

"Don't worry," he says, and his voice is light again. "You don't need to confess that you found me devastatingly handsome on our first meeting."

I chuckle and run the loofah up his knee. "You're not fishing for compliments. Nope."

"I would never."

"Of course you were handsome. You've always been good-looking," I say and let my loofah run up his thigh. To the only spot I haven't washed, yet.

Nate exhales sharply. "Well. We got there in the end."

"I have one more question," I say, moving the loofah around his thighs, his hips, his lower abs.

Nate grits his teeth. "Then the bra is coming off."

"Think you can focus if it's off?"

"I'll do my damndest," he mutters.

I reach behind me and undo the clasp. Slide the straps down my shoulders and slowly, slowly, let the cups fall, leaving me bare.

Nate curses, his eyes turn dark and focused on my tits.

It makes me smile. "You're looking like you've never seen me naked before."

"I'll never be done looking," he says.

I let the loofah drop to the tiled floor and lean against the tub, pushing my breasts up against the edge. The bubbles have mostly disappeared now, and I clearly see his erection beneath the water, resting against his stomach.

I reach down and grip him.

His breathing catches, and his hands tighten on the rim of the tub. "You have the best fucking hands in the world."

"I do?"

"Mm-hmm. Best fucking everything." He leans his head against the rolled-up towel and looks at me with lust-filled eyes. "Ask the question, Harper. Whatever it is."

He's hard in my palm, and grows harder still as I stroke him. I love the feel of him in my hand—heavy, silky, and hot. Have since the very beginning.

And I love the way he looks when I hold him. Like I have his life in my hands. Like I'm the only thing he can think about.

"If you thought I was pretty since, well…"

"For years," he mutters. "Yes."

I feel too hot. From the warm water, his cock in my palm, his eyes on me. The only cool thing is the porcelain against my chest. "Does that mean you've been wanting to do this, too? For years?"

The question hangs in the steamy, scented air.

He doesn't blink. Doesn't look away from my gaze.

"Yes," he says. "I've wanted you from the first moment I saw you."

My hand tightens around him on instinct, and my breath hitches.

He groans. Reaches out to grab me. "Now come here. You're getting into this tub with me, and in return, I'll finally agree that baths are superior."

"I'm still wearing my panties!" But I scramble into the hot water and into his arms.

He pulls me close. "Don't worry," he says. "I think we'll be able to get those off."

Chapter 33

Harper

Sunlight streams in through the gallery's large windows, illuminating the white space. White walls, white floors, white ceilings. The heat wave that kept London in a chokehold for a week slowly dissipated, and now we're back to beautiful June weather.

Aadhya is giddy. I feel it, the emotion radiating from her, even though she's standing calmly beside me. Eitan is talking with two buyers just a few feet away. The paperwork has already been drawn. The pen is out.

I feel the same giddiness Aadhya does. I nudge her, a teeny bit, and she nudges me back.

We just sold a trio of paintings for a number so large, so staggering, that even our tiny cut of the commission will be epic. *Epic.* Kinda like Eitan's approval.

The couple is in their fifties, glamorous, worldly, eccentric. Two married women who appear to be complete opposites but finish each other sentences. They walked in, and Aadhya and I snapped into our roles.

I feel giddy a lot these days. Last night, in the bathtub…

And this morning, when he drove me to work. Completely unnecessary. But he did, and before I got out of the car, he kissed me.

On the street by the Duke of Kent Square, right across

from the Sterling Gallery. Where everyone might see. Aadhya. My other coworkers.

And it didn't bother me as much as it should.

The couple leaves with assurances that the art will be delivered to them later in the week, and Eitan turns to us. He has an uncharacteristically large smile on his face.

"Excellent work, ladies," he says. "Right artwork paired with the right clients."

"We live to please," Aadhya says grandly with a smile.

"And you do," he says. "I looked over the latest plans you two finalized for next week's party. I must say, I'm pleasantly surprised. It's not looking too bad."

That's high praise coming from him.

"Harper, I saw your note about having a guide at hand for those who want to take a more extensive tour of the facilities," he says. "It's… unusual, but it's good."

I'd stolen the idea from the art event Nate and I went to at the London Modern. Our gallery is much smaller, but the work we do and our collection are diverse enough that we can offer whoever is interested a behind-the-scenes tour, and discuss preservation and authentication.

We're still discussing the party, out in the main gallery, when the doorbell rings. The gallery is open to the public, but the door is always locked for safety reasons. Anyone can press the button to unlock it from the inside.

And in walks Willard.

The man I'd spoken to at Nate's party, the nephew of one of Nate's business associates. Outwardly charming. Very easy on the eyes. And definitely someone with ulterior motives.

When I think about it, Nate's jealousy that night had been entirely misguided. This isn't the kind of man I'd ever fall for.

This is the second time he showed up at the gallery.

He smiles when he sees me. "Harper! How lovely you're here. I was hoping you would be."

Willard's voice is soft, accented in such faint traces of

European English that it's hard to place where he's from originally.

"I'll be right back," I tell Aadhya and step out into the lobby. Then, I turn to our unexpected guest. "It's nice to see you again. Came for the tour of the place?"

He nods, and gestures. "Lead the way."

It only takes half the tour for him to open up about why he's really here. There had been hints of it that first time, too, but this is less subtle. He's here with a purpose.

"I've just showed Nate Connovan a Covey," he says.

My eyebrows rise. "You have? When?"

"Just earlier today. I accompanied my uncle to a meeting at Contron," he says. "Then Nate and I took a little trip to where I keep the works I deal with."

"Incredible. And what did he say?"

"That he liked it very much, but that he would have to discuss it with you." Willard's smile widens. "His art adviser."

He clearly suspects we're more than that.

Surprisingly… I'm perfectly fine with the assumption. What I'm not fine with, is the suspicion that Nate buying this art piece is less about the painting and more about solidifying a business relationship.

"I see. Well, I'm happy to view it, too," I say. "I'd also love to see its provenance."

Willard's face doesn't change. Only his voice, which grows a little sly. "Well, that's a funny story. This piece's provenance is rather convoluted."

"Is it?"

"Yes. You see…"

He tells a story that is outlandish enough to be just *barely* believable. A tale of a rich Swiss man who inherited art from his grandfather. A grandfather who had a passion for American impressionists. Who scooped up the works when the painters were still young, when their art was cheap. But the Swiss man is so rich that he has no need for more money.

And, he happens to be the father of one of Willard's old school friends, and so, letting Willard take these works of art to the market.

It's vague.

Vague often suits the world of art, but it doesn't suit me. Not this time. When Willard leaves, Eitan approaches me.

He stares at the door closing behind him. "What was he doing here?" Eitan asks.

"He is trying to sell my client a newly discovered Covey," I say. "But something about his story…"

"Doesn't add up. Yeah. I've heard of him," my boss says with a sigh. "Not that anyone ever listens to me when the possibility of a previously undiscovered painting pops up. People get far too excited."

"Can I do some research on this?"

"Please do," he says. "And let me know what you find."

I head into the back office, where we have access to an extensive online database, and shoot a text to Nate.

Harper: Don't buy the Covey from Willard until we've spoken.

Nate: Has he contacted you?

Harper: Yes, he stopped by the gallery.

There's only a short moment before my phone rings. I look around, but I'm alone in the office. "Hey."

"He stopped by your gallery, *again*?"

"Yes, to convince me to tell *you* to buy his painting."

Nate curses. "He's persistent."

"He isn't interested in me," I say. "He's interested in your money."

"Good. Because that means infinitely less to me."

I smile into the phone, despite myself. "Just promise me you won't buy it without me there, without us speaking about it."

"I'll wait. I was going to make the call this afternoon, but—"

"Don't!" I say. "Wait until I come home. Promise me."

There's amusement in his voice now. "I promise."

"Good. Okay… good."

"Want me to pick you up from work?"

"Do you have time for that?"

"Absolutely not," he says. "But I can make it happen."

I smile at my keyboard and run my thumb along the large *Enter* key. It's nice to hear his voice during a normal workday. "I don't want to inconvenience you. And it's lovely out. I'll walk."

"I'll meet you at home, then."

"Sure you don't need to work late? You mentioned—"

"I'm sure," he says.

I think of what Richard mentioned. That since I moved in, Nate is working less. That he's around the house more. Warmth floods me.

"I'll see you at home."

"Can't wait, baby."

We hang up, and I stare at the screen, unseeing. Wearing a smile on my face, like an absolute moron. It takes me a few seconds to remember why I came in here and what for. Research. *Right.*

Later, when I arrive home, it's with a conviction born out of what I discovered, and the sinking suspicion that it might not matter to Nate. He isn't doing this because he loves art. He's doing this because he wants to sign a business deal.

I'm waiting in the backyard—curled up on the bench under the sun, with a large glass of lemonade and a book—when he gets home. Mom had sent over a copy of *The Professor* by Charlotte Brontë, and I love her thoughtfulness.

Nate doesn't like what I have to say.

I see it immediately when I say the words, the way his mouth turns into a scowl and he crosses his arms over his chest.

"You're sure it's a fake?" he asks.

I give a shrug. "Sure? No, I can't be sure. But the evidence strongly points in that direction. Another gallery sent one of his paintings to an authentication expert a few months back, and the results came back inconclusive."

Nate's eyebrows furrow. "Inconclusive. So?"

"Inconclusive means *fake* in the art world. But, somehow, he's kept going, and I… it wouldn't surprise me if it's all going to come crashing down sooner or later. The police might already be onto him."

"What do *you* think?"

"I think it's suspicious. The provenance story he told me sounds perfectly crafted to get gullible buyers to accept the lack of a legitimate record, and the painting is from a time when Covey did mostly orange abstracts and, very rarely, blues. It just… all of it sounds dubious."

Nate nods and looks out toward the tight boxwood hedge that keeps his backyard fenced. "Right. But you know I'm not really buying this piece because of its artistic properties."

"Nate, you can't ignore it. You *can't*."

He looks at me for a long moment, and there's frustration in his eyes. "If I don't, and if I intimate to Knudsen that it's because I suspect his nephew is a fraud, Contron won't get the contract. He's made it very clear that helping his nephew is the last step."

"Then he's a bully, and that's a bribe."

Nate laughs. It's not a happy sound. "That's my line of work, baby. Contron gets what it wants, either through compliments or careful coercion. Buying a painting from someone's nepotistic nephew is probably the *least* dirty thing we've done to secure access."

"He is a scammer. You buying it from him, with your stellar record of art purchases, will legitimize him." My voice is shaking from how strong I feel about this. Art fraud might not be serious in the grand scheme of things, at least amid all of the world's horrors. But it's one I personally *hate*. It's leeching off real artists' names, using that to feed personal greed.

It's nothing more than a pretty lie.

"Harper," he says with a groan. Runs a hand through his hair. "It's not that I don't agree with you. It's that what you're asking… it would undo almost a year of work."

"It's also the right thing to do." I push off the bench and close the distance between us. Grab his hands and hold them between mine. "I know you're not the kind of man who would turn a blind eye when someone's breaking a law just for profit."

"You *know*," he repeats with a curl of his lips. "I've done a lot of things over the past twenty years to make Contron successful. A lot of things to make…"

He doesn't finish, but I hear what he doesn't say. *To please others*. His father. Maybe his brother, too?

"Fucking hell. You're gonna make me lose a deal that could make my company millions," he mutters.

A pang of guilt flashes through me. "I won't. Your own morals will."

"My morals," he says. His eyes search mine, and there's a cool resignation there. "I have been very immoral, Harper."

I swallow. "I don't believe it."

"Lusting after my friend's fiancée wasn't immoral?" His hand leaves mine to cup the side of my face, and he brushes his thumb against my lower lip. "Because it felt immoral, to have those thoughts about you, when you weren't mine."

I can't speak. Can't find the words.

His smile turns rueful. "I won't rush you. Don't worry. But if you tell me I'm not a bad man, well… wanting you has always been proof that I am."

"You're not," I breathe.

"I won't buy the Covey," he says. "Do you want me to give the police a call? Is it at that stage?"

"It might be. If there's already an ongoing investigation, you could add your statements to it."

"Then I will," he says.

"What about the deal? Don't you think that there's a way to… I don't know. To convince that Danish businessman that you still value his company?"

Nate's smile widens. "I love your optimism sometimes. No, Knudsen doesn't give a fuck about art. He wants to help his wife's nephew establish a career, and I'll undermine that. No, I think the deal will be pretty shot."

"I'm sorry."

"Don't be. You're right. It wouldn't be an ethical move." He wraps his arms tightly around my waist and sighs. I feel the movement through his chest, resting under my ear, and breathe in deep. He smells good. "Coming home to you is becoming my favorite part of every day. Even when you tell me things I don't want to hear."

I make a small humming sound against his chest. Him coming home is rapidly becoming my favorite part, too.

It's a scary realization…

And a wonderful one.

Chapter 34

Nate

Bright midday light streams through the bedroom windows. Thin, gossamer curtains are drawn to obscure the prying eyes, but they don't keep out the sunshine.

It bounces off the white of my comforter. Makes her blonde curls look lighter, like pure honey in the sunshine.

"Hey," she whispers.

I'm propped up on an elbow beside her. The giant duvet is half wrapped around us, only covering me from the waist down. It blankets Harper almost entirely, apart from a single leg she stuck out, the pale skin left bare from hip to toe.

I feel drunk on the sight of her.

"Hi," I say. "Did I miss something, or haven't we been hanging out for… the last… twelve hours?"

"Yes. But you can't be too polite, you know."

"Ah. Right. I appreciate that." I let my gaze wander along her makeup-free, freckled, beautiful face. Down her neck and the collarbone and softly rounded shoulder. Her bare arm is resting on top of the comforter. "You cold?"

"Mm-hmm. No."

"Right." I smile and reach out to trace up her exposed limb. "Because you've been clutching that cover since we finished."

She digs her teeth into her bottom lip. The curls are a riot around her face, mussed and tangled from the early morning sex.

It's a beautiful Sunday in London, and we're checking off another thing from her list. In addition to *stay out all night,* there was also a *spend an entire day in bed.*

Not very hard to do, I'm finding.

"It's very bright in here," she says.

I raise an eyebrow. "Don't tell me you're suddenly feeling self-conscious."

"Suddenly? We aren't usually naked in this kind of intense brightness."

I laugh. "You've got amnesia. The bathroom?"

"Okay, yes, but I used the dimmer on your spotlights."

"Harper," I say. "You look amazing in the brightest of lights."

She shakes her head a little, but she's smiling, and I know she's not taking this too seriously. It's a slight concern, but not a serious one. "You say that because you're biased."

"Of course I'm biased," I say. "But who else is in this room? Who else are you parading around naked in front of?"

She rolls her eyes. "Okay, okay, Mr. Possessive."

I shift closer and run my hand over her thigh. Down the back of her knee, and grab her calf. Pull her leg closer. "Look at this perfection. Creamy skin. Round shapes. I love the length of your legs. They're perfectly wrapped around me, and in a mini skirt when you taunt me, or stretched out in a rowboat before we tip over."

Harper laughs. It cuts off when I drag my hand higher, over the round curve of her ass. "And this… God, I love your ass. Your curves. Not one inch of you is anything but hot."

She rolls onto her stomach on the cover, her fully nude body on display.

If I felt drunk before, I'm high now. Sunlight dapples the skin of her bare back, over the curves of her butt, the length of her legs. Her curls dance across her shoulder blades.

"Feel free to continue," she says.

I laugh and run my hand up her spine. Brush her hair away, and trace her neck and shoulders. "Your skin is so soft. Ridiculously soft, really. I love your freckles here… and on your arms. Love them." My fingers brush down the side of her chest, on the lightly curved breasts, flattening against the comforter. "I love your tits. You know that already. They drive me fucking nuts. When you flashed me on the stairs, I nearly lost it."

"Flashed you? That was an accident!"

"Yeah," I say, but I'm grinning. "Sure."

She shoves my shoulder. "It was. Very ungentlemanlike of you to look!"

"I'm not a gentleman."

"Clearly not," she says. She shifts to her back but snatches up the duvet. It conceals her in a crooked triangle, just barely covering her tits and across her abdomen, hiding the delta between her legs from my view. She puts an arm under her head and looks at me with eyes that make me feel ten feet tall.

"You know what I just realized?" she asks.

"That you're hungry, and we should order takeout and eat in bed."

"No," she says, "but we should do that, too." Her gaze leaves me, wandering to the walls of my bedroom. From one painting to another.

A month ago, I would have avoided showing her this—the full extent of the art collection I built entirely on her recommendations.

The art I bought because she said these works were her favorites.

"You really listened," she says.

"Mm-hmm. You're easy to listen to."

Her smile softens, and she looks intently at the large Ricky Vega on the wall by the couch. "That is one of her largest pieces. It's extraordinary."

"It is. It's grown on me since I bought it."

"I remember when that went up for auction. I followed it from my phone at work. The purchaser was anonymous."

I clear my throat. "Yeah. I like keeping some things private."

"You paid an enormous amount of money for it."

"Worth it," I murmur.

Her eyes land on mine again. "I hope you have everything insured."

"Of course I do."

"And I hope..." a faint blush creeps up on her cheeks, "I hope you might allow me to take a few pictures of them? I can't believe that I'm lying here, amid my favorite art. The sheer monetary value I'm surrounded by right now... is insane."

"And you're naked in front of them all," I say with a tsk sound. "Where's the honor? The respect?"

She giggles. "What they saw earlier today is so much worse."

"Scandalizing the art."

Harper shifts and runs a hand through my hair. My eyes drift close at the feeling. She scrapes her nails gently against my scalp, and I could have her do this forever.

"Tell me," she says softly, "what you'd—"

My phone rings.

It disrupts everything. Blares through the soft intimacy that had settled over my bedroom, the sound of birdsong in the garden, and the tranquility of the cool linen sheets.

"You should have it on silent," Harper tells me.

I roll over to grab the phone from where it's resting on my nightstand. "Trust me, I will."

But the name on the screen stops me. It's Dad. And I know exactly why he's calling. The same reason Alec and I spoke for almost an hour yesterday.

Knudsen.

The phone keeps ringing in my hand. *Decisions, decisions.*

I hit accept. "Hey."

Harper fluffs up a pillow and slides both arms under it. Settles in and looks at me.

"Nate," my father says. His voice is curt. "One of the reasons why we sent you to London was to build relationships with European suppliers."

My eyes are on Harper. "That wasn't the reason I moved to London."

A brief pause. "What? Of course it was."

"I suggested the move."

"Yes, well, it was for the explicit purpose of you handling European deals. I don't need to remind you how important Knudsen's network would be for our—"

"No. You don't need to remind me. I'm aware."

"I tried to speak to Alec about this, but he wasn't having it," Dad says. There's angry frustration in his voice. It's been there for the past six months, ever since Alec had blown up at Dad at Thanksgiving. Almost half a year of the two of them having a strained businesslike relationship.

Although was it ever not strained? Not businesslike?

"I've already discussed this with Alec. There's no need for you and me to go through it, too."

He snorts on the other line. "Yes, there is. I want the reason, and I want to hear it from you."

"Knudsen's nephew is likely a scam artist and a fraud. I wouldn't endorse him as a legitimate art dealer by purchasing from him, and Knudsen didn't handle the news well."

"Okay. But what was the real reason?"

"I just gave it to you."

Dad barks out my name like it's a curse. "Why the fuck would we care? Throw the nephew some money, pat his head, and then shake Knudsen's hand!"

I can't look away from Harper. She's staring at me through long lashes and digging her teeth into her lower lip.

Listening to this entire conversation.

"It wasn't right. And wouldn't look good in the long run."

"That's the attitude of a pussy," Dad says. His voice is heavy with scorn. "You know Contron *needed* that contract. Alec needed it."

"He doesn't need it. He wanted it. There's a difference," I say sharply. "Alec and I have already discussed other potential leads to fulfill what Knudsen offered. None of this will be a problem. And no offense, Dad, but I don't report to you. I report to Alec."

Dad makes a sound most similar to *bah*. He starts speaking again, but this time I cut him off.

"I have to go. It's midday here, and I have things to do."

"Right. Well, I hope one of them is repairing this damage."

"Goodbye, Dad."

I put my phone on silent and toss it across the room, onto the couch in the corner. It hits the soft cushions with a dull thud.

Harper makes a sympathetic sound. "He's angry?"

"Yeah."

"Your brother?" she asks carefully. "What about him?"

I sigh. "He wasn't happy, either. But so what? He understood, and I told him I'd find us another connection. A better one."

"Oh. That's good, right?"

"It is." I raise an eyebrow at her. "Just a year ago, Alec would have reacted differently. But he's gone and fallen head over heels in love, and takes his job slightly less seriously now."

She smiles. "He has? That's great. Sounds unlike him, from what you've told me."

"It is. He even asks me more personal questions now on our phone calls. Sometimes, at least. It's not all about business," I say. I still chat with Connie most weeks—checking in, hearing about her life. We've always had an easy relationship, a good one, but Alec was never one for unnecessary chitchat.

"Have you met her?" Harper asks. "His girlfriend?"

I kiss Harper's shoulder. Her skin is soft beneath my lips,

and fragrant. "Mm-hmm. She's Connie's best friend, so they've known each other for years."

"Wait. Your sister?"

"Yes."

"God, a lot to keep track of." Harper slides her hand into my hair, fingers twisting gently. "And you have a niece, too? And a nephew?"

"Yes to both. And I don't think it'll be long before Connie and Gabriel start up their own baby factory."

Harper chuckles. "You make it sound so romantic."

"I'm a titan of industry, what can I say? Manufacturing is sexy as hell."

I fold the cover back, inch by inch, until her tits are fully uncovered. Push up onto my elbow to get a better look, and she smiles at me, tiny dimples appearing in her cheeks.

"Admiring the view?" she murmurs.

"Always." I tweak one of her nipples, lightly, and feel it harden. Fuck, she's so beautiful. My chest hurts just looking at her. The words want to slip out. All of them. How much I've wanted her for years. Not that I simply found her attractive… but that I saw her first.

That I've loved her ever since.

Not yet, I think. Still too soon. Paris and Dean were just last weekend. We're not in a rush. If I could freeze time, here—in this bed, during a summer day with a smiling Harper… I just might.

I bend down and kiss her left breast. Suck her nipple into my mouth and worry it between my teeth.

She sighs softly and threads her fingers through my hair. "Do you want kids? Like the manufacturer you are?"

The question, while I'm touching her like this, while her naked body is resting right under mine, sends a shot of liquid heat down my spine. My cock hardens in an instant against the linen sheet.

Imagining Harper pregnant with my child. Imagining trying to get her pregnant…

Having unprotected sex with her this week has been the best carnal experience of my life. I didn't know that was a kink I had, something I craved, until her. Until this.

I groan with her nipple still in my mouth.

Harper chuckles, stroking down my neck and over my shoulders. "I can't hear you, Connovan."

I lift my head. "Yes. I do."

Her eyes are soft. "You'd be a good dad."

"Yeah?"

"Mm-hmm."

It's not something I've thought about much. Being thirty-eight and single, I've put that thought at the back of my mind. There hasn't been anyone else since I walked into that bar and saw her. In my despair, by moving to London, in trying to distract myself from her, I did consider the possibility of *maybe*, one day, being able to move on. Hoped for it, even. Freeing myself from the unrequited yearning.

But it never happened.

"And you've got time," she says as if she read my mind. "You're ten years older than me, but you're a man. Nature is unfair like that."

My right hand glides down her body. Pushes the remnant of the comforter away, until she's fully exposed to me. "Yes, it is."

I switch nipples and find the soft skin between her legs with my fingers. She sighs softly and runs her nails along my back.

"I love it when you do that," she murmurs.

I don't stop running my fingertips along the length of her pussy. Teasing, playing. Won't ever tire of that, either. How soft and warm she is, against my fingers, my tongue, my cock.

"Do you want kids?" I ask. Draw her closer and bite her right nipple.

Her breath catches, and she spreads her thighs. "*Oh.* Um. Yes, I do. I've always wanted them."

"You sure have," I murmur.

"What?"

"You're meant to be a mom."

She moans softly when I press my thumb to her clit. "Mm-hmm. Well, I used to want that, soon. Originally… the plan—after the wedding. Like, next year. But now, I don't know anymore. I might want kids in five years. I want to be… free first."

"Of course," I say, and kiss down to her stomach. "You want to complete your list."

"Yes. Exactly… oh." Her words are cut off when I settle between her thighs. She tastes good, and she's warm, and gets wet easily under my tongue. This has been my favorite activity over the past week.

Hearing her moan while her thighs are around my head.

I don't get far before she pulls me. Tells me, with a heated look in her eyes and a blush on her cheeks, that she wants to try something else, something different.

It's a position we haven't attempted yet. I want her to ride me later, in this glorious sunshine… but we'll do this first.

When Harper stretches out flat on her stomach on top of the bedsheets, I reach into the drawer and find the vibrator she bought all those weeks ago. I asked her to bring it up last night, but we haven't used it so far. Hadn't gotten the chance.

Harper's mouth makes an *O* when I hold it up. But then, she nods.

I grin. Slide it under her body, wedging it in place between her clit and the bed. The vibrations make a soft thudding sound on the mattress.

She looks over her shoulder at me, her eyes smoldering.

Fuck, I need to be inside her.

With my thighs on either side of hers, I position myself. Push in slowly. We're both breathing hard at the tightness of the squeeze. With her legs straight and held together, it's like sliding into a vise.

Harper moans when I'm finally, deliciously, fully seated.

She's so tight, it almost hurts, and I can't move a molecule or I'll come.

"On top of me," she murmurs, and right. *Right.* I stretch on top of her so my body covers hers entirely. Use my elbows to brace myself and keep from crushing her. The fit is snug, and complete, and she's mewling beneath me. Her face is turned to the side, and I brush my lips over her cheek.

"Like this?" I ask and start moving my hips. Use my knees against the bed for leverage.

Her eyelids flutter closed. "Yes. Just like that."

I rest my forearms next to hers. Thrust again, slow and deep. Find her hands butted against the mattress and lock my fingers together with hers.

It doesn't take long to understand why she likes this position. Our bodies are touching from head to foot, and I can easily rest my forehead against her neck. Reach her cheek. Kiss the soft skin of her shoulder.

"You feel so fucking good," I mutter into the shell of her ear. "You always do. Like you were made for me."

She moans softly, and beneath our combined weight, the vibrator is a constant low rumble. "I do?"

I close my eyes. Thrusting so slowly is an agonizing pleasure, with her this hot and tight around my cock. The faint throbbing from her clit reverberates through her, and I feel the pulses when I bottom out.

"Fuck yes. This is my favorite… place to be. Inside you."

Her fingers flex around mine. "And to come inside of."

Heat flares at the base of my spine at her words. This previously unknown kink of mine has turned into an obsession over the past week. A compulsion to fill her as much as I can. To see my come dripping out of her.

I dig my teeth lightly into her shoulder, and she chuckles. "Yes," I mutter. "You'll drive me insane, you know. Drain me dry."

"Poor little billionaire," she whispers.

I nip her neck again. Ram my hips sharply against her

round ass, pushing her more firmly on top of the vibrator, and her breaths stutter. *Mine,* I think. Another thrust. *All mine.*

Harper's mouth opens on a moan, and she screws her eyes tighter. "God, that got me so close. Nate..."

"Say my name again."

"Nate," she whispers. "Nate, I need you to never stop, never stop, I'm... oh my God!"

She comes beneath me. Against the vibrator and around my cock. Her pussy is already painfully snug because of the position we're in, but when her walls quiver rhythmically as she orgasms, I can't hold back anymore.

I erupt, pleasure dancing up my spine like flames, and my hips pistoning on pure instinct. Harper is moaning softly under me, and I can't focus on anything—not on holding up my weight, not on breathing, not on thinking.

My forehead drops to her cheek. Our bodies feel fused together, skin bonded with every cell.

I never want to move.

Harper giggles softly. It's a tiny sound, and I feel her breath fanning my skin. "What?" I mutter.

"I think your soul may have just left your body," she says.

"It did. I gave all of it to you." My voice sounds as tired as the feeling in each of my muscles. My heart is pounding, and she must sense that, pressed as I am to her back.

Her back. I'm lying on top of her.

I push up to my elbow. "Shit. You're not hurt?"

Harper smiles and looks at me with her left eye. "I'm the furthest from hurt anyone can be. Come lie on me again."

"I'll crush you."

"No you won't," she says. "And I like it."

I settle back on top of her, still *inside* her, and chuckle hoarsely. "Another one of your quirks. Duly noted."

"Considering one of yours is making me orgasm in a room full of people, mine are pretty mild." She smiles happily and closes her eyes.

I kiss across her cheek. Up to her eyebrow. Her skin is

damp with exertion, the same as mine. Maybe we can leave the bed to have a shower before returning to its comforts once more. Order in some food.

And then do this again.

"Nate," she whispers. "I think I'm falling in love with you. And I don't know what to do about it."

Everything narrows down to this moment. Those words. I press my lips to her cheekbone and try to handle the rush of emotions her confession had sparked.

Her voice was a bit shaky, and hesitant, and I wonder if she's ready to talk about it fully.

"Oh?" I ask. It feels like a beautiful but skittish animal approaching. I don't want to scare it off. "Is that something we should talk about… or keep it in the box for now?"

She smiles against my skin. "I like that box metaphor."

"It's been very useful for us."

"I think it can be in the box for now. For a little while longer," she says, her voice soft. "As long as you know that it's there."

I rest my forehead against her wild curls and swallow hard. "I know it's there, baby. Thank you."

"Mm-hmm. Just a head's up. And how would you… how would you feel about that? Theoretically?"

"Harp," I say. My throat feels tight, and I can't say it to her back, or she'll hear the whole truth in the words. The years of longing and the recent happiness. So I settle on something else. "You own me completely… and that's got a box all of its own."

Chapter 35

Harper

"Okay, there's no way all of that happened in the last two weeks," Aadhya says. We're having iced coffees on the steps of the gallery, having just closed up.

I nod. "Yup. And you know what? The thing I was most worried about; the fact that his best friend was my ex? Wasn't a problem at all."

"Of course it's not," she says. Takes a long sip of her iced cappuccino. "Because he wanted a beautiful woman more than he wanted to keep an old uni friendship. Perfectly reasonable."

I chuckle. Happiness feels like there are soap bubbles inside me, light and floating to the surface. It's a gorgeous June day in London, the gallery's event is coming up, and I'm chatting with a friend. About to walk home through Chelsea and up to Kensington, past the houses I find just as pretty now as the first time I made that journey, to arrive home. Nate will be back at around eight, and we're going to have a date in the garden.

Our first true date.

"I mean, when you say it like that… I suppose it makes sense." I cross my hands and look down at my feet. Stuffed into a pair of navy ballet flats. "Only, do you think it's too soon for me? To get into a new relationship?"

She lifts her shoulder in an elegant shrug. "Honestly? Yes. Maybe. But maybe not. I think a lot of people have hard and fast rules about those kinds of things, but it's always unique to each case. You have to do what feels right to you."

"Yeah," I say and use the straw to stir in my drink. The ice makes soft clinking noises, and, somewhere in the square, a bird trills. "I'm really excited about him and about this. Us. What might happen if I continue down this road."

"Judging by that smile on your face, I believe you," Aadhya says while grinning.

"I used to be afraid that he was too much like my ex. They're both ten years older than me, both quite… well-off. In a way I'm not," I say.

"Makes sense," she says reasonably, "if they have a ten-year head start on their careers."

I nod. It feels weird not to have told her that Nate Connovan, who occasionally buys art from the gallery, is the same man as my "friend-turned-roommate-turned…-lover." But it would be even weirder to confess it now, after all this time.

"And I want independence, you know? At least for now. I want to see more of Europe, and to work here with you, and see where life takes me."

Aadhya unfolds her designer sunglasses and slides them on with practiced ease. "My free-spirited American," she says. "I'm glad they chose you as the new junior trainee, you know."

I pretend to gasp. "A compliment?"

She grins. "You're fun," she says. "Wild, but fun. God help me if I'd been forced to deal with some uppish British girl."

I raise an eyebrow. "Sorry to tell you, but—"

"I know exactly what I said," she says, her smile intact. "And I like being the only me in a room."

That makes perfect sense to me.

We say bye, and I start walking back home. Past the boulangerie with beautiful loaves in the window, past the second-hand shop and the perfume store, and onto the residential streets. I'm not seeing any of that, though. My thoughts are swirling.

The past two nights, I've slept in his bed.

Maybe we should have some kind of boundaries. Maybe it *is* too fast, and maybe I should be more careful, but I don't want to. Not this year. Not this new me. I want to go on wild road trips, embrace spontaneity, and stay out all night.

And maybe, he will want more from me than I can deliver at some point, but that's then, and now's now. The only thing—

My phone rings. It buzzes aggressively in my pocket, and I reach for it.

The number is unknown, but coming from the States. I frown down at it only for a few moments before answering. Between caterers calling occasionally, and my stepdad constantly losing his phone and getting a new one, an unknown number is not that surprising.

I regret answering it the instant his voice comes onto the phone.

"Dean," I say. The bubbles of happiness inside of me pop one by one. I do *not* want to deal with him today. "If this is about my last email, with the payment plan I drew up, I think we should keep that conversation to a written communique. There's no need to—"

"Oh, you're wrong about that," Dean says. "I think there is a need."

I sigh. This is awkward, and painful, and uncomfortable. "I'm sorry about you seeing what you saw, Dean. Honestly. My goal was never to hurt you, just to move on. I want us both to be able to do that."

"Move on. Yeah, I think that's a good goal," he says. "Maybe it was best that I saw the two of you and realized *you* had already moved on. You upgraded to an even richer sugar daddy. Impressive, really."

My stomach sinks. It's just past noon in New York, but I wonder if he's drunk. If he's been at lunch with an investor and indulged more than he should've. "If you called to rant, then I'm hanging up. We'll speak over *email* about my monthly payments—"

"Monthly payments?" Dean asks. "He really hasn't told you. Wow. Well, there will be no need for those." Dean's voice is bitter, and just a tad vindictive. Like he's exhausted but taking pleasure from this exchange. "You see, Nate settled all of it with me."

"What?"

"Oh, yes. Told me to never contact you again. But when your email came in last night, I realized you didn't know."

"He didn't," I say. "He wouldn't do that, so whatever game you're playing—"

"Ask him," Dean says. "He's an arrogant bastard, but he's not a liar. At least, he didn't use to be. Now, I don't know anymore."

I don't know what to say.

Don't know what to think. The last remaining bubbles inside me go off with a pop, leaving me deflated and heavy. I can't imagine Nate would do that. He knows what it means to me to repay Dean for my part. To stand on my own, to stand by my own decision, and to be independent.

To be able to leave Dean *and* his financial manipulations behind.

I'm the one who called off the wedding. I want to pay my half of the costs.

It feels like the easiest concept in the world to grasp, but if he did this, if he went to Dean…

"When?" I ask.

"In London, after you went inside," Dean says. His voice is laced with delight now. "You know, maybe you didn't make a good choice after all, Harper. I would've taken your wishes into consideration. I used to want us back, but now I doubt I'd—"

"You've never once considered my wishes or opinion." I

hang up the phone, my hand clutching it so tightly that my fingers hurt.

He couldn't have.

But he has. It makes sense. A painful, warped kind of sense, and my stomach feels like it has turned to lead. So heavy it's hard to keep walking.

Somehow I do. Somehow, I end up back at home, going through the motions like I do most afternoons. I put on my workout clothes and go knock on Richard's door. Get the dogs, take them for a walk, and chat with our neighbor.

By the time the summer sun has started to kiss the horizon, by the time I'm sitting cross-legged in the garden, it's time for Nate to come home.

A part of me wanted to flee as soon as I arrived at the townhouse today. A part of me wanted to start packing, and I wasn't able to resist gathering my clothes together. Tidying up in the guest bedroom. Throwing the most important things into a bag.

I don't want to be in this position again.

The sentiment is so strong it's hard to keep still on the chair. This situation, this dependence, this kind of relationship. I didn't want to experience it again.

And yet, I have. I've fallen right into it, because it had felt so easy, so *right* with him. Nate had paid for almost everything. I'd tried. He'd accepted on occasion, begrudgingly, but he'd paid for the Paris trip, and for the excursion up north, and the movie premiere, and… and… I let him. I'd gone along with all of it.

Because it felt different from Dean. It felt good.

But maybe, just when I started to figure things out for myself, I'd fallen back into the trap of letting someone else decide for me. And that's one step away from living a life I don't want. Again.

I hear Dean's voice again. The thing he said, that fateful day, when he didn't care about me overhearing him. That he didn't think I was capable. It hurts to think that Nate might feel the same way. That he didn't believe I could repay my debts.

I feel numb when I hear the noise coming from the kitchen. Nate walks out of the open French double doors. He's got a bottle of wine in one hand and a smile on his face.

"Hey," he says. "I'm later than I planned. A work meeting ran over. Didn't mean to keep you waiting."

I shake my head, my hands firmly clasped together on my lap. "That's okay."

Nate frowns. "Everything okay?"

"No. Not really."

He sets the wine bottle down and comes to me. "You look… has something happened?"

"Yes. I have something to ask you."

"All right." His tone is cautious now, and concerned. He sits down on the lawn chair across from mine. "What is it?"

It's hard to get the words out. I feel sad and mad at the same time, and the mix of emotions create a cloying tightness in my chest. "Did you pay off Dean to get him to leave me alone?"

A furrow appears between his brows. "I didn't pay him off. I settled the debts, yes."

I close my eyes. "Oh my God."

"He was using them as an excuse to contact you," Nate says. "It was manipulation, pure and simple, and I saw how it was affecting you. It wasn't right."

"Those were my debts to pay." My eyes are starting to water, and I hate it, *hate* how I cry when I'm angry and embarrassed. "This is *my* life, Nate."

"Harper? It was to help you. To ensure you didn't have to speak to him again unless you wanted to. Don't cry, please."

"I can't believe you did that. I never once asked you to do that for me."

"You didn't have to," he says. The furrow is deeper than ever, his eyes locked on me. There's pained confusion there. Like he truly doesn't understand.

Because this is just what he does. He looks after the people he cares about. And it hurts, like a knife to my chest, that he did this because of how he feels… but the result is still the same.

"I wanted to settle those debts," I say. "It was my way of finding peace with the past and standing up to Dean."

"Dean doesn't need the money," Nate says fiercely. "It's fucking ridiculous that you're supposed to pay *him* for a wedding that never took place, a wedding—by the sounds of it—that he insisted on."

"It doesn't matter! It doesn't matter that he doesn't need the money. It's the principle." I shake my head again, and a tear slides down my cheek. "This was *my* issue to handle, Nate. This is my life."

"I couldn't stand by and let you pay that asshole—"

"Let me? Do you hear yourself?" I can't believe he's doubling down on it. Pressure creeps through my veins, like an itch I can't scratch, and I need to move. I need to escape.

I rise out of my chair and head up the few steps into the kitchen.

Nate follows me. "Harper, it was to help you. He won't bother you again."

"Of course not. Just my conscience will." I round the railing in the hallway and take the steps up to the second floor. To my room.

Only it's not mine. It's his, like everything else in this beautiful house. The house I've lived in rent-free for longer than our agreement from that bet. I went from being under Dean's thumb to a couple weeks of glorious independence to landing right back in the same quicksand pit—moving into the house of another rich man.

I feel so disappointed with myself. I was supposed to *get out,* damn it, to move abroad and be wild and stand on my own two feet and—

"Your conscience? You can't be serious," Nate says. His

voice sounds incredulous. "He doesn't deserve a single passing thought in your head."

"Maybe not, but that's my decision." I reach for the bag. Grab my laptop and slip it inside. The need to flee is so strong, I debate leaving my charger behind.

I fight it. Round the neatly made bed and grab that, too, nearly knocking my head on the nightstand.

"You're packing," Nate says. "No, you're... you've already packed. Unbelievable."

"I need to think. I just need to *think*. That's all."

"Over the money? It's such a small sum, Harper, and what does it matter if it keeps Dean off your back and away—"

"It's not a small sum," I say. My voice is stronger now. Seeing him standing there, blocking most of the doorway, his expression one of pure exasperation... it fuels me. "It's a small sum to you, definitely, and maybe even to Dean, but it's not a small sum to me. Nor to most normal people. And I wanted to be the one to pay it back."

Nate crosses his arms over his chest. "That's not what I meant."

"That was exactly what you meant. God, you and Dean, both so detached. A dollar may have lost its value to you a long time ago, but it's still important to some of us." I swing my weekend bag up on my shoulder and push past him.

He follows me. "That's not true."

"Of course it is. I've seen it every day since I moved in."

"What would you have me do, Harper? Stand by and *watch* as Dean abused you through veiled threats and hints of paying interest?" His voice is angry now, too. Frustrated. "I had to help."

"You didn't *help*!"

"Didn't I? Isn't it better not to have—"

I spin around to face him. "Because now I'm indebted to *you*!"

He stops in the entryway and looks like I've just hit him over the head. "What? Of course, you're not."

"No. *Of course,* I am. And now… I'm gonna have to draw up a payment plan with you. How could you not tell me, Nate? How could you not *ask* me first?"

The words feel like a lead weight, settling somewhere over my ribcage, and a hit of sadness strikes me, strong enough that it feels like a punch to my stomach.

I've been having so much fun with him. I've been feeling like maybe… like we might be… But now, it feels like all of that has been pulled out from under me.

Nate looks at me with sorrow in his eyes, but doesn't give me a response. Even though there is one. But maybe that's part of the box we kept sealed away, too.

The box I can't ignore any longer.

I open the front door and step out into the waning sunlight.

"Harper, you can't leave."

"Oh, that's one thing I can still do on my own."

"Where are you going? Where will you spend the night?"

"I'll figure something out."

He follows me out to the sidewalk. "Let me book you a hotel, at least. Call a cab."

The words make me laugh. It's humorless, and another tear tracks down my cheek. "No, thank you. I think it's time I start paying for things myself."

Chapter 36

Nate

I get very little sleep.

Maybe it's her scent on my sheets. Or the silhouette of art frames on the walls of a darkened room—pieces she picked out without ever knowing all of them were being bought for her. Or, maybe, it's the sickening boulder of guilt inside me.

I don't know where she is.

My mind runs through all the different options in my head. A hotel. *Most likely.* Her friend from work. *A possibility.* The friend she made in Pilates class whose name I can't remember. *Not very probable.*

On a plane back to New York.

Hopefully, *never*.

When I rise in the morning, it's to a pounding headache and a mouth that tastes like ash. I go for a run, shower, and head to work. Contron's London office is modest compared to New York, tasteful and not ostentatious, and I have always enjoyed it. Liked it from the first time I stepped foot inside the old stone building.

Right now, it feels like a corporate prison.

I can't focus on the screen and my emails. Miss whatever my assistant had said so many times that she finally told me she'd write it out for me instead.

I text Harper. Again.

This time, I keep it short. If she's angry, she needs time to cool down, I think. It seems reasonable. At least, I'm hopeful that's it.

Nate: Please let me know you're okay and you found someplace safe to live.

She doesn't answer. Not until after lunch, when I've already decided that the only way to resolve things is to go to her art gallery as she's leaving work, like some kind of stalker.

Harper: I'm fine. Don't worry.

Right. *Easy.* Just don't worry. But right now it's the only thing I can do, and the worry lives right alongside guilt and frustration. What else could I have done? See her suffer with Dean and not stepped in? That feels like an impossible choice.

Maybe it felt too serious. Maybe that's why she'd reacted the way she did. Things with us had gotten deep over the past couple of weeks, and she'd been single only for a few months prior.

I run a hand down the side of my face. *Fuck.* I can't have blown this chance.

When my phone rings around 2 p.m., I can't stop the thrill. But it's not her. It's another name on my screen that I'm distinctly less enthused to see.

But I answer. The habit is deeply ingrained.

"Hello, Dad."

He doesn't bother with a hello back. He asks if I've found someone to replace Knudsen, and I report on the few options Alec and I have already started to work on. Like I did a few days ago.

I'm only a few sentences in when he cuts in, making clear the real reason he called. It comes out as an accusation.

"Neither your brother nor sister have made any plans this summer to come out to the new house in the Hamptons."

I rub my temple with my free hand. "I think they have other plans."

"I bought that house a few months ago to have a spot closer to the city for this exact reason."

"You said the reason was the timing in the market. You'll be able to flip that property in a few years when the housing prices recover and interest rates drop."

"Yes, well, that is also true," he says. There's no lessening of gruffness in his tone. "Talk to them. Tell them I'm expecting at least a long weekend with the entire family gathered there."

"I think you can invite them yourself."

"They'll be more receptive if it comes from you."

"No," I say.

There's a brief silence. "What?"

"No, I think you should tell them yourself."

"Nate," Dad says, his tone implying that I'm being dense. "Talk to your siblings."

"Do you think there might be a reason they're not talking to you?"

"I spoke to Alec just yesterday," he says sharply.

"Yes, but did you really speak?"

"I don't need this attitude from you, too."

I roll my eyes. A bad habit picked up from Harper. "You've offended and hurt both Connie and Alec with *your* attitude toward their life decisions. Their partners. None of us needs to put up with that from you, either."

"I'm your father."

"Yes, exactly. You're our dad. You raised us in your image, and you brought us up to be tough, principled, and not to take *no* for an answer. Can you really be angry at Connie and Alec for standing their ground? That's what you taught them to do, after all. Be proud of them instead."

There's absolute silence on the other end. But the line is still active, and frustration keeps me talking.

"You also taught us to be foot soldiers for Contron. Well, you got your wish, and all three of us work well together to keep this company growing. How many corporate successions are successful, huh? But you managed to pass Contron on to the next generation without a hitch. Now get to know us."

"I know my children," he says.

"You know us somewhat, yeah. But not as adults or what our own interests are outside of Contron. Come to the table without expectations. And apologize to both Connie and Alec."

"I will never ad—"

"Admit defeat, I know. That's your mantra." I look up at the ceiling and the inlaid lights. This conversation is draining the last bit of energy out of me, and I had almost none to begin with today. "But sometimes you need to compromise to make deals. You have done that on occasion in the past. So compromise here, Dad, and get to know your children. We don't need your heavy-handed guidance anymore."

He makes a deep humming sound into the speaker. But he hasn't hung up yet.

"I can't be the go-between between you and your other children forever. Solve this, and maybe, *maybe,* we can move forward. Just respect their choices. They've made them as people you fostered them to become. Bold, smart, and strategic. I have to go now. I need to keep the company you built running."

I hang up. Something I haven't done to my dad in… I can't remember the last time.

One of the reasons my siblings aren't spending time with Dad this summer is because they are coming to London. I didn't bother telling him that Connie and her husband, as well as Alec with his girlfriend and kids, are arriving tomorrow. They are taking the company jet for four days of sightseeing and the kind of family time we've never had before.

I can't remember the last time Alec took his kids on a vacation.

I can't remember the last time *he* took a vacation.

Just a few days ago, I was thinking of how to introduce the idea to Harper. I wanted her to meet them, but worried it might be too soon.

Seems like I don't need to worry about any of that now.

Her gallery event is tomorrow night. I know how much work she's put into it, how important it is to her, and I planned to be there. To watch her impress her colleagues and guests, and to see her shine like I know only she can.

But now…

Showing up might ruin it for her. And I'm not entirely sure how I managed to screw things up already, but I'll be damned if I make her feel uncomfortable on the most important day of her career thus far.

I contact my assistant instead. *Send one hundred pink peonies to the Sterling Gallery tomorrow night.*

Maybe I shouldn't be there. But it won't stop me from making her night a little more special regardless.

Chapter 37

Harper

The gallery is busier than I've ever seen it be. Aadhya and I have been here since the early morning, looking over every last detail, preparing the airy space to welcome all these people.

Now they're here, champagne flutes in hand, heels and dress shoes sounding sharply against the hardwood floors. The main doors are open to the square, and a band is playing soft music in the grand foyer.

And I feel like I'm not here at all.

Like I can't focus, can't think, can't engage.

On my desk in the back office is a giant bouquet of peonies. So large, that it dwarfs my computer; so large, that all of my coworkers had raised their eyebrows and let out soft *oohs* and *aahs* when the flowers were delivered. There was a note attached.

Harp,
Congratulations on the party. I know how hard you've worked on it, and you deserve all the success in the world.

There's a sharp pang in my chest from missing him. It's only been a few days of sleeping in a hotel, of crying in the shower in the mornings, and of trying hard not to think about him. I mostly fail.

Like now.

As I'm looking around the space at the smiling and happily chatting faces, at Aadhya while she's showing off a beautiful Covey abstract to a group of well-dressed attendees… I feel numb.

Staying focused on work has been the only thing keeping me going since I left Nate's townhouse. I've thrown myself into my job and welcomed the distraction from my thoughts.

Eitan comes up beside me. He's been a moving target all night—talking to guests, ensuring that clients who regularly buy from us are happy and feel special. There's a glass of champagne in his hand that he's carried for two hours without taking a sip, from what I can tell. Smart move.

"It's going well," he says.

I nod. "Yes. I think we already have a few purchasing agreements in place."

"We do, yes. The large Jaxon Barn sculpture is sold."

"Really?"

"Yes. And not a day too soon," he says, and we both chuckle. The piece is not only mildly disturbing but is also so large that it occupies half of the West Room in the gallery. "I haven't seen Nathanial Connovan anywhere," he says. "Despite him being confirmed on the guest list."

I look over at the gathered patrons. "Yes, he was planning on coming, but business prevented him from being here tonight. I got a text just a few hours ago."

The lie rolls easily off my tongue. I wonder if that's something I learned from Nate. *False impressions* and all that.

Eitan nods. "It so often does. Well, I hope you've made him aware that he's welcome for a private tour anytime."

"I have, yes. He's always in the market for art."

"The kind of client we like," Eitan says. His voice is warmer today than I've ever heard it before. Still clipped, though, still sharp. "Harper, you've been here almost three months now."

"By July first, it'll be three exactly."

"Your junior trainee position is five months, but I want you to know... We've already started considering offering you a full-time spot on our team."

The words ground me. *Full-time.* Stay in London.

I've been thinking about how quickly my time in London was passing, I found that I wasn't yet ready to leave. I hadn't finished my adventure here.

"Thank you. I appreciate that a lot."

"Would you be interested, then?"

"Most definitely."

He makes a small humming sound. "Excellent. You and Aadhya make a solid team, and you've proven yourself with this bash."

"I enjoy my work here immensely."

"I can tell, Harper. I can tell." He smiles and nods at me, and then he's off into the crowd, mingling again. Always mingling.

I take a long, slow sip of my champagne.

This party is proceeding nicely. I have new friends in the city. The chance at a permanent job. And, after researching for two hours last night, I even have three viewings for new rental apartments lined up.

Life is good. Life should be good.

But I can't shake the feeling of sadness.

Once the event is over, Aadhya comments on my mood. She hasn't said anything all day, but she has clearly noticed. Her voice was soft when she started with a few probing questions while we locked up the gallery and began cleaning up.

"And I heard that you might be offered a permanent position?"

"Good news travels fast," I say.

She shrugs, reaching for another empty bottle of champagne. "It does. People are excited about the possibility. You've charmed everyone here, you know."

That makes me smile. "I really like this place."

"Please stay," she says. "I would hate to have to train another junior trainee."

My eyes widen. "Because training me was so time consuming, was it?"

Aadhya laughs. "God, yes, you had a hundred questions!" she says. "No, no, you were efficient from the start. It's not always like that."

"I would like to stay. I think. It's just complicated right now with… well."

She nods. "Yeah."

I hadn't told her everything. But enough. "I love this city, though. I would love to stay for a full year, at least. Also, it's so close to other places in Europe that I could visit. I didn't realize how many direct flights there are from Heathrow or Stansted. You're so spoiled."

Aadhya laughs again. "Geography, love."

"I need to get out there."

"You were in Paris like yesterday."

"Yes, and it made me hungry for more," I say while grabbing one of the folding chairs we rented for the event. Push it together and lean it against the wall. The janitorial staff will handle most of the clean-up over the weekend, but we need to make sure everything is ready for them.

"Are you going to forgive him?" Aadhya asks. She sets down a big brown paper bag with five empty champagne bottles, and the glass makes an ominous clinking sound.

I sigh. "Maybe. I think… The thing is, I can understand why he thought what he did wasn't a big deal. He meant well, and I know that. I know he's nothing like my ex. But he should have known that it would be a major issue for me. Especially when I'm trying to figure out my own life."

"I get that," she says.

"My last relationship was stifling. My ex always went

over my head, made decisions about money, and set the agenda. He expected me to just roll with it, or worse, be grateful. I lost myself in that, and I never want to lose myself again."

Aadhya puts her hands on her hips. "He demanded gratefulness?"

"Yes. And it's not like I wasn't, but when someone buys you something you've never asked for and then holds it over your head like a weapon…"

"Okay, that sounds awful," she says. "What's the point of dating a rich man if he's going to behave like that?"

A surprised chuckle escapes me. She turns, blinking innocently. "What?"

"I love when you say the wildest things with a perfectly straight face."

A smile curves her red-painted lips. "Have to keep the people guessing."

"You're the best at that."

In the end, we leave the gallery around midnight after locking up and setting the alarm. I walk to the hotel I'm staying at. A rather expensive but absolutely necessary hotel, one that's thankfully close to work.

For the past two evenings, I've walled myself in my room after getting "home" and laid flat on the fluffy bed while watching old reruns of *Friends*. Ordered takeout and tried desperately not to think about anything at all.

Especially not about the days ahead.

I'm running out of clothes. I'd only packed a small bag, and quickly. The majority of my stuff is still in Nate's townhouse. In the room that I've considered mine for a while now.

Tonight, I manage to get inside my hotel room before the first tear falls. It's not the first time I've cried since we argued, but this time, it feels like a release. Sadness, frustration, and exhaustion are mingled together, and I don't even wash off my makeup before collapsing into bed.

The champagne I've drunk should have *stopped* my mind

from racing. But instead, it seems to egg it on. It's as if my thoughts are the bubbles in the sparkly liquid, floating quicker and quicker to the surface, and exposing with a soft pop.

I toss and turn in bed. Try focusing on the TV show on my laptop screen, but I can't. Reposition again. Still useless. Feeling on edge, I reach out and grab my phone.

It's not the first time I've had the impulse, but it's the first time I've given into it.

He answers after the third ring. "Harper," he says. His voice is gravelly. "Are you all right?"

I pick at the corner of the duvet. "Yes."

"It's… nice to hear from you."

"I got the flowers. Thanks."

A rustling sound comes across the line, and I imagine him turning over. Lying on his back in the giant bed I know all too well. "How did tonight go?"

"Really well," I say and clear my throat. "Eitan hinted I would likely be asked to stay in London."

"Oh. That's amazing. Congratulations."

"Thanks." I close my eyes. Press my hand to my forehead. It's delicious to hear his voice. I've missed him. "I think I might need some more stuff from your house."

"Of course. It's all here," he says, but his voice is hushed. It sounds pained. "You're welcome. You still have your key."

"No, I… I left it on the desk in my room when I left."

"Oh."

A beat of silence passes between us. We've never been silent before. It's not us, and it's not the easy, fun dynamic that had made me so effortlessly fall for a man I never planned on loving. I was in deep before I knew I had begun.

Another quiet tear slips down my cheek, and I screw my eyes shut. Why didn't he trust me with the information? Why did he leave it to Dean to tell me?

And is there a way for me to be with Nate *without* giving

up the life I want to live? Right now, I want that more than I want my next breath.

"Maybe I can come by this weekend." My voice sounds soft. Not teary-eyed, and I'm grateful for that. Even if my eyes are more than wet.

"Whenever you want. Just text me beforehand, and I'll make sure there's someone home."

"Oh. Are you traveling?"

"No. My siblings are coming. They're landing in the morning."

"Everyone? Kids, too?"

"Yes," he says.

"It's late, I'm sorry I called. Didn't mean to bother you, I just wanted…"

"I know," he says. He clears his throat, a rough sound that reverberates through the phone. "Harper, I'm sorry."

I swallow hard. Heartache and disappointment form a tight knot in my stomach, and another tear joins its mate sliding down my cheek. In a well-worn path. "I know. I am, too."

He takes a deep breath. I hear the inhale as if he's lying right next to me. "I never wanted to hurt you. Fuck, it was the last thing I ever wanted to do. You… you mean the world to me."

I screw my eyes shut, and this time, I can't stop my voice from wavering. "I'm sorry, too. For everything. I reacted strongly, but… I just need to think about this."

"I understand. Take your time, baby," he says, but he sounds as miserable as I feel. "If I can do anything, anything at all… you tell me. Okay?"

"Okay," I whisper. "I hope you have fun with your family. I know it means a lot that they're here."

"I wish you could meet them."

I blot my cheek with the edge of the duvet. "Yeah. Me, too."

"I'll try to be at the house when you come by," he says, and his voice strengthens.

"Okay. Good."

"I miss you," he says.

If we keep talking, I'm going to burst into sobs. I already feel the quiet tears streaking down my cheeks.

I want him so much, *and* I want my newfound freedom and the ability to explore a stronger version of myself. A new version. "I miss you, too," I murmur. "We should go to sleep now."

"Right. I'll let you go," he says. "Sleep tight, baby."

The familiar endearment hangs in the air between us. "Bye," I whisper and hit the red button on my phone.

Turning over, I curl my knees up to my chest.

I thought I wouldn't feel like this again. *Heartache* wasn't on my "30 Under 30" list. It wasn't planned, it wasn't expected.

And maybe that's why it hurts so much.

I thought I left the pain behind in New York, but it followed me here.

Chapter 38

Nate

Six people are hanging out in my garden. A bottle of white wine is on the table between the four adults, low conversation hanging in the afternoon air.

I lean against the frame of the French doors and just watch them. It feels odd, and almost wrong, to have them here. In this London house that I've made my home, and in this city where I've lived for over two years.

Connie is next to her husband, Gabriel, her auburn hair pulled up into a messy bun. With the warm weather back upon us, she's holding a small water gun that my nephew, Sam, handed her. The kiddo is lying on the grass next to his sister, Willa, and looking up at the fast-moving clouds, another water gun forgotten beside them. Gabriel is nodding along to whatever Isabel is saying. She's sitting next to my brother, her hand clasped firmly in Alec's grip.

It's still strange to see Alec display his affection so casually. He's never done so before. Never been a PDA kind of guy. And to be fair, he still isn't. Not really. But the small touches, his hand reaching for Isabel's or placed on her lower back, continue to surprise me.

I don't want to be bitter.

But it's hard to see my siblings sitting out there, enjoying the sunshine, the company, and being deeply in love with their partners… and to know that the woman of my dreams is as far out of my reach now as she was before she arrived in London. When she was about to marry another man.

"Nate!" Willa says. She pushes up onto her elbows and looks at me with demanding eyes. My brother's eldest is so much like him. "Did you fill the water balloons?"

"I did, yes." I hold up a bowl of ten squashy rubber bombs. As many as I had the patience for. It was a stupid idea that popped into my head while driving past a toy store, knowing that my siblings were coming and Alec was bringing the kids. To get water guns and water balloons.

But the kids have been here for five hours, and they're loving it.

"You're going to spoil them," Alec calls, but he doesn't sound the least bit bothered about it.

"I'm preventing your children from overheating." I set down the bowl between Sam and Willa. "I want you to go really, really crazy, okay? But stay away from the adults and the table… except your father. Hit him. Deal?"

Willa is nodding vigorously. "Deal."

"I hear you, you know," Alec says behind my back.

"Then you know not to duck," I say calmly.

Sam smiles, his grin is wide enough that I see the gap of his missing front teeth. I reach out and muss his hair. This is one of the things I miss because I live in London. I get independence, privacy, distance… but that distance comes with a cost.

The kids resume their game, and I make my way over to the patio table where the grown-ups are lounging. Talking. Laughing. Over the last six months, since Alec and Isabel became a real couple, they've formed this tight-knit little foursome. I'm not sure how it happened. Gabriel and Alec used to be strangers at best, rivals at worst.

Another thing I've missed out on while being here in London.

It must have been Connie's and Isabel's doing. My corporate-minded sister and her ballet dancer neighbor have been best friends for years, and while Isabel's romance with Alec made a temporary rift in that closeness, their friendship now seems to be stronger than ever.

The men, for their part, seem incapable of denying their women anything. So, despite years of barely restrained animosity between our families, Gabriel and Alec found the one thing that cut through all the bullshit of the past.

Love.

"Did you see the schedule I sent over?" Connie asks.

I stretch my legs out and lean back in the lounge chair. "Absolutely not."

"What's the purpose of planning," she grumbles and reaches for her phone. "Okay. We discussed this on the plane, so everyone's already on the same page."

I cross my feet at the ankles. "All right. I guess I don't need to hear it, then, if all I'm to do is follow along."

Alec's eyes narrow. "You okay?"

"Yeah. I'm dandy."

"We're going to see Buckingham Palace first thing tomorrow morning. The kids really want to. And then, we're walking over to Big Ben and Westminster Abbey. Lunch is at The Admiral. We'll get our fill of classic pub fare before we split up. Gabe and Alec are taking Willa and Sam to Madame Tussauds while Isabel and I will hit Bond Street and Regent Street for some shopping."

"Wonder which group I'll go with," I say dryly.

Connie nods. "Yes. You're the tour guide, you know."

"Mm-hmm. I thought the tour guide was called Devon, and he's giving us a private tour of the city on the open top double-decker bus with plenty of snacks for the kids."

"You did read the schedule!"

I cross my arms over my chest. "I did."

"Okay, then you know everything. What do you think? Have we missed anything?"

I think about walks through the park. The movie premiere

at Leicester Square. About the flower market that opens at 4 a.m., and the sunrise breakfast at the Duck and Waffle. And I remember the hours spent in the art museum and laughing so hard that the attendants told us to shush.

"No," I say. "Sounds pretty… comprehensive."

She nods, but she's frowning. I'm not my usual self. I know that they sense it by their heavy gazes. Certain they hear it in my clipped responses. My usual charm is gone. I don't have the energy to make everyone laugh. I can barely focus on the here and now when my mind is a million miles away.

On the sound of her voice last night. Calling after midnight.

When I closed my eyes, it was almost like she was there. Next to me in bed. Talking softly in my ear.

Only her words cut deeper than any knife.

She wants to come over to pick up her things. Tomorrow. Despite my siblings' plans, I know I'll be right here when Harper arrives. I won't miss the chance to see her… to talk to her.

Gabriel clears his throat. "I want to have a James Bond moment. What do you say, Nate? Have you seen those high-speed boats going down the Thames?"

"A few times, yes."

"We could rent one tomorrow night. See the city from the water. Put on tuxes and bring a few cigars."

It's the kind of wild plan that would be expected from me, but Gabriel has the same energy about him. He sees possibilities where others see obstacles. He's great for my sister in that way.

"Yeah. We could do that," I say.

I sound as enthusiastic as a doornail.

Gabriel exchanges a glance with Connie. Alec releases Isabel's hand to reach for his glass, his frown deepening.

Oh for fuck's sake!

I need to pull myself together like I have so many times

before. Let thoughts of Harper go, bury them deep inside. But I can't find the strength to do it. Not this time. It's all gone. She took it with her when she walked out of this house, along with my willpower, my composure, and my happiness.

Isabel stands up from the table. "I need to use the restroom. Were our bags delivered to the hotel?"

Alec nods. "Yes. We'll go there after dinner."

"Great. Be right back," she says and seems to float on her ballet flats through the battle-entrenched children into the house.

Alec and his family aren't staying with me. He has in the past, whenever he came to London for a few days on business. He'd take the company jet and stay in my guest room, and all we'd do was work. Now they've booked into a five-star hotel a few streets over.

Gabriel and Connie have decided to stay here. But I can't let them stay in the main guest room. Instead, they're in another room on the ground floor. The bed is just as big, but the bathroom is smaller. And the view is not as nice.

Harper's room is still Harper's.

Gabriel excuses himself, too, and joins the warring kids. Sam squeals in delight when his new uncle joins his side of the epic conflict. Willa is clearly winning, but both kiddos are drenched in water, their clothes sticking to them. It's perfect in this summer heat.

And I'm left alone with my siblings.

I reach for my glass and take a long sip. We're heading to dinner after this, and I know I should slow down, but there's absolutely no restraint left in me for that, either.

Connie shifts forward. "How have you been?"

"Fantastic," I say.

"You told us someone was living in your guest room?"

They're diving right in. I cross my ankle over my knee, and nod. "Yes. She was. But she moved out a few days ago."

"Someone we know?" Alec asks. There's faint disapproval

in his voice, and it makes me want to laugh. Alec is so Alec sometimes.

"Not in person. No."

Connie makes a low, thoughtful sound. Her green eyes feel far too sympathetic and understanding, and I hate that she's somehow figured me out in just a few hours.

"Must have been nice, having company in this large house," she says. "What made her move out?"

"We had an… argument." I cross my arms over my chest. "It's not something I care to discuss."

"Arguments seldom are," Alec says. He runs a hand over his short brown hair. The furrow between his eyebrows deepens. "Were you involved with her?"

"Sometimes you sound so much like Dad, it's ridiculous."

That makes him silent, and his eyes turn frustrated.

Connie chuckles. "No, it's just his phrasing. And if I can make a guess… was it Harper?"

I tip my head back and look up at the sky. "How'd you know?"

"Just putting the pieces together," she says softly. "You mentioned a few months ago that the wedding was called off, so you wouldn't be coming to New York for it. Then, I heard from a friend of a friend that Harper moved to London. But you never mentioned that during our phone calls."

"Yeah. I guess I didn't."

"Harper," Alec says, sounding like he's trying to remember where he'd heard the name. "Dean Johnson's girl."

I groan. "Don't say *that*."

"All right."

"But yes. She was his fiancée."

"Ah," Alec says, and there's a whole world in that single syllable. Realization tints his tone. "That must have been terrible."

"Yeah. It wasn't… great. Seeing them together over the years."

Connie clears her throat. "Then, let's make sure she moves

back in. How do we solve this, Nate? What was the argument about?"

"I just said that I don't want to talk about it."

"I know, but if we're gonna find a solution, we need to know what we're dealing with."

"When did this become an *us* situation?"

Connie's eyes turn fierce. "When we were born to the same parents. Now tell us. Alec and I are experts at love and relationships now."

Alec blinks. "Uh, yes. That's right."

"Very convincing," I tell him.

He huffs a laugh. "I've got some experience in making bad decisions, at least, and unintentionally hurting people I care about."

I look at them. Sitting in my backyard, and waiting for me to lay it all out there. I can't remember the last time we ever did that. The last time it was the three of us like this.

"All right. So, it all has to do with her ex…" I paint a picture of everything in clear detail, keeping it short and to the point. It sounds no better out loud than it did in my head, getting rehashed time and time again.

When I'm done, Alec nods. "I understand. It's what I would have done, too. He was a threat and you handled it."

"That's what I thought I did. But instead it drove a wedge between us."

Connie blows out a sigh. "Because you went behind her back."

"I know, I should have told her about it right after." I run a hand over my face. Tiredness feels like a lead weight. "The one thing I've ever truly wanted, the one thing I'd give up everything for… and I probably fucked it all up."

"No, no, you should have spoken about it with her *before*," Connie says. Her cheeks are flushed with the heat. "Nate, maybe she's afraid of losing her independence, her agency."

I drop my hand. "What?"

"Her independence. You mentioned Dean used money to

control her, right? To take that sense away from her? And now, just as she's trying to get it back, you swoop in and handle her issues for her."

"I did it because I love her," I say.

Alec taps his fingers along the table. There's a thoughtful frown on his face. "I know all about that," he says, "but I think Connie is on to something here. What you deemed an act of love from your perspective, seemed like you taking control from hers."

"I have never once tried to control her. I don't *want* to control her."

"Then make her understand that," Connie says. "You have to reassure her that she can be with you and still have her independence. Make her feel safe."

I nod, fire bursting to life inside my chest. Fuck. It all makes sense when they put it like that. It wasn't just about the money for her. It never was.

But now, it's there, hanging between us.

"I need to solve the issue of debt first," I say. "She'll always be uncomfortable if we start out with her feeling somehow… indebted to me. It's fucking ridiculous, we're talking about a mere few thousand dollars here, but I get it. It's not ridiculous to her."

"Don't use that word when you talk to her," Alec says. "Just a tip."

"Oh, I won't. But I need to solve it…"

"You could always take her to Vegas," Gabriel calls from across the backyard where he's being pelted with a water gun by a shrieking Willa. "Get drunk, and let one thing lead to another. Bring a ring!"

"Charming!" I tell him, the eavesdropping Thompson who has managed to make my sister happier than I've ever seen her.

He grins at me for a second before his gaze falls on Connie. "It worked wonders for me."

She says something back to him, but I'm no longer listening. Connie's previous words are bouncing through my head instead. *Independence.* That's it. My eyes travel to the kids, the French doors, and the facade of my townhouse. Stop at the half-open window of my bedroom on the top floor. The room that's filled with art I know she loves.

And I think there's a way.

Chapter 39

Harper

Nerves make it hard to think straight. Excitement is there, too, living alongside the jitters in my stomach. I can't deny that I'm not looking forward to seeing him again.

Even if that eagerness is tinged with ache. Even if I don't feel like I know anything for certain anymore, and as unmoored as I did upon first landing in this country months ago.

I walk to Clarence Square on light feet. It's a beautiful day in a summery London, and the tall oak trees in the little park sway softly in the warm breeze. I'd forgotten my sunglasses at Nate's, along with most other things I own. My journal. My running shoes. My watch.

Seeing the townhouse feels bittersweet. It looks the same. Tall, beautiful, white bricks, and the glossy black door with the gold number eight on it.

I texted Nate an hour ago. *Can I come by at noon?* He replied immediately and said yes, the door is always open to me.

I take a deep breath. Knock on the door; the door I used to unlock with my own key.

It takes a while, but then I hear the lock turn on the other side. The door swings open, and my breath catches. It's not him.

Disappointment sweeps through me.

It's a woman. She's my height and around the same age, and has auburn hair pulled into a side ponytail. Curvy, with broad hips that make the simple blue summer dress she's wearing look like a million bucks. Narrow chin, freckles over the bridge of her nose, and bright eyes.

Her face lights up with a smile.

"You must be Harper," she says. "I've heard so much about you."

"I am, yes. Hi. You must be… Nate's sister? Or his sister-in-law?"

"His sister—Connie," she says, stepping back and pushing the door fully open. "Come in, come in. I'm sorry, but Nate isn't in at the moment."

"Oh."

"He wanted to be here when you came," she says, her voice soft and kind, "but he had to put out a fire across town."

"Ah. Contron?"

"Something like that." Connie steps through the large foyer, and I follow her into the space where I used to live. The house I'd fallen in love with, right along with its owner. The beautiful garden and the large living room and the giant kitchen where I loved cooking dinners and watching TV shows.

"I'm sorry if that kept you here just to wait for me," I say. "That wasn't my intention at all. I know you guys are visiting only for the weekend."

Connie waves a hand. "Oh no, don't worry about it. I woke up with terrible nausea today. Typical, right, getting sick on vacation? So I stayed home. If I feel better this afternoon, I'll meet up with the rest of them. My husband wants to drive a high-speed boat down the Thames tonight." She shakes her head, but there's a fond smile on her face.

I smile back. "That might not help your nausea."

"Definitely not. I'll have to cheer him on from the sidelines, I suppose."

"Are you enjoying London otherwise?"

"I am, yes. I love this city. This is the first time we're here all together, though, and with Alec's kids, as well. It's nice to do things as a family."

I think of what Nate had told me—of the Connovans, their relationships, and how they're slowly reconnecting. Taking small steps toward a more relaxed family environment.

One without their dad.

"I think it's great that you're doing this," I say. "It's definitely something Nate appreciates."

Connie's eyes sparkle. "I think so, too. And can I just say… I heard about what he did. Not all of it, of course, but I was curious. Especially since I have met your ex a few times over the years."

I swallow. "Yeah. It's… we're in a kind of weird place right now."

"I know that," she says and blows out a sigh. "And can I also say, between you and me, he shouldn't have paid Dean off. But that's my big brother for you. Actually, both of my brothers are the same. They're loyal to the bone and will die for someone they love. But neither has a ton of emotional intelligence. Nate thought he was helping."

I nod, and look over at the large couch where I lay several times in Nate's arms, watching movies. Talking. Laughing. "Yeah."

"Sorry, I shouldn't be bothering you with my opinions," she says. Her voice brightens. "It's just that, I know my brother, and I've never seen Nate care for anyone the way he cares about you. And while I have you here… I wanted to say, I know love can be really scary. New relationships are terrifying." She chuckles, and I can't help but look at her. She comes alive when she laughs. "Trust me, I know *that* better than anyone. My husband and I had a terrible start. But, sometimes it's worth taking the risk. That's another thing Gabriel has taught me."

I run a hand along my neck. What she's saying makes sense. But she is Nate's sister, and of course, she thinks the best of him. The problem is…

So do I.

That's why his actions hurt so much. Because I didn't *want* to think this way with him. I never wanted to introduce the pain brought on by money, and the unbalance of power and control in our relationship. I want things to be the way they were before he paid off my debt to Dean, without telling me about it. I want our relationship to be as it was before he made the decision for me about my future.

"I'm glad it worked out for the two of you," I say instead. "And I appreciate what you said. It's just…"

"I know," Connie says with a nod. "I do. All in due time. Are you okay, though? Are you staying somewhere safe?"

That makes me smile. "Did Nate get you to ask that?"

"He's worried, yes, but no. I wanted to make sure myself. I know how it can be when your living situation changes quickly. My best friend had something similar happen almost a year ago, and she… Never mind. Are you okay?"

I smile. "Yes, thank you. I'm staying at a nearby hotel. And if you let him know that, please also tell him that he is not allowed to pay for the hotel bill."

Connie grins. "Got it. Now, let's head to your room. I want to hear all about this art collection you've influenced my brother to buy."

That makes me chuckle. "I'm not sure I influenced it so much as he saw an opportunity for investment."

"Uh-huh," Connie says behind me as we head up the stairs. "I think influence is definitely the right word. Tell me about the lady in red in the downstairs guest bedroom. What's the story there?"

"Oh, that's actually a fantastic piece," I say. "The artist worked on a series of paintings referencing the witch-burnings of the Middle Ages, but with modern women in focus, to really highlight to viewers how outrageous it was. Like, they were just ordinary women like you and me, who were punished unfairly."

"I thought her dress looked like flames! I told Gabriel, and he said I was imagining things."

I look over my shoulder at the smiling redhead. "No, that was intentional."

"I win," she says, voice smug. "That's cool."

"She's fantastic."

Connie makes a thoughtful humming sound. "Fascinating. Who's the artist?"

I tell her while packing up the last of my things, and find that I'm actually enjoying myself. Broken heart and all. She's easy to talk to, no-nonsense, and feels more like a peer. A friend. Not like Nate's sister or someone trying to snoop.

"What are you planning on doing, then?" she asks. "Stay in London? It's a fantastic city. Similar to New York in some ways, but very, very different in others."

I nod. "Yes. I've been enjoying my time here and I think I want to stay."

Her smile widens. "That's wonderful."

"But it's not..." I swallow hard. "It's not because of Nate."

"Of course not, no. I understand that. And decisions that big shouldn't be made based on that, either. You're starting over. You're exploring new possibilities." She shrugs, and the movement looks elegant somehow. Like Aadhya's movements. "I'm such a planner, so this isn't me giving advice. It's more like I'm stating something I need to do, too. Which is to be present in the moment and not let the mind run too far ahead."

"Yeah. I've been quite good at that in the last few months," I say and shove my hairdryer down into my giant suitcase. The one that's been banged up and patched together, and had carried most of my important belongings across the pond. The rest are stored at my mom and Greg's house, not that there were many in the end. I thought I had a ton of things. But when I moved out of Dean's, I realized that most things were his, or were gifts from him. I left all of those behind, too.

I zip up my suitcase with a faint groan. "But maybe I need to think a bit more now," I say. "Maybe I've been going with the flow too much."

"There needs to be a balance between the two, that's for sure," Connie says. "Should I call you a cab? That looks heavy."

"Yes, please, I think I'll need one, to get all of this over to the hotel."

I look around the room. This guest bedroom that I'd stayed in, made my own, felt safe in. Somehow, I shoved the notions of me not paying rent and of having moved straight into another rich man's home far back into the recesses of my mind. I consigned those thoughts to that hidden box Nate and I used to speak about. But now that box is open, and I can't ignore its contents any longer.

The room looks like it had when I first moved in. Pristine, luxurious, beige. Empty.

My eyes land on the velvet box lying on the desk. It has an embossed name of the jeweler on the lid.

The diamond and emerald necklace.

I've never worn anything this beautiful until Nate gave it to me, and I doubt I ever will again. The memory of that night brings a smile to my lips. *It was magical.* Despite our current situation, and regardless of what happens between Nate and me moving forward… I will always treasure that evening. Walking the red carpet to watch a world premiere, seeing dozens of celebrities, chatting with the world's biggest action star… and then there was the vibrator Nate brought for me. That led to the earth-shaking orgasm in the back of a car.

I'll have to leave that part out when I tell people about that night.

Connie's soft voice cuts through my reverie. I forgot she

was here, standing in the doorway, so alike her brother. "I think he wants you to have that, too," she says, looking at the jewelry box. "It was a gift."

I grip my bag tight. Turn my back on the necklace and the memory. "It's too nice for me," I say. "But I appreciated the gesture."

Chapter 40

Harper

I'm at the gallery on a sunny day. It's the kind of summer weather that makes work, even work you love, feel like the worst chore in the world. I only want to be outside. Turn my face toward the sun and feel the grass beneath my feet.

The energy at Sterling is restless. Half of the staff are on summer holidays, including Eitan. Everyone but me, Aadhya, Sean from IT, Deana in sales, and Mike the security guard. Vacations are right around the corner.

The apartments I viewed yesterday were pretty good. Two were out of the question, but the third was a definite upgrade from where I lived before Nate's. I gave the landlady—a woman in her sixties, with a spare bedroom and en suite bathroom in her townhouse not too far from here—a tentative yes. She loved it when I told her where I worked.

I need to provide her with a firm response before noon tomorrow.

My mind is spinning with incoherent thoughts as I'm flipping through the catalog in front of me. It lists various art pieces from the Heeler Gallery in Seattle in meticulous order. I'm supposed to search through them for a few up-and-coming artists that Eitan's interested in. See what the comp prices are. But I can't focus. The names bleed together, one into the other.

I truly thought I would see Nate that day.

Connie was lovely. Surprising, even, with how chatty and open she was. A few of the things she said had stayed with me. *I've never seen Nate care for anyone the way he cares about you.*

He showed it. With every action. Each day when he chose to leave work early to come home. By every trip or excursion he planned for us. He showed it. He hinted at it. Said things that implied it.

But the other important issue is also *understanding* me, and he didn't. Not that time. Not concerning my debt to Dean. I'm not sure if I can get over that.

The fear is knotting my stomach. It's the fear of ending up back in the situation I have only so recently gotten out of.

But it's also the anxiety that I'll never feel how I did with Nate. With anyone.

There was such freedom in being with him. The easy conversations and the laughs. How he listened to me. How he opened up to me.

I miss him.

It's only been a few days. Five, in total, and I hate that I'm counting. Three since I heard the sound of his voice. He hasn't called since we spoke on the phone, hasn't texted, and more than anything else, *that* makes me want to sink through the ground.

I had been the one to storm out.

But still…

I flip another page in the catalog and struggle against the pounding headache in my temples. Sleep was hard to come by last night. I called my mom, poured out everything I was feeling and then some, and she listened to all of it. When I told her about Dean and the cancellation fees… she was horrified.

And was furious that she allowed him to call her, had let him make her feel sorry for him.

Why didn't you tell me?

So I told her the painful truth. I was embarrassed.

I was embarrassed about how much I let Dean get away with. By how much I let him pay for, and then he used that to control me. And by understanding too late how he manipulated me, my life, my choices. Our relationship turned unbalanced quickly, and I had no voice, and lost my agency.

But the worst part—I was too blinded to see it because I cared for him. And he used that against me.

Since I moved away to live with Dean in the big city, my mom wasn't around to see all of this unfolding around me. And being a wonderful and constantly busy professor, I didn't want her to worry. But as a mom, she still did, and I told her everything was fine. I was fine. Everything was perfectly, amazingly, *fine.* Until that fine became a cage I couldn't get out of. Because how could I even begin saying that things aren't fine at all?

Mom cried a bit. I cried, too. And she promptly booked a trip to visit me in late July, during her summer break. *Greg could come,* she'd said, but then suggested that it may be more fun for the two of us to drive through the countryside and pretend to be Jane Austen and Charlotte Brontë.

A clearing of the throat a few feet away draws my attention. I look up from staring at a blurry page to see Aadhya standing in the office. She gestures back toward the front of the gallery.

"Your client is here. Nate Connovan?"

I close the catalog with a hollow thud. "He's here?"

"Yes. But he made a strange request…" She frowns. "He said to ask if you'd like to join him for lunch, to discuss a few paintings he's interested in buying, unless you have other lunch plans, that is."

"Unless I have other lunch plans," I murmur. It's hard to think straight. Nate's here. At my work. *Unless I have…* His way of giving me an out? It has to be. Telling me he's here but he'll leave if I don't want to see him.

I rise so fast that my chair wobbles. "I don't have plans."

Aadhya puts her hands on her hips. "Right? That's what I was thinking. When a big client walks in, we're always available."

"He was just being polite."

Her eyes narrow a bit. "You okay? You seem…"

"Yeah. I'm fine. I…" It's a split-second decision to tell Aadhya the truth. But I go for it, jump off the ledge and hope there's a parachute. "He's actually the friend I've been staying with."

Her mouth opens.

"Yeah. I'm sorry I've been coy about it. It's just… with him being a client, too…"

"No, no, I get it." She shakes her head. "It makes sense. For what it's worth, I think that's brilliant."

That makes me smile. "You do?"

"Of course. Marry him, and his art collection is yours!" She winks at me, all Aadhya, calculation and poise and smiles. "Go have fun. I'll finish the Seattle research."

"Thanks, I owe you one."

I cross the gallery in quick steps. Anticipation floods through me, hurrying my pace. And there he is. Standing as he was the first time I saw him in this gallery, months ago, on my second day here.

With his back to me, he's facing a small painting picturing a vibrant blue pattern. Its size is the teeniest we've had in a while, barely larger than a single sheet of paper.

I stop beside him. "The painter was inspired by the broken pottery. The pattern doesn't line up… because the shapes represent jagged shards. But it's pretty."

"It is," Nate says. He's not in a suit despite it being Monday and midday. Instead, he's dressed in a pair of gray slacks and a white linen shirt, sleeves rolled up. But he is carrying a laptop under his arm.

He glances at me, and we stand there, side by side, in front of the tiny painting. "I want to talk to you." His voice lowers, turning intimate. "At the café across the square where we had a drink back in the spring. There are things I want to say, apologies… but only if you're okay with it. I know I showed up here unannounced. One word and I'll leave."

My gaze swims, growing unfocused, and the shards of pottery disappear. "No, don't leave."

"So, you'll have lunch with me?"

"Yes," I say. "I have an hour. Maybe an hour fifteen, if I push it."

"Let's cap it at an hour," he says with a smile in his voice. It makes my chest warm. "Wouldn't want you to get in trouble."

We walk across the square, busy as ever with the summer season. People from all surrounding areas come here to eat their lunch. The restaurants and cafés open up their terraces.

"Are you okay? You found a safe place to stay?" he asks.

"Yes, at a small hotel nearby. Is your family still here?"

He smiles a bit. "Yes. They fly home tomorrow. Connie mentioned… speaking with you?"

"She was really nice. I like her."

"She is. I'm sorry if she said anything that seemed like… pressure."

"No, she didn't. She was just looking out for you."

He opens his mouth to say something, but we're interrupted by a waiter before Nate can get the words out. Our table is in the corner, overlooking the square and the gallery across the way. My second home here in London.

Nate, being the first.

The thought nearly brings tears to my eyes. I swallow hard to chase the emotions away.

"I've missed you," Nate says. "I know it's only been a few days, but…"

I look down at my menu and blink rapidly. "I know. Me, too."

"Yeah?" he asks, and there's such intimacy in his voice that I want to forget about what happened. But it's difficult. It's so burned into me, the fear, the idea that I'll end up in the way I was before. When I had no sense of agency over my life.

"Yeah. I miss the house, our dinners, our life together…" I shake my head. "Moving out was a big step. I know that. But I just needed some time to think."

"I get that." He sets his laptop down on the table between us, like it's some kind of peace offering. Pushes his hair back. "Harp, I've realized I have so many things to apologize for. But let me start with this first… You're right. I shouldn't have paid Dean. What's more, I should have asked you about it, offered my help. And respected whatever answer you gave me."

I dig my teeth into my lower lip. "I know you were just trying to help. Trust me, I do. But it's the last thing I wanted you to do in that situation."

He nods. "I understand that now."

"I want to stand on my own two feet. That's what all of this, *this,* was about." I nod my head across the square, at Sterling. "Dean was my problem to handle."

"Yes. He was. Even if it would have been hard for me to accept and to stand by doing nothing," he says, and leans in closer. His jaw looks tense. "I hate seeing you upset or hurt. It's the worst thing I can imagine. And I absolutely *hated* seeing Dean speak to you the way he did, hearing how he's… It made my blood boil."

"Because you care for me," I say. The words come out softer than I intended, but they come out nevertheless, spoken in the space between us. "And it hurt me because… I care for you, too. And it hurt that you didn't tell me about it."

"Care," he repeats and shakes his head softly. "Yes. That's one way to put it. But I'll say it far more bluntly than that. Remember when you described the kind of woman you thought I would want?"

"Yes," I say. Weeks ago, at a bar right in this area.

"You were wrong. Because the only woman I want is you. I love you, Harper. I've loved you for years."

I blink a few times. "You love me?"

"Yes," he says, that small crooked smile on his face. "I love you, Harper Elliot. And it's been so fucking inconvenient from the start, but that hasn't stopped me. My love for you has only grown. Ever since I saw you at that bar four years ago, I've felt like you've held my heart in your hands."

I can't breathe. "You've… all these years?"

"Yes. Even when I knew I shouldn't. That it was hopeless. You didn't care about me or even noticed me. I knew you were in love with Dean, living with him. And not even seeing his engagement ring on your finger, knowing you were going to marry him, made it possible for me to stop loving you."

His eyes are determined, and there's a pained sheen to them that cuts me to the core. "Every stolen moment I could get, I took. Dinners at Dean's, always hoping you'd be there. His stupid summer parties. The bar hangouts."

"That must have been so hard," I whisper.

"Yeah, I felt like I was dying each time. But I couldn't stop, and the more I got to know you, the more I wanted you. It reached a point where…"

"Where what?"

"I moved to London."

I shake my head slowly. "You couldn't have moved here because of me."

"Dean told me that he was planning to propose to you. I knew, right then and there, that I needed to bury these emotions. That you were going to say yes to him and start a life together—something I couldn't bring myself to stand by and watch. So I pitched the idea of having a Connovan in our European office to my brother. I visited London plenty of times. It made sense."

"I'm so sorry," I whisper.

He smiles, but it's humorless. "Don't be. My emotions were mine to suffer. And as much as it hurt, I've never regretted meeting you."

"I didn't know. I wouldn't have… I didn't know." It feels

like my chest is too tight, too small to fit all the feelings rushing through me. I can't name them all. Can't parse through the maelstrom.

"When I found out that you and Dean had broken up..." His deep voice sounds hoarse now, and almost shaky around the edges. "I felt like an asshole for feeling relieved. For thinking that at least, *at least,* I wouldn't have to see him with you in the upcoming decades. Wouldn't have to know that, even being so unworthy of you, he was still allowed to be at your side... And then, suddenly, you were in London.

"And I just wanted to see that you were all right. That was what I told myself, that I needed to make sure you were okay. To help in any possible way. Help you settle in. Be your friend. And we did become good friends."

"I valued that so much," I whisper. "All the trips we did, the crazy nights, the experiences."

His lips soften into a smile. "So did I. It reminded me what it was like to have fun. I stopped having fun, somehow, over the last five years or so. Put that away like it was a summer jacket in the winter months. But you brought it all back. And then... we became more than friends."

I nod. "We did. It wasn't planned on my part. It was just so easy, and felt so right, and..." My voice breaks, and I have to clear my throat. "I started falling for you."

Nate's eyes are devastating. There's pain there, and such want that it makes my tight chest flush with heat. "I know you were. Until I ruined it."

"You didn't ruin it." The damn inside of me breaks. A tear rolls down my cheek. "You couldn't ruin it. I want this. I want you, and I forgave you days ago."

"You did?" he breathes.

I nod shakily. "Yes. Of course. It's just, this feels terrifying, Nate. All of this. Despite it being everything I want."

This seems like a terrible confession.

His large hand covers mine on the table. "I know it does. Your last relationship was stifling."

"I can't live like that again," I say. "What if I want to… after London… What if I want to move to Paris for six months? Or to Tokyo? What if I want to get a dog or go back to school or not get married for ten years? I might want those things."

Nate's smile widens. "Then that's exactly what you'll do."

"But what about us? If there's an us. I never want to hurt you, either, and—"

"Harper," he interrupts, his voice serious. "I never want to hold you back. If you want to move to Paris, I'll come with you. To Tokyo, too. If you want to get a dog, we'll get a dog. If you never want to get married at all, we'll never get married. Our relationship doesn't have to be like your last."

The picture he's painting seems too beautiful to be real. Could it be? I thought he'd be on a set timeline, have expectations. A man like him…

But he's never once made me feel like that.

Never once hinted at having suffocating demands.

"We can make our own rules," I say.

"We can make our own rules," he repeats. "And then, we can break them. There's no right way to be together. I certainly don't know of one. We can figure it out, build it. Together."

I turn my hand around and grip his fingers with mine. They're warm, holding me steady amid the emotional storm raging inside of me.

"Want to know a secret?" he says. "I'm terrified of this, too."

I look up into his eyes. "You are?"

He nods. "I've wanted this for so long. Want it still, more than ever, and I love you, Harper. But I never want to hurt you again. Never want to let you down, or be less than what you deserve."

Something inside of me aches, and I tighten my hand around his. "You could never let me down," I say. "And as for hurting me… you weather the hurts when you care about one another. That's a relationship. All the good, and a little bit of the challenging."

The corners of his lips tip up into a half smile. "I suppose. But I'm going to try my damnedest to never have it happen again."

I smile at him and steel myself to say the next part. It needs to be said. "The money to Dean, my debt… I don't want to be beholden to you for something that happened before us, before *this*. Can I pay you back?"

"You're not beholden to me."

I forge ahead as if he hasn't spoken. "While I can't pay it all back right away, maybe in a few months? Now that I have a full-time position."

He starts to shake his head, but then he stops. Makes himself nod once. "Yes, if you'd like. It's your choice. But it's not necessary. I used the weekend to run some numbers. You actually don't owe me any money at all. And, if you want it, you're well on your way to never needing a man again. Independence. Right?"

He squeezes my hand, releases it, and opens up the laptop. There's a spreadsheet primed on the screen.

I recognize the names in the right column. Artists. Some of them are my favorites. It's a list of purchases… The prices are in another column. It's his entire art collection, listed out in a neat ledger.

"I purchased forty-two pieces in the last four years, all on your recommendation," he says.

My mouth drops open. I'd known there were a few. But not this much. The numbers on this sheet… I knew, of course. Had lived in that townhouse for months amid all the beauty.

But still.

"I had them all appraised over the weekend. Consulted two independent art experts. I also got an estimate of what I would have paid to you as an art adviser had you been under contract." He scrolls down, to where a sum is highlighted in red.

A pretty large sum.

"That's your commission fee. A fee I never paid you. I used your services without giving you a dime."

"I wasn't consulting officially," I protest. "I was just talking about my favorite artists! Giving you advice and a few recommendations when you mentioned being interested in starting a collection."

"Exactly. Giving advice. My collection has appreciated significantly since I purchased the works. You've *made* me money, in effect, and gained nothing from it yourself. Not even professional credit."

"Nate, I—"

"I'm not wrong here," he says. "I understand if this isn't your cup of tea, but it's an undeniable fact that you should have been paid. Let me deduct what I paid Dean from this amount… and put it into an investment account in your name."

I press my hands to my cheeks. It's all too much, and yet it makes sense. Of course, it does. That's the hardest part. I want to protest, but I understand where he's coming from. And the logic is sound.

"I'll help you long-term with investing and financial planning, if you'd like," he says. "Or I can recommend where to start if you want to do it yourself. Point being, you can build real independence with this. You wouldn't ever need to stay at someone's house. Although I desperately want you to live in mine. But it's *your* choice, Harper. I want you to be happy and independent. And then, I want you to choose me, too."

"This is incredible."

"I was hoping you'd think that," he says, smiling crookedly. "I'm sorry I waited a few days to come tell you this. I wanted to make sure I got the numbers right. But I love you, Harp. And I want you in my life."

I reach for his hand again and grip it between both of mine. "There's something I need to tell you, too."

"Yeah?"

"I love you, too, Nate."

He blinks once. "You do?"

"Yes. It crept up on me slowly, and then faster and faster, until it's all I could feel. These last few days… they've been awful. Terrible."

"The worst," he murmurs. "You love me?"

"Yes. You're everything I never knew I needed. I think that's why I got so scared with the whole money thing. If I'd cared less, it wouldn't have hurt this much."

"I understand." There's light in his eyes that I can't look away from. Happiness. It glows from within and sets off my own until I can't help but smile at him.

He smiles back.

"Are we gonna do this, then?" I ask.

His smile breaks into a chuckle. "Yes, baby. We're going to do this."

He leans over the table to kiss me, and it feels like distilled sunshine, like coming home. Like taking a leap into the void but knowing you'll be caught before you ever hit the ground.

Like new beginnings and adventures yet to come.

Chapter 41

Nate, two weeks later

Harper lies halfway on top of me. Her bare right leg is thrown over mine while dappled sunlight shines down through the tree canopy above us. The blanket we've spread on the lawn of my garden is soft beneath me, but a few sharp blades of grass have poked through. One is tickling my ear.

"Keep going," she says.

I refocus on the list I'm holding and run my right hand along her back. "*Get a tarot card reading.* We never did that."

"No, but there's time left. I found someone on Brick Lane who seems good."

"Seems good," I repeat. "What does good mean here? Do they have great Yelp reviews? Like what's the metric here."

She chuckles and nods, her finger tracing patterns on my chest. "Yes. Four-point-five stars and over three hundred ratings."

"A guaranteed psychic, then." I move on to the next point. "*Stay out all night… spend an entire day in bed.* Both checked off. *Try archery*, checked off. *Visit the Louvre*. Checked off, too. We were really busy there."

"We were," she says.

"You checked off number thirteen," I say. Look at the tiny red check mark she's drawn with pen. *Sleep with someone who is wrong for me.*

She smiles. "Yes. Although now, I suppose, technically, I haven't."

"Oh?" I raise an eyebrow. "And why's that?"

"You know why. Because you're not completely wrong for me. You're actually completely right." Her eyes dance with amusement. "But I don't want to uncheck it."

"I don't think you should, either," I say. "Your list, your rules, right? Besides, baby, I was wrong for you at the time."

"I suppose you were. Off-limits. My ex's best friend." She rolls her eyes. "I can't believe that ever bothered us. It feels like such a nonissue now."

I kiss her. It's impossible not to. I kiss her as often as I can, relishing her softness and warmth. "Agreed."

"So… I've done eight in total," she says. "I have a ton left."

"Some of these are definitely doable." But I frown, looking at that familiar number. My hand splays over her back, my fingers touching the bare skin above her camisole. "But baby, if you're really insistent on number seventeen…"

Her eyebrows rise, and a smile flutters across her lips. "Yes?"

"If it's important to you, I won't stay in your way. We can do it." The idea makes my jaw clench. "It'll be hard for me, though. I have to admit that."

She digs her teeth into her lower lip. "You'd have a threesome just to please me."

I take a deep breath. The mental image that flashes through my mind, of watching another man or woman touching a naked Harper… It makes my stomach turn. "Yes. If it's important to you. But I'd rather not."

"How about with Austin Silver?" she asks. "I can text him."

My entire body tenses. "Absolutely not. Someone else."

Harper smiles and leans closer until our lips are only a few inches apart. "I love you."

"I love you, too," I say. "Does that mean we need to do it?"

She shakes her head, and a lock of curly blonde hair falls to tickle my cheek. "I wrote that list half-mad on a plane across the Atlantic. I was angry and sad, and wanted to shake up my life. I don't actually want to have a threesome."

"Thank fucking God," I say, and my hand tightens around her. Slides down to grip her ass. "Because the idea of sharing you, just about gave me a heart attack."

"You need to say what you want, too."

I chuckle. "I'm not shy about what I want, baby."

She rolls her eyes. "Not just me. But with us, with this relationship. We can work through my list if *you* want to, but you don't have to. We don't need to try… paintballing just because it's something I thought of and wrote while sobbing and watching *Pretty Woman*."

"They still show that movie on the plane?"

She nods. "Yes. I think the other passengers in my row thought I was crying because I was so moved, and I don't know if that makes it better or worse."

I lift my head to kiss the bridge of her nose. The idea of her crying doesn't sit right with me. The idea of her coming to any kind of harm never will, I suspect. It's a new feeling to care so deeply for someone. I haven't done it in a very long time, and never in this way.

"We do things for me all the time," I say. "Besides, all I need is you. Here. This picnic idea is growing on me."

She smiles. "Right? I know you were skeptical, but what's the point of having your own little backyard in London if you won't use it?"

I look past her up at the blue sky. It's a beautiful day in July, a couple of weeks after my siblings departed, and the second day after Harper moved back in with me. Somewhere in the tree branches above us, a bird sings, and the air around us is thick with the scent of freshly mowed grass.

"You were right," I say.

She chuckles. "I know. I so often am."

"Love has made you cocky."

"Do you object?"

I kiss her again. "Not in the least. Now, what are we doing tonight? I know you spoke to Richard about having him over for dinner."

"Yes, but it'll have to be tomorrow," she says. "His brother is actually in London today. Funny story, when he went to the hospital, they notified his next of kin by mistake. Huge breach of privacy, really, but that happened to be his brother… even though they hadn't spoken for years."

I frown. "Damn. Did that bridge the gap?"

"Oh, I don't think it even came close, but it was an opening. Today, they're meeting." Her smile turns warm. "I'm looking forward to hearing about it tomorrow."

"He's a good chap."

"He is," she says, and chuckles. "Chap."

"I'm a Londoner, you know."

"Yes, you are." She rests her chin on my chest and looks at me through long lashes. "It's a shame you never spoke to any of your neighbors for years."

"I needed you to come into my life. Teach me to stop and smell the roses," I say.

She rolls her eyes again. "I think you smelled plenty of roses before me, Nathaniel. A rich bachelor in London, and before that, in New York… Driving sports cars. Tall, dark, and handsome. Charming, and with money to burn…"

I lift an eyebrow. "Nathaniel? And are you implying that I've been around the block, so to speak?"

"Maybe I am," she says. "And I know that's hypocritical, because you had to see me with Dean, which I'm so sorry for now. I never meant… If only I figured things out sooner." She sighs and shakes her head. "The past is the past. But regardless… I don't think I want to know about all the women who've been up in your third-floor suite here before me. Pretend they never existed."

"Before you, I've never slept with a woman in this house."

Her eyes widen. "Never?"

"No. Harper… since the day I met you, I lost interest in others. There haven't been many encounters at all since I saw you at that bar four years ago."

Her green eyes are on mine. There's a soft vulnerability there that I could drown in. "Really?"

"Mm-hmm. Nothing ever went anywhere, because I was emotionally entangled with you. It wouldn't have been fair to someone else, to encourage a relationship when I was in love with you."

She swallows. "I can see that. I'm—"

"Don't apologize again," I say quietly and brush her hair back. "There's no need. You had your journey, and I had mine. And I'm very, very happy with where it led us both."

A smile curves her lips. "You're a romantic, you know."

"I'm well aware," I say with a grin. "It was my bane until it became my strength."

She sighs softly and rests her head on my chest. We lie in soft silence for a bit, my hand stroking along the soft skin of her arm, before she speaks again.

"There's one letter left to open."

I sigh. "I know."

She reaches for the manila envelope lying beside us on the blanket and turns it over to reveal the stamp on the back. The letterhead I recognize all too well. *Contron.* But the name written on the front is mine and it's in my father's nearly illegible scrawl.

I look over at the sky. "If he's resorted to ranting in handwritten letters now, I'm not sure I'm interested in hearing it."

"Have your siblings gotten letters?"

I take a deep breath. "Yes." My group chat with Connie and Alec had lit up three days ago when they got their letters in New York. Mine took longer to reach me across the ocean.

They'd told me to read it. *Wow,* Connie had written. *I need time to process this,* Alec had said. *Let's reconvene in a few days.*

Which could be good.

Or, more likely, very bad.

"You can read it."

Harper's hands freeze on the letter. "Are you sure?"

"Yes. I like your voice." I close my eyes. Listen to the sound of paper being torn, and hear her small gasp of surprise.

"It's not very long."

"He's a concise man," I say dryly. "Now that we've all stood up to him in the span of a year, has he decided to cut us out of his will? Is he making an offer to buy out our individual shares in Contron?"

"No. He's saying he's sorry," she says quietly.

My eyes open. That's impossible. "Read it."

She clears her throat. "Nate. You're my secondborn. The most like your mother. Now you're in London, working for Contron."

"He's starting by listing the facts," I mutter. "This isn't good."

She ignores me. "You had harsh words for me when we last spoke. But some of them were accurate. I have indeed raised all three of you to be firm, independent, ambitious, hardworking. On all counts, I can say that I have succeeded. I've brought up three strong-minded children."

"Yay him," I say.

Harper continues as if I hadn't spoken. "This has caused friction between us. I understand I've had my part to play in this. But I don't want to leave you with just a legacy. I want to leave you with a few good memories, too. This August, I'd like to invite you to the new house in The Hamptons for a small ceremony. I have asked Lauren to marry me. We're currently in prenup negotiations. This will not affect my will."

That makes me chuckle. "Of course. He never changes."

"But this *is* change," Harper says, her voice rising with excitement. "This is an apology. Right? Veiled as it may be?"

"It's the closest he's ever come to one, yeah," I say. "Is there anything else?"

"I know I don't say it often," she continues, "but I am proud of all three of you. Contron is more prominent today than it was during my time, and that's because of you and your siblings. I recently visited your mother's grave for the first time in years. She wanted the world for you. It struck me, how disappointed she would be with me—" Harper chokes up a little and takes a moment to audibly swallow,"—for wasting the God-given time I have with my children in anger, while she was robbed of so much of it with you. The shame I felt then is not one I want to relive."

I blink up at the sky. See my mother in front of me, as clear as if it was just yesterday. With her auburn hair and wide smile, telling me how stylish I looked in my little kid tux. It's my favorite memory of her to return to.

"Finally," I mutter. He's spent so long avoiding talking about Mom. Avoided mentioning that he was dating again when we all knew that he and Lauren from the executive team were closer than mere long-standing acquaintances.

"For a long time, I knew my role. It was to be strong for you. To guide you. But as you reminded me, Nathaniel, all three of my children are now grown. Perhaps, I can afford to take a different approach. Come to the house in August. I'll text the details. Partners are welcome. Dad."

It takes a lengthy moment before I can form a response. "Well, damn," I say.

Harper sets the letter down beside us on the blanket. Her warm hand finds my neck. "That sounds promising. Doesn't it?" she asks softly.

"Yes. Which is why I don't trust it… not yet."

She smiles. "Trust but verify?"

"Something like that. Partners are welcome," I repeat and watch the tender expression in her eyes. "I don't know if I want to expose you to him. He loves to put his foot in his mouth."

Her lip quirks up. "He's not you. I know that."

"He definitely isn't," I say.

"I think it sounds good. Like the possibility of a new beginning." She runs a light finger along my jaw. "And I am a big fan of new beginnings."

Epilogue

Harper, almost two years later

The sun shines down upon us, scorching the Italian countryside. August is the month when Southern Europeans escape their cities for the Mediterranean Sea, and here we are, doing the opposite.

The top is down in the car. Nate is driving, one hand on the wheel and one on my bare knee. He loves to keep it there when he drives, and I love it there, too. And in the rearview mirror, Siena. I look at it getting smaller and smaller behind us as we drive further into Tuscany.

We started our trip up north. Lake Como, Milan, before heading to Venice for a few days. That was amazing. Everything I could have hoped for and more. Then, we drove down to Tuscany.

Which is *also* more than I could have hoped for.

Italy is beating my already high expectations, surpassing them on the regular. It's terribly hot, but I'm enjoying that, too. Living in breezy sundresses and having my curls permanently in a ponytail.

I've rolled down my window, and the winding, narrow road takes us through the groves of olive trees. Old, gnarled, and beautiful. The air smells like heat and dry earth.

"How are you feeling?" Nate asks. "About completing your list?"

I put my hand over his. "Looking forward to doing the very last one tonight."

He smiles at me. "Good thinking saving it for last."

Dancing in the moonlight. We're going to do that right before midnight… The last hour of my twenty-ninth year.

Rolling in with an entirely check-marked list in that final minute.

"I feel good," I say. "Looking back at everything we've done… I can't believe this has been my life."

Every major art museum in Europe that I had on my list is checked off. The crazy thing like *take a hot air balloon* is accomplished, and so is the *sleep in a tent,* which Nate and I did together and vowed to never do again.

"Has been?" he asks. His thumb moves in a slow circle. "You have lots of time. I can't wait to see your '40 Under 40' list."

I smile. "I think I'm done with lists."

"Oh?"

"Yes. After tonight, I've done it all. Well, except for one thing on the list."

"The threesome," he says.

I laugh. "No, that one has been officially struck off the list. No, the whole *buy my first art piece* thing… Maybe it was stupid of me to pull out from the auction last week, but it just didn't feel right."

"Then it was the right move," Nate says. "It *should* feel right."

I hmm a response and look back at the rolling hills of Tuscany. The scenery reminds me of that painting my grandma has, the one that inspired it all. Nate has seen it now, too, back in upstate New York. Introducing him to my family had been nerve-racking… Until they actually met, and I realized I shouldn't have been nervous at all. Of course, he loved them. And they loved him.

He's easy to love.

"I think you're right. When I know, I'll know," I say.

Working with art every day is a privilege, but it's also made me picky about what I want in my own little collection.

Living with Nate has also made me very choosy. I'm surrounded by stunning pieces morning, afternoon, and night.

"The hotel for tonight seems amazing," I tell Nate. Lean out of the car and into the sunshine. It's late afternoon. "Do you think the pool will still be open when we arrive?"

"Might be," he says, but there's something in his voice. A secret…

I look over at him.

He looks at me, a sparkle in his eye.

"What are you planning?" I ask.

His lips curve into a crooked smile, and he looks back at the winding road. "We're not heading straight to the hotel."

Instead, he drives us to a residential address that I don't recognize on the GPS. It's close by, though, that much is clear. The route leads us through a beautiful tiny village with streets so narrow that Nate has to slow the car to a crawl. We finally drive up a cypress-lined road to a small farmhouse.

"Here?" I sit up straighter and peer out. "What's this place?"

"You'll see soon enough," he says warmly. Pulls the car into a parking spot right outside the small dwelling—dark earthen walls and a roof that blends in with the surrounding Tuscan landscape. A few chickens walk by the side of the house, clucking rhythmically as if unhappy with our intrusion into their domain.

The front door is open.

To the right is… is that an easel?

I get out of the car, my eyes wide. "Nate…?"

A woman with curly, gray hair that falls to her shoulders and warm eyes walks out of the house. She has an apron on.

It's covered with paint smudges.

She might be in her sixties or seventies, but there's an ageless beauty to her.

"Signora?" Nate asks.

The woman smiles and nods, and says something in rapid Italian. She calls for someone inside the house, and out comes a teenage boy of maybe fourteen. He waves at us.

"I'll translate," he says in accented English.

The puzzle pieces are slowly falling into place, and I look from the lady to Nate and back again.

"You're Giulia Conti?"

She nods and holds out her hands. They're tan from the sun, with short nails, and covered in color stains. "*Si,*" she says. That's the only part I understand.

Her—is that her grandson, maybe?—translates. "Nonna says your boyfriend here told her how much her art means to you. She's very happy you're here. Come in. We have lemonade inside."

"Come," the woman says in English. "Come, come."

I step after her into the small studio. And everywhere, on the walls and even leaning on the ground, are paintings of the Tuscan countryside. Sun-filled images, or veiled in rain, in winter, and in summer. Rolling hills and olive groves and small picturesque towns.

She's the artist whose painting is hanging on my grandmother's wall.

"Nate," I whisper.

"Good surprise?" I can hear the smile in his voice as he stands beside me.

"The best surprise," I murmur. My eyes have already caught on a large painting overlooking the Tuscan hills at sunrise. I turn to the lady. There are so many questions I want to ask. How she got started, where she paints, who she is… and with the help of the trusty but obviously bored teenager, I get to ask them all.

We leave there an hour and a half later, having been offered drinks and snacks, and with three pairings in the trunk.

I bought one for me.

One for my grandmother.

And Nate bought one for his collection.

He told Giulia that he was an art collector, and her eyes lit up, just as they had when I told her about my job. She didn't have a business card, but I asked her to write her information down for me.

My first art purchase. *Check.*

It's a bit intense. All of it, a full-circle moment, completing the list and being here, in this beautiful environment, with the man I love beside me.

He lets me have it. Looks over at me from time to time on the drive to the hotel, but by now, he knows that it's the weight of the emotions that's keeping me silent.

We check-in at the little boutique five-star hotel. It's on a hill with magnificent sunset vistas.

I haven't gotten used to traveling with Nate, yet. I hope I never will. These hotels, these surroundings... the large rooms and beautiful décor, amazing service. We have dinner right away on the outdoor patio, sitting under the setting sun. Drinking wine and sharing tiramisu for dessert.

It's late when we get back into our suite, and I open the double doors to our balcony. It overlooks the rolling hills, and I breathe in deeply. The air smells like blooming flowers and dry earth. The oppressive heat faded along with the sun, replaced by a warm nighttime breeze.

I lean out over the railing and just breathe. It doesn't take long before a tear tracks a path down my cheek.

Nate is unpacking behind me. I hear him pour a drink, the ice clinking. And then, his approaching footsteps.

"You're enjoying this?" he asks.

I turn to face him. His eyes widen, clocking the tears on my face, but I smile. "Yes. I'm feeling overwhelmed with gratitude right now."

"Oh?"

I pull him closer, locking my hands behind his neck. His skin is tan from weeks in the sun, his hair longer than it usually is. A tendril falls over his strong forehead and across his concerned eyes.

"Two years ago, I was afraid of my career path, unsure about everything, hurt and trying to heal, and… scared about turning thirty. Or rather, about being twenty-eight and starting over."

His lips tilt upward. "Because twenty-eight is ancient?"

"It's not. All my fears were ridiculous. But that's the thing with fears, you know? They don't go away just because you know intellectually that you'll be okay."

"I know," he says and runs a hand along my waist. "Trust me, I do."

"And now, look at where I am two years later. Where *we* are…" I shake my head and smile. Emotion makes my voice shake. "Imagine if I hadn't moved to London. If I got a position in Boston or DC or Paris instead."

He shakes his head, a tiny movement. "I don't want to imagine it."

"Me neither. One wrong move, and you and I might never have happened."

"But we did," he says.

"But we did," I echo. "And I'm so grateful for that, too. With a million possibilities, and billions of people on this planet… I'm so glad I was at that bar that night. Even with the detour I took to get here, where I belong."

Nate's eyes are warm. "I love you, Harp."

"I love you, too. So much." I rise on my tiptoes to kiss him. He kisses me back with soft, slow brushes of the lips while his hands glide to my lower back. And then, he starts to sway.

Oh.

Our dance. I rest my head against his shoulder and close my eyes.

"The final thing on your list," he murmurs. "And with only an hour to spare before midnight."

"Efficient," I whisper back.

He chuckles and runs a hand down my bare arm, raising goose bumps along my skin. In his arms, is my favorite place. Doesn't matter the country, the time, or the circumstance.

"Happy birthday, baby," he whispers.

"You're early."

"I've always been early when it comes to you." His voice is a bit hoarse, and he presses his lips to my temple. "And I'm looking forward to spending your thirties together."

I smile against his skin. There is one thing I wanted to tell him. One thing we'd spoken about over the last few months. Something he told me to tell him. *Let me know when you're ready.*

I reach into the pocket of my linen dress. Pull out the folded list.

He smiles down at it, worn now at the edges. "Time to cross out the last one?"

"I added an extra item at the bottom, to really round out the list," I say. "Even if it happened before I ever wrote anything down."

He unfurls the paper. Narrows his eyes before a smile curls his lips. "Meet the love of my life," he reads.

"Mm-hmm. Sorry. Was that cheesy?"

His smile widens. "I love cheese, baby, you know that. List officially complete, then."

"List officially complete," I say. I fold it back up and toss it in the direction of the bed. Reach for him again.

But he doesn't step into my hold, and his smile has faded.

"Nate?"

"I had something else planned for today, too," he says, reaching into the back pocket of his pants.

"Another surprise?"

His lips twitch. "Yes. Definitely."

There's a velvet box in his hand. My breath catches.

"Harper," he says and drops down to one knee. Here on the moonlit Tuscan balcony, a heartbeat before my thirtieth.

I press my hands to my face. "Nate," I whisper.

"I love you. Even when it was painful, when it was unrequited, when I tried to stop—I have loved you. I can't stop loving you. I never will. Being with you these past two years has been the best time of my life, and by a mile, baby. I can't imagine living the rest of my life without you." He opens the box, his dark eyes on me. There's a ring nestled inside the velvet. "Will you marry me, Harper, and let me spend my life making you happy?"

I can't speak. Can barely breathe. But I nod, another tear running down my cheek. "Yes. Of course, I will," I finally squeeze out.

He smiles—a wide, bright, glowing smile that makes my heart stutter. Slides the ring onto my left hand.

And so, another decade of my life begins.

I have no idea what it will hold… but I know I'm going to make it the best one yet.

Want more Nate and Harper? Join my newsletter to read two extra chapters about what happens a year after the epilogue, during an auction…

Link: https://bookhip.com/TMSRMLC

ACKNOWLEDGEMENTS

This book marks the end of The Connovan Chronicles. This little trilogy where the books just grew longer and longer, the characters more complex, until I broke all my previous word count records. Connie, Alec and Nate just wouldn't be constrained.

I have loved their world. Loved writing siblings with complicated relationships to each other, to their family legacy, to their parents.

Thank you so much for loading their stories onto your Kindle and taking their books into your home.

I love London. The two years I lived there were marked with excitement, in a city so large and so varied that you could live there an entire life and never run out of things to see.

Some places in this book were given fictional names, but they're all based on real areas, squares or places. London in the spring is fantastic!

Nate and Harper's story started from a just a feeling. I knew I wanted London, I wanted spring, and I wanted a slow, delicious shift from friendship into something much, much deeper.

And it took a bunch of people to get it as polished as it is today!

Thank you to my author friends, who never fail to listen, care, and advice on everything from plot and characters to covers. You always help talk me out of plot holes or give me fantastic ideas.

To the fantastic beta readers who give their honest opinions as readers. Thank you! It's invaluable to me. Thank you Andie, my editor, who always polishes and strengthens my stories.

Thanks to Yoly for the beautiful ebook cover, and Books & Mood for the stunning paperback cover.

I loved Harper's journey in this book. Her writing a 30 under 30 list inspired me to write my own, and there are some areas where we overlap (not number 17, I promise!) Rediscovering fun is part of her journey to rediscover herself, and I loved writing that journey. New and challenging experiences can shake something loose that we didn't know was there all along.

As always, thank you for reading my books. It never stops fascinating me that I get to do this for a living. Every day, all the time, and I never take it for granted. Thank you!

I've always loved exploring the intersection of ambition and love. Maybe that's why it's been at the core of every single one of my billionaire books.

So what's coming next?

More of just that. Ambition and love, complicated friendships, buried secrets, and lots of rich men spoiling the women they never knew they needed. Who just walk into their world and turn it upside down.

The next series is coming… and I can't wait to bring you along with me. It's going to be the biggest series yet.

OTHER BOOKS BY OLIVIA

LISTED IN SUGGESTED READING ORDER

The Connovan Chronicles

Best Enemies Forever
Gabriel and Connie

The Perfect Mistake
Alec and Isabel

One Wrong Move
Nate and Harper

The New York Billionaire Series

Think Outside the Boss
Tristan and Freddie

Saved by the Boss
Anthony and Summer

Say Yes to the Boss
Victor and Cecilia

A Ticking Time Boss
Carter and Audrey

Suite on the Boss
Isaac and Sophia

12 Days of Bossmas
Christmas anthology

The Seattle Billionaire Series

Billion Dollar Enemy
Cole and Skye

Billion Dollar Beast
Nick and Blair

Billion Dollar Catch
Ethan and Bella

Billion Dollar Fiancé
Liam and Maddie

Brothers of Paradise Series

Dark Eyed Devil
Lily and Hayden

Ice Cold Boss
Faye and Henry

Red Hot Rebel
Ivy and Rhys

Small Town Hero
Jamie and Parker

Standalones

How to Honeymoon Alone
Phillip and Eden

Arrogant Boss
Julian and Emily

Look But Don't Touch
Grant and Ada

The Billionaire Scrooge Next Door
Adam and Holly

ABOUT OLIVIA

Olivia is a hopeless romantic who loves billionaires heroes, despite never having met one. So she took matters into her own hands and creates them on the page instead. Stern, charming, cold or brooding, so far she's never met a (fictional) billionaire she didn't like.

She picked up the pen in 2019, and she hasn't put it down since. With over a million books sold, Olivia writes fast-paced, swoon-worthy stories filled with banter and spice. Join the heroes as they meet, clash with, or stumble into the ambitious heroines that make them fall, and fall hard.

Join her newsletter for updates and bonus content.
www.oliviahayle.com.
Connect with Olivia

facebook.com/authoroliviahayle
instagram.com/oliviahayle
goodreads.com/oliviahayle
amazon.com/author/oliviahayle
bookbub.com/profile/olivia-hayle

Printed in the USA
CPSIA information can be obtained
at www.ICGtesting.com
JSHW022344260424
62001JS00007B/18

9 789198 927191